THE LIFE AND TIMES OF
PERSIMMON WILSON

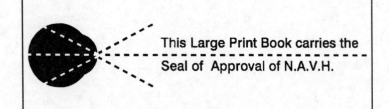

This Large Print Book carries the
Seal of Approval of N.A.V.H.

THE LIFE AND TIMES OF PERSIMMON WILSON

NANCY PEACOCK

THORNDIKE PRESS
A part of Gale, Cengage Learning

GALE
CENGAGE Learning·

Farmington Hills, Mich • San Francisco • New York • Waterville, Maine
Meriden, Conn • Mason, Ohio • Chicago

GALE
CENGAGE Learning

Copyright © 2013, 2016 by Nancy Peacock.
Thorndike Press, a part of Gale, Cengage Learning.

Thorndike Press® Large Print Basic.
The text of this Large Print edition is unabridged.
Other aspects of the book may vary from the original edition.
Set in 16 pt. Plantin.

LIBRARY OF CONGRESS CATALOGING-IN-PUBLICATION DATA

Names: Peacock, Nancy, author.
Title: The life and times of Persimmon Wilson / Nancy Peacock.
Description: Large print edition. | Waterville, Maine : Thorndike Press, 2017. |
  Series: Thorndike Press large print basic
Identifiers: LCCN 2016053151 | ISBN 9781410496782 (hardback) | ISBN 1410496783
  (hardcover)
Subjects: LCSH: Large type books. | BISAC: FICTION / Historical.
Classification: LCC PS3566.E153 L537 2017 | DDC 813/.54—dc23
LC record available at https://lccn.loc.gov/2016053151

Published in 2017 by arrangement with Atria Books, an imprint of Simon & Schuster, Inc.

Printed in the United States of America
1 2 3 4 5 6 7 21 20 19 18 17

Dedicated to my siblings:
Lance, Meg, and Ed
My favorite wild bunch

April 1, 1875
Drunken Bride, Texas

I have been to hangings before, but never my own. Still, it should be some comfort to me that except for the noose around my neck, and the drop that will take my life, I know exactly what to expect two days hence. I know there will be a crowd like there always is at a hanging: picnics, baskets lined with checkered cloths, the smell of fried chicken, and the noise of children. There will be, like there always is, a preacher, and a group of white women dressed in black, singing me to their god.

I expect the day of my execution to be a beautiful day. It hasn't rained lately, but that could change. Some old Indian could show up, do a rain dance, and the whole thing might be postponed. I doubt it though. I've never heard of a hanging rained out. It seems to me like the white god smiles on a

7

hanging, just like he smiles on making money.

There will be plenty of opportunity for making money on the day of my death. Merchants selling warmish lemonade by the dipperful from a barrel, food for those who didn't bring their own, slices of pie and cake for dessert, trinkets to commemorate my demise. And there should be, I hope, at least one industrious young boy out in the crowd, hawking souvenirs, competing with the adults' business, selling miniature nooses with my name written across them.

I saw those little nooses when I was just a boy in Virginia, at the hanging of a man named One-Eyed Jim. Jim was a slave who killed his overseer in the middle of the night while the man slept. Jim used a shovel head and his bare hands, and rumor had it that he killed the very man who took his eye out. I was nine, maybe ten, years old the day Jim got hung, and a slave myself, owned then by a man named Roland Surley.

I was brought along that day to help out Surley's lady friend, Miss Fannie Sims, with the picnic. I was there to carry the basket, spread the quilt, fetch things, and if she got too hot, whisk a big fan back and forth to cool her. I saw the white boys winding their way through the crowd calling out, "Nooses.

Get your souvenir nooses right here." Roland Surley flagged them down and bought a little noose to give to Miss Fannie, but she thought it was maudlin and refused to accept it, so he flipped it to me. "Here, Persy, I reckon it's yours." A little noose with the name One-Eyed Jim written in lumpy ink letters across the rope, a memento of that day that I have kept all the rest of my life. It's dirty and grimy now, and the letters are faded away, but all the same I keep it.

I'm picturing those little nooses at my hanging, and the little white hands that ought to be making them. Maybe two boys working together, debating which of my names to use, then ending the argument by making some of each. I figure on at least a dozen with my slave name, Persimmon Wilson, and another dozen with the translation of my Comanche name, Twist Rope. Kweepoonaduh Tuhmoo.

Persimmon is the name my mama gave me, after the fruit she stole off a tree down in the woods while she was carrying me, and Wilson is the name of the man that last owned me. I don't want to call that man master here, but for the purpose of making this easier to read than its content might allow, I will. Master Joseph Wilson owned me

9

down in Louisiana, owned me as best he could, and I reckon I was owned as best I could be, till the Federal government and General Butler decided I couldn't be owned any longer.

There's folks that'll be reading this after I'm dead, who'll be looking for me to say, at the mention of Master Wilson's name, "God rest his soul." So here you go: God rest his soul. He died by my hand, although I really shouldn't take all the credit. In spite of being a heathen, I do know something about etiquette, and because of that I have to admit I had some help from my friends, the band of Comanche warriors I rode and raided with. Many of them are dead now, or else corralled onto a pitiful plot of land the white folks have not decided they want yet. Me, they saved for hanging.

Which brings me back to those little nooses I hope some boy is peddling. As I said, a dozen with my white name — Persimmon Wilson — and another dozen with the translation of my Comanche name. Twist Rope, the black Indian. That's what they call me, when they're not calling me nigger.

There is no shortage of irony in this world — white people calling me the black Indian and Indians calling me the black white man.

10

And the hell of it is, we had five or six white Indians riding with us, men who'd been captured young, raised in the tribe, turned to warriors like every young Comanche boy is.

Irony — now there's a word I'm not supposed to know, being a nigger and all.

You've probably already picked out a few words that trouble you for a black man to be using. Big old words. Thought-heavy words. Dangerous in the wrong head, and mine is the wrong head, isn't it?

I know too much. All the more reason to put a noose around my neck. Never mind that my last request was paper and ink and to be left alone to write this. Never mind that my jailer Jack laughed at the idea of a nigger writing. It was a novelty to hand me paper and ink and see what I'd leave behind. It might be something to sell, might be worth something later on, or it might be something to burn. It shouldn't matter to me. If I learned anything at all from living with the Comanche, it is this: words don't mean a thing unless they're true. So you do what you will, burn my words if you want to, set them loose into the air. Nothing would make me happier than all of you having to breathe this story, this truth of what I am about to tell you. Nothing can kill truth, not even white men.

Master Wilson did not know he was buying an educated nigger. He'd likely not have bought me had he known. He might wish now, if the dead wish at all, that he hadn't bought me. But I didn't kill him because I was educated. I killed him because I had the chance, and I took it, and it's not as though educated was listed as one of my assets when I got to the slave pens in New Orleans.

"Prime Young Buck. Strong. Seasoned. Lots of years left on him. Just look at those muscles."

No one asked, "But can he read?"

I could read. And I could write. More than just my name, as you can see. I was taught when I was a boy. Taught by an old spinster white lady I was hired out to. Miss Clemons was her name. She hired a boy named Bessle and me from Master Surley every winter for twelve years. She worked us by daylight: bringing in firewood, hauling up water, mending up fences and digging her garden for spring. No one knew that by night, every night, she gave us lessons, teaching us first to read and write, and then in subsequent years adding on layer after layer of knowledge, until finally, that last year before I was sold, I could speak and write and read as well as or better than most any white man. Out in the field I had to keep up appearances though. I had to pretend I didn't know anything more than the hoe and the mule, just like I had to keep on saying yassuh and nawsuh.

Slavery still has its supporters. Some might think while reading this, it was the education that ruined me and made me want to bolt. But it wasn't the education; it was the whip, and a woman named Chloe, and the idea of a life spent taking orders from a man who didn't deserve to own a mule, much less a human being.

Most all my life I took plenty of orders, from sunup to sundown. I was born to slavery, and just when I was feeling like a man, I was sold from the Surley place, along with every other slave I knew. Liquidating the estate it was called, and it had to be done when Roland Surley died, six years and four children after marrying Miss Fannie. Worse than just dying was that he died owing money all up and down the county. The sale of his slaves was meant to make up for that. My mama and daddy were sold separately, her to a local man, my daddy to a trader. My sister, Betty, was sold upstate. I got sold to another trader and taken downriver for profit. Bessle, the boy I learned reading and writing with, was sold to the same trader. There were a whole lot of others sold, too, to a whole lot of places, but I won't go into that here. I haven't the paper or the time for it.

Bessle and I were walked to Richmond, and transported by ship down the James River, then off to sea to New Orleans. The trip took three weeks. Once a day we were let out of the hold and brought up top for air. When we docked at New Orleans we were loaded off the ship and chained at the ankles. The air smelt of fried fish and was thick and heavy, like something that needed to be spooned instead of breathed.

We were marched through the streets and then locked into a yard surrounded by walls twice my height, and stinking of sweat and human waste. On the other side of the walls we could hear conversations, shouts, and the whistles of steamboats along the river.

For the next week I was fattened and toned for market. I was fed bacon and butter and bread, and five times a day made to run laps around the perimeter of the yard with the other men. Then the day came that I was washed, greased, and walked through a door on one side of the compound to a clean wide room. I was stood up against a wall with other slaves for sale. Women were on one side of the showroom and men on the other, and all of us were arranged by height.

I spent three days in that showroom and each day was the same. White men coming along, taking my fingers in their hands and moving them back and forth, checking for nimbleness. They ran their hands up my legs, along my arms, across my chest and abdomen, looking for tumors, hernias, and wounds, anything that would bring my price down or make them decide not to buy me. They pulled my lips back and looked at my teeth. I was told to strip that they might check my back for the marks of the lash. I was told to dance a jig that they might see for themselves that I was spry and able.

I was seventeen, eighteen maybe, I don't know.

The grease the trader had smeared on my skin, and polished in to make me gleam, made me hot. My skin felt closed up, like my whole body was wrapped in tight leather on a sweltering day. All I could do was stand there, let the white men look, and answer their questions.

"What's your age, boy?"

"Can you drive a buggy?"

"Ever had chicken pox, whooping cough, measles?"

"Where did you live before?"

"You got a wife?"

"Would you like to come home with me, boy?"

We'd been told what to say. Old men were told to say they were younger. There were skills we didn't have that we were meant to claim. Our health was good, always. Scars and missing fingers were explained away, not as punishment, but as mishaps with machinery. The farther we came from, the less likely we were to run. The same for being unhitched. In answer to that last question, would you like to come home with me, boy, the only reply a slave could give was yassuh.

Yassuh, I answered the gravelly voiced man who had prodded at me for the last hour. It was then I raised my head slightly, and got my first look at Master Wilson, the "innocent" man I would kill ten years later. He was short and round. Two days from now I will be dead, hanged for his murder, and the kidnapping and rape of his "wife."

You who find this, I know what you will be thinking. You will want to take those words, "innocent" and "wife" out of quotation marks. You will think that I, a nigger, a heathen, a horse thief, a murderer, a kidnapper, a rapist, do not know the meaning of

16

what I have just written, but you will be wrong. I know its meaning. Innocent in quotation marks means that he was not innocent, and I tell you, sir, that he was not. And wife in quotation marks means that she was not his wife, and I tell you, sir, that she was not. She was his former slave, Chloe, and she is dead now.

I write this for Chloe. It is my urgent task these last few days of my life. I write this that she may be known for who she was, and not for who you think she was. She was not Master Wilson's wife. She was not white. She was a former house slave, and I loved her, and I love her still.

The first day I saw Master Wilson was the first day I saw Chloe. She stood across the showroom from me, just opposite, wedged between two dark-complexioned women, one wide and old, the other young, scrawny, and thick veined. Chloe was smooth and young, with soft curly brown hair pulled back into a braid, wisps of it escaping to frame her face. Her skin was light, the color of pinewood, and the contrast made her seem all wrong and out of place, as though a white woman had gotten in among us and somehow made herself for sale.

There was not a man in that room who did not notice Chloe, those that were buying and those that were being bought alike. I heard our trader call her a fancy, which meant she would most likely be sold for some man's pleasure.

I was no different than the other men in that room. I noticed her. And I watched as the man who had just purchased me walked up to her and began asking his questions. In the scuffle and noise of the showroom, I could not hear her answers, but her carriage was demure and subservient. Master Wilson made her lift her skirt and he felt of her legs. He next felt of her arms and pried her mouth open to examine her teeth. Female slaves, as well as males, were asked to strip to the waist, and Master Wilson indicated that she should do this, and she did. When he was done examining her she shrugged the bodice of her dress back on and buttoned it up again. It was easy to see that Wilson liked what he saw. Without much bargaining he purchased Chloe. With some more bargaining he also purchased my friend Bessle and a man named Henry.

It was November of 1860. The freedom war had not yet started. As Master Wilson chained us together at the wrists and loaded us into the bed of his wagon, there was not, in any of our minds, a hint of the things to come.

Besides his cargo of human beings there were also two barrels of flour, a bolt of cloth, and a sack of coffee. Chloe leaned against the sack of coffee and the rest of us sat as comfortably as we could on the hard uneven planks of the wagon bed, Bessle and

I propped against the back, and Henry leaned up against one of the barrels. Henry was a big man, with muscles that strained against the thin cloth of his shirt, and legs that took up most of the bed. He closed his eyes and fell asleep immediately, but Bessle, Chloe, and I stayed awake and watched the landscape go by.

Louisiana was a watery place. The road we traveled was built on the crest of a long ridge of packed earth. Down below, on one side was the Mississippi River, and down below, on the other side were swamps and channels of water, and where there wasn't water there was land, but the land seemed almost as though it didn't belong. The fields of stubbled cotton and corn, already harvested, were like something laid on with paint. And then there were fields of something else, something I had never seen before, something tall and grassy that waved in the breeze. This plant I would learn, all too soon and all too well, was sugarcane.

The fields we passed were full, not just of cane and channels of water, but also of slaves. Armies of slaves moved as one, men and women felling the crop with large-bladed knives, and children following along behind, gathering the fallen cane into bundles, carrying these bundles on their small shoulders to a waiting cart. Even over the rattle of the wagon I could hear the rustle of the cane and the sound of those knives whacking into the plants.

It takes four strikes of the blade to bring down one cane plant; two downward strokes to each side in order to strip the plant of its leaves, one to cut it at the ground, a fourth to take off the immature top. Even though I did not yet know this, it was easy to hear a rhythm in the work. Whack, whack, whack, whack, and then the slaves moved on to the next plant and the next quartet of strikes.

Besides cane and slaves and water and fields, we passed the occasional plantation house, each one seemingly larger and grander than the last, almost all larger and grander than anything I had seen in Virginia. One had gnarled oak trees along either side of a drive leading to its entry, and the trees bent into a canopy and were hung with veils of drooping moss. Another had two curved staircases sweeping down from the gallery. There were houses with double chimneys on either end, houses with galleries high in the air, houses with columns lined up like sentry guards against all invaders.

I felt a thump on my knee and looked up to see Bessle leaned over writing something in the dust on the wagon bed with his finger, holding on to his chains with the other hand to prevent them from rattling. "Good master?" the message read.

Chloe quickly looked away, as if the devil himself had come to sit down next to her and tempt her into trouble. My previous master had told me that God had an especially fiery room in hell for any nigger who even thought about learning to read or write. If that is true, then I sealed my fate a long time ago. During our lessons Miss Clemons assured Bessle and me that reading and writing were not sins, but would instead be our salvation should we ever be freed.

Freedom and salvation seemed a long ways off the day I was sold to Master Wilson. Hell seemed much closer. I shrugged my shoulders, not knowing the answer to Bessle's question. Bessle quick-scraped his foot across the message, and it was just then Master Wilson spat off into the weeds and looked over his shoulder at us. Just as quickly he turned back around and chucked at the horses, lifting the reins and giving them a light slap in the air.

We had set out from New Orleans late in the day, and had traveled only a few hours before we stopped at a plantation, a place called Lidgewood, where we stayed the night. Master Wilson went inside the big house and supped with the other white folks, and was given, I am sure, a nice warm bed made up with linens and quilts. Bessle, Henry, Chloe, and I were made to stay in a barn, still chained together, Chloe to one side of me and Bessle to the other, and Henry chained to Bessle.

A boy brought us some plates of food. It wasn't much — bacon and biscuits, a bit of potato, all of it cold and greasy — but we were hungry, so we ate and licked the plates to get every scrap we could. After we ate, we were let off the chains to go relieve ourselves. Then we were locked together again, given one blanket each, and the lantern was taken away.

We were not in total darkness however. Outside there were torches, and through the slats in the barn their light jumped and flickered against the walls. A strange burnt scent filled the air, and I heard wagons rattling past, and a little ways off the plodding feet of horses, and what sounded like wooden gears turning one against another.

"What's going on out there?" I asked.

"Grindin' season," Henry answered.

"Grinding what?"

"Cane."

"How late are they going to work?"

"Maybe all night. Maybe till midnight. Then back befo' dawn. It won't be over till a frost come or the last plant get cut." Then he picked up his chain and rattled it, laughing. "Welcome to cane country, boys. If the work don't kill you, the skeeters will."

I rose up and twisted my body to look out through a crack in the wall. Another wagon rattled past, the bed heaped with stalks of cane.

"Sunup to midnight?" I asked.

"If you lucky," Henry answered. "Befo' sunup in some places."

Bessle stirred beside me and he, too, tried to rise up and look out. "You worked cane before?" he asked.

"Cane, cotton, rice. You think cotton kill you? You think rice hard? Cane kill you faster than anythin'. You learn soon enough."

Bessle and I eased back down and leaned against the wall.

"They ship it out downriver," Henry said. "That road we up on, that be the levee road. You take a look tomorrow and you see a dock fo' every big house."

"I seen 'em," Chloe said.

"That right. Every big house," Henry said. "Boats come up the river, pick up barrels of sugar. You see."

I watched the torchlight dance against the walls of the barn and listened to the creak of the gears and wagon wheels, the shush of cane being unloaded.

Henry kept on. "That levee hold back the river," he said. "They ain't even supposed be no land here. That river flood and break the levee, the whole mess gonna get washed away. Us too. Us first prob'ly."

I squeezed my eyes shut. I could feel them wetting up on me. I don't know why, but I'd thought of Mama just then. I hadn't thought of her since we'd stepped off the boat and been herded into the pen. Before that, if she'd come into my mind, I'd pushed her away. Henry must have felt some change in me, because he said, "Where you came from, Sprout?"

"Don't call me Sprout," I said.

"All right. Ain't no need to get yo' hackles up. I call you Shoot. That suit you? You big on the outside, but you ain't quite growed on the inside. That the way I be lookin' at it."

Chloe said, "I wish I warn't growed."

But Henry was looking at me. "What 'bout you, Shoot? You growed all the way on the inside yet?"

"I reckon not."

"Ain't none of us growed," Henry said.

"We all massuh's little chirren. Me too. Big old man like me cain't even keep hold of his family." He sniffed a little, and then asked again, "Where y'all came from?"

That was when we talked some. Bessle and I told our stories. His family had been sold all over the place too. We'd both watched our fathers chained together into a coffle that was led down a road heading south.

"Trader," Henry said.

I nodded dumbly.

"Papa's trader took him by land. Ours took us by ship," Bessle said.

"He prob'ly bringin' 'em here," Henry said. "They might get sold close by. Most of this land be sugar, and sugar need slaves."

Bessle gave a choked little sob and then was quiet.

Henry added, "Aw, fo'get 'bout it. You ain't never find him."

I asked Henry where he came from and he said a place in South Carolina where he worked rice. But then he was sold downriver. He'd worked cotton some, and cane for two years, tried to run away twice, was sold for that. He had a wife and two children he'd left behind in South Carolina. He heard his old master had died, and the slaves were sold, families split up just as

26

mine had been. He reckoned his wife had taken up with someone else by now. He couldn't blame her, he said.

Chloe told us she came from a place in Alabama where she'd been a house servant. She'd left behind a sister and a niece. She'd been used hard, she said, and she hoped things would be better with Master Wilson. We all knew what she meant by used hard, and we didn't answer, the three of us, as if by being male, we were as guilty as any white man who had taken her that way.

The silence grew and Chloe started crying. We could hear her snuffling and sniffing and trying to keep it quiet. I could feel her shoulders shaking next to me and with each shake our chains rattled just a little, and against this sound was the background noise of the sugarhouse and the work going on there, the torches outside flicking a little light against the far wall. Finally Henry said, "God help us."

At the beginning of that day I had believed in God. But that night in the barn at Lidgewood I could feel God leaching away from me, just like the warmth in the air leached away as nighttime trenched itself in.

Off in the distance we heard a wild scream.

"Panther," Bessle said, and this stopped

Chloe's crying and caused her to pull her body closer to mine.

I smelt the scent of coffee left in Chloe's hair from the sack she'd leaned against in the wagon bed. After a while she fell asleep and her head dropped against my shoulder, and I dared not move for fear of disturbing her. Henry soon knocked off with deep, resonant snores that Bessle and I stifled giggles against. Then Bessle nodded off and I was left awake.

Besides us, there were animals in the barn that night: a cow with a bleating calf, horses and mules, rats and mice whose feet scurried and scratched in the darkness, mosquitoes and gnats and spiders, an owl that had swooped out at dusk and would swoop back in at daybreak. I flicked something away from my face, flicking, that is, as best one can with heavy chains on the wrist. Chloe sighed in her sleep and threw her one free arm around my waist. Finally I, too, slept, with the scent of coffee lingering in Chloe's hair so close to me, and the sounds of wagons going by and the cane being ground, gear squeaking against gear, and the endless plodding of hooves.

Was it the silence that woke me? Or the barn door screeching open? All I know is that suddenly my eyes were awake and there was a man with a lantern standing in the opening of the barn door. I was struck by how quiet it was, all the work outside having ceased. The man came closer and held the lantern up over us and in its light I saw that it was Master Wilson.

He set the lantern down and pulled a key from his pocket and leaned over, unlocking Chloe from me. The chain he loosened from her wrist thudded to the ground.

"Massuh?" Chloe muttered sleepily.

And then he had her by her arm and pulled her to her feet. "Get the lantern," he said.

Chloe picked it up and he dragged her away from us, the light and the two of them disappearing into an empty stall. Through its slats I could see their shadows as Master hung the lantern from a beam.

"What's he doing?" Bessle asked.

"Don't be stupid," Henry said in a rough whisper. "Be quiet."

And so we were quiet.

What else could we do? The sounds coming from the stall where Master Wilson had taken Chloe said everything that needed to be said. Grunts. Scuffling. A slap. Flesh smacking against flesh.

I cannot say that soon it was over, although that is most likely true. But it is also true that in that moment time was stretched taut. It was as if time would pull itself into forever, that the sounds of Master Wilson taking Chloe would never end, and when they did finally end, it felt like time could have snapped and thrown us, like a slingshot would, through the roof and into the dark sky. "Get dressed," I heard him say.

Chloe was returned, chained to me once more. I kept my eyes closed, but as Master Wilson left, taking the lantern with him, I opened them and I saw by its swinging light one piece of straw hanging from Chloe's hair. And then it was darkness again. I felt her move away from me, but I tugged the chain and pulled. I just wanted to comfort her, to put my arm around her and let her cry, but Chloe gave a hard yank on the chain and curled alone into the straw. She did not cry.

Eventually I heard Bessle's breath slowing, and Henry's deep snores again. I sat in the dark listening. I could tell that Chloe did not sleep and she could tell the same of me, for after a while she asked in a fierce whisper, "Ain't you gonna sleep?"

"I can't," I said.

She laughed a little. "Uh-huh. You gonna stay awake and protect me?"

"I wish I could," I answered.

30

She was silent then. The calf in the stall at the end of the barn bleated once and then rustled in the straw, snuggling up to its mother, I presumed. And then briefly, once again, I thought of my own mother and how I had snuggled up to her as a young child.

I heard the straw shift beside me and felt the chain go slack. Chloe moved closer. She leaned her head against my shoulder. "I wish you could too," she said. "Protect me."

I awoke just before dawn to the sounds of cane work starting back up. The clink of tack, the snorts of horses, the crack of an axe splitting wood for fires, and the four-whack rhythm of cane being cut for the mill. Eventually Chloe stirred, then Bessle, and finally Henry, and we sat there, quietly talking as morning came on, and the slaves outside worked. Chloe stayed close to me during this time, still resting her head on my shoulder. The scent of coffee was gone from her now, replaced by the smell of hay, and beneath that, the swampy scent of Master Wilson.

Henry gave us a brief description of grinding season; of steam or horses turning the rollers that smash the cane stalks, how the juice rolls into a vat and is heated in a large kettle, the impurities skimmed off. Always, just at the right time, the juice must be moved to the next kettle, from cooler to hotter fires until finally it is ready for striking, being drawn off and poured into the cooling vats.

"Most likely we gonna work cane," Henry said. "You get a feel fo' it. You mess the whole batch if you ain't got no feel fo' it. White man lose money, they hell to pay then."

"You ever tasted sugar?" Bessle asked.

Henry said he'd tasted raw cane and molasses. Bessle and I had never tasted sugar, or syrup, or honey, but we'd had molasses. Chloe said she'd tasted sugar once, when she stuck her finger in the sugar jar and licked it off.

"You get caught?" Bessle wanted to know.

"Naw," Chloe answered.

"This place puny," Henry said. "You hear those horses goin' round? That the mill. Steam mill a whole lot mo'work. Gotta keep the boiler fed, and the cane comin' in faster. All the coast turnin' to steam these days."

"Coast?" I asked.

"That what they call it. It short."

"Short for what?"

"German Coast," Henry said. "This side of the river be the German Coast, and it all goin' to steam." He shook his head and added, "Steam-powered sugarmill, hell on earth."

After a short time a white man came in and let us off our chains to go relieve ourselves and walk around briefly. We were then shackled up in the same order as before, and a young boy brought us plates of food, and we ate with our fingers again and cleaned the plates with our tongues. The sounds of the sugarhouse continued monotonously, the horses plodding the mill into action, wagons coming and going, while in the fields the cane was cut. Daylight came on stronger, and soon enough Master Wilson came to load us once more into the wagon. The four of us were still in our places: Henry resting his arms on his knees, Bessle and me, the same, and Chloe curled into me again with her head leaned on my shoulder.

There would be many times to come I would feel something like a spirit, cold and hateful, passing between Master Wilson and myself. I would feel it the day I killed him, just as I felt it on this day, when Wilson saw Chloe curled against me. That dark spirit coiled between us, touching me with the frosty points of its fingers. Chloe straightened up and moved herself away from me. "Mornin', Massuh," she said, lowering her eyes to the ground.

"Get up."

We rattled our way into standing positions, and stood facing Wilson. He slid his fingers into the pocket of his shirtwaist, extracting once again the key to our shackles. Chloe stiffened as Wilson lifted her wrist, mine along with it, and pawed the key into the lock and turned it. My own body went taut, as if I might spring on him this time, as if I might not allow him to rape her again. As if . . .

I would do nothing. I would stand there, in my place, and listen to the same sounds coming from the stall as I had listened to the night before. Master Wilson led Chloe away, and the space where she had been emptied, like air rushing across the cavity left by a pulled tooth. Their feet crunched in the straw, and then stopped. At the other end of the line Master Wilson chained Chloe to Henry. I felt a sudden exhaustion at the relief of this, and without thinking I shook my head to clear it. Then I shook my arm, where Chloe had been chained, to get the blood flowing again.

Wilson stepped back to me and leaned into my face. "You like that, boy?"

I wasn't sure what he was asking. I wasn't sure if the correct response was yes sir or no sir.

"Yassuh?" I ventured.

35

I suppose I guessed correctly, for he went on to say, "Uh-huh. What's your name again? Persimmon?"

"Yassuh."

"Persimmon Surley?" he said.

"Yassuh. Folks call me Persy, suh."

"Is that right? Well, you're a Wilson now, boy. Persimmon Wilson. Has a better ring to it, don't you think?"

"Yassuh," I answered truthfully, for what did it matter, trading one white man's name for another, as if I didn't already know my position in life. I felt that spirit swirl between us again.

"To the wagon," Wilson said.

We walked in a line outside. The sun was bright now, and I blinked against it.

"Get in."

We loaded ourselves into the wagon bed and nestled among the cargo. Wilson climbed into the driver's seat and chucked the horses into moving forward. Chloe now sat across from me. She looked up and gave me a sad smile, and shook her head, for she already knew her future with this man.

It was early evening when Wilson finally turned the wagon off the levee road and down onto a tree-lined lane. As the wagon dipped lower I felt the air grow still. The breeze we'd felt on top of the levee disappeared among the fields where crews of Wilson's slaves slung their knives into felling cane. I strained to get a look at the big house at the end of the lane. Like all the rest I'd seen, this one was two stories with a large gallery along each floor. On the upper gallery I could see open double doors with white curtains hanging limp in the heat. As we pulled closer the curtains parted and an older slave woman stepped out and walked to the railing, where she looked at us before turning around and stepping back inside, the curtains falling behind her to droop once again in the humidity.

Master Wilson pulled the horses to a halt, and a young boy stepped out of the shadow of the house to take the reins. "Get out," Wilson said as he swung his legs off the wagon and jumped down.

Our chains clanked as we unloaded ourselves and stood before him. Wilson took the key out of his pocket and unlocked each one of us. We stood there rubbing our wrists where the shackles had been. "If you try to run," he said, "you'll get a whipping like you've never seen. I don't tolerate runaways. And I don't tolerate shirkers. Do your work and you'll be treated well."

"Yassuh," we muttered.

"You're on Sweetmore Plantation, boys.

Stand here. Someone will be by to get you. Chloe, come with me."

And with that, she left. I watched as she followed Wilson, three steps behind him, to the back of the house. Her homespun dress swayed with her walk, the worn soles of her shoes showed with each step. Her braid fell down her back and swung across her shoulders in rhythm. Around the corner and she was gone. I would not see her again for over a month.

Did I think of her during this time? Only a fool would think I did not. I will not endeavor to tell you how much, or how often, only that I thought of her during every particular I had to learn about this new place and the work I would be doing there. Chloe haunted me. She haunted me even more than my own mother, and this is true to this very day, where I now sit in a jail cell listening to the nib of my pen scratch across the paper.

I was occupied, of course. I was thrown into the tail end of grinding season, and during those two months the lessons, the things I had to remember, came at me like a flood. There was the primary concern of how best to do my work each day, which turned out to be two nine-hour shifts of fieldwork, one cutting cane, the other hauling it to the sugarhouse. We did not take Sundays off during grinding season.

On the first day of cutting cane I was handed a long-handled knife. I learned how to hold and wield that knife. I learned the four strikes it takes to bring down a cane plant. And once it was down, I learned to move quickly and fluidly, with the least amount of effort, on to the next plant.

Sweetmore Plantation did in fact have a steam-driven mill, with two chimneys on either end of its sugarhouse spewing dark columns of smoke into the air. I suspected that Henry was right; I would have preferred the plodding pace and rhythm of a horse-powered mill. I came to think of the sugarhouse itself as some demonic creature from the depths of hell, a creature that spewed smoke and ate up firewood and wagonloads of cane for eighteen hours every day. A creature that ate up lives as indiscriminately as it ate the cane. We worked seven days a week, as I have said. There was no break, no rest, our only consolation was that rations were plentiful, the food cooked for us three times a day and served in the fields.

I would not feel we'd made any progress at all except for our midnight walks back to the quarters, where I would finally see in the moonlight — if there was any, and in torchlight if not — fields of cane already cut, the stubble poking above the ground like hard little sticks. The next day, before dawn, we were marched out to the fields again, and there was more cane ready to be cut, its leaves rustling in the breeze as if to taunt us.

In my first few months at Sweetmore, I learned a few of the names of my fellow slaves, but certainly not all. There was a fellow named Sup, whom Henry, Bessle, and I bunked with in a cabin at the back of the quarters, and a woman named Sally, who cut cane faster than anyone else, and a solemn little girl named Peach, who served us our three meals a day out in the fields. But in the sugarhouse and on the boiler gang there were faces with names I would not learn until the end of grinding season.

In the few early-morning hours between the end of work and the beginning of work, a blaze guttering in the fireplace of our cabin if it was cold enough, I learned about my new white people from Sup. He told us that Master Wilson's wife, Missus Lila, was a thin, sickly woman, not suited to the climate of Louisiana, not suited to much of anything according to Sup. The couple had one son, whose name was Gerald. He lived with his young bride at a plantation called

Ashleaf, farther up the river.

"It when young Massuh Gerald get married, Missus Lila get sick," Sup told us, continuing the story from one morning to the next. "She couldn't stand to lose him. Cried and wailed when he married Miss Emma. Wailed on like he dead, fo' god's sake." Sup shook his head and poked at the fire before tossing on another log. "She never did get seasoned into this place. Lost her some babies when she first come here down from Maryland. Lost three." He stood and walked to his pallet, lay down and crossed his arms behind his head. "Make her kind of tetchy, if you ask me."

While cutting cane I had looked up as often as I dared toward the big house, hoping to catch a glimpse of Chloe stepping out the back door, or carrying dishes of food from the kitchen house to the big house. But the distance was too great. Now I reached into my pocket, for I slept in my clothes, as we all did during grinding season, and fingered the little noose from One-Eyed Jim's hanging. When I looked up, Sup was staring at me, leaning on his elbow, the thin gray blanket falling from his chest. "What you know?" he asked.

"Nothing," I said.

"Somethin' troublin' you?"

I took a deep breath and stared at the ceiling, at a hole where the moonlight shone through. At the foot of my pallet Bessle shifted on his moss-stuffed mattress. "There's a girl named Chloe," I said. "Came in the same day as us."

From his pallet across from Bessle's I heard Henry groan. "Fo'get 'bout her, Shoot."

"What 'bout her?" Sup asked.

"Master Wilson," I began. And then I fell quiet.

"Take a likin' to her, did he?"

"Yeah."

"And you too?"

"Yeah, he did," Henry said. "Now y'all go to sleep. Long day tomorrow. Long day fo'ever. Damn shit."

"Not the way he did," I answered Sup.

"Naw, I reckon not." Sup lay back down and crossed his arms behind his head again. "I heard of her. A fancy is what I heard."

"Do you know what Chloe's doing?" I asked.

"Workin' as a nursemaid to the missus. 'Spect come grindin' season over, she be seein' a lot mo' of him."

I knew from my shifts driving the wagon, hauling cane to the sugarhouse, that Wilson was there most of the time during grinding season. I'd seen him talking to his overseers and drivers. I'd seen him leaning over the steaming kettles of cane juice, gauging the efficiency of the slaves working that station. I'd seen him pacing up and down with his thumbs tucked into his suspenders.

Christmas came. Wilson did not shut down the sugarhouse as I heard some did. On Sweetmore we worked as if there had never been a savior born, as if there was nothing to celebrate, and no god to pray to.

It was not long after Christmas that a man named Breech got his hand caught in the rollers at the mill, mangling it so badly, Henry told me, that it looked like bagasse.

"What is bagasse?" Bessle asked.

"Pulp," Henry said. "Pulp left over after the cane get smashed."

"Breech a dead man now," Sup said. "Been here fo'ever and 'bout wore-out anyway. They ain't gonna do nothin' fo' him."

Two weeks later Breech died from the infection that set in after the hand went untreated. We were called away from our work to see him buried in the slaves' cemetery along the edge of the swamp: overseers, drivers, house slaves, and field slaves, all but those working in the sugarhouse where the grinding and the boiling of syrup must go on. By the time my gang arrived a grave had been dug, and Breech lay on the ground beside his pine casket, his right hand wrapped in a blood-slick feed sack.

It was plain to see that Breech wasn't going to fit in that casket. His feet lay on the ground a good two hands' length beyond its end. I'd heard from Sup that Master Wilson kept a stockpile of coffins for the slaves stored in a barn. A man named Jonas built them off-season. I would see them later on. Coffins for children of all sizes, infant on up, and coffins for adults, but no coffin that would fit Breech, and apparently no time during grinding season to build one. Behind me I heard the stifled weeping of Breech's widow, Harriet, and his child, a girl sixteen or seventeen years old named Sylvie.

Wilson was not there yet, and I took the opportunity of his absence to search for Chloe in the group of house slaves opposite us. I found her, clothed now as the other female house servants were, in a plain dress with a full apron, her hair swept up and pinned beneath a little frilly cap, holding on to one elbow of Master Wilson's wife. It was my first look at the missus, and she was a sickly looking thing, skinny and pale, with a face that seemed as though it might draw up and cave in on itself with the next disappointment. Her lungs were good though. She leaned against Chloe for support, and dug her clawlike fingers into the sleeves of Chloe's dress, and fairly shouted, "Chloe, why did you bring me here?"

"A man die, Mizz Lila. We here to see him buried."

"Who?" Missus Lila said. "Who died? Someone I know?"

"Yesem. A man named Breech, what I hear. Worked in the sugarhouse."

"Pshaw. I don't know any of those niggers."

"Yesem," Chloe said, but she made no effort to leave. Instead she looked up and scanned the group of slaves across the yard from her, and when her eyes landed on me, they rested there.

Master Wilson showed up, anxious to get the ceremony under way so we could get back to making his sugar. He strode between the two groups of slaves, not noticing why Breech was lying on the ground instead of in his casket. "This nigger Breech," Wilson said, pacing back and forth, "was a good worker. A hard worker. God rest his soul in heaven. Amen. Now someone put him in, we got work to do."

"Amen," we muttered, standing there staring at Breech's body and the casket.

"Someone put him in and let's get this over with," Wilson said.

An overseer stepped up. "He ain't gonna fit, sir."

"What?"

Chloe looked up at me, Missus Lila still clawing at her sleeve. "Why don't someone put him in?" Missus Lila yelled.

"He ain't gonna fit, sir," the overseer repeated.

"Chloe, I'm cold. I don't need to see this nigger buried, I need to go back to bed." Missus Lila again.

"Yesem," Chloe answered, but again she made no move to leave. She shook her head slightly at me, and smiled a little, as if to say, "These damn fools."

I smiled back. It was the wrong thing to do, for Wilson looked up and caught the moment between us. He turned to me and said, "Persy, stomp his neck."

"Suh?"

"You heard me, boy. Get over here and stomp his neck. Break it."

"Suh," I said again.

"You disobeying me? You want a whipping? Now get over here and stomp this nigger's neck. Any fool can see he won't fit otherwise."

Harriet gave out a low moan. "Naw," I

heard her say. "Naw."

I handed my cane knife to Sup.

In my mind it is better to bury a man with no casket at all than to break his neck to make him fit. But Master Wilson prided himself on being a Christian, and whatever else that meant to him, his dead slaves got caskets.

"Persy, stomp his neck," Wilson said again.

"Oh, naw. Naw, naw, naw," Harriet moaned.

"Mama," Sylvie said. "Don't look, Mama."

I walked over to where Breech was lying. I lifted my foot. Breech's eyes were open. Harriet and Sylvie had been working in the fields when he died in their cabin. No one had been there to close his eyes, and now those eyes stared at me in frozen disbelief. I brought my foot down hard on his neck. I heard the crack of bone, and the wail of Harriet, and I felt Breech's neck shift beneath my boot. His head lolled to one side. As I walked back to my place in line, I saw that Harriet had slumped to the ground and was crying in her daughter's arms. All the other slaves gathered on my side of the grave had their heads lowered and were looking intently at the ground. I dared not look up to see the house servants' side of the grave, for fear of looking into Chloe's eyes.

"Persy, you about the stupidest nigger I ever saw," Wilson said. "You think he gonna jump in that casket all by himself." He laughed. "Come over here and load him in. Henry, you take his feet."

Henry and I did as we were told. We lifted Breech. His head hung off his broken neck and swung heavy, like a ball off a chain. We laid him in the casket, and when Breech's head caught on the edge of the wood, I folded it down to his shoulder to make him fit. We set the casket's lid in place and nailed it on. Using ropes, Henry, Sup, Jonas, and I lowered Breech into the ground.

"Get back to work," Wilson said. "That mill ain't running itself. Peach, you take Harriet back to her cabin. Harriet, you take a few hours off. Sylvie, I'm sorry about this. Best thing for it will be a little work. Persy, you fill in this hole after your shifts."

It was a thin waxing moon that night. I was given a lantern to work by, and I stood in its meager light scraping my shovel into the pile of dirt beside Breech's grave, tossing it onto his casket. The Comanche speak of tears as belonging to women, but they are warriors. The Comanche's solution to grief and sadness is warfare. I cannot see that white men are any different. But working beside Breech's grave that night, I was not yet Comanche, and I would never be white, and I am not ashamed to tell you that I cried. When I was finally done filling in the grave, when I had finally tamped it down and pounded in the nameless wooden cross so thoughtfully provided by the Christian Wilson, I sat down in the dirt and sobbed. I rolled onto Breech's grave and begged his forgiveness. I begged Harriet's forgiveness. And as I lay on my back beneath the cross and fingered the little noose in my pocket and watched the sliver of moon march across the sky, I thought of Chloe, and I prayed to my remnant of a god that she had not watched me break a dead man's neck. And still I cried, on into the dawn when the bell rang and the work began again.

I address you now, you who are the first to read this after I am dead, you, white man. Perhaps you are my jailer. Perhaps the preacher who sometimes visits in the hope of saving my soul. Perhaps the newspaperman who drops by my cell, wanting an interview that I will never give. Whoever you are, laugh once at this passage, and I promise I will haunt you. I will haunt you until the day you die. I will never let you sleep without some visitation from me. I will form myself into a body like Breech's, with a head that lolls to one side. Do not tempt me. I have no shame for crying that night. And in this narrative I am to cry many more times, yet I tell you this about me, Persimmon Wilson, Twist Rope, Kweepoonaduh Tuhmoo: in two days I am to hang and I am not crying now.

Grinding season ended in mid-January. I remember cutting my last plant that afternoon, then standing in the field hunched and ready with my knife in my hand, looking for the next one. But there were none. None in my field anyway. As my gang slowly realized this, we straightened and looked at each other questioningly. "Last plant," the driver called out. "We done. Sup, you go get Massuh. The rest, follow me." We trudged behind him in a row.

My whole body was tense, each muscle coiled, wanting it to be over, yet not believing that it was. The cane knife felt heavier in my hand than it had on that first day. Where were we heading? To another field? We must not be done. I could feel my muscles spasm with disappointment.

As it turned out, three fields over, there was one cane plant left. The largest cane plant of the harvest held out from all the rest stood lonely in a field of stubble. "Hold off fo' Massuh," the driver said, and we stood around this plant, staring at it. The other gangs drifted in, joining us, until all the field workers were there, staring at the cane plant. Finally I heard the sound of a horse at a gallop and Master Wilson came riding up to us, dismounting in a great hurry. In his hand he carried a streamer of blue ribbons, which he tied onto the lone cane plant, the hardest work I'd seen him do yet. Then he stepped back and said, "Sally?"

Sally, the fastest cutter at Sweetmore, was given the "honor" of cutting down the now-decorated last cane stalk of the season. Whack, whack. The leaves. Whack. It fell to the ground. Whack. The top came off.

A great cheer erupted from all the field hands gathered round. Master Wilson mounted his horse again, and Sally carried the cane plant to him, still tied with the stubs of ribbon that had now been severed by her knife. I leaned down and picked up a strand of ribbon that was left on the ground and slid it into my pocket without notice.

We followed Wilson to the sugarhouse, where, again, a great cheer went up among the workers when they saw that final plant. Grinding season was over, but the next day, the bell rang again before dawn. This time Master Wilson had us all standing in the quarters, while he stood on the stoop in front of one of the cabins. The weather was cold now and we stamped our feet for warmth, an unhappy clump of slaves: the sugarhouse workers, the boiler gang, the field hands, the wagon drivers. Our dissatisfied breath puffed into the air in front of us. Master Wilson held his hands up and said, "Go back to bed. Rest up. Y'all got a party tomorrow night."

I am sure that Wilson did not feel the beat of annoyance in his slaves before him. In his feeble mind he was playing a good-natured joke on us. How clever to make us believe that we would be working that day, when in fact he was sending us back to bed and telling us that we were to be rewarded with a party. We played our roles, every one of us. We set up another loud cheer and tossed our hats, those of us who had them, into the air. But Master Wilson hadn't gotten us out of bed to tell us anything we didn't already know. There had been talk among the slaves about sweeping and scrubbing the sugarhouse clean, and who would be preparing the food for the party, and what most likely would be served. A slave from another plantation, Sally's husband, had been hired to play the fiddle for us. We knew all this, but we went along. We cheered and hoorayed, and Wilson raised his hands again, and patted the air with his stubby, sausage-like fingers, indicating that there was more he wanted to say.

"Every one of you worked hard," he said. "We had a good season. We made five hundred forty hogsheads of sugar and one hundred eighty barrels of molasses, and every one of you deserves a week off after the party."

Another cheer. More hat tossing. The week off, like the party, was presented as a reward for all our hard work, all our "loyalty," but we would not be spending it in rest. We would tend our winter gardens, fish and hunt for extra meat, gather moss with which to re-stuff our mattresses, split wood for our fires. Now that grinding season was over our rations would be cut by a third. We all knew this. Even Bessle and I knew it, for Sup had told us. Still, we played our roles. We made Master Wilson feel like a hero as he stepped down off the cabin stoop.

"Thank you, suh," we said.

"Much obliged, Massuh."

"Bless you, Massuh. Bless you."

He held up his hands again, as if to ward off our phony gratitude, and made his way, chuckling, to his own house, to his breakfast cooked and served by slaves, to Chloe if he wanted her.

I looked for Harriet. Even though she and Sylvie lived in the cabin next to ours, I had not talked to her since Breech's death. There hadn't been the time, and I hadn't had the nerve, but the event weighed on me and I needed to say something, no matter how inadequate I knew it would be. I caught sight of her hurrying away with Sylvie, and I worked up my courage to call out to her.

They stopped and turned, and waited for me until I reached them. But once there, once facing the wife and daughter of the man whose neck I had broken, I could not speak. I just stood there and shook my head. I stammered, "Breech. His neck."

Harriet placed her hand on my arm. "Warn't yo' doin'. Don't think no mo' 'bout it." She turned and left me standing there, Sylvie following along behind her. At their cabin door Harriet stepped inside, but Sylvie stood on the stoop and stared my way before slipping inside herself.

My fellow slaves poured along beside me, heading to their cabins, wanting to get some sleep before the sugarhouse party.

Henry came along behind me. "What she say, Shoot?"

"She said don't think about it anymore."

"Then that best be what you do. What Sylvie say?"

"Nothing."

"Come on. Let's snore."

Henry, Sup, Bessle, and I slept, as I believe every sugar worker on Sweetmore did, all that day, on into the night, and all the next day, waking up at last to the ringing of the bell announcing the party.

It was not the first time I had seen the inside of the sugarhouse. On occasion, while hauling cane to the mill, I had stepped inside to help with one task or another. I already knew the cast-iron kettles lined along a brick wall with a ledge in front that could be stepped up on, and I knew the dirt floor so busy with people that their shoes had raised dust and dug furrows. But now the floor was even and tamped and swept, the marks of a stiff broom crisscrossing it. Along the walls, pine-knot torches gave light, while also giving a dark, pitchy smoke that rose to the ceiling and hung there like a thundercloud. A long table was spread with a patched red cloth and covered with platters of food, food like I had never seen offered to slaves before. The abundance alone was startling. There were hams and chickens and sausages, plates of greens and potatoes, and bowls of stewed apples. There were pies and cakes, and jugs of cider.

"Eat up, Shoot," Henry said. "Rations goin' down." He slipped two potatoes into his pocket, before loading his tin plate with slices of ham. I followed his lead and slid two potatoes into my own pocket.

We piled the food onto our plates, mounding it into little hills to fit on as much as possible. To a man and to a woman, the slaves ate ravenously, leaning against the walls of the sugarhouse, or sitting on the ledge in front of the kettles, barely talking as we did so. We ate plateful after plateful, each of us going back for more as if we could somehow swallow away the entire grinding season, its long days, and the seemingly endless labor.

As the food disappeared Jeff the fiddler came out and stood on the ledge in front of the kettles. He raised the instrument and stuck it under his chin, poised the bow over the strings before striking a note and stamping his feet and wheeling his way into a lively tune. Soon the floor filled with dancing couples, men swinging their women around and around, and women's skirts flying out, like fully opened morning glories.

We had been left to eat alone and in peace, but once the music started Master

Wilson and the missus paid us a visit. They stood to the side, Wilson delivering a benevolent smile and occasionally clapping his hands to the tune, his wife holding on to her husband's arm as though she might fall into a faint. Missus Lila looked worse than she had at Breech's funeral, her face still a caved-in looking thing, falling in on itself like a spoiled apple. She tugged on Master's sleeve and said something to him, and after a short time of standing there and being seen, and receiving more of the Bless you, Massuhs, and Thank you, Massuhs that he so craved from us, Wilson led Missus Lila out, and up the lane to the big house, the full moon lighting their way. I watched them as they left, Wilson round and sturdy with Missus Lila tottering along beside him, occasionally stopping to lean down and catch her breath.

I looked for Chloe, even though I did not expect to see her. The house slaves did not mix with the field slaves, and even if that had not been so, I was sure that, as nurse to Missus Lila, Chloe would be held back and kept in the big house. But still I looked. I could not help but looking.

A girl asked me to dance, and I went out on the floor and swung her around. And then another girl asked me to dance, and I swung her around. I danced quite a bit, with many girls, and I could feel, as I held each girl's hand, the rough calluses of grinding season in her palm. I learned their names that night. Jenny, Bea, Louisa, Alice, Linda.

The moon marched across the sky, full and bright, its light casting whiteness to the ground outside, making it look like new snow. I stepped out into it to catch my breath. I saw a group of men gathered in a circle around a fire, a jug being passed around.

"My man, Shoot," Henry hollered from across the fire. "Come on over here. Give yo' thirst a drink. You got the gals after you tonight, don'cha?"

I laughed. "Don't know, Henry."

"Mmm-hmmm." That was Sup. He took a swig on the jug and passed it to me. "This child's got it bad fo' that gal Chloe, work in the big house takin' care of the missus."

"Best stay away from her," another man said.

"What'd you hear?" I asked.

"Massuh Wilson's," he said simply.

"Fo'get 'bout her, Shoot. Don't be courtin' trouble. Here. Take another swallow."

I stayed and drank a little before wandering back into the sugarhouse. I was standing at the table, gnawing the marrow out of a bone, when I felt a tug on my shirttail. I looked down to see Peach, the girl who'd brought us our meals out in the fields.

"You Persy?" she asked.

"Yeah."

She crooked her fingers and wiggled them toward herself, indicating that I should lean down. "Chloe say fo' you to meet her," she whispered in my ear, "in the quarters. You in that last cabin? With Sup?"

"Yeah."

"That what I told her."

The full moon made the whitewashed cabins shine. A thin trail of smoke rose from Harriet's cabin next to mine. As I hurried down the lane, Chloe stepped out from the shadows, pulling her arms close around her and holding them to her chest. "Come in," I said.

Inside I built a fire to take the chill off and while we waited for the air to warm we stood in front of it, holding our hands out to its heat, our breath puffing in clouds between us.

"I brung you somethin'," Chloe said, reaching into the pocket of her apron, pulling out a small book and handing it to me.

I folded my fingers around it, feeling its cloth-covered binding, and the warmth on one side where it had pressed against her body. It had been a long time since I'd held a book in my hands, or a woman. "Chloe," I said. I took a deep breath. We both knew the rest of what I was about to say. She shouldn't have done this. It was dangerous to steal a book. She had taken too great a risk. "Won't this be missed?" I asked. "Won't you?"

"Massuh don't read," she said. "Only Missus read and she too sick to notice. She sleepin'."

"What about Wilson? Is he sleeping too?"

"He gone. Took off to see a fella next place over."

"There's no place to sit," I said apologetically, sweeping my hand in the air, showing her the four pallets nailed against the walls.

"Which one yo's?" she asked.

I pointed.

"That'll do."

She sat on my pallet. I laid another log on the fire and then sat beside her, turning the book over in my hands, not able to read its title for the feeble light inside, and the fear and the excitement I felt at sitting next to her again, unchained this time.

"I have something for you too," I said, and I pulled the blue ribbon from the last cane plant out of my pocket and handed it to her. "It's not much."

61

She took the ribbon and fingered it lightly.

"It'd look pretty in your hair," I offered.

"I cain't take it. Massuh see I got it and want to know where from."

I nodded. "Missus Lila will notice this gone when she gets well," I said, holding the book up.

Chloe shook her head. "She ain't gonna get well. I know it. Everyone know it. Massuh know it." She lowered her eyes to the ground. "Missus dyin', Persy. I don't think she dyin' fast enough fo' him, or fo' her either. I never been in such a house as this. Feel like the whole world jest waitin' on her to pass over."

I leaned against the wall behind me. I remembered all too well the death of Master Surley, and the auction of his estate where I had stood alone on an overturned crate, for sale as a single unit. But perhaps little would change if a mistress died rather than a master. How dense I was, how ashamed I am now to think of it.

"You supposed to be at the party," Chloe said.

"No one's going to miss me there." I reached up and brushed a strand of hair off her cheek. "Does he bother you?"

She shot back quickly. "What it matter to you what he do?"

"It matters," I answered. "I just can't do anything about it."

"Then maybe it best you don't know." She shrugged her shoulders and looked away from me.

In that moment I envied the wild animals whose first thoughts in danger are always of flight. A wild animal will chew its own leg off to get free of a trap. My instincts told me to go ahead and chew my leg off, to run, to take Chloe to a safer place, but there was no safer place to go to. Big plantations, water, white folks surrounded us. Our only recourse, I thought, would be to live in the swamps as Sup had told me some were doing. A wild animal would have taken Chloe there.

"They might miss me soon," Chloe said. "Missus might wake up needin' somethin'."

I nodded. She leaned over and kissed my cheek, and pressed the blue ribbon back into my hand. "I cain't keep it," she said. "I wish I could. It real purty."

"It's all right," I answered.

I put my arm around her, and we fell together onto my moss-stuffed mattress. Our coupling was desperate, made as much of fear as of heat. Fear and heat tangled together into a stew of passion. We were afraid, not just of getting caught, but of never being able to make this choice again. We pulled at each other's clothes. We tugged each other's bodies closer. We thrust and we pressed into each other until it hurt, and until it released that hurt.

The ribbon drifted to the floor. The book Chloe had given me slid with a thump off my pallet. The potatoes I had stolen at the party rolled out of my pocket and lumped softly across the uneven planks toward the fireplace.

Afterward Chloe fell asleep in my arms, and I pulled the thin gray blanket that had been issued to me over her shoulders to keep her warm, and watched the firelight flicker across her face. That sleep. I wanted it to last as long as she needed it to. And when she woke up I wanted to wind our fingers together and talk quietly and softly, the way I'd heard my mother and father talk together in our cabin at the Surley place. I wanted to see morning with Chloe, but she could not be missed in the big house. We could not be caught together like this.

The fire sputtered and gave one last flicker of flame before it bent itself to glowing coals. I heard drumbeats starting up outside the cabin. It sounded like many drums and the beating was at first disorganized, but gradually it coalesced into an unrelenting rhythm.

I did not know it then, but many of the men who had been on Sweetmore for several years had used their weeks off at the end of grinding season to make drums out of barrels and hollowed-out logs with animal skins stretched taut across them. Now they were gathered around a fire, beating on those homemade drums, harder and faster and wilder, while some of the women danced, gyrating, moving to the rhythm as though the drums were inside them. I would experience drumming and fires with the Comanche, but before that night the only drumming I had heard was at One-Eye's hanging, a solemn beat on a single drum as he was led out of his cell with his hands tied behind him, into the waiting crowd, and up the steps of the scaffold.

Now Chloe stirred and woke. "I gotta go," she said. She pulled away from my embrace and hurriedly began picking up her clothes and putting them on. "That drummin' gonna wake Ol' Miss. Mean ol' thing, she scared to death of everythin'." She buttoned the bodice of her dress, and tied on her apron, and plunked the little frilly cap that house slaves wore back on her head. Then she sat down beside me again and pulled on her stockings and shoes and began lacing them up.

The fear of getting caught was thick and palpable in the air now. It hung in the room like the heavy smoke from the pine-knot torches at the sugarhouse party. The drumming outside was becoming wilder and wilder, and only now do I imagine how the sound of this drumming must have felt to the white people as they lay in their beds in their big houses, surrounded as they were by all their trinkets and fine linens and gleaming wood and delicate china and silver polished by dark hands. How frightened they must have been that their slaves were becoming African again.

"You took a big chance," I said as Chloe laced the last of the grommets on her shoes.

She leaned over and kissed my cheek, and I selfishly tugged her back onto the bed, our lips meeting. She pulled away quickly and smoothed her hair. "I take a chance again, Persy," she said. "How I look? Not too messed up, I hope."

I sat up and tucked her hair behind her ears, and she leaned forward and kissed me once again. She stood and crossed the cabin floor. The sound of the drums leaked in louder as she opened the door, and then muted as it thudded softly behind her.

After Chloe left, I got up and dressed. I picked the potatoes off the floor and brushed one off and ate it, and then I ate the other one. I stoked the fire and kicked up the flame. Then I picked up the book Chloe had given me and by the light of the fire I read its title. *Sonnets from the Portuguese.* A book of poetry by Elizabeth Barrett Browning. I opened it and read a few lines.

I thought once how Theocritus had sung
Of the sweet years, the dear and
   wished-for years,
Who each one in a gracious hand appears
To bear a gift for mortals, old or young

I closed the book and ran my hands along its cover. I opened it again and smelt its pages. A scent of perfume wafted into my nose, no doubt the smell of Missus Lila in better days.

Perhaps if I had been a different person, perhaps if I had not been born a slave, perhaps if I had been white and educated and slept in a feather bed, perhaps then I would not have picked up the green sapling we used to poke the fire, and lifted the burning log, and wedged the book beneath it. I tossed the blue ribbon in behind it, and watched it curl and blacken and turn to cinders.

At the end of the week Master Wilson culled his slaves. Bessle was among the five chained and loaded into a wagon for transport to New Orleans. I stood with the others watching the wagon with its load of chattel rocking away from us along the rutted lane that led to and from the quarters. Behind me I heard Ida, the mother of another boy being carried away, sobbing. Bessle lifted his hand, chained to a man as old as his pa, and waved.

We returned to work on Monday. My first job was hauling wagonloads filled with barrels of sugar up to the levee road, and then rolling those barrels down to the quay and loading them onto a waiting steamboat. My second job was hauling and rolling barrels of molasses. Then sugar again. All day Monday we rolled the barrels.

And then on Tuesday I was given a task that would not end until March, digging furrows and planting cane. Tuesday and Wednesday I worked the plow, while behind me flowed a wide swath of slaves, bending and stooping, placing and then covering with dirt the sticks of cane with nodes budding on them. On Thursday, Friday, and Saturday I was taken off the plow and set to planting, and then it was I who followed behind, bent and stooped, a sack full of rattling cane sticks hanging across my body. Master Wilson had opened up two new fields to be planted, and we planted them, thinking of the extra work this would make for us at grinding season.

It was now January 1861. Do not think that just because we were slaves we were ignorant of the turbulence between North and South, although the white people always did their best to keep things from us. Nevertheless, all up and down the river, these same white people talked freely with one another in dining rooms, and in parlors, with whiskey and cigars, or tea and cakes. All the time that they talked there was a slave or two standing by to serve them, to keep them comfortable, to place logs on the fire, to pour that whiskey or that tea, to snip the ends off those cigars or replenish those cakes. But lately word had been coming to the quarters by way of slaves who visited from other plantations that something had gone strange with the white folk. Conversations were suddenly checked in servants' presence. Talk was now held behind closed doors. Voices were lowered and sometimes words spelled out.

At Sweetmore there had always been a dearth of information, as Master Wilson and his wife entertained not at all, and barely talked with each other, certainly not on matters such as politics. But still, we learned things. We were not ignorant. Every Sunday when Jeff came to visit Sally, he brought what news he had heard, and he had heard plenty. His master was in the habit of reading the newspaper aloud to his wife, and several of the slave children had taken to hiding beneath the house and listening and memorizing and reporting what was said to their elders. It was through Jeff that the slaves of Sweetmore learned that Louisiana had left the Union.

We weighed our odds of course, as we had always done. In my own cabin, Henry said he had heard there was talk of war, but the white folks said it would be short and quick and the South would be victorious.

Sup mentioned a Federal invasion, but Jeff's master had dismissed the notion as absurd. The states above Louisiana, Jeff explained, would take the brunt of the fighting and would cushion the state from any danger.

"What about the river?" I asked.

"Cain't get through the river," Jeff answered.

"Why not?"

"I jest sayin' what the white folk say. Cain't get through the river. They ain't gonna run short of nothin'. Goods gonna come in through New Orleans. Sugar get shipped out. I hear Massuh say two forts guardin' that river and cain't nobody get up there if they ain't supposed to," Jeff said.

"Aw, Shoot," Henry said. "I'm tellin' you, they gonna work somethin' out. You think white folk up nawth gonna do without they sugar? Without they cotton? Hell naw."

This is what Henry told himself, and this is what the white people told themselves as well. It might have been the only thing that Henry and the white people ever agreed on. If ever there was a safe place to be, the white people assured themselves, or a place where nothing would change, Henry said, Cane Country was it.

And nothing did change, except that as a precautionary measure, the reins that kept us in slavery were tightened. It was not long after Louisiana had seceded that Master

Wilson rallied us around him at the end of a workday. He stood again on the stoop of one of our cabins, and held his pudgy fingers up, just as he had done when he'd announced the sugarhouse party, but this time his face was a grave mask, as if to emphasize the seriousness of what he was about to say.

"There are going to be some changes in how things are done," he said. "Patrols are going to be increased up and down the river. Passes are going to be asked for and scrutinized. If you are caught off my property without a pass, you will receive twenty lashes, to be administered immediately by the man who apprehends you."

Among the slaves there was a slight, almost imperceptible stir. We were usually so skilled at keeping our feelings and thoughts to ourselves, but this news that we could be whipped by anyone caused a small fissure in our composure. I glanced over at Henry, barely turning my head as I did so. His face was sculpted again into his mask for white folk, but his fists clenched by his side.

"Husbands," Wilson continued, "from another plantation can see their wives but twice a month, no more." Sally straightened her spine and narrowed her eyes.

"Marriages will no longer be approved between plantations." I watched Lucy, whose beau lived on another sugar farm several miles downriver, blink twice at this news and heave her chest up once, her mouth tightening into a stick-straight line.

"Furthermore, any white man can inspect any Negro's cabin at any time. Now I don't expect any of this will make much difference to you, as long as you do your work and behave."

This is what white people always told us. Work and behave and nothing bad would befall us, as though being a slave was not evidence of something bad having already befallen us.

I saw the patrollers more often now as I worked in the fields, groups of white men on horseback, riding back and forth along the levee road, looking down on us as we worked. I could see the whips coiled and at the ready, snugged into the hand of one, or against the leg of another. Sometimes Master Wilson was among them.

Several times a day these patrollers passed by now, and at night I occasionally woke to the thunder of horses' hooves as they rode unrestricted through the quarters.

While we were repairing the levee one day, a group of white men stopped and spoke to

74

us, telling us that we had best behave ourselves, that word again, telling us that we had best obey our master who feeds us and clothes us, telling us not to be getting any crazed ideas about freedom in our woolly little heads. "Ain't no Yankee soldiers gonna come down here and save your sorry asses," one of them said.

"Yassuh. Yassuh," we replied.

They rode on, and we kept on packing dirt into the levee crack, saving their sorry asses from the river, should it decide to rise anytime soon.

More bothersome to me than the increased patrols was the decrease in rations. My stomach growled as I worked, and it growled as I watched the big house for signs of Chloe, and it growled as Master Wilson rode here and there, stopping in the road to talk to patrollers or a neighbor, or riding along the lanes that ran beside the fields, watching his slaves stoop and dig his crop in.

On Sundays Wilson gathered his sickly wife up like a heap of silk and lace, put her in the buggy, and drove to church. When it wasn't Sunday Missus Lila most likely languished in her bed, and Chloe most likely carried her food in and her slop out, wiped her brow, made her comfortable, waited by her side, and held her papery hand.

It was March before I saw Chloe again, and again it was Peach who brought me the message. "Chloe say meet her in the sugarhouse, Sunday mornin', after Massuh and Missus leave fo' church."

On the appointed day, I watched for his carriage pulled up to the house, for the careful way he led Missus Lila down the steep front steps, for the way he helped her into the buggy and took the reins from the waiting slave and chucked the horses into moving.

The sugarhouse was a long ways off from the big house, with nothing but a yard and the Wilson family cemetery and cane fields between the two, the cane plants a mere blush of green across the brown landscape now. I worried that it was too far for Chloe to make it safely during the day. Our master might be gone, and patrollers might not be in sight, but there were others who would betray us. Overseers, drivers, slaves as common as me who might tell Wilson of our tryst in the hopes of some scrap of a favor from him. But if she was clever, and if she stayed low, and if she skirted the edges of the fields, alongside the swamp, there was a chance, I thought, that she could make it. I, too, looked around, and made sure I wasn't being watched as I scurried up the lane toward the sugarhouse.

Chloe was there when I arrived, sitting on the ledge in front of one of the kettles. She came to me, and I went to her, and we met in each other's arms in the middle of the floor. I kissed her lips and then she pulled back, still holding on to my waist, and looked at me. "Lets us go to New Orleans," she said quickly. "They's plenty free niggers there. We pretend we free, get us a little house, start us a bakery. I good in the kitchen. You make us up a pass, Persy, you know how to write, make us up some of them papers say we free. That all you got to do, 'sides go with me."

"Chloe." I shook my head.

"I steal us some food," she kept on. "Massuh give me all the food I want. I pocket some away. You need food?" she asked. "You hungry?"

"I'm fine," I lied.

Chloe ripped out of my arms and began walking back and forth in front of the kettles. "You don't know what it like," she said. "You don't know. I trade places if I could. I plant cane. I work the field. Those long days." She beat one palm against her chest. "Ain't nothin' longer than my day.

Since grindin' season over, he pawin' on me all the time. He want . . ." Her voice cracked. "He say, 'Come here,' and I got to go there."

"Stop," I said.

"I standin' in his doorway pretendin' what 'bout to happen ain't gonna happen. I say, 'Massuh, you want I should stoke the fire? You want I should bring you a brandy or some tea?' He laugh and say, 'Chloe, you coy thing.' "

"Stop," I said again.

"He pat the bed fo' me to come over there. His wife, next room over, dyin'. He don't care. He pat the bed like I a little dog." Her voice grew louder as she talked. "He tell me she gonna die soon, and we be alone together all the time. Like what we doin' somethin' we both want."

I covered my ears. "Stop," I said. "I can't hear anymore. Please."

"He say after she dead, I sleep in her bed. He come visit me there. No one need to know. Like all those other house niggers don't already know what goin' on. Like they ain't lookin' at me now like he favorin' me somethin' good. Like he tellin' me, 'Chloe, close the do',' somethin' fun goin' on. Like I want it."

"Chloe, stop," I yelled. "Stop. Please. I

78

can't hear anymore." I put my face into my hands. "I can't hear anymore," I repeated.

When I looked up she was staring at the floor. "You all I got, Persy," she whispered.

"That's a shame," I answered, "because I am nothing but a field nigger."

"That right," she said. "I ain't got nothin'."

"You got food," I snapped. "Be grateful for that."

"And you ain't got Wilson humpin' on you all day, all night," she snapped back.

I took a deep breath. I did not want to think about that.

"He on me all the time," she whispered. She stopped her pacing and sat on the ledge in front of the kettles. I could see her shoulders tremble as she stifled tears. Finally she wiped the hem of her apron across her face, and looked up. "I don't reckon it matter."

"It matters."

She steadied a gaze at me, and said nothing. If I had thought what she told me with her voice was bad, what she told me with her eyes was even worse. Prove it, they said. Prove to me that I matter.

I took a deep breath and said nothing. Chloe continued to stare at me for what seemed like an eternity. I withered under

79

her gaze, and then, when she looked down, away from my eyes, I withered even more, for I could not bear the pain of disappointing her. I could not bear Sweetmore without the promise of her affection, and I found myself saying what I did not know I was going to say. "If we run away, we've got to have a plan. We can't just take off without thinking it through. You've got to go back to the big house." My own voice cracked at the thought of it. "You've got to go back to the big house," I continued. "You've got to . . ." I broke off my sentence, unable to say what it was she had to do.

"I know," Chloe said. "I gotta go back and make him think everythin' the way it always been. I do that, Persy. I strong. I been pretendin' all my life. But jest give me some hope. Jest a little hope to live on."

In that moment, when Chloe mentioned hope, I told myself that this was perhaps all she needed of me, to tell her a story, to comfort her with a lie.

"All right," I said. "Don't talk about this to anyone."

"Naw," she said. "I ain't no fool."

"I'll think of something," I told her. "I'll send word through Peach," I added to make it sound believable.

She stood up and came over to me, and

placed her hands on either side of my face. "I be a good woman to you, Persy."

I took her. I roughly shoved her clothes aside. I hurriedly unfastened the buttons on my britches. I took her and she gave herself to me on the sugarhouse floor, and for all his property rights Master Wilson could not buy what I had that Sunday, and yet I had bought it. I had bought it with lies.

It is not that I wanted to stay on Sweetmore. It is not that I didn't want to take Chloe away from that place, away from Wilson and his endless pawing at her. It is not that I didn't desire to take care of her, just as every man desires to take care of his woman. It is just that I was a slave, and I knew that New Orleans was not far enough away for safety, yet it seemed as unreachable as Africa.

In spite of the patrollers, and the danger, Chloe took the chance of meeting me three more times before the cane had grown above my head. Our passion fulfilled itself once again on the sugarhouse floor, once screened from view by the smaller levee that bordered the swamp, and once in the loft of one of the barns, above the stash of coffins Jonas had made.

Each time we were together I lied to her. I told her I was forming a plan for our escape.

I told her I was working on forged papers. I told her that it took time to make them realistic. I told her I thought we could make it to New Orleans and pass as free coloreds, find a little house the way she wanted, sell her baked goods on the streets and earn a fine living. I told Chloe whatever I thought she wanted to hear, and in the brief time we had together, she told me her own stories, stories that I didn't want to hear, stories that made me even more ashamed of what I was doing, and what I was not doing.

She was born on a plantation in Georgia called Collinswood, to a woman named Anna, and the man she called Papa was named Jason. "But I think Massuh Collins be my daddy," Chloe said. "I think Ol' Miss don't want me round no mo' 'cause I 'mind her of her husband." I stroked the skin on her arm and wondered at the generations of masters breeding with their slaves that had resulted in its color.

"I 'bout seven when I taken to Alabama, and I miss Mama and Papa, but things be all right 'cause I with my sister again, and she have a baby, and I in the kitchen now with Dicey May and she teachin' me to bake. She teach me everythin' 'bout bakin'. I good at bakin'. Then I gets a little bigger and Massuh Dan start with me. I ain't but eleven or twelve."

I pushed a curl of hair from her face.

"It go on fo' years, Persy." Her voice cracked. "I jest little when it start up, and I jest take it, then I gets bigger, and then one day I gets sold 'cause I . . ." She paused and looked up at me.

"What?"

"I crack a broom 'cross Massuh Dan's head. He fall on the flo'. I think I done kilt him. I run down the road and into the woods and it get to be dark. I hear the dog man comin' and I gets caught, but no one whip me. 'Stead I get brought down here to where . . ." She paused again, touching my face with her fingers. "Where I meet you," she whispered.

It was a whisper that made me ashamed, holding as it did all her hopes and dreams, as though meeting me could end this string of events in her life, as though I could somehow turn us both into free and respected colored folk, as though that little house she wanted was just waiting on us.

All this time the work of Sweetmore went on. There were, of course, the cane plants to tend to, and the repairs to the levee, but this was not the sum of it. I planted corn and sweet potatoes. I fed and watered the stock. I worked on a gang that graded and

83

repaired the roads left rutted and worn from their use during grinding season, and turned to ribbons of mud during the previous rains. And always there was wood to be cut and hauled from the swamps to feed the boiler of the sugarhouse mill for the next grinding season.

For this work of standing in swamp water, felling cypress trees, we were paid in credit, fifty cents per cord. It was the first time I had ever been paid for work in my life. This overwork, as it was called, came at night, after our day in the fields, and we volunteered for it. We piled into flatboats and pushed out into the swamps, one lantern held high for every six men, the light reflecting eerily in the dark rippling water as we moved along, the whole scene ghostly and surreal as we stepped into the water to cut the trees. Oftentimes a snake would come swimming along, carrying its body high, and we would clamber and splash away from it, fighting each other to climb up on a cypress knee. The snake would pass and we would slip back into the swamp and swing our axes against the very tree that had just protected us.

I do not think the mosquitoes in Louisiana ever truly went away. In the swamp the air was alive with them. We slapped at our bare arms and faces, and cursed the damn devils, and kept on with our axes and our muscles and our sheer determination that we might use our credit at Sweetmore's commissary to buy gaily colored swatches of cloth for our women, or a drinking gourd if ours had cracked, or a spoon with which to eat our cush-cush if ours had been lost.

Once a month I visited the store, and stared at the things I would like to buy for Chloe. A bolt of calico. A bonnet. Another ribbon for her hair, prettier than the one I had burned. I bought nothing. Now I do not even know why I went into the swamp so willingly, except that not doing so would have brought attention to me, as every able-bodied young man ached for the chance to earn something for his labors, and to buy something to call his own.

My credit at the commissary built, and built some more with each cord of wood I delivered. I could have bought a fry pan, a blanket, leather with which to repair shoes worn-out with the running from baying hounds. Instead I let my credit grow, and continued to assure Chloe that I was working on a plan for our escape, a plan so clever and perfect, I told her, that it would seem to Master Wilson we had merely floated away over the cane, its green leaves waving goodbye to us as we glided right into the heart of safety and freedom.

Chloe always looked at me when I said this, her eyes gone soft with love, and awe, and wonder. It was a look that I craved.

In May or June, I do not recall with certainty which, a local militia was formed to fight for the Confederacy, and Master Wilson's son, Gerald, signed up, as well as three of Sweetmore's four overseers. I had not seen Gerald Wilson the entire time I had been at Sweetmore, but Chloe told me he and his wife had come to Sunday dinner several times. Missus Lila, Chloe said, rallied to the table on the days that Master Gerald visited, dusting herself with powder for color and having Chloe dress her in her finest attire. Then she made her way down the staircase with the help of the banister at one side and Chloe at the other. At the bottom of the staircase her son was always waiting.

The newly formed Confederate militia made a grand tour of each plantation along the coast, marching in line and performing drills in their unsullied gray uniforms. It was, I suppose, for the glory of the cause and the entertainment of the ladies. These ladies, the young unmarried ones, followed the men from big house to big house, each buggy driven by a slave wearing a top hat and white gloves and holding the reins in stern profile. Sitting behind him, the ladies waved their handkerchiefs in the air, their pastel gowns spilling over the sides of the buggy like icing on a cake. Occasionally they broke into some rousing song about their sweet homeland, and Jefferson Davis, and hanging Abraham Lincoln from a sour apple tree.

At Sweetmore our work was stopped briefly and we, too, were rallied together on the lawn of the big house to watch these new, some of them barely whiskered, soldiers perform their marches and drills. We gave our own performance of mute subservience, our hoes and shovels and axes still in our hands or resting against our hips.

It is hard to say what I felt in that moment. It was, I think now, a mixture of things. These men were showing off their might and their power, as white men have always done, yet this grand display only told me that my enslavement was not such a certainty any longer. I could not, of course, articulate this in that very moment.

I thumped Sup on the hand. "Which one is Master Gerald?" I asked.

Sup scanned the soldiers. "All look the same to me," he said. He looked harder.

"He that one, behind the one carryin' that flag."

I looked closer. Gerald, for I will not call him master here, was tall and thick boned. He looked in the face like neither his father nor his mother, but he marched perfectly, rested his rifle on his shoulder perfectly, held his head up in perfect Confederate pride, never once glancing toward the porch of Sweetmore, where his father stood with a few house slaves gathered behind him, or to the balcony where Chloe stood, holding a weeping Missus Lila in her arms.

I could see Chloe talking to Missus Lila. Perhaps offering gentling and unfelt condolences of comfort as Missus Lila's only son marched off to war. Whatever Chloe said, it did not please Old Miss, for she abruptly gathered her body up straight, and her arm rose up, and her hand slapped Chloe across the face. I felt Sup grab my wrist and in that instance Chloe bowed her head, and I could see her lips moving in apology.

The soldiers finished their display. Master Wilson and the pastel ladies clapped their hands and Chloe led Missus Lila back into the house. Chloe turned once, as she was about to push the curtains aside, and scanned the slaves gathered on the lawn, but she could not immediately pick me out of the crowd of faces, and our eyes did not meet. The curtains closed behind her, and moved ever so slightly as they settled into place.

The militia marched down the lane to the road. The buggies rolled by, filled with ladies. Master Wilson held up his hands. "Back to work," he said.

I returned to the cane field and my hoeing. As I worked, with the sounds of mosquitoes circling my head, and fifty hoes chopping against the ground around me, I kept on seeing Missus Lila's withered hand rising up and landing across Chloe's smooth skin.

I had seen my mother slapped once when Miss Fannie had deemed the cake too dry to serve at her wedding party. She had landed her blows once across each cheek. I was a boy at the time, but even as a boy I felt that surge of manhood inside me that wanted to protect my mother.

I was trained though, as every slave was trained, to witness such things and do nothing, even though doing nothing felt like a sickness inside me, a parasite that would devour me until I was but the husk of a locust. It was no different on Sweetmore. On the day I saw Chloe slapped, I felt that parasite gnawing away at me. It felt as though I would be eaten from the inside out, and I could not bear it. I could not bear the knowledge that I was a man only in body, able to work hard and swing an axe in a cypress swamp, yet unable to keep one feeble-bodied old woman from laying a hand against my Chloe. It was this parasite that caused me to begin believing my own lies, for as long as I convinced myself that I really was making a plan, I was doing something, and as long as I was doing something, I was a man.

Chloe began sneaking food out of the kitchen house and bringing it to me whenever we met, and we began to meet far too often and far too regularly. We were giddy with these false plans of mine. It was as though our talk of escape had loosened something in our minds, as though we had folded our caution into tight little bundles like feed sacks tucked into the cracks of logical thought.

We had our occasional trysts at night, but they were random and scattered and we could not depend on them with any regularity. And so we began to meet each Sunday morning, in different places, after Master Wilson and Missus Lila had left for church. It was foolish to do so, foolish to meet each other with such clockwork precision, foolish to fatten each other's chimera of leaving, foolish for me to let Chloe steal so much food. But I was hungry. And I worked hard.

And I told myself that I deserved it.

However, if I am to leave an honest account here, I must admit to you that I felt a certain clandestine thrill in eating Master Wilson's food, and in the way that his fancy willingly gave herself to me. It is crude of me to speak so of Chloe, and in the affairs of her I do not care to be crude, but just this once, I will, because I know of no other way to show you what a diminished man I had become.

By July the cane plants had grown over my head, and the coast had emptied of its young white men. I would not have noticed their absence were it not for the fact that along the levee causeway young women now rode in their buggies without the accompaniment of young men, and along that same road, the ranks of patrollers were now greatly reduced. Chloe noticed this also, and she talked incessantly of our escape. She dreamt out loud of the little house we would have, and the goods that she would bake and put up for sale.

"Pies," she said. "All kinds. Blueberry, peach, apple. With crusts all buttery and flaky. I make a good piecrust, Persy. You see. And cakes. All kinds. Chocolate, white, fig. And biscuits. I love to make a biscuit. These biscuits they servin' here, they ain't nothin' 'pared to mine. You see. If Massuh had any sense, he put me in the kitchen and Katy in his bed."

One awkward laugh escaped her after saying this, and then she fell silent. Without discussion we had chosen to never mention Master Wilson's penchant for her company, and this slip of her tongue fell between us like a thunderclap.

It was nighttime, one of our rare evening visits. Master Wilson was serving with the patrollers and an hour earlier Chloe had climbed the ladder to the barn loft, balancing a tin plate of chicken in one hand. I had taken that plate from her and set it on the floor and then I had begun unhitching the buttons of her dress. A half moon, leaking through the slats of the barn wall, felled its light across her skin in stripes. I moved her here and there that her body be illuminated in different places, and I touched those places with my tongue until she cried out a slave's secret passion, a cry that must remain, for the purpose of safety, quiet and muffled.

Afterward I had lain naked on a horse blanket and gnawed on the chicken while watching her get dressed. I was ravenous. I remember that. "You best put yo' britches back on," Chloe had said, reaching between my legs and giving me a playful tug. "You don't want Massuh catch you without yo' drawsies." I'd laughed and obediently dressed.

Now I reached over and rubbed Chloe's shoulder, but her mood had changed, and she shrugged my hand away. She stared hard at her shoes and began toying with the grommets. "When we gonna leave, Persy?"

"Soon," I answered.

Chloe said nothing.

"We can't rush," I added.

Still she was silent. Her fingers walked along her shoes, from grommet to grommet. She did not look at me. It was bad enough, I suppose, to hear my lies, but to watch me telling them would have been even worse.

"The time has to be right, Chloe. You know that."

I felt her take in a deep breath and let it out, and in that moment I knew. I knew that she had seen me for exactly who I was. I had no plan for her, no forged papers, no prospects of getting her away from Master Wilson's lasciviousness. I had no way to fly us over the cane fields.

The cane plants were filled out now, with emerald-green leaves that would wave in the slightest breeze, and when they did the entire field undulated, making it seem like a bright green sea. I suppose it might have been pretty to someone who did not work it. It had been pretty to me in the dream I'd had the night before, a dream in which I actually was flying with Chloe's hand in mine, and we were looking down over those fields moving in the breeze and Chloe had said, "That our wind makin' 'em go like that. Look at it, Persy. That our wind."

In the loft of the barn that night, the caskets stacked in a stall down below us, I turned to look at her, and although I could not see her face clearly, I knew that she was crying, softly and silently, the worst kind of tears, the kind that come from knowing that nothing is going to change. "I reckon you doin' the best you can," she whispered.

I sat with Chloe's moisture still caught between my legs and a tin plate of chicken bones sitting at my feet. I felt as though someone had turned the flame of an internal lamp up, and now it blazed brightly enough for me to see my own cowering soul in the corner of my being. I could not continue this way. I could not go on lying to her. Above all, I would not let Chloe buttress my manhood for me. I would not let her pretend that she did not know I was a shuck of a man, a charlatan, a fraudster. I picked a small stalk of grass from the leg of my britches. "I don't have papers," I confessed. "I don't have a plan."

I could feel her sniffling beside me. It was my punishment to sit and listen. I did not think I should be forgiven and so I did not apologize. Chloe's sniffling continued, and then, out of the corner of my eye, I saw her wiping tears away with the hem of her dress. She reached out and touched me. I felt her fingers through the rough linsey of my shirt. Her small, slim fingers that had caressed me, that had held me, that had wandered across my body and up my neck.

"Don't forgive me," I said. "I do not deserve to be forgiven."

I was thinking only of myself. It would have been easier if she had been angry, if she had slapped me hard across the face, if she had left me sitting in the barn loft alone, as I deserved, but this is not what she did.

"All those pies you talked about," I said, "all those cakes. The little house."

"I ask too much," she whispered.

"The food you bring me." I kicked at the plate of chicken bones and tipped them into the straw. "You over there having to . . ." I could not finish.

"I ask too much," she whispered again.

"We ask too little," I answered.

"Persy, it not too late." Chloe pulled away from me, forcing me to sit alone in a slat of moonlight that fell across the horse blanket. "We start plannin' now. Now better than ever. They not so many 'trollers. Yankees comin' to set us free anyway."

I shook my head. "You don't know what it's like in those swamps, and that's where we'd have to go. There are snakes. Gators. Mosquitoes. Panthers. It's putrid. It's damp, Chloe."

"I reckon I know a swamp is damp."

"You don't know what it's like in those swamps," I repeated. "I know. I cut wood there."

"And you don't know what it like in the big house," she said with so little inflection that I felt a chill go up what was left of my spine. She leaned against the back wall. "Missus Lila gonna die soon. They gonna come a day when she don't go to church. I won't be seein' you on Sundays no mo'. I won't be bringin' you no food. It gonna happen soon. Ever since her son left, she been doin' worse poorly. She don't eat much. Her skin all pale and drippy. I ain't told you this. I don't know why." She looked down and her fingers found the grommets of her shoes again.

I knew why she had not told me. It was

because she trusted me, and because she did not want to burden my "perfect plan" with the pressure of moving too fast. She would endure whatever she had to endure in order to help make our escape sound, and had I been paying attention to anything but the plates of food she brought me, and the comfort and release she gave me with her body, I would have known this. Chloe had told me of Missus Lila's attachment to Gerald, and now without her son close by, Old Miss had little reason to live, and Master Wilson, once free of his wife, would have little reason to dampen his desires for Chloe.

"Chloe, I —"

"Shhh. Quiet," she whispered, holding her finger up and cocking her head to listen.

Outside, the ground crunched.

We froze.

The ground crunched again.

I felt my body instinctively wanting to move deeper into the loft, to crawl under the horse blanket, out of the moonlight. But afraid that moving would cause a rustle that might be heard, I stilled my body's urge. I turned my face to the barn doors, and watched, and waited.

The ground crunched twice more. The doors twitched. I told myself that a cow must have gotten loose. I listened carefully for the ripping of grass that would indicate this as true, but there was none.

Again the sound of something stepping, and then, through the crack between the barn doors, I saw a shadow slip by. Chloe's hand went to her mouth and covered it, and she hid her face in my shoulder. Then the ground crunched again, and then again, and again, the sound moving away from us now, as whatever it had been left the barnyard.

My breath went out of me. I fell limp against the back wall, still holding on to Chloe. My heart seemed as though it had left my chest and lodged in my throat where it now hurriedly throbbed like the heart of a panicked bird. Slowly, I felt Chloe's shoulders relax and the fear unfasten itself from her body. "I'll do it," I whispered. "I'll get us out of here."

She reached up and stroked my cheek. I raised my hand to meet hers, to turn her hand over, to kiss her palm. "I know you will," she said. And then she added, "I gotta go."

I nodded.

"I cain't stay no longer."

"I know. You leave first."

She smoothed her hair. "How I look. Am I all messied up?"

I smiled. "You look beautiful," I said.

She picked up the tin plate. "You bury 'em," she said, pointing to the chicken bones lying across the loft floor. "I ain't got nowhere to put 'em won't be seen." I scooped the bones up and jammed them into the pocket of my shirt. She scooted herself to the edge of the loft, holding the tin plate in the fingers of one hand. "Careful," I said as she swung her legs onto the ladder. The soles of her shoes squeaked against the rungs. When she'd reached the bottom I could hear her hitting her hands against her dress, trying to remove any dirt or dust that clung to it. I pictured her running her hands through her hair, straightening it the way she always did before leaving me. And then I thought of the dream I'd had, of flying over the cane fields with Chloe's hand in mine, of watching our wind make a churning sea of those leaves.

I did not know how I would achieve it, but I vowed that I would get Chloe off Sweetmore. I vowed that I would take her away from Master Wilson. I vowed that I would be true to my word.

Chloe opened the barn door and in the shaft of moonlight that was let in, I saw her turn and look toward the loft. I held my hand up to bid her farewell, but she could not see me. She let herself out, the tin plate hitting softly against the wood of the door as it shut behind her.

I waited. It would be safer if I did not leave right behind her. I waited until I was certain that Chloe had had enough time to reach the big house, and to let herself inside, and to make her way to her pallet at the foot of Missus Lila's bed.

And then I folded the horse blanket we had used to lie on and swung my legs off the edge of the loft onto the ladder. I placed the folded blanket back where I had found it, draped across one of the stalls. A mule blew out a huff of air as I passed by. "Easy fella," I whispered. "Ain't no one here." I pulled the barn door open and stepped outside. The moon had hidden itself behind a cloud. I could make out only dark shapes. A hedge. Another outbuilding. A wagon. One step, then two, and then a third, and my foot landed on something and caused it to flip up and hit me lightly in the shin. I leaned over to pick up the tin plate that had held the chicken Chloe had brought to me.

"What you doing, Persy?" Wilson's voice came to me from the hedge of shrubbery.

I turned to the sound of it. "Massuh," I answered. I hated the cower in my voice, the quiver, the instant subservience that I

101

used in addressing him. "I's checkin' on one of the mules," I said. "It limpin' this evenin' when I put it up."

"Mighty late to be checking on a mule."

"Yassuh. I's worried 'bout it. It a good mule," I added. "You don't want to lose it, Massuh. I jest lookin' after it."

"Don't be giving me that shuffling nigger crap, Persy." The clouds left the moon and Wilson stepped out of the hedge holding Chloe by the arm. He shoved her to his side. "Get on back to the house," he told her.

"Naw, Massuh," Chloe said. "You come on back with me. Let's leave this nigger be and go on back to the house together."

She touched his arm. I looked at her fingers on the sleeve of his shirt as they trailed seductively upward to his shoulder. How I hated him, how I hated all the white men making their little mulatto babies down in the quarters. And I almost, in that moment, hated Chloe, too, for touching him willingly this time, for using his lust in an attempt to save me.

Wilson coolly tilted his head down and looked at her hand. "Get on back home," he said again, "or maybe you want to watch me give this nigger a lesson."

"Naw, Massuh."

"Chloe, go to the big house," I said,

slowly, deliberately, as if I were giving orders to a child. And with that Master Wilson landed a fist in my gut. I felt the breath go out of me. The tin plate slipped from my hands. My body folded over with the impact and the chicken bones rattled from my pocket and fell to the ground.

Wilson grabbed me by the back of my shirt and shoved my face against the barn door. I could feel him behind me, leaning into my back. I could smell the scent of cigars and liquor on his breath. "She ain't yours to give orders to," Wilson hissed, turning me around now to face him.

Chloe was on him, clawing at his sleeve, begging, "Massuh? Massuh? Massuh, come on back to the house with me."

"Naw, Massuh," I hollered. "I jest checking on a mule."

"Mule, my ass."

"Massuh. Massuh. Come on to the big house with me." Chloe's fingers raked at his jacket, and as he pushed her away, I felt, ever so slightly, her fingers stumbling across my own skin as she fell. Master Wilson stepped back and hit me again in the gut. And then again and again.

I fell onto the grass and curled into a ball to protect my stomach, my groin, my organs. Dimly I saw Wilson's black leather boots flying toward me as he delivered kick after kick upon my person. And dimly I was aware of Chloe, up off the ground now and returned to pawing at him, and saying, "Massuh. Stop. Stop, Massuh. You gonna kill him."

"She ain't yours," Wilson kept hollering. "She ain't yours. You got that, nigger. She ain't yours and she never will be." The kicks flung into my arms, my legs, my ribs. He circled, working one side and then the other.

"Massuh, you gonna kill him," I heard Chloe say again.

And then Wilson roared, "By God, I will kill him. The damn nigger son of a bitch."

He placed his boot against my side and pushed until I rolled over, exposing my gut.

"Naw," Chloe said. "Naw."

I rolled quickly over once more, again curling to protect myself, and as I did so I saw a flutter of cream that I took to be Chloe leaving at last, her dress billowing as she ran to the big house.

Wilson stood back from me now. "Stand up and fight," he said.

"Suh?" I managed.

"Stand up and fight me. You're man enough to be telling my wench what to do, then you're man enough to fight me."

"Nawsuh," I said.

"No sir, what?"

"Nawsuh, Massuh, I ain't man enough to fight you."

"Stand up." He pulled me up by the back of my shirt until I was upright and swaying before him. "You a goddamn mess, Persy. Just look at you. You think she wants you? You just a common field nigger. I'll teach her who she wants."

Before I knew it I had hit him. It was a punch that landed Master Wilson on the ground, and once I had committed to it, I pounced on him, and I pummeled my fists against him. Even as I did so I knew that I would be killed for this. I would be flogged to death, or hanged, or tortured. Whatever the method, I would die for this action, and because I knew this, it did not matter what I did. I would die defending Chloe's honor, not that it would do her much good in the long run. But still, I could not stop. I felt my fists sink again and again into his puggish flesh. I felt the breath sink out of him. My muscles coiled like snakes, striking and striking and striking and striking. Through my cottony mind I heard voices. My name repeated again and again and the word stop. "Persy. Persy. Stop. Stop, Persy, stop," and then I felt hands pulling me away, hands pulling me back from the job I had started and was bent to finish.

Henry had me by the arms and he flung me against the barn door and held me there. He shook his head. "Shoot, you dumb son of a bitch, you done it now."

I heard Sup say, "Massuh? Massuh, you all right? Here, lemme help you up."

My left eye was swollen shut but through the slit of my right eye I saw a lantern sitting on a stump, and by its light, Sup was helping Master Wilson off the ground, their shadows thrown large across the hedge of shrubbery. Wilson stood and brushed Sup's hands away from him. I had not beaten him as badly as he had beaten me. I had not had the time for it.

Henry held my arms and Wilson took one step toward me, his boots crunching into the chicken bones that had fallen from my pocket. He looked down, and noticing the tin plate, he picked it up and held it between two fingers. "I caught this nigger with stolen food," he said. "And then he went crazy on me, cussing and trying to hit me. I got the best of him though. You can see that."

"Yassuh," Henry said, looking me over. "Look to me like you did."

"Fifty lashes," Wilson said, pointing one plump finger at me. "To be administered Friday afternoon. Holmes will do it. Take him back to the quarters, Henry."

"Yassuh."

Sup leaned down and picked up Master Wilson's hat. He brushed at it, his fingers raking off the leaves and grass that clung to it. "Yo' hat, suh." Wilson grabbed it, glowered at me once, and then stalked off to the big house, hat in one hand, and tin plate in the other.

The power I had felt while beating Wilson was gone now, dribbled out of me like pee. On one side, Henry got an arm around me, and on the other, Sup, and with their help I began limping my way back down the lane to our cabin.

"Chloe," I said, my own voice coming to me as if from inside a hollow tree.

"That filly done got you in a heap of trouble, Shoot."

"Is she all right?"

"Last I saw her," Sup said. "Come and got us. Save yo' life. Look like she save massuh's too." He chuckled.

"Why the whipping?" I asked.

They both stopped. It was Sup who answered. "You think you gonna do somethin' like that and not get a whippin'?"

"No, I mean, why aren't I going to hang?"

"Aw, damn, Shoot." We started our movement toward the cabin again. "That ol' buckra got some pride, don't he? He cain't let folk know you was humpin' on his fancy."

I reared up at this manner of talk about Chloe, reared up as best I could, which was not much, as the only response to it was Sup saying, "Easy there, stud."

"What kind of food you steal?" Henry asked.

"I didn't steal any food."

"Someone did."

"Chicken," I said. "I stole chicken."

"Fifty lashes mighty much fo' stealin' chicken," Sup said. "Maybe he givin' you half those fo' not sharin' with us."

"Damn, Shoot. I got half a mind to hang you myself, hungry as I am."

"I'll bring you some next time Chloe and I meet."

"Y'all ain't gonna meet no mo'. Leave it be, Shoot. You got any damn sense at all, you leave that gal be."

Sup let go of my shoulder long enough to ease the cabin door open and help me inside. I collapsed on my pallet and closed my eyes. I heard the sound of hands dipping into the water bucket, and wringing out a cloth, and then I felt cool moist fabric laid gently across my swollen eyes. I felt someone untie and then remove my shoes. "Rest up, Shoot," I heard Henry say. "Gotta work tomorrow. Gotta work all week, then they gonna be a whippin'." I heard him laughing to himself as he crossed the floor. The moss inside his mattress sighed as he lay down. "You got yo'self a beatin', then workin' all week in a cane field, then a whippin'. All that worse than hangin', if you ask me."

I believe Henry was right. At my whipping I would be made to lie facedown on the ground. My hands would be tied to two separate stakes, spread apart. My feet would be tied together onto one stake. I would be stripped to the waist that I might receive my lashes without ruining my shirt. The man doing the whipping would count out the number with each delivery.

I had seen such a whipping on Sweetmore the year before, required, as I was a part of the quarters, to witness the punishment of a young girl named Jilly, accused of insolence. I had heard the talk of what transpired to cause her punishment, but I cannot recall now the specifics. I do remember that she was young, and very pregnant, and that I had been given the task of digging a hole that her belly might rest in it while she received her punishment, thus protecting Master Wilson's future property. I had closed my eyes to the whipping and lowered my head. If I could have covered my ears without notice, I would have done so, but I could not, and the sound of Jilly crying and screaming, and the whip whistling through the air and then landing on flesh was a cruel concert. As Jilly's skin opened up the sound changed, and the liquid notes of blood and the moans of the slaves added themselves to this awful symphony.

I could barely move the morning after my encounter with Master Wilson, but I pulled myself out of bed and made my feet get inside their shoes, made my legs line up outside with my gang. I made my arm reach out to take the hoe. I made my fingers wrap around it. I said nothing to anyone that day, but I could feel the news of my crime, stealing chicken, and my punishment, fifty lashes, make its way through the cane plants and jump the ditches from one field to the next. By the time the day was over everyone in the quarters knew what had really happened.

I barely ate the cush-cush Sup offered me that night. I lay on my bed and closed my eyes, but it was not long before there was a knock on the door. I heard it open and then the sound of Sylvie's voice. "I reckon his ribs might be broken, some of 'em," she said. "Might help to wrap 'em."

"Persy," Sup said. "Sit up. This lady gonna tend you, not that you deserve it."

I groaned as I raised my body up to sit on my pallet. "Take yo' shirt off," Sylvie demanded. I tried but my fingers felt like nubs of clay. I could not make them work the buttons. "Here," she said. "Let me." And she knelt before me and reached out, her fingers shuttling at the front of my shirt until it fell open. Sylvie stood, and resting one hand on my shoulder, she helped me slide the sleeves away until my shirt lay in a rumpled landscape behind me. "Raise yo' arms," she said, and I did so, painfully. Sylvie knelt again before me and began binding my torso with a cloth. She looked into my eyes as she did this, and I met her gaze. She was, I saw, a beautiful girl. "They's perfectly good womens round here, Persy. Massuh be happy fo' you to have any one of 'em. You ain't gotta take what his."

I looked away, and did not answer, and she cinched the cloth around my torso a little too roughly, causing me to draw in a painful breath.

"Too tight?" she asked.

I nodded.

"Well, I jest have to loosen it then." And she did, and then bound me once more. "Better?" she asked.

I nodded again.

"I don't see no fancy down here takin' care of you," Sylvie said.

Every day that week I dragged myself through my work. I winced with each beat of the hoe against the earth. I cursed the sun hammering down on my back. I cursed the mosquitoes that stung me without mercy. I cursed the cane plants and their precious sugar. I cursed the white people and their precious way of life.

Master Wilson did not come around to the fields that week as he usually did, nor did I see him riding anywhere. The big house loomed quiet and sullen. The only life I saw there was the occasional slave walking from the kitchen house to the back door, carrying a platter or a tureen of food.

All I could think of was what punishment Master Wilson might have meted out to Chloe. He would not whip her; I knew this. Her skin was too soft and smooth and inviting to him for whipping. I could only imagine that he forced himself upon her more often, and perhaps more brutally. She was not mine, he had said, she was his. He would teach her, he'd said, whom she wanted.

I obliged myself now to think of those particulars that Chloe had told me of during that first meeting in the sugarhouse, the particulars that I had previously given myself the luxury of keeping out of my mind. I drove myself to remember Chloe telling me of his calling her to his chambers, and of her standing in the doorway offering to bring him a cup of tea or a tumbler of brandy, hoping to turn him away from his lechery. I thought of Master Wilson patting the bed he sat on, as though Chloe were a small dog delighted to leap up next to him.

These thoughts made me physically ill. More than once I bent over and vomited beside a cane plant, then straightened, spit once, wiped my mouth, and continued hoeing. Yet still I forced myself to remember. I felt nothing but contempt for my selfishness, my egotistical need to embellish the lies I had told Chloe, my need to make myself feel like a man while doing absolutely nothing for the woman I claimed to love. I almost welcomed the lash, believing that at least I would suffer during my whipping as much as she suffered every day. The only consolation I allowed myself was the knowledge that house slaves were not required to witness whippings, and therefore Chloe would not be among the wincing faces watching the flesh fly off my back.

The day came. Master Wilson did not attend. It was Holmes, as Wilson had named, who would do the job of punishing me. Holmes was Sweetmore's only overseer who had not signed up for service with the Confederacy. He was thin and lanky, with a slab of dark hair falling from beneath his hat. I did not judge him to be particularly strong, but truthfully it did not matter as the whip was designed to do most of the work.

I remember raising my arms while the cloth that Sylvie had bound around my torso was unwound by one of the drivers. I remember the cool ground against my chest and stomach as I was made to lie down. I remember that there was a line of black ants marching across the dirt in front of me.

If I allow myself to, I can feel the roughness of the ropes as they were tied around my wrists and ankles, staking me into place. I can hear the slice of held breath behind me where my fellow slaves were gathered, and the voice of Holmes saying, "For the crime of stealing food, Persimmon Wilson, you are to receive fifty lashes," and then the unfurling of the whip behind me, the tip of it dropping to the earth with a light smack.

Fifty lashes. I did not know what I was in for. The first lash stung. I thought I could bear it. The fifth lash caused a warming sensation. At ten I begged for mercy. At twelve I swore into the dirt to the god I did not believe in.

Holmes counted out loud. I remember puffs of dust erupting in front of my mouth, as I blew air out with each lash. I remember grit settling in my nose, my eyes, my mouth. After a while I felt my flesh split open.

"Oh Lord," someone said behind me. "Oh Lord."

The slaves began to moan. Their voices rose and fell into crescendos and valleys as each blow fell across my back. I felt another strip of skin peel away. I felt air move across muscles and tendons. I felt hot rivulets of blood pour down my sides. I saw a piece of my flesh plop wetly into the dirt in front of me.

I do not know at what count of the lash I went unconscious. I do not know where my mind went or how it could have gone anywhere at all while my body endured such treatment. Time passed. Flesh peeled off my back. The slaves moaned. More lashes were delivered. The counting continued, but I could no longer hear it.

After it was over Holmes must have commanded that someone cut me loose. He must have coiled the whip, and handed it to a slave to be put away. He must have daubed his hands, wet with my blood, on his pants legs.

I came to as I was being laid into the bed of a cart. I lay on my side as the cart bumped down the lane. Each squeak of the wheels tore into my brain. Each jolt of its hard wooden shelf ran through my body like bolts of lightning. "Is he dead?" someone asked.

The cart came to a stop. I was lifted from its bed. I opened my eyes and saw that we were at our cabin, that Henry was holding me in his arms as if I were a sack of potatoes, that Sup was standing at the door, one hand on its wooden knob, my shirt and the cloth that had bound my ribs in the other.

"Goddamn," I heard Henry say. I remember feeling the deep resonance of his voice vibrate through his shirt where my ear rested.

"I'm not dead," I tried to tell them, but the words did not come. I tried again to speak and nothing. I began to wonder if perhaps I was dead. Perhaps I had died on the ground ten or twenty lashes before the end. "Chloe," I tried to say, but the only sound I heard was a wet garble.

"I get the brine." A woman's voice. I know now that it was Harriet.

"He ain't gonna be able to work next week," someone else said.

"Naw. That must of been some chicken," and there was a smattering of laughter, and then the door opened and I was carried inside. I felt Henry lower me onto my pallet, and then turn me over so that my back was exposed. "Goddamn, Shoot."

If I had any doubts about whether or not I was alive, they were immediatcly expelled when Harriet sopped a cloth soaked in brine across my back. It was fire, pure, hot, blueflame fire, as if kerosene had been poured across my skin and then lit with a match. I jerked trying to get away from the pain. "Easy," Harriet said. She pushed her hand against the back of my neck. "It bound to burn, but it what you need. Massuh sent it."

"Good of him," I heard Sup say from off in one corner.

Harriet peeled the cloth off my back. I heard her dip it in the brine again. I heard the brine drip as she lightly squeezed the cloth. Once more she sopped it across my shredded skin and again I jerked. I felt her cool hand on the back of my neck. My eyes watered with tears. The pain of the brine across my raw back was as bad as the whipping, yet it is never the brine that I think about, only the whip. I heard the door open and Henry say, "Y'all go on home now."

"Persy gonna be all right?" someone asked.

"He be all right," Henry said. "Jest a whippin'," and he closed the door and said to himself, "jest a goddamn whippin'."

Harriet sat with me throughout the night, keeping the cloth on my back from drying, constantly peeling it off and wringing it out with more brine, then laying it on again. After some time my back numbed to the burning, and I became accustomed to the sound of the wringing cloth in the brine and the feel of the air across my lacerated skin as the cloth was changed, and after some time I was able to sleep.

I dreamt, I remember, not of Chloe, but of my mother working in the field, heavy and pregnant with my sister, and dropping one day to her knees as her labor began. I dreamt of my pa tending the garden behind our cabin by the light of the moon, that we might have a little extra food besides our rations. I dreamt of the morning glory vine that grew outside our cabin door, how Mama had trained it to grow up the cabin walls by way of sticks jammed into the cracks between the chinking.

"Yo' mama ain't here," I heard Harriet say, so I must have called out in my sleep. I opened my eyes. The cabin was dark. I heard Henry snore and Sup roll over and punch at his mattress. I felt Harriet peel the cloth away from my back. Then I heard her plunging it into the bucket of brine and wringing it out before I felt it laid across my back again. "Go on back to sleep," she said. "You get some rest. Best thing fo' it."

Hours later the bell rang, calling the slaves to get up and ready for work. I felt Harriet rise from the side of my bed. "Change his dressin' befo' goin' to the fields," she said, and then I heard the door open and close as she left. I felt the movement in the cabin as Sup and Henry pulled on their britches and shirts. I heard the fire crackling and a spoon hitting against the sides of a bowl, then the sizzle of grease as someone dropped batter in to cook.

"You hungry, Persy?" Sup asked. "You want a hoecake?"

I shook my head.

"You ought to have you some water," Henry said. I made myself prop up and drink while Henry held a gourd full of water to my lips. Then he changed the dressing on my back, as Harriet had instructed. "Don't let that dry on you," he said. "Pull it off you feel it dryin'. You hear?"

I nodded.

The bell rang again, and Sup and Henry left for the fields. I drifted in and out of sleep. When I felt the cloth drying on my back I twisted my arm that I might grab its corner and pull it off. It scraped tortuously across the raw meat of my spine, and it was some time before I could drift again into sleep. I awoke, I do not know how many hours later, to the sound of the door creaking open.

"Day over?" I muttered, expecting the rough, hard steps of Henry and Sup coming in from the fields, and then feeling confusion that the light was too bright for the end of the day, and the footsteps that traversed the cabin floor were too light and soft.

"Persy?" I heard. "Persy? I got somethin' fo' you."

I recognized the voice of Peach and I turned my head to find her standing at the side of my pallet. "This from Chloe," she said, and she pried my fingers open and placed a piece of folded paper inside my palm. I closed my eyes as my fingers wrapped around this bit of paper.

Peach stood beside my pallet, then leaned over and picked the cloth up off the floor. I heard her dip it in the brine, and wring it out, and then felt it being laid across my back. "Thank you," I said.

Her feet crossed the floor again, and the door creaked open. "You look right bad," she said before stepping down onto the stoop and letting the door fall shut behind her.

I told my fingers to open this paper and see what was there, but I could not get them to obey the command. And so I merely held it. I could not imagine what message it could possibly contain, as Chloe could not write, and I did not know of anyone in the big house who would write a note for her. Finally, as the light was fading, I again sent the mental commands to my body. I forced myself to roll to my side. I forced my fingers to unfold the piece of paper. I forced my eyes to focus in the dimming light and read what was there, but there was nothing there in the form of words. Only the embossed initials of Master Wilson at the top of the page, and then marks of ink, slanting to one side and broken up by spaces, as if in imitation of writing, one final mark at the end, as if a signature. Judging from this last, Chloe imagined her name to be long and florid, and this made me smile.

I turned the "note" over and over in my hands. I reached with one finger to feel the indentations on the page where Chloe bore down with a pen. I did not need to be either literate or illiterate to know what was written there. It was a note of love, a note of sorrow, a note of passion, and it meant more to me than any words I have ever read.

Before Sup and Henry returned from the fields I hid the folded paper, sliding it into the seam at the head of my bed, where wall met floor. There I could reach for it while still lying on my pallet. And I did just that on Monday morning, alone in the cabin once more while the others worked. I touched those "words" again and again.

Four days after my whipping Master Wilson paid me a visit. It was in the middle of the day, the cabin quiet and empty, while off in the distance the rhythmic thuds of the slaves' hoes hit against the earth. I was lying on my pallet, still on my stomach, touching the words on Chloe's note, when I heard his footsteps on the stoop followed by the scrape of the door against the floor. Quickly I slid the note beneath my body.

"Persy," I heard him say.

"Yes, Massuh."

"How are you feeling?"

"Right po'ly, suh."

I heard the squeak of leather as he crossed the floor. I could see the tops of his boots as he stood beside me. They looked to be new, shiny with brass buckles, not the boots that had kicked me.

"Well, yes, I'm sorry to hear that," Wilson said. "But I suppose you've learned your lesson."

"Yassuh."

"You'll not be stealing any food from my larder again."

"Nawsuh."

"Very good, then." There was a long pause. "Harriet and Sylvie have been taking care of you?"

"Yassuh. Every night."

"Using the brine I sent along, I hope."

"Yassuh. I's grateful fo' that, suh."

"Well, let's have a look."

Master Wilson probed his pudgy fingers into my back, kneading at my wounds. He asked me to move my head this way and that, and he picked up my arms and moved them back and forth. He held my hands and manipulated my fingers. I prayed that he would not ask me to roll over, or get up, that he would not see Chloe's note which I felt pressing against my chest, causing a small patch of skin there to sweat.

"Well, I don't see any real harm done," he finally said. "This is scabbing up quite nicely. You'll be back to work next week." He stood up straight again so that I again saw the tops of his boots.

"Yassuh," I said to his knees.

"It's a hard way to get a week off, Persy."

"Yassuh. Sho is."

"I'll have Katy send some extra rations to your cabin. Biscuits? Do you care for biscuits?"

"Yassuh. Thank you, suh."

"Pies and cakes? Do you care for pies and cakes?" I was silent. He knelt down beside me so that now we looked each other eye-to-eye, man-to-man, except that he was master and I was slave and I knew to look down, away from him, and this I did. "Blueberry?" he taunted. "Apple? Fig?" Again I did not answer, for there was no good way to reply. "I expect you back to work on Monday," Wilson said. "Full days."

"Yassuh."

"You're not getting off of this plantation, Persimmon Wilson. Ever. You'll die here. I'll make sure of it. Do you hear?"

I did not answer.

"Look at me," he said.

125

I did as I was told. I had never looked so closely into Master Wilson's face, or any white man's for that matter. His eyes were black as coal. His nose mapped with broken veins. There was a large mole at the base of his jacket collar that I had never noticed before. I held the bile down in my throat as thoughts of Chloe surfaced, Chloe having to be as close to him as I was now. Closer. Him inside her.

"Do you hear?" Master Wilson repeated.

"Yassuh," I answered.

"I'll send Peach with those biscuits."

"Much obliged, suh."

He rose and looked about the cabin.

"You boys keep a neat place."

"Yassuh," I said.

"That's good. I like that." I heard him dip the cloth into the bucket of brine and wring it out. He laid it across my back. "Don't forget what I told you. I'll kill you myself." He crossed the floor and opened the door.

By Monday the lacerations from my whipping had formed scabs that felt tight across my back and itched as I worked. My shirt scraped across them during the first part of the day, but by the afternoon my wounds split open, and by the end of the day the flies that tortured me while I worked had become so drunk with my blood that they fell off me onto the ground.

I washed my shirt every night, and then tossed the bucket of blood-tinged water out the door. Every morning I put my still-damp shirt back on to repeat the process. As the weeks went by, under Harriet's care with the brine-soaked cloth, the lacerations on my back changed slowly, first from a solid crust of joined scabs, then to rivers of finger-width scabs, then to trickles of thin incrustations, until finally, by the end of August, my wounds had healed into a landscape of soft ridges, and I still had not seen Chloe.

The cane plants were ten feet high now and grinding season was upon us. I began to turn my attention to serious thoughts of escape. I began to wonder if now was the time, just before Master Wilson became entrenched in the busy work of making sugar. It is ironic, after all my promises to Chloe of creating a perfect plan, that I had no plan. A plan almost seemed farcical to me now, a thing that could only go wrong, that could trip us up, like the hem of a long ridiculous coat.

I had devised no way yet of getting a message to Chloe, but all the same, just before sugar making was to start, I paid a visit to Sweetmore's commissary with the intention of purchasing a few things with the credit I had accumulated by cutting wood in the swamps. Holmes stood behind the rough wooden counter when I entered. I asked him, addressing him in the usual way, "Suh, has I got enough to get two blankets and a fry pan?"

"You going somewhere, Persy?" Holmes asked.

I laughed and grinned. "Nawsuh. I's jest gettin' some blankets fo' the winter, and a fry pan fo' the fish I gonna catch come holiday after grindin' season done ended. I bring you some them fish, if you like." It galled me to talk like this.

Holmes reached beneath the counter and pulled out a large ledger, making a show of slapping this book onto the counter and sighing heavily as he opened it to look up my name. He flipped the pages, one after another. I saw my name go by. Then he started at the beginning again, this time running his fingers down the list of names and marks on each page before turning to the next one. I saw my name again as Holmes's finger slid over it, written in Master Wilson's florid script. I saw the marks next to it, each one representing a cord of wood, which I had delivered, cut and stacked, to the sugarhouse yard. "You're not listed, Persy," Holmes said.

In October Jeff, the fiddler, received his last pass of the season to visit his wife Sally and spend a weekend with her at Sweetmore. He had taken a shine to Henry, Sup, and me, and during these weekends, he spent at least a few hours sitting around our fire, smoking his pipe, and delivering whatever news he had garnered during his trips as a fiddler up and down the river. Jeff prided himself on gathering up white folks' news and spreading it among the coast's slaves, and well he should have been proud. His was a service we needed, especially on Sweetmore, where the chances of overhearing an informative conversation were next to none.

"Rations goin' short this grindin' season," Jeff told us during this last visit.

"Why that?" Henry asked.

"Blockade," Jeff said, nodding to himself.

"Blockade?" Sup said. "What the hell a

blockade?"

"A mess of Yankee ships, what I can tell," Jeff answered, "blockin' them Rebel ships from gettin' to New Orleans, and blockin' everybody else from gettin' out. That block-ade makin' the white folk run low on every-thin'."

"Everythin' 'cept meanness," Henry said.

"They low on food, we lower on food," Sup observed.

"They might run low on somthin' else," Jeff said. "Three families 'long the river done lost they boys. Niggers comin' home without they massuhs, if they comin' home at all. One nigger up on Lastola Place got hisself a whippin' fo' not bringin' his mas-suh's body home. He told me warn't nothin' left to bring home. Some battle up Virginia. Rebels sayin' they won that one. Nigger say he couldn't get outta that place fast enough. Pieces of people flyin' everywhere. Wudda had to scoop up some mud and guts and call it the right mess of bones to make his-self a massuh." Jeff shook his head, leaned down to the fireplace, and lifted a burning stick to the bowl of his pipe. He puffed on it till the smoke was going strong, then he dropped the stick back into the fire and shook his head again. "White people killin' white people like heaven to me."

"Why that nigger come home at all?" Henry asked.

"Wife and younguns. He figure he be gettin' a beatin' when he get back."

"They can't ship out the sugar?" I asked.

Jeff shrugged. "Don't look like it."

"What we growin' it fo'," Henry asked, "they cain't sell it?"

Jeff shrugged again. "Don't know. But this as pretty a crop as I ever seen. I reckon they gonna cut it and grind it like always, figure somethin' to do with it later. Cain't have no sugar dyin' in the field. Cain't have no bunch of niggers doin' nothin'. Naw siree, cain't have that."

"Them Yankees gonna come upriver and set us free?" Sup asked.

"White folk say it ain't never gonna happen. Cain't nobody get upriver fo' them forts I told you 'bout. White folk say we safe."

"Who they talkin' 'bout bein' safe?" Henry said. "They talkin' 'bout theyselves bein' safe. Ain't no nigger safe."

"I jest sayin' what the white folk say. They ain't always right. I know somethin' else though, 'bout that fancy in yo' massuh's house."

I looked up to find him regarding me. "What about her?" I asked.

" 'Bout a month ago, she start askin' 'bout cotton root bark."

"Cotton root bark," I repeated.

"You know what it fo'?" Jeff asked.

"Yes," I whispered. "She's pregnant."

"Not no mo' she ain't," Jeff said. "I get the cotton root bark to Sally, Sally get it to Peach, and Peach get it to Chloe. She ain't pregnant no mo'."

"Is she all right?"

"She sick awhile," Jeff said. "We don't tell you till now. She all right now." He stood up from the stump he was sitting on and stretched, his fingers easily touching the ceiling of our cabin. "I reckon I better go see that gal of mine. But you watch. Rations this grindin' season ain't gonna be like last."

"You gotta leave that filly be," Henry said after Jeff left. "What you reckon would've happened if she'd birthed yo' child?"

"He'd have killed me," I said.

"Damn right, he'd kill you. You gotta leave that gal alone."

But I had no intention of that if I could help it. All I could think of as I tried to sleep that night was Chloe being sick, aborting a baby. Even though it was dangerous to do so, she was wise to rid herself of it. I wished I could see her. I wished I could hold her hand. I wished I could comfort her. I wished

I knew that the baby was Wilson's child and not mine.

Our decrease in rations was noticeable on the first day of cutting cane. Our breakfast was cush-cush, our dinner had no meat in it, and the slabs of pork that were cut for our supper were grainier than they had been the year before. Each day out in the fields we ate our portions of food and hungered for more. I was accustomed to being hungry. We all were. But this was different. This was harder. In the months before grinding season we worked ten- and twelve-hour days, sometimes only eight, and we had Sundays off. Now we worked eighteen-hour days, seven days a week. Our stomachs grumbled and complained. Three people collapsed during the first week, two during the second week, and five during the third, but in each instance they were returned to the fields before the end of the day, and soon enough we adapted. We found our rhythm. Four whacks to the cane plant and move on. Swaths of cut cane lay behind me in the path I forged.

I could not help but wonder, as I worked, if those Yankee ships anchored downriver might mean Chloe's and my eventual freedom. There was talk of this in the quarters of course, when there was talk at all during grinding season, which was only early in the morning after our shifts or if it rained too hard for us to work the field. Even on rainy days, surprise days off, we were too tired for deep discussions, and so our mentioning of Yankees was reduced to occasional mutterings.

"I wish they come on, if they comin'," Harriet said.

"Damn Yanks," Henry said. "Ought to come durin' grindin' season, at least. Even if they lose the damn war, might get a extra hour off one day."

All my days, rainy or not, were spent missing Chloe. I had not known, until her company was taken away from me, how much I had come to depend on our visits to lift my spirits and make me feel like a man. And now there was this news of the cotton root bark. I had noticed of late that Peach would no longer meet my eye when she served me my food out in the field, and this concerned me. I had not seen Chloe for four months now, and with Peach looking away from me every time I stepped up to her food cart, I became obsessed with the notion that Chloe no longer cared for me. Or, and this I found much worse to contemplate, that Chloe thought I no longer cared for her.

November. December. We worked through Christmas day, just as we had done the previous year.

The bell rang nine times each day to clock our lives. Once in the morning to get us to rise, a second time to tell us to line up for work, once each for our meal breaks, and again to tell us that this respite was ended, and finally at midnight to tell us to return to our cabins and sleep. The next day would bring it all again. It was no different from the previous year, except in two things. Our rations were cut, as you know, and this grinding season lasted much longer.

January came, and the year turned to 1862. It was warm that winter in Louisiana. No frost as of yet, and the cane fields remained lush and green. By mid-January we were three-quarters through with the cutting, and still the weather stayed unseasonably warm. We worked all through January and into half of February until finally we'd cut all the cane plants, save one, the one that Master Wilson decorated with ribbons, and that Sally cut down, the one we cheered for as it was handed over to the sugarhouse workers and put into the grinder.

My second grinding season had come to an end, and I swore to myself, as I stood there cheering with all the rest, that there would not be a third. I swore to myself that if Chloe were still willing to place her trust in me, I would get us free of this place. I would do this if I died trying, and if Chloe died trying, well then, at least she would not die on Sweetmore with Master Wilson's fingers on her body.

In spite of the food shortage, we were still given our sugarhouse party. The philosophy of the white folks seemed to be that they should keep appearances as normal as possible in order to avoid alarming us, or leading us to believe in any way that the blockade cutting off their supplies was a concern to them. They went so far as to act as though we had no knowledge of it at all. I do not know if they themselves actually believed this or if it was only for show, but had they stopped to consider it, they would have realized that we knew something was amiss. After all, a slave notices a shortage of food before anyone else.

The table in the sugarhouse was spread with the same patched red cloth as last year, but with fewer dishes. An attempt had been made to disguise this fact by decorating it with a centerpiece made up of cane leaves and moss.

"Cain't eat no cane leaves. Cain't eat no damn moss," Harriet muttered as she stood next to me and forked a thin slice of pork onto her plate.

The year before there had been food left over, enough for Henry and me to pocket a few potatoes, but this year after we had filled our plates there was nothing left but empty platters and bowls, some of them swabbed clean with pieces of bread and fingers.

Jeff stepped up onto the ledge in front of the kettles and tucked his fiddle under his chin. I danced with the girls. I swung them around, smiled and laughed, but they did not interest me. All I could think of was Chloe, and the message she had sent to me through Peach at the last sugarhouse party, and that night in my cabin with Chloe lying on my pallet, her skin in the flickering firelight. I ached to see her again, to hold her, to tell her of my renewed dedication to escaping this life.

Master Wilson and Missus Lila came to watch our dancing, but they stayed hardly any time at all before he took her arm and led her outside, her balance and breath so rickety now that twice she had to stop to rest before reaching the waiting buggy. And this was another difference between last year and this. Last year Master Wilson and his wife had walked from the big house to the sugarhouse.

I made sure that Wilson saw me dancing with the girls. This and the food had been my sole interest in the sugarhouse party of 1862, and after Wilson and Old Miss left I, too, left, stopping to swig at a jug going around by a fire, but still firmly making my way to my cabin.

Even though I'd told myself repeatedly, as I made my way down the lane, that Chloe would not be there, I felt my disappointment as a palpable thing when I swung the cabin door open and found it empty. I built a fire and then slipped Chloe's note from its hiding place. I sat on my pallet and ran my fingers across the marks, feeling each one, and grazing the longest across the last, Chloe's "signature." I will teach her to read and write, I thought. I will not let those hands always be plunged into biscuit dough.

During our week off I fished with Sup and Henry, but I was poor company, quiet and sullen. Continually they asked what was bothering me, but I had no answer for them, and eventually they ceased asking and merely let me be. The task I most wanted to do during my holiday was split wood, and I spent a great deal of time at it. The strength it took to wallop a log into several pieces was solace to me. No one spoke with me as

I bent to this task, and therefore I was left alone to stew and to brood, and yes, to plan. If only I could somehow think of a way to reach Chloe and speak with her again.

We began planting cane immediately after our week off. We did not spend any days rolling barrels of sugar or molasses down to the quay. We did not load them onto a waiting steamboat. There was no waiting steamboat. There was no exchange of money through white hands. The barrels of sugar and molasses that we had worked so hard to make were stored in a barn. Seven hundred and sixty hogsheads of sugar, two hundred and fifty barrels of molasses, and a grinding season that had lasted four months instead of three. A barn full of sugar, yet still we planted.

The weather was cold now. The ground wet and freezing against my fingers. As I walked back to my cabin with the others at the end of the day I glanced at the big house. It seemed more closed off to me than ever before, its shutters drawn tight. Inside somewhere was Chloe. I wondered if she could see me, if she could pick me out in this surge of slaves as we filed in from the fields. I wondered if she even looked.

Another month passed. I planted the cane. I helped repair the levee. I leveled and filled the wagon ruts in the roads. I tended the stock and planted sweet potato slips. I did everything but enter the swamps and cut wood again.

Toward the first of April the weather warmed and the rains began, and on the other side of the levee I could hear the roar of the river. Out in the fields the mud sucked at our feet with each step, as though the earth wished to haul us down into hell itself, not knowing we were already there. My shoes became wrapped in mud, until my feet felt like clubs on which I must somehow stay balanced and walk. Each night, I sat outside on the stoop of our cabin, shoulder to shoulder with Henry and Sup, each of us with a stick in our hands scraping the caked mud away.

The cane plants did not seem to mind the rain. The fields were designed so that any excess water was channeled off to drain into the swamps, but the swamps were now creeping higher and higher. So much so that one day, I was put on a gang to raise the smaller levee that bordered them. Another day I was ordered to walk that levee and check for cracks, and as I did so I looked fearfully into the dark waters, remembering the summer I had cut wood and the snakes that swam with their bodies riding high.

Chloe and I would have to enter those swamps in order to get away, and I wondered if the spits of land it was rumored runaway slaves lived on were still dry.

I reported to Holmes that I had found nothing along the swamp levee to cause concern, and he sent me back into the field to plant more cane. At midmorning I noticed as I worked, a large flock of vultures flying along the road that ran through the swamps behind Sweetmore. There were fifteen, maybe twenty, and they took turns dropping down from time to time and then suddenly flapping back up. I was not the only one who noticed this. In fact it was such an odd sight that we all stopped to look; we could not help it, Holmes and the driver included. "What the hell that?" Sup asked.

Soon we saw a colored man wearing clothes so torn and ragged that they waved in the breeze like banners billowing behind him. He pulled a narrow cart, struggling to haul it along the muddy road, and at the same time fighting the buzzards away by swinging a stick. The man turned up the lane into Sweetmore, and as he did so I caught the scent of rotted flesh in the air.

"This don't look good," Holmes said.

"Don't smell good neither," someone said.

"Y'all get back to work," Holmes ordered, but we didn't. Not one of us moved. We stood in the mud and watched as Holmes rode out to meet the man, who had stopped his cart beneath a live oak tree, the buzzards settling into the branches with the heavy beating of their black wings. I could now see a pair of puffy, black feet sticking out the back of the cart. A buzzard dared to drop on one and the man swatted at it with his stick and the bird flew into the tree and preened its wings.

"That Peter," Sup said. "Massuh Gerald's nigger he took to war."

"Then I reckon that be Massuh Gerald in the cart," someone said.

"That a nigger in the cart," another person argued.

"That Massuh Gerald," Harriet answered. "He dead. He been dead so long his skin done turned black." I looked over to see Harriet nodding to herself.

Holmes held a handkerchief to his nose as he spoke to Peter, then he wheeled his horse around and rode off in the direction of the big house, leaving Peter to beat away the buzzards as they took turns landing on the body in the cart.

"This gonna be the thing kill Ol' Miss," Harriet said.

"Sho is," someone else agreed. "She love that boy mo' than she love life itself."

Chloe's voice suddenly came to me.

He tell me she gonna die soon, and we be alone together all the time. Like what we doin' somethin' we both want. He say after she dead, I sleep in her bed. He come visit me there. No one need to know.

"Can't be him," I said quickly. "Must be some other nigger. Some other corpse."

I felt Sup looking at me. "What some nigger gonna bring his dead massuh here fo' it ain't Wilson?"

I shrugged.

"Besides, what it matter to you who it is? You ain't never even met Young Massuh." I shrugged again, but I could feel Sup's eyes boring into me.

All this conversation caused the driver to come out of his stupor and tell us to get back to work, but his words had no bite in them, and we still stood there watching as Master Wilson came running from the big house to meet Peter and his cart. Wilson fell onto the grass at Peter's feet and began sobbing and then vomited. I watched his back arch as he retched again and again, his hands pressed into the wet earth, mud getting on the knees of his britches, Peter standing above him swinging his stick at

144

every buzzard that dared to drop onto his master's body.

Holmes came riding back to the field. One man in our crew was told to stop work and go build a casket. "Measure him first," Holmes said ominously. "Don't get one out of the barn. You, go dig a grave," Holmes said to another man, "and you." He pointed to someone else. "Ride down to Ashleaf and find an overseer. Tell him Mrs. Wilson's a widow now." He reached into his pocket for a scrap of paper, scribbled a pass and handed it to the man. "All the rest of you, get back to work."

And so we began to work again, digging furrows and dropping the cane sticks into the ground, scraping the dirt over them, planting Master Wilson's fortune to the background of his sobs and retching.

Gerald Wilson's body was too far decayed for anything but immediate burial. My heart soared at the thought, for even though I worried that the death of Gerald Wilson might have an adverse effect on the health of Missus Lila, I was certain that I would finally see Chloe, for surely she would be required to attend the funeral. It had been eight months since I had last seen her, eight months since our tryst in the barn that had earned me my whipping, but today a grave was being dug, a casket built, a widow told that she was a widow, and a sort of giddiness overtook my mood as I planted cane and waited for the bell to ring that would signal us to stop work and pay our respects to the deceased.

Gerald Wilson was buried after our dinner break in the Wilson family cemetery, a small plot of land surrounded by a wrought iron fence, with a live oak tree spreading its moss-draped branches for shade.

The field hands gathered in a loose semicircle, outside the fence, our feet still clubbed with mud, while the house slaves and the family and Peter, still in his ragged clothes, stood inside the fence. Even the buzzards came to say their goodbyes, hulking in the branches of the oak tree, disbelieving, I thought, that such a fine meal was taken away from them.

Chloe was there, as I had hoped she would be. She stood on one side of Missus Lila, holding her teetering charge by the elbow, while Master Wilson stood on the other, no longer crying, but grave faced and red eyed. Missus Lila was, of course, sobbing, as was her daughter-in-law. The stench of rotted flesh seeped from the casket and the preacher delivered the ceremony holding, at times, a handkerchief to his face. He said a few words and read a passage from the Bible. "Let us pray," the preacher said, and everyone lowered their heads and closed their eyes.

Everyone except Chloe and me. We stood looking at each other over the bowed heads of our fellow slaves. I wanted to go to her, to take her hand, to hold her. I wanted to stroke the strands of hair from her face, to touch her cheeks and kiss her eyes.

Chloe smiled at me, but the smile itself was no smile at all, so wrought with sadness it was, so filled, I thought, with resignation that I could barely bring my own lips up into an answering smile. In delivering his prayer the preacher held the handkerchief to his nose and rushed his muffled words, but Master Wilson was so entangled in his own grief and shock that, for once, he paid no attention to Chloe or me. We stared over the heads of everyone, into each other's eyes. We knew we had little time before the prayer ended, and we each tried to glean what we could from the other's face.

And then one of the vultures swept down off its perch and landed on the casket and began strutting back and forth and pecking at the wood. Chloe raised her one free hand up to her mouth and I could see the laughter in her eyes. I smiled at her now, our separation having been narrowed by the sharing of this sight of the vulture strutting along Gerald Wilson's casket. I even dared to mimic the bird, cocking my neck out and pretending to peck, but by the time the preacher was closing his prayer, our heads were bowed with all the rest, our smiles erased once more into the unreadable faces of slaves.

Two days after Gerald Wilson's funeral I hobbled my mud-caked feet in line toward Peach's cart. As she dished my food onto my plate, she raised her solemn face and stared directly into my eyes, as she had not done for months. Peach then lifted her spoon and gave it a few swats in the air, indicating that I should move on and let the next man up for his grub. As I ate I watched her closely. She did her work as usual. Serving, clearing, taking the tin plates from those who had finished eating and giving those plates a quick slosh in the pail of water that sat at the rear of the cart. I felt sure that Peach had a message for me from Chloe, and I made certain to linger over my food that I might be the last to return my plate to her.

Peach turned to the side as I approached, keeping her face away from Holmes while busying herself with running the spoon along the inside of the kettle. "Sugarhouse, Sunday mornin'," she whispered, and then my plate was in her hands and plunged into the pail of water, and I was hurrying along to pick up my bag of cane sticks.

All the rest of that day I had to concentrate at keeping a smile from forming on my face, at hiding any hints of joy from Holmes, and even from my fellow slaves, for I did not wish that anyone would notice a difference in my demeanor. Yet I wonder now how they could have not noticed, for I was so feverish at the thought of seeing Chloe again that I fairly planted up a storm that day. First up one row and then down another, I barely felt the cane sticks in my hand, I barely felt the sun on the back of my neck, I barely felt the mosquitoes, freshly emerged in the warm weather, biting at my bare skin. It was Wednesday when I received this message through Peach. I had three days to wait, but those three days felt like an eternity.

I counted them as they went by. I had never before welcomed the sound of the bell that woke us up in the mornings, but now I did. One more day begun, and then gone by, before I could see Chloe again.

At last it was Sunday and the day woke up cloudy, the sun barely reaching the earth to warm it, and certainly not reaching through the walls of the sugarhouse. About the time that Master Wilson and Missus Lila would be going to church, I eased the door open and stepped inside to the cool dank air. I searched the darkness looking for her shape, the light color of her dress against the gloom, but she was not there yet.

I sat on the brick ledge and waited. It was some time before I heard the door creak open and saw a little light let in, briefly framing Chloe's silhouette before the door closed behind her. I stood up from my perch. "I'm here," I said, and then she was in my arms, her skin against my skin, my face nuzzled into her neck, our lips meeting at last. Tears stung at the rims of my eyes, and then, no longer able to contain them, they spilled down my cheeks and wetted the collar of her dress. Chloe pulled back from me and tenderly wiped them away with her sleeve. "Oh, Persy. I so sorry what they done to you."

I could not think what she was talking about. The most that I had suffered had been her absence, but then I remembered the whipping and Master Wilson's beating the last time we had met. I shook my head. "That's over," I said.

"I heard it," she said. "I heard it from his room."

She did not need to say more. Those words, that phrase, "from his room," told me how Master Wilson had spent his time while the whip whistled through the air and landed on my back. Chloe had lay beneath him while he grunted and fucked and she listened to the moans of the slaves as they witnessed my punishment, to every smack of the whip as it landed on my skin, to my own cries for mercy. I shook the image away.

"Are you all right?" I asked. "The cotton root bark, I heard about that."

She lowered her eyes. "I all right," she said. And then she raised her eyes and looked into mine.

"Will you still leave with me?" I asked.

"I still wants to go. We gots to go quick. Ol' Miss not even goin' to church today. She gettin' worse, Persy. Peach watchin' her now."

"When can you get away?"

"Next Sat'day night. Katy say Massuh goin' out that night. Playin' poker at Lidgewood. Take his mind off Massuh Gerald dyin', Katy say."

"Meet me here. I'll be waiting for you."

Chloe slyly looked at me. "You got a plan now, Persy?" she asked.

"I plan to take care of you," I answered. "I plan to never let anything bad happen to you again. That's the only plan I've got."

"That be good enough fo' me." Chloe lifted her sleeve and dried my face once more. "I sorry it been so long. I ain't able to get away from him after we get caught. He watchin' me night and day. It only since Massuh Gerald die he let up some."

"I missed you," I said. "I was afraid . . . I was afraid you didn't love me anymore."

"Naw, Persy. I love you."

Chloe took me by the arm and led me to a darkened corner behind one of the kettles and there she placed my hands on the bodice of her dress and closed my fingers upon the top button. I undid that button. And I undid the next and the next, taking my time, letting her dress fall open slowly. And when I was done I held my hands against her breasts and kissed her there, but she pushed my head away, and reached for my shirt. She unhitched each of its buttons, letting the cool air fall across my skin as slowly as I had let it fall across hers. The shirt at last fell fully open and Chloe put her hands on my chest and then moved them gently to my back. I felt her fingers softly tracking the scars that had been left by the lash, and then she slipped my shirt off and turned me around and traced each path of that awful violation with the tip of

153

her tongue.

We parted with vows to meet the next Saturday in the sugarhouse. "Tie your clothes into a bundle to carry with you," I said. "Steal some food if you can. Don't bring anything extra, nothing that will weigh us down."

"I ain't own nothin' to weigh us down, Persy. Jest myself." Then she laughed. "Don't even own myself, I reckon."

"You will," I told her. "I promise that you will."

I kissed her again and nuzzled my face into her neck once more before letting her slip out the door and into that cloudy Sabbath day.

On Monday I was put with the hoe gang out in the sweet potato field. On Tuesday I was in the cane fields again. On Wednesday I began to worry about the high water in the swamps. I could not swim, nor did I think that Chloe could swim, but I pushed this thought down into the fathoms of my mind. I told myself that I would not worry. I told myself that I would not be stopped by unpredictable concerns. I would not feel this paralyzing fear any longer. We must escape and we must do it Saturday night while Master Wilson played poker at Lidgewood. Thursday I was put on a gang to repair the levee. The river had not risen as the swamps had, but even so I stood on the levee's crest and gazed at that rush of brown water. A whole tree floated slowly by, and then a dead cow, its feet stuck straight up in the air.

"Spread out in twos," our driver said, and the slaves made themselves into pairs and skittered down the levee toward the river, each pair moving upstream or downstream searching for crevasses.

I paired with Henry, and soon enough we found what we were looking for. We began digging our shovels into the ground and moving the dirt into the cracked levee, tamping it down with our feet to seal it up.

"What's on the other side?" I asked Henry as we worked.

"Other side of the river? Mo' of the same. White folk, planters, cane, cotton. Nothin' good on either side of this damn river, and nothin' in between but water."

"Can you swim?" I asked.

"Naw." Then he stopped working and lifted his head. "That the bell?"

I ceased shoveling and stopped to listen. The river lapped at the shore, and for a while this was all that I could hear. I strained my ears, blocking out all sound and then, just barely, I heard it. The bell clanging back and forth, calling the slaves in from their work, for what reason, I did not know.

"Back to quarters," the driver yelled down to us.

We climbed to the crest, making sure not to drag our shovels or shove them into the dirt for leverage, lest we be accused of causing further damage. Then we scaled down the other side of the levee and began the trudge back to quarters, merging with other gangs leaving their own work and moving in the same direction.

"Ol' Miss," I heard someone say.

"She dead I bet," another said.

"She been 'bout half-dead all her damn life, what I hear," Henry said, but no one dared to laugh. The death of one's white person was rarely a good thing. We could so easily be sold, or inherited, moved like furniture into another room. "Too soon fo' her to be dyin'," Henry added.

"Massuh Gerald ain't been in the ground that long," another said.

"Too soon," Henry said again.

I barely felt my feet meeting the ground with each step, barely felt the shovel I held in my hand or noticed the other slaves drifting along with me toward the sound of the bell. Wilson stood on the stoop of one of the cabins, as he always did when he had an

156

announcement for us. We gathered around as we were meant to, crowding around him like cows waiting to be milked. Some of us pasted on our anxious, concerned masks. Others looked as impassive as always. I stood at the back of the crowd, not wishing to be in Wilson's sight if this announcement was what I feared.

Master Wilson raised his hands. "I have some very sad news," he said. "Your kind and gentle mistress has passed away. I know that you all share in the sorrow I feel."

A proper murmur ran through the group of slaves. I tell you, we were such good performers. A few cries of "Oh no" and "Lord have mercy" rose from the crowd. A few sobs were heard and a few heads were lowered into the skirts of their owners, the grief, it would seem, too much to bear. Perhaps some of it was real. I cannot say for sure.

Harriet said, "I knew her when she come here a young bride, Massuh."

"She a kind and gentle mistress," someone else said, echoing Wilson's own words. "Sho was."

"Her sufferin' over now, Massuh," another person intoned.

Without discussion or plan, we formed a line, and one by one, we shuffled by Master

Wilson and hung our heads and gave him our condolences.

"I sorry fo' yo' loss, Massuh," I said.

"Thank you, Persy." And as had happened before when in Master Wilson's presence, I felt that cold spirit there between us, touching my chest with its bony fingers and extending the same, I suspect, to Wilson, who reached out and gripped my shoulder. "I know you will miss her," he said pointedly.

After we had filed by and given him our shows of sympathy, Wilson held his hands up again to silence us that he might say more. "This is hard news for you to receive in the middle of a workday," he said. "I know that it pains every one of you to think of your mistress passed away, and of the loss to me of my companion in this life. I know that your grief is excruciating, as is mine, but the best thing for you in this time of loss, the best thing to help us heal our wounds, is to just do our work. This is what God wants of you, that you just do your work."

There was a response of, "Yassuh. Yassuh. Yassuh." Those who were crying, or pretending to, wiped their eyes. We drifted away from the yard like a flock of moths.

All the next day a throng of white people

came and went from the big house, buggies pulling up, colored coachmen standing by, waiting for their masters and mistresses as they paid their respects to Missus Lila and gave their condolences to Master Wilson. Sylvie was pulled from the fields and given a clean dress and told to help serve the guests and clean up after they had left.

"Missus Lila," Sylvie told us that night as we gathered in her cabin, "layin' out in the parlor, wearin' a blue satin dress. She look good."

"Better than when she alive?" Henry asked.

Sylvie giggled and the others laughed. I sat with my head bowed, unable to think of anything but Chloe and our plans of escape the following night.

"Chloe grievin' hard," Sylvie said.

I looked up, and found that she was staring at me.

"She grievin' hard. Stayin' up all night with Missus Lila. She'd of stayed with her all day, too, 'cept all the white folk."

"They buryin' her tomorrow," Harriet said. "Chloe's grievin' come to an end after that."

"Uh-huh," Sylvie answered, still staring at me.

"Grievin' come to an end," Harriet repeated, shaking her head.

I had so utterly failed Chloe. I had so utterly let her down. I had lied to her, I had deceived her, I had delayed all chances of taking her hand and flying over the cane fields to freedom, and now I doubted that Master Wilson would be going to a poker game the next night. I doubted that Chloe would be able to meet me in the sugarhouse. I doubted that we might ever get as clear a chance for escape again, for as soon as Missus Lila was buried, Chloe would lose the only protection she ever had from Master Wilson's lasciviousness. She would belong to him more than she had ever belonged to him before.

I plan to take care of you.

My words echoed back to me.

I plan to never let anything bad happen to you again.

"They somethin' goin' on with the white folk," I heard Sylvie say. "They all agitated. They come to pay they 'spects to Missus Lila but they standin' round talkin' 'bout somethin' called a 'bardment. Yankees done barded they way up the river what I hears. I tellin' y'all, they's mighty antsy over that 'bardment. Doin' some mighty large frettin' seem like to me. Massuh too."

I lifted my head to hear more.

"What gonna happen them Yanks get through?" Sup asked.

"Gonna be free," Harriet said. "Yankees gonna set us free."

"Sound like they done got through," Sylvie said. "Broke through somethin' called a boom."

"What did you say?" I asked.

They looked at me blankly.

"Sylvie, what did you say about Yankee ships on the river?"

"They down below New Orleans, white folk say. Broke through a boom, they sayin'. Got past two 'federate forts. White folk right jumpy 'bout it."

"Wilson too?"

"He jumpy fo' sho. He pacin' in front of Missus Lila casket all day long. It a sight to see. Her layin' out, him and all the other white folk standin' round talkin' 'bout 'bardments and booms like she ain't even there."

"What you think it mean, Shoot?" Henry asked.

I shook my head. "I do not know."

The following day Holmes was free with his whip. It snapped beside us if it was deemed we were not planting fast enough. It slashed across our backs if we stopped to wipe the sweat from our brows. It popped left and right as Holmes rode through the fields on his horse. "You goddamn niggers," he said more than once. "You think you gonna be free. I'll show you free at the end of a rope."

The whip landed that day twice across my own back.

"You fucking niggers," Holmes kept saying, as if the war, as if the ships Sylvie reported on the night before, as if every perceived injustice done to white people was the fault of the enslaved.

Late afternoon a wagon rolled into the lane and rambled up to the cemetery, where it stopped. The driver was a colored man, and he jumped down and began to wrestle with dragging something off the wagon bed.

"Persy," Holmes said. "You go over there and help that boy, and be quick about it."

"Yassuh." I pulled the cane bag off my shoulder and trotted across the grass. The item the man was struggling with was the tombstone for Gerald Wilson's grave, lying, I saw, in the wagon bed in front of two others.

"Reckon we'll be needing another one ourselves," I told him as we slid the slab of stone off the back of the wagon. "Our mistress died this week."

"Might not get it," the man said quickly.

"Yankees at New Orleans now. Name's Joe," he added.

In the short amount of time it took us to move the tombstone off the wagon and lean it inside the wrought iron fence, I learned that Joe belonged to a man whose home lay between Sweetmore and New Orleans. He was being sent upriver to deliver and collect on three tombstone orders, after which he was to return to his master as fast he could with the money. "Massuh say we gonna refugee," Joe said. "Him, me, all the slaves 'cept the oldest and the youngest goin' to Texas."

"What about his wife?" I asked.

"He say she be all right stayin' on. He say he got to 'tect his property, and she stay here, make sho the house don't get burnt down."

Just then the lash whistled through the air beside my ear and landed next to me, spitting up a clump of grass at my feet. "You taking too long, Persy," Holmes said. "You, nigger," he said to Joe, "you done your work. Now get on out of here before I whip you myself."

"Yassuh," Joe said, "but I supposed to collect on this from Massuh Wilson."

"Get on up to the big house, then, but stop your jabbering here."

"Yassuh." Joe climbed into the wagon seat and chucked the mule into moving.

I returned to the fields and whispered the news to Henry as we knelt down to plant. "Yankees at New Orleans now," and then Henry whispered it to Sup, and Sup to Sally, and Sally to her neighboring planter until it had spread across the fields like water. Holmes continued to lash with his whip like a madman, but he couldn't be everywhere at once. He could not stop this whispered knowledge from spreading among us like gospel. By the time Missus Lila was buried that evening the slaves fairly vibrated with what we were not supposed to know.

Perhaps, I thought, it was the perfect night after all, for Chloe and me to escape. Perhaps Master Wilson would be so distracted by this new development that Chloe would be able to sneak away. Perhaps we could avoid the swamps altogether, and make it downriver to the Union lines.

We gathered graveside just as we had for Gerald Wilson, many of the hands this time showing stripes of blood through the backs of their shirts, but still our elation could not be contained. We stood in our mud-caked shoes and our bloodstained shirts at the grave of our former mistress, and I swear that we could barely keep from rolling onto our toes and dancing a little jig. We twitched, we scuffled, we jittered, and whenever a white person looked our way we quickly stilled ourselves and hung our heads and showed the proper sadness at the passing of our "dear and kind" mistress.

Chloe stood with the small group of house slaves behind Wilson and his daughter-in-law. Chloe's head was bowed and her hands clasped in front of her, and this time she did not look up. None of the house slaves looked up. They stood still and solemn and I wondered if they knew as much as we did, and then I wondered if they perhaps knew more. I stared at Chloe as much as I dared. I tried to will her with my eyes and my heart to look at me, to give me a smile, to assure me in some way that we would be meeting in the sugarhouse that night. But she and the other house slaves kept their heads down, although I saw that Wilson looked up plenty. He and all the white people, including the preacher, kept glancing nervously toward the river, and then the road, as if Yankees might invade at any minute.

The same preacher who had presided over the service for Gerald Wilson delivered words for Missus Lila, and he was even quicker in his delivery than before. A short reading from the Bible, a scant few words on the goodness of the dearly departed's character, a hasty prayer for her soul, and then four slaves grabbed the ropes that were snaked under the casket, lowered Missus Lila into the ground, and began shoveling the dirt back into the grave.

"Get to your cabins," Wilson said to the rest of us. "If any of you are outside tonight we'll shoot you down dead."

As I turned to walk away I caught Chloe's eye at last. I gave her a smile and a barely perceptible nod toward the sugarhouse. She returned my gesture with one slight shake of her head and then looked down again. We walked in opposite directions, away from each other, always away from each other it seemed. Holmes came riding up beside me. "Get going," he said, and he lashed the whip into the mud, spattering it against my legs. "Get to your cabin and stay there. All you niggers," he hollered as he spun his horse around. "Get to your cabins and stay there."

Henry built the fire up and as he laid sticks on the crackling flame he asked, "What you think it all mean, Shoot?"

"They're nervous."

"Jittery as hell look like to me," Sup said.

"Ought to be jittery." Henry again. "Judgment day comin'." He paced across the floor. "Ought to be layin' down on the ground beggin' fo' mercy, you ask me."

Sup mixed up a batter and cooked the hoecakes for our dinner. We sat on the edges of our pallets eating. There was nothing more to say, although Henry occasionally shook his head and muttered under his breath, "Judgment day comin', Massuh," while Sup added a chorus of, "Yankees comin', Massuh."

I could barely contain my glee at the thought of leaving Sweetmore with Chloe that night. Her shake of the head, her looking down, the house slaves' somber demeanor, were all signs I refused to read. She would be there. We would leave. We would go to the Yankees. Somehow we would find our way to them, to freedom, and to a little house of our own with Chloe baking in the kitchen and children crawling across the floor.

Sup stood and put another log on the fire. We lay down for the night, but I kept myself awake, waiting to hear the slowed breath of my cabinmates that I might at last slip out the door and sneak away to the sugarhouse to meet Chloe and disappear into the night. I was tense with excitement. My skin felt as though it would crawl away without me if I did not leave soon.

Outside an owl hooted, and I heard the rustling of some creature along the exterior wall behind my head. The insects started up their din of song. Then the pounding of someone riding a horse through the quarters. Holmes most likely, patrolling, I thought.

The fire sputtered and gave away in the grate, yet Henry's and Sup's breathing did not deepen and I knew that they, too, lay awake listening to the horse pounding past our cabin. How could any of us sleep, I thought; how could we not lay awake and wonder what this increased surveillance meant to our lives. To their lives, for it would mean nothing to me. I would be leaving with Chloe. Even if Henry and Sup never fell asleep, I would fly this coop. When I heard the horse ride through again, I began to silently sing to myself the verses of my mama's favorite song, thinking to use each chorus to mark the amount of time between one ride-through and the next.

Children go where I send thee.
And how shall I send thee?
I'm going to send thee one by one,
One for the little bitty baby
Born, born, born in Bethlehem.

Now children go where I send thee.
And how shall I send thee?
I'm going to send thee two by two,
Two for Paul and Silas,
One for the little bitty baby,
Born, born, born in Bethlehem.

It was a good song to gauge time by, building on itself the way that it did, plus it was a strengthening song, for tonight, the night of my escape with Chloe, I almost believed in God again. By the time I reached "five by five," *five for the gospel preacher, four for the four that stood at the door, three for the*

Hebrew children, two for Paul and Silas, one for the little bitty baby, Holmes rode through once more. I judged it was just enough time between his rounds to make my way to cover, if not all the way to the sugarhouse.

I reached behind me and tugged Chloe's note from its hiding place and in the dark I ran my fingers across the indentations of its marks, lingering as always on her "signature." I determined that I would take the note with me, that it would be something I would show our children when I told them about slavery times, about what it had been like to belong to another man, about loving their mother, and how much this note had meant to me as I lay on my pallet with my back raw-open from a whipping.

I would tell our children everything. Chloe's and my children would not grow up lacking for knowledge. I would hold nothing back. I wanted them to know what a brave, kind mother they had. I wanted them to know how much I loved her, and how we had risked our lives to leave a place called Sweetmore. I pictured them asking, "Where is it?"

"Gone," I would answer, "it's gone. Once the slaves were no longer there to work the cane and repair the levee, the river rose and broke through and swept it out to sea."

I practiced the words in my mind. *Gone. Swept away. Out to sea.* I pictured the levee breaking and the water pouring over the land, covering the cane fields, lapping at the wheels of carts and wagons, seeping beneath the doors of the sugarhouse, rising to the lips of the kettles, flowing up the steps, one by one, of the big house.

I folded Chloe's note and slid it into my pocket and as I did so I felt the little noose from One-Eyed Jim's hanging. I still carried it every day, although I had not fingered it in a long time. My mind of late had stayed so thoroughly saturated with thoughts of Chloe and escape that I had simply forgotten it. It had become something that I owned, something that was always in my pocket, but not something that I ever thought of, and I wondered at that. How could I, a slave who owned so little, not give thought to what little I owned, while the white folks, it seemed to me, owned a great deal, and thought about it with debilitating constancy?

I lay on my back and held the little noose, rubbing it as I had once done for comfort. I inserted my finger into its loop, and pulled on the rope, causing it to tighten. Then I loosened it and ran my fingers once again along its knot.

I heard the rustle of Sup swinging his legs off the edge of his pallet. "I cain't sleep," he said. "Holmes ridin' through keepin' me 'wake."

"Ain't none of us sleepin'," Henry said.

Sup stood and stoked the fire, and soon got it going again, the room lighted with its shuddering glow.

"What you got there, Shoot?" Henry asked.

I turned to face him. "Little noose," I said.

"Lemme see."

I reached across the space between our pallets and passed the noose to Henry. "Where you get this?" Henry asked.

I sat up, swinging my legs off the edge of my pallet, watching as Henry pulled on the rope and closed the noose around his finger. I told him about One-Eyed Jim's hanging, the single drumbeat, the boys selling these as souvenirs. We heard the sound of the horse riding through the quarters once again. Henry sat up and handed the little noose back to me. "You best get goin', Shoot, if you goin'." He reached out his hand and I grasped it in mine. Sup too.

"How did you know?" I asked.

"Jest knew," Sup answered.

"You might fool them white folk, but you cain't fool us," Henry said.

172

I put the little noose in my pocket. I pulled on my shoes and tied their laces. I rolled up my blanket and tucked it under my arm. I shook their hands once again. Henry stood and pulled me into an embrace.

"Good luck to you, Persimmon Wilson," Henry said.

"Be safe," Sup said.

The night was cool and misty and I made my way from shadow to shadow, sliding between the cabins, hiding behind trees and whatever else I could find. I was behind a wagon when I heard the sound of an approaching rider. It was Holmes, all right. I could see him as he passed. He would have to stop this patrolling at some point, and when he did it might be Master Wilson who took over riding through the quarters.

Once Holmes had passed, I sneaked along, hiding here and there, behind whatever cover I could find, sometimes flattening myself on the ground along the edge of the cane field, other times hiding behind barns. Twice more Holmes rode through, and twice more I eluded him until at last I reached the sugarhouse and slipped inside its darkness.

She was not there. I called softly to her, but there was no answer. I waited beside one of the kettles, my body tensing at every sound. Once the doors to the sugarhouse creaked and swayed slightly as if they were about to be opened, but it must have been the wind. I reached into my pocket and fingered the little noose, and felt the folded paper of Chloe's note. An hour passed. Another. My muscles cramped and I stood to stretch. I judged it past midnight now, and still there was the sound of Holmes circling the property. I sat again. I listened to him go around and around, and waited and waited for Chloe to appear.

With each circle of Holmes on his horse, hope seeped away from me and pooled at my feet, as useless as spilled blood, until finally all hope was gone and I knew that she would not be coming. The hours of darkness before dawn, hours of darkness we needed in which to escape, were too few now.

A horse neighed outside and I shrunk behind one of the kettles. The door opened. I saw the outline of Holmes standing there, legs spread wide, the whip coiled in his hand. He peered through the darkness, then he stepped back and let the door shut behind him, and soon I heard him ride away, this time toward the stable. I listened closely for the sounds of his replacement but there were none. No voices of Holmes and Wilson discussing events of the night, no jingling of tack as a horse was mounted, no pounding hooves circling the quarters and the fields any longer. Master Wilson, I was sure, was sleeping soundly, and could not be bothered with patrol. And Chloe, I was sure, lay awake beside him.

I heard the sleepy peep of a waking bird and could dimly see a change in the light through the crack in the sugarhouse door. I must return to my cabin; I must not be caught outside. Even though there was no patrol that I could determine, I crept again from cover to cover, for a slave who was not where he was supposed to be could never be too cautious. Finally I made it to the quarters and slipped between the cabins until I reached the last one along the lane. The land was hung in a heavy gray mist, and just before I opened our cabin door and tucked inside, I looked toward the big house, shrouded in this mist like a veiled heathen monster.

Henry and Sup still lay in bed. They were awake, and they watched me brush the dirt from my clothes. The fire was dead, but I did not stoke it. I unfurled my blanket and spread it across my bed. I pulled my shoes off. I unbuttoned and tugged off my shirt. Then I pulled the note from Chloe out of my pocket and slid it again into the crack where wall met floor. "I sorry, Shoot," Henry said.

I nodded and lay down, and rolled over, away from the room, away from Henry and Sup, away from my life here at Sweetmore. I closed my eyes. I could not bear to think of Chloe, nor could I avoid it. Her face, her hair, her laugh, her fingers unbuttoning my shirt all floated into my mind, and as if they were inexorably entwined, Master Wilson floated there too. I could see his fat pudgy hands as he held them up to tell us that Missus Lila had passed away. I could see his boots that had kicked me, the spittle coming out of his mouth as he declared my punishment of fifty lashes, the mole on his neck. I thought of his penis, which he forced into Chloe night after night and I wanted to castrate him. I wanted to hang him. I wanted to let his body swing in the air above his wife's grave, and may the buzzards feast on his putrid flesh.

Lying on my pallet, in the cabin I had hoped to leave behind, I vowed that I would not give up, that I would not let him win, that I would see her again, that we would get away. I told myself these things again and again and again until at last I tired of my own thoughts and finally drifted into a troubled, hot sleep.

The bell awakened me, calling us into the yard.

"It goddamn Sunday," Henry said. "Ain't no fuckin' workday."

We pulled on our clothes and our shoes, and we stepped out into the lane and lined up with all the rest. Holmes walked along in front of us, a ledger tucked under his arm, pointing to each slave and counting out loud as he did so. I could see the dark circles under his eyes from lack of sleep. "Two missing," Holmes said. "Which ones?" We looked straight ahead, no one answering. Holmes opened the ledger. "Say here when I call your name." He began his inventory, a chorus of "Here, suh. Here, suh," following.

I looked up at the big house. There was a buggy, not belonging to Master Wilson, pulled up out front. Then I saw Wilson and a man step out onto the porch.

"Persy."

"Here, suh."

"Jonas and Timothy," Holmes said at last, closing the ledger. Jonas and Timothy, the coffin builder and his son. "Missing," Holmes continued. "Anyone want to tell me about that?" We were silent. "Didn't think so. Get back to your cabins. Don't let me see you outside today, you hear. Not a one of you."

"But it Sunday, suh," some poor fool ventured to say.

"I don't care if it's Christmas. Get on back to your cabin and stay there." Holmes held his coiled whip in the air, and then opened his hand, letting it unfurl, its tip smacking the ground. "Lest you wanting this?"

"Nawsuh, nawsuh, I bc goin' on."

Sup built up the fire and we sat on the edges of our pallets without talking. Finally Henry let out a sigh. "Christmas," he said. "Like Christmas somethin' special fo' a nigger round here." He lay back on his pallet and put his arms behind his head. Then he rose up, punched at his mattress, and lay back down.

Sup looked at me. "What you want to do, Persy?" he asked.

"Eat something," I answered.

We boiled a ration of bacon and ate it with our fingers, Henry rising out of his bed just long enough to share in this meal and then return to lying down and punching at his mattress again.

"What now?" Sup asked.

"Nothing to do," I answered.

Sup lay back on his pallet and sighed. He stared at the ceiling. I had the good fortune that day of being exhausted from my night of waiting for Chloe in the sugarhouse, and I fell easily asleep, but once again the bell awakened me.

Midmorning, noon, twice in mid-afternoon, the bell rang, the slaves lined up, Holmes counted us and then reminded us what a sorry bunch of niggers we were, reminded us that he had the whip, reminded us that a runaway could be hung, reminded us that we would never be free, reminded us how good we had it here at Sweetmore, taken care of, fed and housed, and then told us to return to our cabins and not be seen outside. We were counted four times during the day, and each time I noticed that there was a different buggy or horse not belonging to Wilson, pulled up outside of the big house. The last time I saw a man leave, Master Wilson followed him down the steps and shook his hand while standing in the yard. Between the inventories, I slept. But it was never enough, for it seemed as soon as I had drifted off the torture of the bell rang again.

It rang a final time that day in early evening, just as Sup was stirring up cush-cush for dinner. "Damn shit," he said. "We done stayed in. It supper time now."

We tromped outside once again. Master

Wilson was there this time, standing on his favorite cabin stoop. Holmes counted us and reported that, minus Jonas and Timothy, we were all present. Wilson held up his hands.

"My good people," he said.

I turned to look at Henry standing beside me. He gave a slight shrug of his shoulders. No white person had ever before called us people, and the word good had only been said when prefaced by the word be — Be good — unless a slave was dead or being sold, and then he was a good worker.

"My good, good people," Wilson continued. "Our very life, your homes, your livelihood, your rations, your women folk, your babies are at this moment under threat of attack. I will not lie to you; the Yankees are close by. They are just downriver at New Orleans. I know that some of you believe that the Yankees are here to set you free, but have I ever lied to you?"

He had done nothing but lie to us, but we nodded and shuffled among ourselves and answered as expected.

"Nawsuh."

"Nawsuh."

"You's always been truthful with us," Sally hollered out for good measure.

I was afraid that my distaste for this

theater was becoming unmanageable, for as we stood there listening to Master Wilson extol his virtue of honesty I could barely contain my rage. I could not help but imagine the scent of Chloe still on him, and of him on her.

"No, I have never lied to you," Wilson continued. "I have always treated you fairly, kept you sheltered, and fed you well, but now all that is threatened. These Yankees that are coming up the river, do not believe that they are friends to the nigger. They are not your friends. They will rape your women. They will steal your children. They will hitch you to a cart and make you pull it. You must know that yours is, unfortunately, an inferior race. You must know by now that I . . ." He beat his hand on his chest. "I have protected you and kept you safe. But I can no longer do that here."

Again a murmur went through our ranks.

"I can no longer protect you from the scourge that is about to plague our land. We must leave here. It is imperative that we do so. I have arranged to keep you safe, every one of you. At great expense to myself I have done this for you, but it requires that we leave Sweetmore, and all that we love about this land."

A wave of movement undulated through

our group. Again we murmured and whispered among ourselves.

Wilson held up his hands and announced, "Tomorrow morning we will begin the long journey to Texas. It is the safest place for us. We will board a steamer, which I have commissioned to take us across the river. We depart first thing tomorrow. It is, as you know, a very sad day for me, for I have just lost my dear, sweet wife, and not long before that, my only son. Besides my family, and you, Sweetmore" — Wilson's voice cracked — "is what I have always loved the most. I suppose I should be thankful that my wife and son are not here to see this. I know that it is a sad day for all of us, for all of you, for I can imagine that you do not wish to leave the cane that you took such care in planting, and that you will miss seeing all your hard work come to fruition. But we must be strong and brave together. Return to your cabins now, pack up your belongings, get plenty of rest. We leave first thing tomorrow morning."

At this Wilson stepped down from the stoop. Several of the slaves surrounded him. "Naw, Massuh. Naw. This here my home."

"My husband jest downriver," Sally said.

"My daughter down at Lidgewood," another said.

"Pa too old to make that trip," someone said.

Back at the cabin Sup built up the fire again and cooked the cush-cush. We ate, sitting on the edges of our pallets, listening for a long time to the crackling of the flames as they consumed the logs. Finally Henry spoke up in a fierce whisper. "Now the time to run, Persy, if you goin'."

"I'm not going without Chloe," I said.

"I goin'," Sup said.

"Me too," Henry said. "Tonight. You come with us."

I shook my head. "Not without Chloe."

I stood and went to the hearth. I poked at the fire and a spray of sparks rose up, then I lay another log on and watched it catch.

"She'd want you to be free," Sup said.

"I want her to be free."

"Ain't nobody gonna hunt us down," Henry said. "They too busy leavin'."

"Yeah." I stood at the fireplace staring into the flames. It was the perfect time, what I had been waiting for all along.

"If only you was in love with a field nigger instead of a house nigger, Shoot."

I shrugged. "But I'm not."

"So you goin' to Texas?"

"I reckon so. If Chloe's going. And I don't see she's got much choice about it."

"Naw. I reckon she don't."

"If I don't ever see you again . . ." I could not finish my sentence. I had been so brave the night before, when I had been the one doing the leaving, but now it was Henry and Sup who would be gone, and I who would be staying behind, who would be traveling to Texas with Master Wilson, who would be choosing slavery and servitude over freedom.

The bell rang long before daybreak. As soon as I woke I knew they were gone. The cabin felt like an empty husk without them, void of their breath, void of their spirits, no one here to call me Shoot or to cook the cush-cush. I got up and stoked the fire and by its light I saw that their blankets were stripped from their pallets, their shirts gone from their pegs. Henry's hat gone too. One hoecake was left in the fry pan, and I sat on the edge of my pallet and ate it. I rolled my blanket up and slipped Chloe's note into my pocket. I pulled on my shoes and laced them.

Outside Holmes stood in front of one of the cabins with his whip coiled around one arm and his book of recorded names resting open in the crook of his other arm. A young boy held a lantern over the book that Holmes might see by its light, but it was easy to tell, even in the darkness, even

185

without the book, that there were fewer of us than there had been the night before, gaps in our line where whole families once stood.

Henry and Sup were gone of course, but also Sally; Jilly and her baby; Harriet and Sylvie; a man named Willis and his wife and two children; another man named Andrew, his wife, their newborn girl; another named Jacob, his wife, four children. Twenty in all stole away from Master Wilson in the night.

Holmes made his marks in the ledger and then closed it with a heavy thump. "All right, you niggers," he said, "what's left of you. First thing we got to do is get the livestock onto the boat." He started bellowing out orders, pointing directions with the handle of his whip. You here. You there. You get the horses. You the mules, the cows. Leave the chickens be.

We spread out to the barns. I was assigned to help bring in the cows and we roped our animals and led them along the lane toward the quay. We stood on the levee waiting our turn, watching as lanterns swung wildly down below, illuminating pieces of the scene as horses and mules were pushed and cussed and tugged into walking the planks that ran from the quay to the deck of the boat. Lantern light flashed on a face, and then on a horse's ass, then Holmes and his whip, a slave's hand, little waves in the river reflecting the gleam like a thousand twinkling stars. I heard a splash. "Nigger overboard," Holmes yelled, and then a lantern was held close to the water, and I saw a man floundering in the river, and then a slave I knew as Blake lay stomach down on the deck of the ship and reached out that the man might grab hold of his wrist. Blake pulled him up and the man lay panting and coughing on the deck and I heard Holmes say, "Damn niggers. Can't swim. Falling in the fucking river. Don't be falling in the river no more."

"Yassuh." The lantern swung away.

I stood my turn, holding a cow and her calf by ropes tied around their necks. The calf leaned over, nudged my arm with her cold nose, and licked my hand with her soft tongue. I offered it a pair of fingers, and she sucked on them greedily as if they were a teat.

It took hours to load the stock, but at last each horse, mule, and cow stood on the deck of the steamer, tied closely to the railing. Next loaded was a wagon, pushed and pulled by seven slaves, not horses or mules, lest a horse or a mule panic and fall into the river. I could see that the wagon was filled with meat from the smokehouse, saddles and tack piled into a mound beside it, along with one trunk, filled, I presumed, with a few of Wilson's personal possessions. And then it was our turn, the slaves.

The only boat I had ever traveled on was the one that had brought me to market in New Orleans. It was named *Deliverance.* I do not know what this boat was named, for it was dark still, and although I could see that there was printing along its side, I could not read it. It was not a huge steamer. It was midsized, with a paddle wheel on either side, extending up through a boxlike structure at the center of the deck, which was open on two ends. The large black smokestack rose above everything like a single tree left standing after a forest fire.

For the most part I had been confined in the hold on the *Deliverance,* chained to an iron ring bolted to the floor. At that time, I had not feared the sea, or thought of drowning, for I could think of nothing but being sold down South, where I knew we were headed. But now as we were told to crowd together onto the deck, chained to nothing, I remembered the pitch and sway of the other ship, and as I walked the plank to the deck I felt unsteady, frightened that this river might swallow me up and take my life in desperate saturated breaths.

I was not the only slave who feared the water. Few of us could swim. The activity had been discouraged, and in some cases, forbidden, lest we get any ideas of drifting downriver away from our captivity. As we vied to distance ourselves from the edge of the boat, a collective moan rose from our ranks like a wave. It was not unlike the moan I had heard as I was being whipped, except that this moan was punctuated by the bellowing of cows, the bleat of calves, the whinny of horses and mules, and the occasional plop of steamy animal shit onto the deck.

"Sit down. Sit down," Holmes hollered. "Every one of you just sit down. You won't fall off."

We sat like obedient dogs. In spite of my fear of drowning, I allowed myself to be edged away from the center, angling closer to the railing that Chloe might be able to sit next to me when Wilson brought the house slaves down.

The sun now crested the horizon and pinked the mist that lay on the water. I peered through this mist to the shore, but was unable to see much of anything. The dock, a tree at the base of the levee, Holmes standing at the end of the quay, now looking in the same direction as I was, his hands on his hips, the whip coiled and held to one side. Waiting. We were all waiting, and watching the shore as the mist changed from pink to yellow to cream, and then I heard Master Wilson's voice. "Come on now, Katy. Come on. There's nothing to be afraid of. Texas is a fine land; now come on."

Katy. I remembered the name. She was the woman Chloe had said made biscuits that were not as good as hers. I tried to peer through the mist but could see nothing.

A female voice cut through the fog. "Katy, come with me, honey. I be with you. Boat ain't gonna sink. Massuh make sho of that."

Master Wilson hollering again, "You don't get a move on, Katy, I'll shoot you here on the spot."

"Katy," the woman pleaded. And then, "Naw, Massuh. She jest scared. Katy, come on now."

From the other side of the levee a pistol fired, and I felt the girl next to me quiver. A cow plopped a pie out right behind me, and it splattered onto my shirt. "Lord have mercy," a woman whispered. The pistol fired again.

"Shut your trap," Holmes yelled, stomping back onto the deck, "or I'll whip every damn one of you."

We shuddered quietly together, watching and waiting. The group that Master Wilson led suddenly came in sight through the mist at the end of the dock, like a congregation of ghosts. I peered hard to make out Chloe among them, and at last I saw her, walking slowly, one arm draped around the shoulder of a woman who was crying into her apron.

The group was herded onto the boat with the rest of us. The invisible boundary that had always separated field slaves from house slaves could no longer be upheld, and I saw Chloe scanning the faces, looking for me. I coughed and she looked my way, her eyes finding mine. She picked her way toward me, still holding on to the other woman, whom she pushed down to sit. And then Chloe boldly sat down beside me reaching under her apron to brush my thigh with her hand, and then letting that hand wander to the bodice of her dress, to a small rip where a button had pulled off. She fingered the rent cloth. She was wearing, I noticed, new shoes. The woman beside her buried her face in her apron, and her back heaved up with each silent sob. "Hildy," Chloe said to me in a hoarse whisper. "Katy's mama. He done shot Katy, Persy. I believe she dead." Beside her Hildy let out a wail.

Wilson stood before us now. He held up his hands like always. "Now listen here," he said. "Some folks have run off, and I'm just going to have to leave them behind. That's right. I just got to leave them here because I need to protect the rest of you. Those folks staying behind," Wilson continued, "God rest their souls. God rest their souls, that's right."

Hildy let out another long wail.

"Shut that bitch up," Holmes yelled, and Chloe roped her arm around Hildy's shoulder and pulled her closer until she fell into a soft whimper.

Wilson kept on with his little speech. "No one is looking after them now. They got no home, no food, no master. How do you think they're going to survive?"

Chloe shifted closer to me so that the length of her thigh lay against the length of mine, one arm still around Hildy, and the fingers of her other hand still on the bodice of her dress, prowling nervously for that missing button.

"They're going to live," Wilson continued, "for as long as they do live, in the swamps, hunted down by the Yankees. If the Yankees don't get them, the swamp fever will, while the rest of us get on to the safety of Texas."

The crew moved about, starting the engines up. Smoke billowed from the smoke-stack. There was the feel of machinery firing up beneath the deck. The whistle blew long, three times. Chloe pressed her leg into mine. I dared not look at her, but I leaned her way, my shoulder against her shoulder. The ropes were untied from the dock and the steamboat pulled out into the current. The engine chugged. All around me the slaves started moaning and crying again. Chloe let out one small mewl and then fell silent.

Holmes paced across the deck. "Sit still and shut up," he yelled. "Y'all be all right. You don't fall in, you can't drown. You know what's good for you, you'll just sit still."

Wilson did not pace. Nor did he look at us. Instead he stood at the stern, his hands gripping the railing, his eyes watching the shore retreat as the boat pulled away. The engine churned, and the paddles slapped the water, and still Wilson stood there and the boat moved farther and farther out into the river, until we were far enough out to see beyond the levee to Sweetmore. The newly planted cane fields, the barns and sugarhouse, the wrought iron fence surrounding the graves of Wilson's wife and son, the quarters, the big house with its chimneys rising into the air, smoke still puffing out of one, like a lady waving her handkerchief goodbye.

I suppose if there was ever a moment to feel something for Master Wilson, it would have been this one. You may take it as a testament to the cruelty of my heart that I felt nothing for him as I watched his back, his coattails billowing in the breeze, his empire receding from his life, possibly forever.

"I cain't swim," Chloe whispered.

"Me neither," I whispered back.

Her body began to tremble. She leaned into me now with all her weight. Her fingers still wandered the bodice of her dress, searching for that button.

We were far out in the river now. Sweetmore was barely recognizable, and still Master Wilson stood and looked its way, and then he turned, turned away from Sweetmore, away from the shore he was leaving to scan the faces of his slaves. He pulled a pistol from his shirtwaist and pointed it at us, letting it roam across our entire group. "Naw, Massuh. Nawsuh, Massuh." The pleading came from our ranks as if we were one. We cowered before him. "Naw, Massuh, naw." And then Chloe buried her face into my shoulder and began crying and Wilson pointed the pistol at me.

"Stand up, Persy."

"Yassuh."

I untangled myself from Chloe's grasp and stood. Hildy lifted her head and began sobbing uncontrollably.

"Come over here by the railing," Wilson said.

"Nawsuh."

"No? Are you disobeying me?"

"Is jest I cain't swim, suh. I scared."

" 'Is jest I cain't swim, suh. I scared,' " Wilson mimicked. "Get over here by the railing." His voice was low and flat. Chloe stopped crying. I could hear her breath held, as I could hear all the slaves not daring to breathe, lest they, too, be chosen. "Get over here," Wilson said again, and then he leveled the pistol at Chloe.

"Yassuh," I said.

As I moved, the gun moved with me, away from Chloe until I was positioned against the railing and the pistol pointed solely at my chest. Master Wilson's hand was as steady and unmoving as a cane kettle.

"Sir," I heard Holmes say.

"Shut up," Wilson snapped, and he wheeled and pointed the gun at Holmes, "or I'll shoot you too."

Holmes held his hands up and backed away, and Wilson again turned and pointed the pistol at my chest.

"He's my nigger. I reckon I can shoot him if I want to."

The engine churned on indifferently. The paddle wheels slapped at the water. A cow bellowed. The Confederate flag flying above us slapped its lines against the pole. And then I heard Chloe's voice. "Naw, Massuh. Naw."

Wilson spun and pointed the gun into the group of slaves. "Nawsuh, Nawsuh," they pleaded. While his back was turned I caught sight of Chloe, but she was not looking at me. She was looking at him. She had pulled away from Hildy and was kneeling, her hands clasped together as if in prayer, but it was not God she beseeched. "Massuh," she said. "Massuh. I do whatever you ask me. Please leave him be." Someone snickered behind Chloe, and Wilson laughed, if you could call it that.

"Sir," Holmes tried again, coming up beside him. "We've had our fun now, sir. I'm going to need your help with these niggers."

Wilson turned and pointed the gun at him and again Holmes held his hands in the air and backed away. And then the gun was on me. The boat churned farther and farther away from Sweetmore. Sweat trickled down my face, gathered beneath my arms and along my back. Wilson laughed again. "Persimmon Wilson," he said, and then I saw his finger squeeze against the trigger and I heard the gunfire and felt a stinging in my shoulder and I fell backward over the railing and plunged into the river.

The water enveloped me and I felt the wake of the boat as it pulled away. I sank deeper and deeper. I beat my arms against the river, and something lifted me to the surface, where I gulped air before sinking again. A red trail of blood billowed away from my right shoulder, like a scarf. Something brushed against my leg and I kicked it away and again I popped above the surface and gulped another measure of air before sinking. I sank and kicked and punched at the water until somehow I made surface again. Each time I did, I saw the boat pulling farther and farther away from me until it was a tiny speck and then gone. And then I saw, in one of my mad gulps for air, a log lazily floating my way. I sank again and when I rose next above the water the log had gone by out of reach.

My lungs strained for air, my limbs cramped, my right shoulder ached dully now, and my arm felt like a club that I could not detach myself from. I resurfaced and sank, and resurfaced and sank, plunging again and again into the river, and breaking the surface again and again. Twice I saw logs or pieces of wood float toward me, and twice they drifted beyond my reach.

The sun was higher now. The mist had burned off. The brightness hurt my eyes whenever I surfaced, and it seemed that every time I plunged below, I submerged deeper than before, and that to rise again required more and more fight, until I felt I could fight no longer. I broke surface once more and the day seemed less blinding, and finally I slipped cozily, peacefully into letting myself drop.

I remember looking up at the sun shafting through the water and I thought, how beautiful. How beautiful this place is. It was exquisite the way the light flashed, the beams of sunlight gleaming all around me. One strand of light landed on my face and I remember feeling warm and comfortable. Particles of dirt and vegetation drifted in front of me like a dance performed solely for my entertainment. A few fish gathered around and watched my descent, their mouths opening and closing, their gills folding in and out, their eyes watching me, one swimming up to me and taking a cautious nip at my finger. Something bumped against my body. A fish nibbled at my finger again. Another took a tug at my hair. And then I heard Chloe's voice.

Biscuits. Pies. All kinds. Blueberry, peach, apple. With crusts all buttery and flaky.

I thought I felt her hand against my thigh. I thought I felt her tongue tracing the scars on my back. Something floated in front of me and I lazily put my hand out to it. A piece of paper. It unfolded itself before me. I gazed at the writing there, only it was not writing. It was marks. Chloe's marks. Chloe's signature. Chloe's note. I reached out to touch its message as I had done so many times before, but beneath my fingers the marks seeped away from the paper in rivulets of ink. I watched the note drift up, away from me, above me to the surface, into a slant of muted light. And then I remembered Chloe kneeling before Master Wilson, pleading with him, promising him anything he wanted from her, if only he would not hurt me.

I spoke to my legs. I spoke to my arms. I spoke to the dull ache in my right shoulder. I even spoke to God and then suddenly I was moving upward again. I broke through the surface, gasping for breath, and just as I did so, something bumped into my chest, and whatever it was, I grabbed it and wrapped myself around it and began to drift downriver, coughing and sputtering, spitting up water and gulping for air.

There are things I know now that I did not know then, things that I must tell you that you may understand this story, understand that Chloe was never who you think she was, understand that, yes, I killed Master Wilson, but I did not kill her husband.

I know now that when I went into the river Chloe screamed, that she jumped up from her begging and ran to Master Wilson and beat her fists against his back. I know now that while I floundered in the river Wilson grabbed Chloe and held her against the railing, held her by her hair and forced her to watch me thrash and flail until I sank and was not seen again.

And I know now that when Master Wilson and his livestock and his slaves reached the opposite shore they stayed the night at another plantation, the slaves and livestock in a barn with Holmes watching over them, Master Wilson in the big house talking to his host and hostess. I imagine the woman of the house, her pale white hand fluttering with emotion at her bosom as Master tells his tale of woe. I imagine a lamp held by a slave as he is led to a comfortable bedroom upstairs. I imagine his bed; dark polished wood, a mattress soft and puffy with comfort, a white counterpane folded gently back for his solace.

I do not have to imagine Wilson rising from that comfortable bed in the dead of night. I do not have to imagine him lighting a lamp or making his way to the barn where his slaves were kept. She was crying when he came for her, crying over my death, and he took her into a stall, and he raped her, just as he had done that first night at Lidgewood. I do not have to imagine this, for Chloe told me its truth.

As she sat in the straw still sniffling and buttoning the bodice of her dress, he reached out and fingered the cloth with the missing button torn away and he said, "You can have it this way, Chloe, or we can make other arrangements." And then he gripped his fingers around another button and yanked it off, dropping it onto the straw.

Halfway to Texas Chloe left the coffle of slaves she traveled with and she climbed onto the wagon seat beside Master Wilson and she became his "wife." This is how it happened that her skin became lighter to you, that she became white in other people's eyes, that she became your "Mrs. Joseph Wilson."

From that moment forward Chloe was transformed into a white woman. And once she was white, Chloe could never be anything else to you.

I do forgive her. She only wanted to ease her own life. She believed that she would be a slave forever. She believed that Master Wilson would rape her forever. She believed that if she became his "wife," he might be gentler to her; she might have things such as clothes, and furniture, and a big house like Sweetmore. At the very least, she could ride in the wagon and would not have to walk to Texas with the rest of the slaves. She believed I was dead, but I was not dead.

The wood I clung to in the river was slick with algae. I grasped my fingers around its rim, for strangely, it had a rim. The top was rounded, and underneath it was hollowed out, and as my fingers felt along, I realized that this thing that had saved me, that had drifted, half-submerged, into my body just as I broke the surface gasping for breath, was an old dough bowl turned upside down. I lay my head on my craft and fell asleep and as I did I heard Chloe's voice once more: *Biscuits. Pies. All kinds. Blueberry, peach, apple. With crusts all buttery and flaky.*

It was night when I awoke. I lifted my head but could see nothing save the faint light of stars reflected in the lapping water. I could feel, though, that I was no longer adrift. A hard twisting form pressed against my back. I reached out with my left hand and felt along it, judging it to be a spine of tangled branches and logs that I had caught against. I dropped my legs deeper into the water, searching for solid footing. My feet sank into mud, and then I was wading, pushing my bowl in front of me, coasting it against the shore like a little boat, and then I climbed onto the beach, where I collapsed facedown.

When next I woke it was to the heat of the day. I rolled over and gazed at a cloudless sky. I sat up and looked around me. At my back were trees and thick vegetation. In front, the river lapped peacefully against the shore. I recognized nothing. I probed at the wound in my shoulder, and a sharp pain rocked through my arm. My joints ached. My skin felt hot. I collapsed again onto the ground, curling against the dough bowl and clutching it to my chest as if it were a woman.

The day passed and as the sun left the earth, a deep and gelid cold crept from the ground into the very marrow of my bones. I curled into a ball, hugging what little warmth I had into me, wafting in and out of consciousness. Then I found that I was walking, then crashing through the under-brush. Behind me I heard branches snapping and the crunch of boot against ground. I stopped moving and leaned against a tree. The sound stopped. Sweat bloomed on the back of my neck and across my chest. I reached up and wiped the moisture from my brow. I heard the bell ring. *Too sick, Massuh,* my own voice said. *Too sick to plant cane, suh.*

A blue cloud of smoke rose through the woods farther ahead, and I went in that direction but found nothing, not even embers, not even a clearing. Then I heard Henry's voice.

Damn, Shoot. You done it now.

I spun to the sound and saw him standing just a few feet away, laughing at me, pushing his hat back on his head. I went to him. I clung to his waist, but after a few minutes I found that I was only clinging to a tree. A snake slithered across my foot. I reached out and grabbed it just below its head, then squeezed the breath out of it while its body thrashed and curled around my arm and finally stilled.

"He seem 'bout half-dead," I heard a woman say. "Where you say you find him?"

"Down by the river in the rain, holdin' on to a dead snake," another woman answered.

"Snake? What kinda snake?"

"Cottonmouth."

"Cottonmouth? Lord. He bit?"

"Naw. He jest got that wound in his shoulder."

"He walk up here?"

"Barely. Leanin' on me, but we made it."

I heard movement, and then the crackle of a fire.

Sup. Sup always stoking the fire, always cooking the cush-cush and the hoecakes. Good old Sup.

"What day you find him?" the voice said.

"Thursday."

Thursday. Just two more days of work and I can rest. Bell ain't rung yet. Did I sleep through? *Oh naw, Massuh, don't whip me. Please don't whip me. I jest didn't hear it. I*

205

jest didn't hear that ol' bell.

"Hush now. Ain't nobody gonna whip you."

Hands on my chest gently pushing me back down.

And then I was in the river again, and Chloe's note was unfurling in front of me. But it was a dream. I woke to the sound of Sup stoking the fire, mixing up batter for hoecakes.

Hoecake, Sup. Can I have a hoecake?

"Ain't got no hoecakes," a woman said.

I opened my eyes. I was lying in a large bed covered with a blue counterpane. I looked around at dark cabin walls, just like my cabin at Sweetmore, but here there was a wingback chair covered in light blue fabric pulled up to the hearth, and an old Negro woman sitting in it. "He awake," she said.

And then I saw a younger woman turn from stirring a pot by the fire. She had skin like polished walnut, and her left temple glowed, lit up from behind like a lantern. "What yo' name?" she asked me.

"Persimmon Wilson," I heard myself say.

"That quite a name."

"Persy." The word scraped like grit against my throat as it came out. It was so hard to speak. "Folks call me Persy," I croaked.

The younger woman came over and laid a

hand on my forehead, and then my cheek. "Well, Persy, you still got the fever. It better, but you still right hot. You want you some water?"

I nodded, and she reached to a table next to the bed, picked up a cut crystal goblet. I tried to rise up but found that I couldn't.

"Here," the woman said. She slipped one arm behind my head, lifted me up, and held the goblet to my lips.

"Thank you."

"Right mannered nigger, ain't he?" the old woman in the chair said.

"Get some rest," the other said, and she lowered me back into the bed and set the goblet down on the table. The skin on her temple glowed and flickered and caught the light.

For three days I slept and woke. Sometimes I felt my head held up and broth spooned into my mouth. Other times I felt a cool cloth on my brow. When they were not tending to me the two women talked, and snippets of their conversation floated into my semiconscious mind.

You ought to of let him die, Silla. He jest dirtyin' up yo' new bedcloths. And what that out of his pocket? A little noose? What he carryin' a noose fo'? And what he doin' with a snake in his hand? I tell you, Silla, you done caught yo'self a witch doctor. He still callin' that name over and over? Chloe? That it?

When next I opened my eyes the old woman was still sitting in the wingback chair, but now there was a matching chair beside it, and the younger woman sat in it, sewing. "He awake again," the old woman said.

The younger one put down her work and got up and came to me. She laid one hand on my forehead as she had done before, and as she did so I saw that the glowing place on her temple was a large flat scar, the skin thin and taut, pulling her left eye up a little higher than it should be and reflecting the light of the lamp beside me. "How you feelin', Persy?" she asked.

"A little weak," I answered.

She smiled and nodded. "I 'spect so. I'm Silla," she said, "and this here my mama, Lizbeth. You want you some tea?"

Lizbeth chuckled to herself. "Massuh left it behind." She stood and took a fancy cup and saucer off the top of a polished dresser, and then poured from a kettle into it, and brought it to me.

"Here, baby, let me sit you up," Silla said.

She plumped the pillows behind me and helped me prop against them. A jab of soreness coursed through my right shoulder as I moved. I winced and lifted my left hand to it. Turning to look, I found bandaging there, neatly wrapped, clean and white except for one small spot of yellow blooming through the cloth. Lizbeth handed me the cup and saucer and I took them delicately, their diminutive size nearly swallowed by my hands.

"Mama dressed yo' wound," Silla said.

"Look like you got shot. Bullet went right through I reckon, but that wound nasty. Full of pus. Smell to high heaven."

"Where am I?" I asked.

"You on a plantation called Sou Sou," Silla answered.

"Does your master know I'm here?"

"Jest listen to him. He talk like a white man," Lizbeth said.

"Massuh gone," Silla answered. "He done run off from the Yankees."

"We free." Lizbeth laughed and pointed at me. "You free. You lucky you alive too. Silla done found you by the river with a snake in yo' hand. What you doin' with a snake in yo' hand?"

"I don't know."

"Who done shot you?"

"My master. He shot me and I fell into the river." I took a sip of the tea. I was surprised that it was sweet. "You have sugar?"

"Five hundred and thirty hogsheads of sugar," Lizbeth said. "Molasses too. Massuh done left it all behind. Now where you come from? Who yo' massuh?"

"Wilson, of Sweetmore."

"I heard of it. That where Jeff the fiddler wife live. Sally her name."

"Mama, let him rest," Silla said. "He ain't up to you askin' all these questions."

"I jest want to know what he doin' with a snake in his hand and a noose in his pocket. I tell you, Sill, you done caught yo'sef a witch doctor."

"He jest a sick man," Silla said. "Now leave him be."

"How sick was I?" I asked.

"Mighty sick, child." Lizbeth again. "Mighty sick. Yo' skin like fire."

"I 'spect you need you some food. I made a stew. I get you some." Silla went to the hearth and dished out a ladle full of steaming stew into a china bowl, into which she plunged a bright silver spoon.

"Are you the only ones here?" I asked.

Silla nodded and handed me the bowl. "Now hush up and eat. You ain't had nothing but broth since I found you. They's meat in that stew. Eat up."

"What day is it?"

"Lord, I don't know, child. That bell stop ringin' us out to the fields, I done lost the days in my head." Lizbeth chuckled and plopped herself down in her chair again.

"Wednesday," Silla answered. "I done found you on Thursday. You been gone out fo' near a week. Now eat, and rest. You ain't well enough fo' a social yet."

Wednesday today. Thursday when I was found. It had been Monday when we boarded the boat. I counted in my head. Ten days. Ten days since I last saw Chloe.

"Who Chloe?" Lizbeth suddenly asked as if she had reached into my head and pulled out the name.

"Mama!"

"I jest askin'. Save the man's life, I reckon I got a right to know who he callin' fo' in his sleep."

"My wife," I answered quickly. "Chloe's my wife. Wilson took her across the river to Texas and shot me and left me to drown."

"Nothin' these white folk do surprise me." Lizbeth shook her head. "But I reckon you best fo'get 'bout her. She over there and you over here."

"Over here?" I asked.

"Where else you be but over here?"

"I think he wantin' to know what side of the river he on. Is that right, baby?"

I nodded.

"You lucky to be on the New Orleans side," Lizbeth said. "You on the side with the Yankees."

"Our massuh took everyone to Texas too," Silla said. "We run off and hide in the swamp. Come back after they gone."

"Got Missus china and beddings. Tea, sugar, meat. Chairs." Lizbeth ran her hands along the blue fabric upholstery of the chair she sat in. "Fine chairs. Comfortable."

"Food gonna run out soon enough," Silla said. "We sittin' pretty now, but it ain't gonna last fo'ever." She nodded at me. "We share what we got. You eat up now." Silla waved her hand at the bowl I held. "You still weak."

"I need to get across the river."

"You ain't gettin' 'cross no river," Lizbeth said. "Rebs over there. Yankees over here. You free here. You jest another nigger slave over there."

"Chloe. I have to find Chloe. I have to get her away from him."

Lizbeth snorted. "Ain't none of our people in the right place no mo'. Fo'get 'bout that gal. Look after yo'self."

Silla laid her hand on my chest. "Mama's right," she said. "Now eat up."

I did not argue. I had no strength for arguing. I needed to get well again for the trip across the river, but the food lodged in my throat and I had to force every bite. My teeth were sore and the meat hard to chew, but I ate and I swallowed and I kept it down, although the knowledge of what they'd said made me feel sick, as if a black bile ponded in my stomach. Chloe on one side of the river and me on the other. Ten days apart.

Over the next week, I could barely get out of bed to relieve myself, and I did not rest easily. Each night I felt myself tossing in that sea of bedding, and I heard myself moaning, and I woke more than once, calling for Chloe. But Chloe was not there, and Silla was.

She changed the bandages on my shoulder each night. The wound still wept a bit, but Silla pressed the pus out and bathed it with brine. Once she ran her fingers lightly along the scars on my back and asked, "Wilson do this?"

"Had it done," I told her.

"That the way of it," Silla replied, touching the scar at her temple.

Gradually I got well enough to go outside

and sit in one of the wingback chairs pulled into a patch of sun. And then well enough to walk a bit around the empty quarters, and then to explore further afield, the barns, the big house, the river. As I stood on the banks of the levee looking out over the river, I wanted to cry. I wanted the release of tears spilling down my face, but too much had been wrung out of me for that. Making a life with Chloe seemed hopeless now. How could I ever get across the Mississippi River? How could I ever get to Texas, and once there, how could I ever find Chloe? I stood still, staring out over the water. A Yankee gunboat came into view. The men on deck waved to me and I lifted my arm and waved back, the ache in my shoulder almost gone now.

I moved into the cabin next door to Silla and Lizbeth. I plundered the big house and dragged furnishings into my new home: a feather mattress and a bedstead nearly as large as the cabin, a dresser crammed beside it, two chairs with backs curled like question marks pulled up to the hearth. I found a quilt, dishes, cutlery. I found stockings and shirts and britches, boots to replace my ruined shoes. I found a room in the big house filled floor to ceiling with shelves of books, a ladder that rolled along on wooden wheels to help in reaching the topmost ones. In this room was a large table with chunky legs, and on it spread a map of the United States and its territories, or what had once been the United States. It was two countries now, torn by war.

It was raining the day I noticed the map. I lit a lamp and set it on the table to see by. The rain pattered softly in the trees and thrummed on the porch roof. On the map, I traced my finger from Virginia, along the James River, and then out to sea and down to New Orleans. From there I ran my finger up the river to where I estimated Sweetmore to be, and then across the Mississippi, to the other shore, and west across the rest of Louisiana and on into Texas. My finger trawled that state, from the perimeter to the middle until finally I had touched every inch, and somewhere in all that, my finger had touched the land that Chloe was on.

I turned the flame of the lamp up and looked more closely at the rivers. Were I to go looking for her, these would be my greatest obstacles, I thought. The Red River, which flowed into the Mississippi, was something I could avoid if I crossed below it. But the land between the western shore of the Mississippi and the border of Texas was mapped with rivers, and along the Texas border there was a river called the Sabine, and beyond the Sabine more fingers of water crept across Texas like veins. I leaned closer and read the names of the few towns in Texas that were marked on the map. Liberty, Houston, Port Caddo, Fredericksburg, and above Fredericksburg, an arm of Texas that seemed empty of everything, and across this patch of nothingness one word, written in capital letters. COMANCHES.

The map was large, too large to fold and carry comfortably in my pocket, and so I tore out the states of Louisiana and Texas, and this swatch I did fold and put into my pocket where it nestled against the little noose.

I held the lamp aloft and wandered along the shelves of books, finally selecting one and then snuffing the light. I had taken to reading to Lizbeth and Silla each night after we shared a meal, and eventually, perhaps it was inevitable, Silla followed me to my cabin and lay with me in my large feather-bed.

I cried the first time, the tears breaking through when I felt the comforting arms of a woman once again. Silla rocked me like a baby. She stroked my neck and muttered softly, "Po' Persy. Po', po' Persy."

I took from Silla love and succor, solace

and companionship, food and nurturing. I took these things, and delivered words read from books, and firewood, split and stacked, and buckets of water drawn from the well and left on the stoop of their cabin. I learned to set traps and snag rabbits for dinner. I baited deer with salt, and learned to make friends with them before I chose one and slit its throat, and hauled it home for dressing and cooking. I allowed the men that passed through, Yankee soldiers and runaway slaves, the occasional planter or former overseer, dippers of water from our well, and I watched them closely to make certain that they left the plantation. I protected Silla and Lizbeth and Sou Sou, and every day I stood on the levee and gazed across the river to the other shore.

April had turned to May while I was sick, and now May turned to June. The air grew stagnant, hot and steamy. I raided the big house once again and stole sheets to hang in the open doorway of my cabin in the hopes of letting in some of the cool night air, but now the mosquitoes found their way inside and whined in my ears all night long. Still, Silla came to me, and each night we went at each other.

I had become rough with her. I gave no thought to her needs or pleasure. This was my brief life on Sou Sou. I did my chores. I read my books. I fucked my woman. And then one night after I had finished my business with her and rolled away to face the wall and sleep, Silla let out one long breath and said, "I ain't comin' back no mo'." I didn't answer and after some time of silence she asked, "Did you hear me?"

"I heard you." I turned to face her, and in the faint moonlight that slipped its way between the cracks in the wall of my cabin, I could see the dampness on her face. "Why?" I asked.

She put her arms around me and pulled me to her, trailing her fingers along the ridges of scars on my back. "Persy, I done ask you 'bout yo' scars. I know you got 'em from a whippin'. I know what you was accused of. I know Chloe ain't yo' wife. She Wilson's fancy. I know all that 'cause I done ask you 'bout yo' scars. But you ain't never, even once, ask me 'bout mine." Her hands left my back and traveled to her face. "It like you don't want to hear my story. Like I jest here to be yo' fancy. I ain't no whore, Persy."

"Chloe's not a whore," I said.

"I ain't say she was. I say I ain't."

Silla was a beautiful woman. If I have not described her thus, then I owe you, and her, an apology. Even the scar contributed to all that was Silla, to all that was her beauty, this large flat scar like a large flat rock I remembered in a field at the Surley place in Virginia, a rock that we plowed and planted around, and that I had played on when I was just a shirttail boy too young to work. "I'm sorry," I said. "Please, tell me now."

"Kitchen fire," she answered, without inflection. "I got this goin' into the kitchen house and pullin' out a little white baby. Save that child's life. Chrissy her name. I her gal. Then I too ugly to be a house slave no mo', too ugly to be her gal. I get put out in the fields."

"I'm sorry, Silla. I'm sorry I never asked." I held my hand against my forehead, staring at the ceiling.

"You call fo' her in yo' sleep. You call her name. 'Chloe. Chloe.' Every night. I cain't listen no mo'."

April 2, 1875

I have written well into the night. Outside my barred window the pink light of dawn has given over to the white light of morning. Jack, my jailer, told me when he brought my breakfast that I am to be measured for my casket today. I will not be surprised if the newspaperman also pays me a visit, begging once again for my story, and of course, the preacher might stop by, begging once again for my soul. I will tell everyone but the casket maker to go away.

My hand is cramped, my forearm knotted with the effort of unceasingly moving pen across paper for twelve or more hours. I have called to Jack during the night for more ink, more paper, more fuel for my sputtering lamp. I have little time in which to live now, one full day and part of another in which to complete this account. I do not mind dying. Perhaps I even deserve it, although you hang me for the wrong crime. The death of Wilson is nothing. It made my heart glad to kill him. The person I have failed is Chloe, and I cannot die until I have completed her story.

You call her now "the most tragic figure of the frontier," a "white" woman degraded not just by an Indian, but also by a nigger. You say that Chloe was my slave, and I write this to disavow you of that thought.

There is so much more truth to tell, and so little time left in which to tell it. And so I ask your forgiveness for the literary pace with which I write this section, this narrative that bridges my life as a field slave on a cane plantation along the Mississippi River to my life as Kweepoonaduh Tuhmoo, the man you are about to hang.

I have many years to cover and a short time in which to do it, and I am in this moment still a man with a body that protests for food and rest, a body that cares not that tomorrow it will be dangling and jerking from the end of a rope. My body wants only for its immediate needs. It screams at me to stop this foolishness, this ridiculous writing. It screams at me to eat, to sleep, to massage my hand and forearm until my muscles relax again. As a Comanche I learned to set aside the needs of the body. Today my heart burns only with the wish to complete this narrative and to still be able to stand up straight enough to die.

I joined the army after I left Sou Sou. I had heard from passersby that a regiment of Negro soldiers was being formed, and I walked downriver to Camp Parapet and presented myself to the first white soldier I saw. He took me to his captain and I was signed up. I was told that yes, I would be sent across the river to Texas to fight. It was not true. I was not sent to Texas, and my plan to desert my post once there and begin my search for Chloe was thwarted.

I spent the remainder of the war serving the Union, serving the country that had brought my ancestors here as slaves, and had then regretted that decision enough to now allow black men to fight and get shot at. It was as safe a place to be as any for the next three years. At least I had a gun and was surrounded by other men with guns. At least I was on the side of the white people who would not re-enslave me once the war was over.

I will tell you only two stories from this time.

While still in Louisiana along the German Coast above New Orleans, I made a survey with my captain upriver. He was fond of me, as I was literate and, he said, intelligent. He was a kind man, far kinder than the white soldiers who taunted and swore that "Niggers won't fight." I had lied to him, telling him that I knew the land, therefore he chose me often to go with him on these little excursions into the country. On this particular exploration we rode our horses a long ways up the levee road. We passed many plantations with the cane gone long in the fields, the weeds lapping at walkways and steps leading to high and once mighty verandas, the morning shadows falling across busted windows and doors left ajar. Not all the plantations were abandoned by their owners, but the vast work-packs of Negroes were missing, and the fields left unattended. As we traveled upriver, a white man or woman would often step out onto the gallery of a big house and glare at us.

In the afternoon the levee road became familiar to me. I recognized the bend in the river where Henry and I had worked to repair the levee the day Old Miss died. A little later I saw the quay where I had once rolled barrels of sugar and molasses, and where I had waited on the deck of the steamer for Master Wilson to bring Chloe and the other house slaves to board. In the other direction I could see all of Sweetmore, the quarters, and the fields, and beyond the fields, the sugarhouse, and beyond that, the big house with its four cold chimneys. Beside the lane leading to Sweetmore was a grave marked with a wooden cross, rocks mounded like a tumor on the land. We reined in our horses and sat in the saddles looking down at the tilted cross. An animal had pawed at the earth, and a hole was partially dug along one side of this last resting place.

"Sir," I said. No sentence shaped itself. I swallowed a great lump that had formed in my throat. "Sir," I said again.

My captain looked at me. His name was Captain Wiel. "Is this your old place, Persy?" he asked.

"Yes sir."

"I'll hold your horse," he said, and he reached out to take the reins.

I dismounted and clambered down the bank of the levee. There was no name on the cross, but this would be where Katy, Wilson's cook, fell when he shot her five months earlier. I wondered who had buried her, Henry and Sup perhaps, or one of the others who had run off into the swamps. I pushed my boot against a rock that had been pawed away from the grave. I straightened the cross and wedged another stone against its base to hold it upright. Behind me the fields of cane, their plants taller than me now, waved and undulated in the breeze.

When I looked up I saw that Captain Wiel was making his way down the side of the levee, leading my horse as he sat astride his. He stopped before me. "I could use a little break," he said, dismounting. "I'll just sit in the shade here." He led the horses to a live oak tree and tied the reins to a low-hanging branch. "Take a look around if you want to."

"Thank you, sir."

I turned downstream a ways and followed a footpath into the quarters and pushed open the door of my old cabin. The smell of damp disuse rose to meet my nostrils. There were four pallets lined against two walls. Ashes filled the hearth. I shoved the toe of my boot against a partially burnt log and wondered if it was from the same fire I had stoked the morning of our departure, the morning I woke up to find Henry and Sup gone. I touched the peg where Henry had always hung his hat. I walked to the pallet in the far corner of the front wall and lay facedown on it. I ran my fingers along the crack where the floor met the wall, as if Chloe's note would materialize at their touch. I rolled over and looked at the ceiling, my movement stirring the scent of mold.

I stepped back outside and headed up the lane, past the bell that had called me to work, tilting now on its post, past the stoop where Master Wilson had stood to make his little announcements, past the wagon I had hidden behind while making my way to the sugarhouse, past my hopes of ever escaping with Chloe.

I pushed the door to the sugarhouse open. The ghosts of grinding season were thick here, the boiling kettles, the rollers crushing the cane, the feet scuffing paths from task to task until the dirt floor was ridged like a washboard. And then the ghosts of our sugarhouse party made their way onto the floor, the table covered with the patched red cloth and laden with food, the couples swinging and dancing to Jeff's fiddle. The door behind me heaved and creaked. I turned, but nothing was there. Nothing but ghosts. They owned this place now.

They jingled tack as I passed the stable where the horses had been kept. They bleated as I passed the milking barn. They moaned as I approached the whipping place, the three stakes in the ground where I had been tied. I kicked at one of the stakes. It did not move. It would not move.

I turned to face the big house, and it loomed as ominously as it ever had, towering in the landscape, towering over the cane plants, towering over me. I walked toward it.

Parts of the picket fence that surrounded the big house had been kicked over, large sections of it lying on the ground with tangles of thick weeds punching their way through the slats. The gate still stood and I pushed at it, but it hung by only one hinge and I had to lift it in order to scrape it across the ground.

I had never before approached the front door of Master Wilson's house. With each step closer the house grew larger and larger, its windows like accusing eyes staring at me, as though the house itself would punish me for daring to verge on such directness. I stood now at the foot of the steps, looking up at the veranda, at the chairs and couches pulled into a circle as if they expected a slave to step forward with tumblers of bourbon, a box of cigars. My eyes wandered to the front door, left slightly ajar, creating one slant of darkness that revealed nothing of the interior.

I placed one foot on the first step and stood, not moving, until finally I placed my other foot on the next step, and so I climbed to the gallery, slowly, and then stood on the gray-painted floor facing the dark green–painted front door. I had always thought it black from a distance.

I told myself that there was no reason to feel such trepidation at entering the big house of Sweetmore. I reminded myself that I had entered and plundered the big house of Sou Sou plenty of times. I had dragged out furniture, rifled through books and papers, stolen dishes and clothes, the very boots on my feet, the piece of map I still kept folded in my pocket. Yet this felt more dangerous, and I swear that as I set my hand on the latch of the front door, I felt once again the chilled fingers of that spirit raking across my skin, always, it seemed, connecting me to Master Wilson. I pushed the door open and stepped inside, finding myself in a wide front hall, doorways to rooms in every direction except directly in front of me. There, a curved staircase rose as if to some clouded, exalted place in the sky.

I smelt him here; his stinking breath, his flatulence, his sweat, his semen. I suddenly felt ill and leaned over and vomited in one corner of the hall. I straightened and wiped my mouth with the back of my hand. "You bastard," I said out loud, my voice echoing against the cold white walls.

I walked through the lower rooms first, my boots thumping hollowly across the floor, leaving prints in the dust that coated everything. In the dining room nothing had been touched, not the large table with the twelve chairs pulled up close to it, not the china soup tureen with a ladle jutting out from under its lid, not the thick spiderweb that filmed from the ladle to the windowsill.

In the parlor were two chairs with curved backs. One was pulled up against the wall as if waiting for a firing squad; the other lay on its side in the hearth, partially burned. There were three upholstered settees, a knife slash running through each, horsehair spilling to the floor. Tables, once polished, were now sheeted with dust, and a lamp sat on one, its globe clouded with soot. In another room books were spilled onto the floor, and some piled in the fireplace, but in the study it looked as if nothing had been touched. An inkwell, a pen, and stationery were arranged on the desk in an obsessively meticulous line.

I ran my fingers across one sheet of the stationery, over Master Wilson's embossed initials, the same stationery on which Chloe had written her note to me. I opened a drawer. There was nothing in it. I rifled through the rest of the drawers in the desk, searching for anything that might tell me where he had gone in Texas. There was nothing. A receipt for Gerald Wilson's headstone. A wax seal. A strip of ribbon curled into one corner, gritty with dust.

I climbed the curving staircase to the upstairs rooms. There were five in all, and I went first to one and then to the next, peering into the doorway of each, not sure what it was that I sought, then realizing that the room I most wanted to visit would be Missus Lila's room, where Chloe had spent most of her time. But which one was it?

I thought about the placement of the windows that I had studied so much from down below, and the balcony I had stared up at so often. I walked to the western side of the house and entered the last bedroom. I opened the doors to the gallery and stepped outside, looking out over the yard, and beyond it the fields, the sugarhouse, the levee, and the river. I saw Captain Wiel sitting beneath his tree, his hat pulled down over his eyes. I returned my gaze to the yard and recognized the tree I had stood beside with Sup while witnessing the newly formed Confederate troops march and drill. I turned back to the room, knowing that this was indeed Missus Lila's quarters. A four-poster bed, thick with lace and ruffles and comforters. Rugs. Dressers and armoires. Tables. Two chairs were pulled up to either side of the bed, and at its foot, a pad made of an old quilt. This, I was certain, was where Chloe had slept, but it told me nothing of where she had gone.

I went to the next room. Another four-poster bed. Less lace, fewer ruffles. I opened the armoire. It was filled with men's clothes, a pair of boots. This was his bedroom, his bed, where he had patted his plump hands as Chloe stood in the doorway. This was the place where Master Wilson had repeatedly raped my woman. My rage released itself like a bear finally let off its chain.

I picked up a chair and threw it into a mirror, glass splintering across the floor. I rocked the armoire back and forth until it crashed down with a loud crack, a cloud of dust rising from the floor and then settling. I pulled my pistol and fired three times into the mattress, and feathers puffed out into the air. They drifted onto my uniform, onto my hat, onto my boots. I leaned down to brush one away, and there on the floor I saw a small shadow in the low-slung afternoon light that cast itself where the armoire had stood.

You will perhaps think I have gone mad if I tell you that the world became quieter then, not just because I had ceased my rage, but because the birds and the insects, so incessant in Louisiana, stopped singing. The air grew still, as though every spirit who had ever crossed the cane fields of Sweetmore was now behind me, pushing me, guiding my hands toward this small object with the long shadow. I knelt down and touched it. I picked it up. A button, plain and unadorned. I held it in the palm of my hand, and remembered, as we sat together on the deck of the steamer, Chloe's fingers wandering at the rent of fabric on her dress.

How many times had she let me unhitch this button from its fastening? How many times had I spread the fabric of her dress apart? How many times had I slurped at her love like a hungry calf, and what had she received from me but semen, and empty promises? I closed my fingers around the button and I swore that, somehow, I would find her. As I did so I heard Captain Wiel's boot steps on the stairs. "Persy," he called. "Persy, are you injured?"

"No sir," I said.

He stepped into the room and saw me kneeling there amid the feathers, the overturned armoire, and the splinters of mirror glinting across the floor. "Perhaps it's time to leave," Captain said.

"Yes sir." I slipped the button into my pocket.

It was September 1862. I had not yet seen battle, but that would soon change. As my regiment advanced on Port Hudson in the spring of 1863, a shell hit a man in the head and his brains splattered across my uniform. He was the color sergeant, and his name was Anselmas Planciancois. When he was hit two corporals to either side of him seized the flag to prevent it from touching the ground.

That night I served as assistant to a surgeon, who was not really a surgeon but was merely a hospital steward. All the white doctors had refused to attend to the colored troops, but this man could saw through bone as well as any, and that seemed to be all that was required.

We worked in a small shack on a spit of land inside a swamp. The floor around us was slick with blood, the air slick with screams and moans, pleading and suffering. Our patients were laid out on an old pine table, and the steward's apron was covered in blood, as was my own. We administered chloroform, and when the chloroform ran out we administered muscle, holding the men down on the table as they writhed and screamed, and as the surgeon plied his grisly trade. With each limb he sawed off I took hold of it and tossed it out the back door like a stick of firewood.

When we had finished our horrible task I wandered out into the night. There was a small campfire close by and I went to it and sat on a log, listening to the snores of the sleeping men all around me, and picking pieces of Sergeant Planciancois's skull from my uniform. I felt in my pocket for Chloe's button, and was relieved to find it still there, nestled against the little noose.

I did not want to risk losing it and so I wandered back to the makeshift hospital, and I found a man who had died in the night. I loosened the buckle of his belt and slid the belt from his pants. I then took the belt outside and held it against a stump as I cut from it a thin strip of leather. On this I strung Chloe's button and tied it around my neck.

If I were a gentler person, a man of sentiment and poetry, then I would tell you that it was only my love for Chloe that kept me alive during the war. I have read enough books to know that it would make a good story. But truthfully, it was also my hatred of Master Wilson. I nursed that hatred, and it became the strength with which I dug the trenches for latrines, the ferocity with which I built breastworks and went into battle, and the desperation with which I survived.

At the end of the war the entire nation was desperate — some folks for food, others for shelter, almost all to be with loved ones again, if the loved ones were still alive. I was no different. I was desperate to find Chloe. It pained me to think that she might remember me as yet another man, no different from the rest, who had used her for his pleasure. I was as desperate to prove to myself that this was not true as I was to prove it to her.

It had been three years since I'd last seen Chloe. That she might not remember me at all, that she might not love me any longer, that she might have married another man, that I would not even be able to find her; these were thoughts I would not allow myself as I caught a steamer across the Mississippi River and began walking. It was October of 1865. I slept in burned-out houses and abandoned barns and along spits of land inside the swamps. I looked out for snakes and battled swarms of mosquitoes and ducked under my worn wool coat during thunderstorms, and shaded my face from the sun with an old hat I'd found along the road. I ate what I could find. When game was scarce I ate bugs and for nourishment, drank a tea brewed from lichen or pine needles. I foraged for persimmons and wild grapes. I caught crayfish and snapping turtles. These last I threw directly into the fire, and when they tried to crawl out, I poked them back in with a stick, later scooping the cooked meat out of the shells with my fingers.

I was given, on occasion, a ride in the back of a wagon, or passage across a bayou on a flat boat. I was given, on occasion, a meal sneaked to me out the back door of an old plantation by an ex-slave who had stayed on with a former master or mistress. I saw that the loss of the war, the loss of crops and prestige, the loss of slaves and property had stricken some white people with what is politely called "a case of the nerves." Those who were stricken as such became harder than they had ever been before. I wondered at times if Master Wilson had succumbed to such a disorder, or if he had somehow righted himself, as a cat that tumbles will always land on its feet.

I asked about him wherever I went, as I inquired also about Chloe. A light-skinned colored woman I said. Last seen traveling with her master in 1862, on their way to Texas. He was short, and round. A large mole right here. I pointed to my neck, just below Chloe's button.

Last I saw her, my wife, I added, she had long wavy brown hair. She usually wore it in a braid. Slight of build, I said. Strong arms. Her name is Chloe. My wife, I said again. I am searching for my wife.

I was met with women like Lizbeth who told me I was on a fool's errand, and that I would never be able to find her. Texas, I was told, again and again, is a big place. "Better get yo'sef a new wife. That one done gone."

But I was also met with sympathy, a shake of the head, a pitying look, and a hand reaching out to take the empty plate from my lap. "They been several mo' like you come through here lookin' fo' wives, or chirrens, or mamas or papas. Somebody always lookin' fo' somebody. Now you best get on fo' my mistress see you. Somethin' fo' yo' travels." And this kind woman would hand me bit of bread, and bacon perhaps, wrapped in an oil-stained cloth. "Get on now, fo' we both in trouble." And on I went, to the next barn to sleep in, the next back door to inquire at, the next begged meal, if I could find one.

I had traveled two weeks, maybe three, when I met a black man along a lane, walking in the opposite direction. We nodded to each other, and stopped for conversation. "Name's Zek," the man said.

"Persy," I told him.

"Where you headin'?"

"Texas."

"You almost there. Not too late to change yo' mind."

"Why would I change my mind?" I asked.

He shook his head. "White folk in Texas ain't givin' up so easy. 'Mancipation come late fo' 'em. They still some slavin' over there, and some may as well be slavin' fo' all the diff'ence they is. They still whippin' in Texas," Zek added.

"That can't be legal," I said. "We're free now."

Zek laughed. "You sho talk purty, but legal and free two diff'ent things." He shrugged and pointed down the road. "Don't matter to me. Sabine River 'bout three miles off. You almost there. Don't ask to cross at the ferry. They'd soon drown you. Travel down-river a ways, find a colored man named Lester. He take you 'cross if you hell-bent on it."

"I am," I said. "My wife —"

He cut me off. "I got me a wife. I got three, all diff'ent places fo' I get sold on to the next place. Even if I thought I could find one, I wouldn't know which to look fo'. They was all fine women," he added.

"I've just got one."

"You talk educated," Zek observed.

"I can read and write."

"I wouldn't let on 'bout that if I was you." He nodded. Lifted his hat. "Good luck to you, then. Lester'll take care of you."

It was late afternoon when I found the man Lester along the eastern bank of the muddy and flat Sabine River. He rowed me across for the last bit of money I had in my pocket. "You change yo' mind now, I row you back," he said. "Ain't no extra charge fo' changin' yo' mind. Ain't no shame in it neither."

"No, thank you," I said.

He pulled the skiff ashore and I climbed out. "Now listen here," Lester said. "You in Sabine County. You follow that path." He pointed to a footpath cutting through the bottomland and into woods. "Where it fork, you go left. Not right. You got that?"

I nodded.

"Left, not right," he said again. "Right lead you to the big house of a place called Shambleville."

"A town?" I asked.

"Ain't no town. It jest a cotton farm be-longin' to Massuh Shamble. You don't wanna mess with him. He mean as hell befo' his slaves run off. Now he meaner."

"They're free," I insisted. "A free man can't run off."

He gave a little huff at that. "Tell it to Massuh Shamble if you want to. I jest tryin' to help you keep a rope off yo' neck." I looked at him. He nodded gravely. "I ain't lyin' to you," he said. "They hangin' niggers fo' lookin' at white people wrong. Massuh Shamble's niggers done left befo' he could get up a gang to quit 'em from it. He fired up 'bout that. Got cotton in the field need harvestin' and no niggers to work it.

"I take you back," Lester offered again. "No extra charge. I goin' back anyway."

I shook my head.

"You one determined nigger," he said, and then reminded me about the footpath. "Go left at that fork. You still be on Shambleville land. Quarters that way. If you don't light a fire or lamp, I reckon you could stay in one of them cabins fo' a night. They a woman named Hannah still there. She 'bout to pop a baby. Husband done left her. You find her, she help you know where to go next."

He nodded and shoved off, and I turned away from him, gazing at the bottomlands and the path leading through the woods and listening to his oars dipping into the water behind me, growing farther and farther away.

I took the path as instructed, turned left instead of right, and arrived at nightfall along the edge of a cotton field, and beyond the cotton, the rows of cabins. I crossed the field, the plants scraping against my shirt and trousers, and as they did so I remembered one of the men I had served with at Port Hudson. He'd told me that as New Orleans fell, his master had also fled, taking his slaves to his second plantation, a cotton farm in Texas. I had not heard of Master

241

Wilson owning any other plantation, but perhaps he did. Perhaps he had come here. I entered one of the cabins and there I spent my first night in Texas, falling asleep on a pallet similar to mine at Sweetmore.

I found Hannah the next morning standing with her hand on her back, watching the sunrise. She did not seem surprised when I called out to her. "I reckon Lester send you," she said. "I reckon you lookin' fo' somebody." I nodded, and introduced myself, and gave my descriptions of Chloe and Master Wilson, and asked if she knew of a farm belonging to a man by that name.

She shook her head and said, "Nobody by Wilson round here."

"Did you see someone fitting his description?" I asked.

Hannah sighed. "It been a long time since them folk started comin' from Lou'siana. I seen a bunch of 'em, lines of slaves walkin' behind a wagon or two, but I cain't rightly 'member any 'ticulars." She moved her hand from her back to the mound of her stomach. "Massuh Shambles be hirin' out Massuh Wilder's niggers startin' tomorrow mornin'. I gotta cook fo' 'em. They be a mess of 'em stayin' in the quarters." She sighed heavily again. "Overseers too. You cain't stay here."

"I didn't intend to, but who's going to help you," I asked, eyeing her belly, "after the baby comes?"

She gave a sad little laugh. "Nobody. Nobody gonna help me befo' or after."

"What will you do?"

She turned and looked at me. "I do what I have to do. Whatever that be. Don't worry 'bout Hannah. You got yo' own woman to worry 'bout." She ran her hands across her stomach. "It kickin'," she said. "You wanna feel?" She reached out for my hand and took it and laid it on her belly, and beneath my palm I felt the rumblings of her child. Hannah smiled and moved my hand away.

"Do you think I'm a fool," I asked, "to look for her?"

Hannah reached over to me again, and this time laid her hand on my arm. "I think you a good man fo' lookin'." She squeezed her fingers into my skin and repeated, "You a good man." And then she let go and the warmth of her hand was replaced by the cool, indifferent Texas air.

"It ain't gonna be easy to find yo' Chloe," she said. "But here what you gotta do. You gotta stay away from white folk if you can. Unless you know fo' sho they kind. You talk to black folk, what you do. You find the next colored person and ask where you go, who you go see, who you ask 'bout yo' Chloe, which white man give you work and be fair."

"But where do I go now?" I asked.

"You go six mile west. Stick to the woods. You find another quarters. Look fo' Levi. He help you out."

I hesitated. It seemed as though she would give birth that very day. She read me. "Ain't nothin' you can do fo' me," she said. "Jest get on. It make me happy to know they a man out there lookin' fo' his woman."

"I imagine there are a lot now that the war's ended," I said.

"Some givin' up. It too hard. White people too crazy 'bout losin' the war. They takin' it out on everyone but theyselves. Go find Levi. Stick to the woods. Don't take the road if you can help it. You see white men, get out of they way. Don't let 'em see you. You ain't supposed to be travelin' without no pass."

"A pass? I'm a freedman."

"Depends on what you call free," Hannah said. "I told my man to leave me here. Jake's his name. I told him to get out and take our other chirren. Two boys." Her voice cracked. "Joey and Billy. Save the chirren, I tell Jake. Save yo'self. I don't reckon I ever see 'em again. Now go." She pushed against my chest. "Go. Get out of here."

I left her there crying at the edge of that yet to be harvested cotton field. I found the man named Levi, and from there a man named Cor, and from there a woman named Hester, and on I went, from Negro to Negro, seeking now not just information about Chloe, but also information about how to stay safe.

By the end of November, by carefully staying off heavily traveled roads and away from towns, by following the network of former slaves, one to the next, I had made my way safely to what is known as Hill Country. All along the way I asked about Chloe to no avail.

Winter came, and I found work, herding sheep. I slept in one corner of the farmer's barn, bedded down in hay with an old worn quilt donated by his wife. The wind blasted through the slats of the barn. Come spring I moved on, traveling to the next settlement I'd been told about, working once cleaning a saloon in the mornings before the drinking began, another time as a grave digger in a town hit by cholera, once more herding sheep, another time teaching school, but the school was burned down.

Occasionally I met a freedman who had a copy of the *Colored Tennessean* newspaper. Whenever it was available I read the advertisements placed there by a man or a woman searching for their loved ones. Sometimes I read them to myself, and sometimes out loud to a family I was staying with.

"Information wanted of the children of Janie Smith, sold to John Webb when they were nine, six, and three. Names Noah, George, and Mary."

"Information wanted of my sister, Martha Ginger, mother's name Collie Jones."

"Information wanted of my mother, Libby Monroe, last belonging to Henry Wallace."

"Information wanted by Kansas Barks on the whereabouts of her children, Eliza, Jimmy, Lina, Sarah, and Adam, sold in auction in South Carolina. Ministers, please read the above to your congregation."

My heart jumped one night when I read the name Chloe by the light of a fire in a slave cabin. "Information wanted about the mother and father of Chloe Simmons."

Simmons. The name did not fit, but names among the enslaved were fluid things. I read the details. I tried to remember the names of her mother and the man she'd called father. Anna? Jason? None of the names in the ad fit. The white men who'd once owned this Chloe did not fit. I read the rest of the ads in the paper and found nothing. The next day I headed on.

Months passed. Seasons passed. Seasons added into years and they too passed. There was no method to my wandering, no logical approach to finding Chloe. There was no way to have a logical approach, or a plan. I knew in my mind, even in my heart and my soul, that I should end this search. Texas was too large. I would never find her. I knew this as well as I knew anything, yet I could not stop.

Time and again I took the piece of map I'd stolen from Sou Sou out of my pocket and unfolded it. It was now thin and creased from carrying it so long, and I trawled my finger over its soft, frayed paper, as if it could somehow give up the secret of where she might be. I trawled my finger even across that empty swath of land labeled Comanches.

As I traveled I heard stories of the Indians. It seemed unbelievable to me that outside of Saline 2,100 cattle were taken during a daytime raid, along with fifty-four horses. A few months later a man and his son were killed, the man found with twelve arrows bristling in his back, the boy with his throat cut, both scalped. Two children were captured near Comfort. A woman was raped and scalped, her son taken — Saline again. A man and his sister were killed in Gillespie

County, the man's wife and five children captured. Another man in Mason heard sounds outside, and upon investigating, he shot the figure he saw creeping around his barn, his own son it turned out, mistaken for an Indian.

Somewhere outside of San Antonio, in June of 1867, as the land gave way again to hills of grass, I heard a wagon rattling up behind me. "Name's Mo Tilly," a man hollered out. "You wantin' a ride?"

I looked up into the face of a white man whose skin had been sunned the color of caramel, and whose cheeks looked withered as a dried leaf. He grinned at me with gummy, stained-black teeth, and then turned his head and spat tobacco juice off into the weeds.

"Yes sir," I said. "Thank you, sir." And then I froze, for without thinking, I had spoken normally to this man.

"Well, what you waitin' fo'?" he said.

I went to the back of the wagon, but the man stopped me.

"Set up here by me," he said. "I could use the comp'ny. Besides, you set back there you liable to get hit when I spit my tombaccer juice." He let another stream fly, and then wiped his sleeve across his mouth. "Where you headin'?"

"Texas," I answered.

"Ha. You in Texas." He gave the reins a light slap and the mules plodded forward, twitching their ears against the flies.

"Yes sir. I'm looking for my wife."

"Ah. Got split apart, did you?"

"Yes sir, during the war."

"What yo' name?"

"Persy."

"Well, what her name? Who she belong to? I might know somethin'."

I told him.

He shook his head. "Naw. Don't know no one by name of Wilson, but Texas a big place. You plan on coverin' every damn inch of it?"

"It feels like I already have."

"How long it been since you seed her?"

"Five years." I began rolling the button between my fingers, and then, I cannot explain it, I told this man, this white man, Mo Tilly, whom I had just met, everything. The story poured out of me unbidden, and Mo Tilly sat there listening, slapping the reins against the mules' backs every now and then, swatting at the flies, spitting, and occasionally interjecting commentary, kindly, so as to ease the parts that were clearly painful for me.

"Listen here," he said when I'd finished.

"You ain't no crim'nal or murderer, are ye? We get along jest fine, providin' you ain't no crim'nal or murderer. You ain't, are ye?"

"No sir."

"All right, then. You a liar though. This gal Chloe, she ain't really yo' wife."

"No sir." I shook my head and wiped my sleeve across my face. "I'd like her to be."

"Five year a long time," he said.

I nodded.

"I hates to say it, but she might not even be alive no mo'. That damn war . . . I reckon you noticed a whole messa folk got theyselves kilt."

"Yes sir."

"If she alive, she might not want you no mo'." He spat and wiped his sleeve across his mouth.

"I know."

"Gal as good-lookin' as all you say bound to 'tract some 'tention."

"Yes sir."

"Might be married to someone else."

"I hope to someone good," I said.

"Or she might be lookin' fo' you while you lookin' fo' her, and you be goin' 'long in Texas and she be travelin' back to Lou'siana, and y'all pass each other a hunderd miles apart."

I nodded.

"Lot to think 'bout."

"Yes."

"All them pos'bilities. It enough to make a man profundy tired. Why don't you get on back in the wagon and lay down. They some blankets and such. Make yo'sef comfortable. I try not to spit on you."

I was tired. I felt ashamed that I had exposed myself to Mo Tilly, that I had not been more careful in dealing with a white man. As I crawled into the back of the wagon and rolled myself into a cocoon of blankets, I thought of Henry and Sup. I missed them. I missed the camaraderie we had shared. I covered my head with the blanket, only wanting to escape into sleep. Above me Mo Tilly chucked at the mules and talked to them — Gee — Haw — Come on now, Jenny, gitty up — and I fell asleep, the wagon creaking and rocking me farther along, to where, I did not know.

When I woke it was dusk and the wagon had come to a squealing halt. I sat up to see Mo Tilly jump down off the seat and stretch his back. Sitting as he had been, I had not noticed his stature, but now I saw that he was chunky and short, about as tall, it almost seemed, as a pair of men's knee-high boots. "Come on now, Persy," he said. "We got to make camp."

A creek bubbled nearby and we drank deeply before pulling weeds away from the ground to make a fire pit, and gathering wood, then setting a blaze going, which I tended while Mo Tilly hunted. Before long he had shot a rabbit, skinned it, and had it cooking on a greenwood spit. He pulled out a jug and took a swig, then offered it to me. I took a swig and passed it back. I had never shared a jug with a white man before, or since, but it was comfortable sitting around the fire with this man, listening to the rabbit drip grease onto the sizzling coals.

Mo Tilly told me he was heading off to foreman a ranch for a Yankee man who'd purchased it sight unseen. His first task was to winter over on the ranch, repairing what needed it, and building new where that was required. "Them plains is full of longhorns jest free fo' the takin'," he said. "Now listen here, Persy. I been thinkin' 'bout yo' sit-chiation. You cain't jest be wanderin' Texas lookin' fo' this gal. You been doin' it, what? Almost two years now? And you ain't found her yet, and it a wonder you ain't been kilt. It don't make no damn sense the way you goin' 'bout it. You got to have you a base of op'rations."

"You think I can't find her," I said.

"I didn't say that. You might find her. You

might find her, and she might still be wantin' you. Y'all might get married and have babies and yo' son become the prezdent of the United States."

I nearly spat my swig of liquor out laughing. "I doubt a nigger's going to be president of the United States, Mr. Tilly."

"Naw, I reckon not, but that ain't the pint. The pint is you gonna get yo'sef kilt wanderin' round out here. Like I say, it a wonder you ain't dead yet. It plain to see you ain't got no sense. You got to have yo'sef a plan."

"No plan is perfect," I answered, thinking of the way I had stalled Chloe at Sweetmore.

"Didn't say it was. But some plan better than no plan. 'Specially out here. No plan'll get you kilt."

"And what sort of plan ought I to have, Mr. Tilly? Texas is a big place. Everyone tells me that. What am I supposed to do? Give up? Make it smaller?"

"Ain't no need to get testy. By god, you talk to every white man the way you talkin' to me, you gonna get yo'sef hanged. Not everybody in Texas enlightened as I am." He pulled another swig on the jug and jammed in the cork. Then he stood up, all four and a half feet of him, lifted the rabbit

253

off the fire and dropped it onto a tin plate that sat between us. Mo Tilly sat back down again and ripped a leg off the steaming rabbit and began eating. "Hot, hot, hot," he said. "Help yo'sef, Persy."

I did so, tearing at the meat and blowing on it to cool.

"Now like I was sayin'," Mo Tilly continued. "You need yo'sef a base of op'rations. You gonna need you a job, Persy. You gonna need you some money. It ain't jest findin' her you got to think on. What if you do find her? You cain't be askin' her to wander round Texas eatin' rabbits and bugs."

"How'd you know I ate bugs?"

"Everyone starvin' eats bugs. One of the things I like 'bout you. I can see you resourceful. Besides, you tol' me. Now listen here, how you gonna set her up, once you find her? What you got to offer?"

I shook my head. "Nothing."

"Exactly right. And there she might be havin' some other fella champin' at the bit to marry her, and he offerin' her somethin' and you there offerin' her nothin'. Which you think she gonna choose? You ain't that good-lookin', Persy, so you better have you somethin' to offer."

"So what do I do?"

"You sign up with me. You come to the

ranch and winter over with me. Help build the place back up. Come spring, you work the longhorns. You any good on a wild horse?"

"I haven't had much occasion to find out."

"Well, you talk like a learned man, maybe you can learn to break horses. You be worth yo' weight in gold, you break horses. White men look up to a nigger can break a horse. You gonna need you a skill."

"Where is this ranch?"

"Well now, you gonna think that be a problem, but it ain't no problem. People gonna come through there all the time, been everywhere. You ask 'em 'bout Chloe. Let the travelin' come to you, 'stead a you doin' the travelin'."

"Where is it?"

"Yep, folk gonna come through all the time," he said. "Soldiers be nearby. I think we can sell beeves to the fort there. That what I tol' Mistah Spencer. We take the beeves to market and you can ask them soldiers. They goin' everywhere lookin' fo' Indians."

"Where is this ranch?' I asked again.

"Well now, I don't think it much fo' you to worry 'bout, Persy. Indians don't like nigger hair. They be lookin' fo' white hair." He reached back and flipped his greasy hank of

255

hair like an angry squirrel's tail. "Flows purty on they shields, you see."

"You haven't told me where it is."

"Now, I knew you'd be fixated on that. You jest a damn greenhorn, Persy. You need me. You may not think so, but Texas . . ."

I finished the sentence with him. ". . . is a big place."

"All right. The frontier be where we goin'. The Travelin' S Ranch."

"Close to what town?"

Mo Tilly ripped another hunk of meat off the rabbit and started gnawing on it. "You so damn green, Persy. Frontier. You deef or somethin'? Frontier mean they ain't no town nearby. Well now, that ain't exactly true. It depend on what you call a town. Ain't no town like Austin or Galveston or Santone, but they's a little settlement called Drunken Bride sprung up at the edge of the prairie, 'long the Colorado River. They some fellas there tryin' they hands at farmin' and ranchin' and such."

I laughed. "Who would name a town Drunken Bride?"

Mo Tilly shook his head and leaned back. "Don't rightly know the story round that." He reached into his haversack, pulled his knife from his belt, and shaved a chaw off his block of "tombaccer."

I reached into my pocket and pulled out my piece of map, unfolded it and placed it on the ground between us.

"Well now, looky here, ain't you come prepared?" Mo Tilly laid another stick on the fire for light and then leaned over and peered at the map. "This here Walker's Creek," he said, pointing to the water we were camped next to. "It be 'bout here." He stabbed his stubby finger on the map above San Antonio, then traced west and then north, and stopped uncomfortably close to that word Comanche. "Fort Concho 'bout here. Concho gonna be a brand-new fort 'long the North Concho River. We goin' 'bout here." He punched his finger to an empty spot east of Concho. "Mo' or less," Mo Tilly added. "The ranch be 'bout fifty miles east of the fort. We gonna sell the beeves to 'em. They be needin' meat. But first we gotta get down here." He trailed his finger to the bottom of Texas, southeast of San Antonio.

"That's got to be a hundred miles from here," I said.

"Eh. Seventy, eighty, ninety maybe."

"Why should I do this?" I asked.

"I done tol' you why. You need you a plan. I jest tryin' to help. You gonna get kilt wanderin' out here by yo'sef. You damn lucky I the one came 'long and pick you up. You jest a greenhorn nigger, Persy. You might of been somethin' out there in them cane fields, but here you ain't shit."

"I wasn't anything in the cane fields but another slave."

"And now you jest another ex-slave. That don't buy you nothin' in Texas."

"I noticed."

"Then I ain't tellin' you nothin' you don't already know. Finish off that rabbit, Persy."

I reached over and picked up the carcass, pulling off the meat with my teeth. Mo crammed the tobacco into his mouth and started chewing and, soon enough, spitting. I could sense he was waiting for an answer from me.

Everything he said was true. I was free now, but I had been free for two years and what had it gotten me but traveling secretively and furtively, going only where other freedmen said it might be safe.

I gnawed on the rabbit and pitched the bones off into the weeds, and Mo Tilly spat and the fire guttered and the shadows danced and neither of us talked until finally he said, "Pay thirteen dollars a month. Payday don't come till after we sell the beeves. You ain't the only nigger gonna be there. I got one other hand, name of Sedge, gonna be workin' fo' me. He break wild horses. I'm on my way to pick him up. He teach you that skill, you have work in Texas fo' as long as you hang on to yo' bones. You make you some money, Persy. Plenty wild horses out there. Take care of that gal, Chloe. I believe you gonna find her. I believe you gonna find her and get married and have you a mess of little Persys runnin' round. By then you be done fo'got 'bout yo' ol' friend, Mo Tilly."

I had known Mo Tilly for less than a day. That he should refer to himself as my old friend astounded me. Yet I had told him everything there was to say about my life. I turned to look at him. He spat and wiped his sleeve across his mouth. Then he took his plug out, pitched it into the woods, and lay down, pulling the blanket over him and punching his hat into a pillow. I put another stick on the fire and folded my map and returned it to my pocket before rolling into my own blanket. I could hear by his breathing that he was not yet asleep. "Have you ever been married?" I asked.

"Once," he said.

I stared at his back, at his lank tail of dirty blond hair spilling over the edge of his blanket.

"You wouldn't be bunkin' with the white

259

hands," he said, "if that what you worried 'bout. You and Sedge be bunkin' with me. I already got it set up. That the only way Sedge agree to come."

"That's not what I'm worried about."

Mo rolled back to face me. "You worried 'bout yo' hair? I tell you, Persy. Them redskins don't like nigger hair. I got mo' to worry 'bout than you."

"No," I said. "I'm worried I won't find Chloe."

"That gonna be yo' worry wherever you go."

"What happened to your wife?" I asked.

"She died." He rolled over and faced away from me again.

The next morning I unfolded my piece of map and looked at it. Mo took one look at the map, then walked off to hitch the mules to the wagon. When he was done he came back over and picked up his haversack, a plug of tobacco already moiling around in his mouth. He spat. "I doubt she be in the plains," he said. "They's nothin' there 'cept that settlement I tol' you 'bout, a few ranches, and them red devils."

"Then why would I sign up with you?"

" 'Cause I the only friend you got in Texas, Persy."

I committed to nothing more than riding with Mo Tilly to Sedge's place, a journey of seven days. From there, if I chose to join them, we would travel two hundred miles north to the Traveling S Ranch, abandoned for five years now, and unseen by Mo or its new owner.

"This country almost tame befo' the war," Mo Tilly said. "Rangers 'bout had the Indians licked, then all the fightin' men leave. I reckon the Indians give that rancher some trouble, so that why he leave too. He damn lucky Mistah Spencer be willin' to buy that ranch, and Mistah Spencer damn lucky to have me.

"Spencer a damn fool, Persy. He say he ain't scairt of no backwards, primitive people. He say folks in Texas jest overreactin' to the Indian trouble. Jest a bunch of pussies out here. He say that to me." Mo thumped his thumb against his chest. "To me," he repeated, and then spat twice and shook his head. "Long as he stay outta my way and let me do my job I reckon we get along. But I ain't got much 'spect fo' a man say the Indians ain't no trouble out here. He ain't seed what I seed.

"Now, Persy, like I say, I don't think you got nothin' to worry 'bout. Indians don't like nigger hair. No offense to you, but it ain't purty on they shields."

"None taken," I assured him.

"But they's some things you ought to know jest in case we have us a run-in. First, you don't want to be taken alive. Kill yo'sef befo' you let 'em get to you."

"Kill myself how?"

"Save a bullet fo' yo'sef. That rule number one." He held up one gloved digit.

"I don't have a gun, Mr. Tilly."

"I getcha a gun, Persy. I won't be leadin' you out there without no gun. Now, rule number two, if you do get taken alive, they gonna torture you. And when they do, you jest take it, you hear? Don't be callin' out fo' yo' mama. Don't be callin' out fo' yo' god. You jest buck up and take it, whatever they do. You hear?"

"What are they likely to do?"

"Well now, like I say, I don't think you got much to worry 'bout. They don't care fo' yo' hair. But they admire courage. So if you get captured, jest don't be screamin' and hollerin'. Jest take it and they might ease up on you. I knowed a rancher once got captured and he so brave they let him go. Jest let him go, that how much they admire courage."

"What happened to him?"

"He quit the frontier. Couldn't take it no mo'. Went back east."

"No, I mean what did the Indians do to him?"

Mo leveled a long look at me. "They devils, Persy. They likely do anythin' they think of. Break yo' fingers. Cut you little bit at a time till you bleed out. Saw yo' limbs off, startin' with yo' dick and endin' with yo' nose. If you ain't dead yet, they might drag you behind a horse. Burn you. Pull you apart. I seed it. Corpses burnt slap up. Tied to wagon wheels and pulled apart.

"They cut up the dead, Persy, enemy dead. I seed it. Legs and arms hangin' in the trees. Heads rollin' round like cannonballs. Torsos like stumps on the ground. Ain't so bad if you dead, I reckon. Hell of a thing if you alive though. Jest 'member rule number one, kill yo'sef first.

"Now, in Texas," Mo Tilly went on, "the main tribe causin' all the trouble be the

Comanche."

"I read their name on the map," I said.

"Ye did, did ye? Well, that right. Comanche. And some Kiowa. Some Apache. Comanche and Kiowa rides together sometimes. They steals chirren."

"Some got captured down near Castell," I said. "And Gillespie County, along with a woman."

"I heard that too. That woman utterly degraded now. Rurnt. Some men, if they wife get captured by Indians and then returned back to civilization, they won't even take her back."

"I'd take Chloe back, no matter what."

"Yeah, well, you and me, we enlightened. Most men ain't, you know."

"Would you take your wife back?"

He paused and then answered quietly, "I would. I sho would."

We rattled on in silence for a while and then Mo spoke again, shaking his head. "Them chirren. Folks won't never see 'em again prob'ly. They do, they wish they hadn't. Kids be heathens by then. Hate everythin' 'bout white folk. I seed it. Little gal name of Cynthia Ann Parker kidnapped back in '36, rescued in '60. Never was right after that. Had a little Indian daughter, name of Prairie Flower, died a few years back. Tore Cynthia Ann up, what I hear. She livin' with relatives now, but she ain't never been right after livin' with them heathens. She run off all the time. They brung her back. She sleep on the floor 'stead of a bed. She don't even know she white anymo'. She with them Comanche" — Mo Tilly spat — "how many years it be?"

"Twenty-four," I provided.

"Twenty-fo'," he repeated, shaking his head. "She mo' Comanche than white now."

"Why doesn't she go back to the Indians?" I asked.

"She white, Persy. It ain't right fo' no white woman to be livin' with them heathens. 'Course now she rurnt, like I say. Ain't no man gonna want Cynthia Ann after bein', well . . ." He stopped off delicately. "Hands as big as paddles I hear. From all that work they make her do, besides bein' . . ." Again he cut off his remark, and then finished under his breath. "Utterly degraded."

"Why didn't the Indians kill her?"

"She jest a youngun when she captured. They don't kill younguns. They raise 'em up, turn 'em into Indians."

"Then she's an Indian."

"Goddamn it, Persy, you 'bout thickheaded." Mo Tilly spat off to the side. "She white. White, white, white. She jest don't know she white and she refuse to learn it, but all the same, that what she be. She ought to be grateful to be back with her own people."

"Even though her own people don't want her anymore?"

"They want her."

"But not the men. Not for a wife."

Mo Tilly ignored this. He jumped back in to telling me how to behave should I ever be captured. "Now, listen, here somethin' else to know, jest in case it ever reach this far. If the Indians ever offer you somethin' to eat, you take the raw meat, you hear? I hear they likes raw meat. They might like it if you do too. Cain't hurt to try. They think you part Indian maybe. 'Course by the time they sittin' down to dinner, you prob'ly be the dinner. Ha."

Sometimes I rode in the back of the wagon, rolled in a blanket, pretending to sleep, just to avoid Mo Tilly's constant chin-wag. Sometimes I walked just to feel the earth beneath my feet. Sometimes I rode next to him and endured his endless tute-lage. Thrice more I mentioned Mo's wife, asking about her: how long they were married, where they had met, how long he had been a widower. Each time he turned away and spat, wiped his sleeve on his mouth, and handed me the reins, jumping off the moving wagon with his rifle to go hunt. By the time we reached Sedge's place I was sure that I'd heard every story and opinion Mo Tilly had to offer, including all the things he claimed to have "seed," but I had not heard this one, his story and opinion of the woman he was once married to.

The Double H Ranch, where Sedge lived, was a tumbling, destitute-looking place down in the flat, scrubby land of southern Texas, not far from the border of Mexico. The barns, three of them built in a row, looked as if they were heading toward imminent collapse. Each one leaned in a different direction as if they were a trio of old sots, holding each other up as they crossed the street. The house was not much better, a small frame structure with windows so insignificant they barely glanced the Texas sun off their panes. The only things the Double H seemed to have of any value were several well-built corrals full of sleek and spirited horses, and its only worker, Sedge himself.

Sedge was a sinewy, dark-skinned man, arms like ropes of muscle, and legs as springy as a jackrabbit's. "Mistah Tilly," he hollered, bounding toward us as the wagon

267

rattled into the yard, " 'bout time you got here. What you do? Whore yo' way 'cross Texas?"

"You know better than that," Mo said. He pulled the mules to a halt and handed the reins to me before jumping down. The two men slapped each other on the back, clouds of dust rising off each of them before being blown away in the wind. "This here Persy," Mo said.

Sedge reached up and shook my hand. "Pleased to meet you. Mistah Tilly give you that bullshit about Indians not likin' nigger hair?"

"He has."

"Don't believe it."

"Don't flow purty on they shields," Mo said.

"Put it in they shields. Stop bullets," Sedge answered.

"You had any trouble with 'em lately?"

"Not lately. It been quiet here, mostly. Attack a few counties up, I heard. Man and his son out wintering with they cattle got kilt."

"Scalped?"

"Yassuh."

Mo shook his head, gave a mandatory spit. "White, I bet." Then he changed the subject. "Persy signin' up with us. Cain't do shit though."

Sedge looked up at me. "Why'd you hire him on, then?"

"I got a soft spot in my heart fo' him. Prob'ly regret it. Thought we'd teach him a little 'bout breakin' horses."

Sedge grinned. "Yassuh. He gonna need somethin' to know."

Just then, a decrepit voice, long and stringy, drizzled out to us from inside the cabin. "Sedge. Who's out there? Who you talking to?"

"It's all right, Mizz Doreen. They friends of mine."

"You don't have any friends."

"Yesem."

"Don't you be jabbering all day long. There's work to be done."

"Yesem," Sedge called. Then he turned back to Mo, slapped him again on the back, and said, "Don't pay her no mind. She stuck back in slavery day, but she won't cause no trouble. That voice be the only strong thing she got no mo'. 'Sides me."

Mo looked down at his boots and kicked at the dirt. "You still the only one here?"

Sedge nodded. "All the rest took off. Never came back."

"Who gonna take care of her after you go, Sedge?" Mo asked.

"She don't own me no mo'," Sedge said. "I go where I want."

"I know that."

"Take care of herself, fo' a change." Sedge looked at one of the horses circling a corral. "She dyin', Mistah Tilly. Takin' everything down with her. This whole place dyin'. We runnin' outta feed. Horses gonna die if we don't turn 'em out to graze." He turned his face to look at Mo. "I ain't goin' down too. Them horses means too much to me. I broke every one of 'em. I let 'em go befo' I let 'em die."

"I don't jedge you fo' it," Mo said.

"Nawsuh. I don't reckon you do." Sedge looked down into the dirt. "I's hopin' she die befo' you get here, but she ain't. It sho woulda made it easier."

Mo nodded. "We stay a little while, Sedge. She prob'ly die befo' we leave." Sedge bobbed his head and swallowed hard. His mouth opened as if he wished to say more, but he closed it. Mo reached up and patted him on the shoulder. "We got a little while. Couple of weeks, maybe. Grain hold out that long?"

"Yassuh, I think so."

"We gotta get there well befo' winter though. I ain't seed the place. We might not have us a bunkhouse. Might have to build one. Corrals too." Mo spat again, this time into a clump of weeds, and looked at the corrals and the barns. "Plenty of lumber here," he said.

"Yassuh. I reckon we could take some with us." I thought I heard doubt in Sedge's voice.

"Wagon?"

"We got a wagon," Sedge said in the same tone.

"All right. Get this one unhitched. Put the mules up."

"Yassuh."

Sedge and I unhitched the mules and gave them some grain before leading them into one of the crumbling barns. If Mo was concerned about timbers falling on his animals, he did not show it.

I followed Mo and Sedge toward one of the corrals, and as I did so, I turned to look back at the house. It could not have been more than two rooms. The front door was flung open. A chicken pecked in the dirt, and then hopped the step and strutted its way inside. "Sedge," the stringy voice called. "Sedge, come get this damn chicken outta here."

"Hold on a minute, Mistah Tilly." Sedge returned to the cabin, and soon walked out holding the squawking bird, which he tossed

271

in the yard, closing the door behind him. I could hear her before the door shut. "Who's out there? Don't you be jabbering all day long. You got work to do."

"Don't pay her no mind," Sedge said again. "It like this all day long. As weak as she is, I don't see how she got the energy to complain so much. Sometime I think that the very thing what keepin' her alive." And then Sedge did a perfect imitation of the voice inside the cabin. " 'Sedge, don't you be thinkin' jest 'cause the war over, I don't own you. I own you top to bottom, jest like I owned yo' daddy, and yo' mama, and my daddy owned yo' daddy's mama, and all the way on back to the little nigger Adam and Eve.'

"That on a good day, Mistah Tilly, when she know the war be over. Mostly she think it still goin' on and Massuh Hill gonna come back home one day. I don't even tell her no mo' he done come home and shot hisself in the head."

Mo kicked at a small stone and sent it tumbling across the yard. "She do anythin' fo' herself?" he asked.

"Nawsuh. She bedridden."

"Well," Mo said. "Maybe she die befo' we go."

"Yassuh, I hope so."

"If we got to leave her here, then we got to leave her here. I don't jedge you fo' it."

"Nawsuh."

"What kind of horses you got?"

Sedge perked up at the mention of horses. "Lot of horses, Mistah Tilly. We catched 'em back when we had a crew here. We find out we free, and everyone go, but the horses too wild fo' anyone to take with 'em. I work on gettin' 'em broke. Then I trade 'em fo' mo' wild ones. I always get mo' wild ones than I trade out broke ones."

I could hear the pride in Sedge's voice over this enterprise.

"Way I figure it," he said, "I break 'em, they mine. That right?"

Mo nodded.

"This one I want to show you, she a purty girl. Green-broke."

"Ain't quite got her trained, eh?"

"Nawsuh. She be good one fo' Persy to ride."

We approached a corral in which a single horse circled, stomping and neighing, tossing her mane. As she went around and around she eyed us suspiciously.

"Named her Spring Dance," Sedge said. "She in one of the last herds I trade fo'."

"She don't look green-broke to me. She look like an outlaw."

"Nawsuh. She like me purty good."

"She take a saddle?" Mo asked.

"Yassuh, I get a saddle on her."

I watched as somehow Sedge coaxed a blanket and a saddle onto this horse, and cinched it up tight, and added the reins and bit in her mouth. She allowed him that, and he held out his hand to give her a treat, although what treat, I could not guess, for I had yet to see a garden on the Double H Ranch. But it must have pleased her, for Spring Dance nuzzled Sedge's armpit and let him lead her into a chute. Once Sedge closed the gate behind her, she could move neither backward, nor forward, nor sideways. No longer Sedge's friend, she now stomped and neighed and snapped her teeth in the air.

"Sedge always did have a way with horses," Mo said admiringly.

"Is he going to break her?" I asked.

"Naw. You are."

"I don't know anything about breaking horses."

"We gonna teach you."

"No sir, I ride just fine once they're broke."

"You 'bout thickheaded, Persy. What the hell you think I been tellin' you all this time? That you need yo'sef a skill. And this here the skill we gonna teach you."

"Mr. Tilly, sir . . ."

"Aw, crap," Mo said, and he spat again, this time close to the edge of my boot, a little puff of dust rising up where he hit his mark.

"I have a skill, sir. I can read and write."

"Ain't no little schoolhouse where we goin'. Ain't no little chirren needin' no lessons."

"I wished I could read and write," Sedge interjected.

"Well, good," Mo said. "Y'all trade off. Sedge teach you to break horses, and you teach him to read and write. In my 'pinion you gettin' the better end of the deal, Persy. Now get on."

I hesitated.

"Get on, or you can stay here with Mizz Doreen."

Still, I did not move to mount Spring Dance.

"Persy," Mo said, a tinge of forced patience in his voice. "I don't know if you aware of this, but you a nigger. Sedge a nigger. All the other hands gonna be white. They gonna be a rough bunch. They jest lost a war. They gonna hate you, mark my words. They gonna be havin' breakfast while you and Sedge be toppin' off six or seven broncos. That jest the way it is. I didn't make the rules."

"Topping off?" I turned to Sedge.

"Breakin' the horses," Sedge provided. "Mistah Tilly right. White man don't have to be as good as a black man. White man white. That good enough fo' most of 'em."

"So you see . . ." Mo spat. I jumped back and his brown tobacco juice hit the dirt where my boot had been. "I tryin' to make it better on you. Now, get on the damn horse or else go in there and carry out Mizz Doreen's slop, and wipe her ass while you at it. We gonna break you and the horse together."

"Spring Dance a good girl," Sedge said. "Jest a little spirited is all."

I fingered Chloe's button and climbed over the fence and lowered myself into the saddle. Spring Dance threw her head back and snapped the air, as close as she could get to my flesh. I grasped the reins and held on to the saddle horn. Her muscles rippled beneath my legs, and I could feel her wanting to buck. Sedge opened the gate, and as soon as she had room to move I was pitched off and onto the ground, rolling away from Spring Dance's stomping hooves and snapping teeth, escaping under the fence.

I tried once more, with the same results,

before Sedge said, "Let me show you somethin'. You gotta let yo' body go with what she doin'. Be a part of her. Don't be a man tryin' to hang on to a horse. Be the horse. Let yo' spine go loose or else you gonna break yo' back. Dig yo' legs around her, hang on there too." He climbed onto Spring Dance, and Mo let the chute open and I watched Sedge ride her. She bucked as badly as she had with me, but Sedge gripped the saddle horn and reins, and wrapped his legs around her tightly. His spine was pure poetry. Even Sedge's hat stayed on until he was thrown. But Spring Dance did not stomp around him and take nips at him the way she had me. Instead she leaned down and nuzzled his neck.

"I believe she sparkin' with you, Sedge," Mo said.

Sedge got up and leaned over to grab his hat and dust off the knees of his britches, and as he did so Spring Dance butted her snout against his rear.

I climbed onto this horse three more times that day. I learned to hold tight with my legs, and to loosen my back so that it felt like we were one, bucking together. Each time I mounted Spring Dance, I stayed on a little longer, until finally she accepted me and we rode around the corral. When I dismounted, Sedge slipped me a sugar cube and I held it out in the palm of my hand to her, and rubbed her nose. And then he led Spring Dance away and brought out another wild horse. He'd named this one Cups, for the blaze of white teacup shapes across her shank. I fared a little better with Cups, and after only two rides she calmly walked around the corral.

"I believe you gonna do," Sedge said as we put up the saddle and curried the horses together. "Cups be yo' horse now."

"I think she likes you better."

"They all like me better. She warm up to you."

That night I eased myself down on my bedroll beside Mo in the yard, a fire prickling in front of us. I felt as sore and stiff as if I had worked a long day of cutting cane. Every one of my bones felt as if it wanted to break loose from the cartilage that held it in place, as though my own skeleton had turned on me for doing this, and now wanted a more trustworthy human to reside in. Besides that, I was dizzy from the jolts of being thrown, and I lay down with a wet bandana across my eyes. "You meant it when you said you were breaking me," I said to Mo.

"You get used to it."

I groaned.

"Man been whipped like you been can take on a few wild horses."

Once he'd tended to his charge inside the cabin, Sedge came out to join us. I kept the bandana over my eyes and listened to him spreading his bedroll out beside mine. "Don't you have to stay inside with her?" I asked.

"I go back in directly. She sleepin' now."

"We stay awhile, Sedge," Mo said. "She die, we bury her, and then you can move on. Don't be worryin' 'bout it."

"Thank you Mistah Tilly. I much obliged."

"Eh." I heard Mo spitting off. "From what you tell me, she die any minute now. Ain't nothin' to stay and wait it out."

"That what I been tellin' myself fo' over a month now."

"You keepin' her too well fed, Sedge. Now listen, Persy here lookin' fo' a gal."

"We ain't got many gals out here, lest you want the one in there."

"I don't," I said.

"He lookin' fo' a gal named Chloe. Light-skinned. Long brown hair. Short, but not as short as me. Belonged to a man name of Joseph Wilson."

"Wilson," I heard Sedge say. "Name kinda ring a bell."

I sat up and let the bandana slide from my eyes.

"Years back a man come through name of Wilson. War ain't been goin' on long. He come through here with a messa slaves. He and his wife stay in the cabin with Mizz Doreen. Overseer stay in the barn with the slaves. I took some food out to 'em, but I ain't seen no light-skinned gal."

"Wilson wasn't married," I said. "His wife died before they left."

"Well, maybe it ain't him. Or maybe he pick him up a wife 'long the way. She a good bit younger than he. Seem a little unsure of herself. Never talked."

"No." I shook my head. "He didn't have a wife."

"Shit, Persy," Mo said. "You know how some men cain't get 'long without a woman. He prob'ly like that. First one die, he got to go get another. Like goin' to the sto' fo' another block of tombaccer after you done chewed yo's up. That jest the way some men be."

"He didn't need a wife," I said. "He had Chloe to . . ." I could not finish my sentence.

"Sound to me like he didn't have Chloe," Mo said. "Sound to me like she 'scaped."

"No light-skinned girl with the slaves?" I

280

asked Sedge. "Pretty. Prettiest one there."

"I'd of noticed purty. Warn't no slave like you describin'. I heard him say he done lost some 'long the way. Some died. A few more made off in the night. They was gonna settle here, but he decide to move on up north. Mizz Doreen told 'em not to. Told 'em the Indians bad up there. He won't listen. Had him some idea 'bout a ranch up there."

I lay back on my bedroll and raised my hand to finger Chloe's button. "He didn't have a wife," I said again.

"Must notta been him, then." Sedge shook his head and looked back toward the house, where a dim light shone from one of the tiny windows. "She don't die, I ain't never gonna be free. War never be over fo' ol' Sedge."

"Here, Sedge. Have some tombaccer. Make you feel better." Mo reached over to his haversack and shaved off a plug, the first time I'd seen him offer any of his precious "tombaccer" to anyone.

Sedge accepted the plug and popped it in his mouth, and through moiling it around he said, "Folks act like the niggers 'sponsible fo' keepin' all the white folk alive, and niggers dyin' all the time tryin' to take care of these buckras."

"We have you outta here in a few days,"

Mo said mildly.

"What 'bout her?" Sedge asked, cocking his head toward the cabin.

"She die. Everybody die 'ventually."

"What if she don't die? What if we jest leave? You reckon they could hang me fo' murder if I jest left her here?"

"Prob'ly. They hang a nigger fo' less than that."

Sedge spat, and Mo spat, and the fire spat, and I sat up and laid another piece of wood across it.

"It be pretty cold leavin' her here," Sedge said. "She jest starve to death. I feed her by the spoonful. I wipe her ass. Who gonna do that after I gone?"

"Nobody," Mo said.

They talked some more. I vaguely listened, but I could not pay much attention. My thoughts were too strong on Chloe. My fingers worried at the button, and then, after a while, for some reason that I do not know and cannot explain, my hand left my throat and wandered into my pocket to extract the little noose. I rubbed it and turned it over and over, occasionally pulling it tight on my finger and loosening it. Mo pulled the plug out of his jug and passed it to me. I propped myself up and took a swig and passed it to Sedge. I looked at the sky. It seemed so unfair that these stars, these cold points of light that cared nothing for Chloe, knew exactly where she was.

The next day we broke more horses. Sedge had an endless supply, it seemed, of green-broke horses, horses he could get a saddle on but could not always ride. I rode them. I rode them that day and the next and the next as we waited for Miss Doreen to pass her last breath so we could put her in the ground.

Sedge divided his time between answering Miss Doreen's calls, getting saddles on and off the horses I was intended to ride, and a never-ending list of chores. Over the time we stayed there I saw him hunting, cooking, boiling laundry and hanging it out, washing dishes, watering the pitiful garden out back of the barns, emptying Miss Doreen's chamber pot, feeding the chickens, and feeding and grooming the horses. Occasionally I caught him standing still, looking out toward the horizon with a bucket in his hand or a saddle in his arms, just staring

out into the scrubby flatlands that surrounded the Double H Ranch, looking, I
thought, to anything that might hold a different life for him.

He had been the only hand on this ranch
since news of the war's end reached them, a
good three or four months after the fact.
Miss Doreen had been sick, off and on, for
almost two years and her husband dead for
one. There had been children of this union.
Two were buried in the small plot next to
their father, one dead of smallpox, the other
died an infant. Two more, I learned, had
been carried off by Indians.

Miss Doreen's reedy voice crept out of
the cabin often, always calling for Sedge.
He could hear her from anywhere, even
from the corrals with the horses thundering
their hooves in the dirt. "Yesem," he'd hol-
ler. "I comin'." And he'd take off in a sprint.
Her voice was surprisingly strong for a dying woman, and it did not weaken over the
time we were there. After he'd reached the
cabin I could hear her complaining, "What
took you so long, Sedge?"

Sometimes Sedge simply rode away, out
into the wild lands surrounding the ranch.
He would be gone for hours, and while he
was gone Mo and I would ignore Miss
Doreen's calls. When Sedge returned he did

not say anything about his absence, but would always go straight to the cabin and check on her.

I once helped Sedge change the sheets on her bed so he could wash them. I discovered that I had been wrong about the cabin. It was not two rooms but one long one, Miss Doreen in her iron bed at one end, a round table beside the bed, and on the table, a huge globe lamp painted with a hunting scene. At the other end of the cabin, the fireplace, kettles and fry pans, a rocking chair, and a small table next to it. In between the two ends of the cabin were a braided rug, a trunk, the pallet where Sedge slept at night, and columns of dust motes drifting in dim shafts of sunlight from the little windows.

Sedge told me that Miss Doreen was once a large woman. Now she was skeletal, her hair a wispy cloud on the pillow, her skin blooming with brown spots, two thin arms on top of the covers. A sour smell permeated the house. Miss Doreen raised her head and pointed a finger at me. "Who is this nigger?" she asked.

"This Persy, Mizz Doreen," Sedge said. "You 'member Persy. You got him back in New Orleans, jest befo' you married Massuh Hill and come here."

I looked at Sedge and shook my head. I did not care to be a slave again, pretend or otherwise. He waved his hand at me, dismissing my discomfort. Miss Doreen squinted, as if trying to recall. "I remember," she finally said, and laid back on the pillow and closed her eyes. "Paid good money for you, nigger. Where you been, Persy? You run off or something?"

Sedge nodded at me to answer, and I swallowed my pride and went along. I did it for Sedge. I did it for the entrapment he felt in taking care of this bag of bones clad in white skin.

"No ma'am," I said. "I have been right here."

She raised her head again and narrowed her eyes at me. "Huh. What'd you do? Get you an education while I lie here sick?" She cleared her throat, a huge, wet and viscous noise coming from the depths of her lungs as she held up one finger to Sedge. He leaned down and brought up a bowl, helped her rise up so she could spit into it, something stringy and yellow. Sedge wiped her mouth with a nearby cloth and eased her back onto the pillows.

"Persy gonna help me change yo' sheets, Mizz Doreen. He gonna pick you up while I change 'em. I gots some clean ones right here." He patted at the folded linens he had set at the end of her bed.

"All right," she consented. "About time. I can't believe how you let me lie in my own filth the way you do. When Mister Hill gets home I'm gonna have him cane you."

"Yesem," Sedge said. He pulled the covers back. She had on a thin white nightgown through which I could see her sagging breasts, the dark circles of her nipples, and the bare, sparse triangle of pubic hair. I turned my head away and reached under her and lifted her into my arms. She weighed nothing. That she was alive was a cruel miracle.

Sedge made quick work of stripping the bed and replacing the dirty linens with the clean ones. Miss Doreen fell asleep in my arms and stirred only a little as I placed her back in the bed, and Sedge pulled the covers up to her chin. He was tender with her. He was tender and gentle and I wondered for the way she treated him. She was, I suppose, out of her mind, and Sedge, having known her prior to this, understood it better than anyone.

We stayed three weeks. Our days were spent with the horses, our nights in camp out in the yard, or if the weather was bad, hunkered down with the mules in one of the barns. During these three weeks it seemed that nothing changed with Miss Doreen. Every day Sedge carried food in and slop out. I thought of Chloe of course, and of her time spent caring for Missus Lila, of the duties she performed, of the hours spent sitting passively by Missus Lila's bedside. I thought of the scent of that room, the sun shafting through the windowed doors that led onto the balcony. I wondered if Chloe ever rose from her chair while Missus Lila slept. I wondered if she ever stepped out onto the balcony and tried to find me among the slaves in the cane fields, or driving a wagon to the sugarhouse, or perhaps, at midnight during a new moon, if she stood there and watched the torches bob as we made our way back to the quarters for a few hours' rest.

The time came, about two weeks into our stay, in which I had ridden every horse on the Double H. They were broken, all of them, and I was broken too. I had a skill, and while it was not one that I had ever wanted, it was one that I was proud of. I could see that knowing horses could serve me well. I could also see that Mo was feeling restless to move on.

Each night by the campfire, before Sedge came out to join us, Mo spat and tore at his food and looked at the sky and said, "Winter comin' on." It was August. Hot as blazes. I could not see that winter was any sort of threat to us, but Mo insisted that it was. "Gotta get there," he'd say, spitting, always spitting. "Gotta build some corrals fo' the horses." Spit. "Gotta have us a place to stay." Spit. "This takin' too long. How long it take a ol' woman to die, anyway?"

Each night Sedge came out to briefly join us by the fire, and Mo asked if anything had changed and Sedge would shake his head, look down at his feet, and say, "You go on, Mistah Tilly. I catch up to you."

"I ain't lettin' you travel alone out there. Indians."

"I could at least make it safe to Drunken Bride."

Mo spat. "Maybe. Prob'ly not. Don't matter. I ain't hunkerin' down in that shit-hole, waitin' on you. You got every right to leave here."

"Yassuh. That what I tell myself. I cain't do it though. You go ahead. I catch up."

And so they went around like this for several nights until Mo said, "I reckon after she die we be wantin' to take some lumber with us."

Sedge nodded. "Yassuh?"

"Well, Persy and me ain't got much to do

right now. We could be takin' down one of them barns. Speed things up a little if we ready to go."

Sedge looked sadly at the barns, each one a dark smudge leaning against the night sky. I looked at them, too, with alarm, for I did not relish taking apart a building that threatened to tumble on me at the first tap of a hammer. "Which one?" Sedge asked.

"That one on the end there, to the west. I been lookin' at it. It ain't got much stuff in it."

"It ain't my barn," Sedge said.

"Whose barn is it, then?"

"It Mizz Doreen's. You know that."

"Mizz Doreen? Mizz Doreen who 'bout to die any minute now?"

"I cain't let you take down that barn, Mistah Tilly. I cain't let you steal lumber while she alive."

Mo spat. "Did I say somethin' 'bout stealin' lumber? Shit, Sedge. You 'bout thickheaded. You ain't understood a word I say. I wants to take down that barn so's we can repair the other two. It jest make good economic sense to have two good barns 'stead of three bad ones. And Persy and me ain't got nothin' to do. Might as well help out round here."

Sedge looked up and grinned. "Yassuh.

That be a big help. That be real fine."

And so the next day we began moving things out of the barn and dismantling it. Mo sent me, against my protests, to the roof to pull the tin. I could feel the structure sway in the wind. "You're going to kill me," I yelled down to Mo.

He spat and hollered up, "Careful, Persy. You ain't no use to me dead."

As I threw down lumber, Mo sorted it, pulled the nails out, and loaded the best pieces into the Double H wagon pulled close by. The bent nails went into a bucket, which he wedged in beside the wood. He covered the wagonload with canvas. And still Miss Doreen lived. Even over the banging of our hammers as we knocked boards apart, and the screech of nails as we yanked them out of the wood, I could hear her voice drifting across the air. "Who's out there, Sedge? What are they doing? About time you niggers did some work."

And then the barn was down, and Mo began the task of casting around the ranch for anything we might use on our journey. We cleaned and oiled old saddles, snapped the dust out of horse blankets, cleaned and repaired tack and re-braided lariats.

In all this exploration I found three whips, coiled and hung on nails inside what had been the middle barn. The whips were just like the ones at Sweetmore, just like the ones the overseers had carried before most of them had left for the war, just like the whip Holmes had used to deliver my fifty lashes. I reached out and touched my finger to it. And then I lifted it off its nail and held its handle and let it unfurl into the dirt at my feet. Mo walked by carrying a kettle. "Take 'em," he said. "Might come in handy."

I shook my head and coiled the whip again, hung it back on its nail. "No."

Mo shrugged. "All right. We ain't wantin' to be too burdened down with stuff, anyway." He walked off to put his kettle in the wagon.

Mo and I made camp out in the yard that night, the sky clear, the moon full and casting shadows across the ground. The shadow of the corrals laid stripes in the dirt. The shadows of the two remaining barns were solid and black, like the block of tobacco Mo carried in his haversack. The moon was so bright that I could even see the shadow of Mo's spittle whenever he let one fly. We'd eaten a chicken for dinner. Mo had killed it in spite of Sedge's protests that Miss Doreen needed the eggs. Something had shifted in Mo. The wagons were packed. He was ready to travel. "We done all we can here," he said too many times.

We heard the cabin door squeak open and close. Sedge was preceded by his shadow as he loped out to join us. "She sleepin' now," he said as he sank down beside the fire.

"Dark clouds over there," Mo said. "Storm comin'."

I rose up to look. The horizon had become inky black, but it was so far off, it did not seem a threat. I lay back down.

"We runnin' outta feed, Mistah Tilly," Sedge said.

"Yep." I heard Mo spit.

"You oughta take the horses and go on without me. I don't want them horses to die. They needs pasturin'."

"They do," Mo said. "I ain't goin' without you, Sedge."

"I ain't goin' till she do."

They fell silent and then Mo said, "Comin' closer."

I sat up again, propping onto my elbows. Far off, lightning flashed and illuminated the underside of dark roiling clouds. But here the moon still shone, and the storm seemed faint, and faraway, almost like a dream.

"How long you think befo' it get here?" Sedge asked.

"We know soon enough."

The lightning off in the distance snaked down to the earth in bright jagged spears. Each time it struck, a golden hole opened up where it pierced the clouds. We watched for a long time as it crept its way across the land, like an animal come down from the heavens to stalk its prey. A breeze occasionally brought the sound of thunder to us, and then suddenly the stars and moon were gone, replaced by a sky as black as any I had ever seen, and then just as quickly the wind smacked into our campsite, and pelts of rain came stinging down upon us. "Wrap it up," Mo yelled, as if we weren't already grabbing bedrolls and running to shelter. Sedge and I veered toward one of the barns, but Mo headed toward the house, and without having time to think it over, Sedge and I changed directions. We joined Mo as he threw the door open and tumbled in behind him, slamming it against the rain and dumping our bedrolls on the floor.

The lightning flashed wildly now, and the thunder pounded simultaneously. Between the bright, white flashes Miss Doreen's lamp cast a dim flickering circle of light onto the table next to her bed, the shadows of the painted hunting scene against the wall.

"Who are these people?" Miss Doreen called out in her thready voice.

"We jest takin' shelter from the storm, Mizz . . ." Sedge answered, his sentence lost at the end in another boom of thunder.

"Who are these niggers?" she asked.

"One a white man," Sedge replied.

Miss Doreen raised her head to look at us. The lightning flashed and made the interior of the cabin once again visible, and then suddenly it disappeared into darkness, save the lamp on her table.

"They look like niggers to me," she said. "One looks like a dwarf. You know I don't let any niggers in here but you. You and Janie. Where's my gal Janie?" In the next flash of lightning I saw that she had laid her head back on the pillow.

"She done run off, ma'am."

"Run off?" A boom of thunder. "I'll have the hounds after her. I'll have her whipped."

"Ain't no hounds, ma'am." Boom. Boom.

"Mister Hill will know what to do. He'll know what to do when the war's over." Boom. "Meanwhile, we just have to hang on, Sedge."

The lightning flashed. The cabin shook with each roar of thunder.

"Yesem," I heard Sedge say. In the next flash of lightning I saw him slumped down

against the wall, sitting on the floor with his
head between his knees. I sat down beside
him, not wanting to take the only chair, the
rocker that was pulled close to the hearth.

"Get some rope, Sedge," Miss Doreen
called. "Make me a noose. I believe I'll just
hang the bitch." Boom. Boom. "Is that the
Yankees?" she asked. "Is that the Yankees
coming here?"

"No ma'am. That jest a thunderstorm,"
Sedge whispered.

The lamp beside the bed sputtered its last
flame and went out. Beside me I heard
Sedge sigh. And then in the next frame of
illumination from the lightning I saw Mo sit
down in the rocking chair and pull his hat
down over his eyes, resting his hands on his
stomach. Soon I heard him snoring. There
was more lightning and thunder. Miss
Doreen muttered a few more sentences
about the Yankees, and not to let them catch
her. Sedge rose and went to her bedside.
He held her hand and stroked it. "It jest a
thunderstorm, Mizz Doreen. It be over
soon." He kept stroking her hand, and after
she had fallen asleep he moved to his pallet
and lay down, pulling the covers up over
him, and soon I heard his own snores winding in with Mo's.

I could not sleep. I stayed sitting on the

floor. With each flash of lightning I noticed something new about the cabin. A vase of weedy wildflowers Sedge had brought in and placed on the mantel. A letter half-written on the small table next to the rocking chair, a pen and jar of dried ink sitting next to it. A man's coat hung on the back of the door. And then Mo pushed his hat back. The cabin fell dark. In the next flash of lightning I saw the empty rocking chair moving back and forth. Darkness, and then Mo was walking across the floor toward Miss Doreen. In the next flare he was by her side. And darkness. And Mo was holding a pillow over Miss Doreen's face.

Her hands came up to grip his wrists. Her legs kicked. Her body shuddered. In the next frame of light she lay still. Mo removed the pillow and gently lifted her head and placed it beneath, and then darkness. I heard him walk across the floor and stop in front of me, and squat down. Lightning flashed and I saw him there, looking at me, and then darkness, and he was gone. There and not there. There and not there. "Persy, you awake?" he whispered.

"Yes sir."

"Do you know what jest happened?"

"Yes sir."

"Tell me."

"You killed her," I whispered.

"That ain't what happened." Mo leaned forward. Lightning flashed, his face close to mine now. "That ain't what happened," he said again.

Darkness and he wasn't there anymore, but I could feel his breath, smell his tobacco.

"She died in the night," Mo said in the darkness, and then there he was again. "You understand?"

Not there.

I didn't answer.

There again.

"Goddamn it, Persy. You understand?"

"Yes sir," I said.

"I'm trustin' you to understand."

"Yes sir."

"Tell me what happened."

"She died in the night."

"Go to sleep." He stood and went to the rocking chair, and settled in, stretching his stubby legs out in front of him and pulling his hat down over his eyes.

The storm stayed with us. I slept fitfully, the booms of thunder waking me up again and again. Each time I woke I watched in the flashes of lightning to see if Mo or Sedge had wakened. They slept through. It was not until the storm had moved on and morning dawned that Sedge discovered

Miss Doreen's death. I watched him cross the floor and go to her bed. He called her name softly. He lifted her hand and called her name again. He leaned over and laid his head against her chest, listening for her heartbeat. Then he stood straight up and looked at her, and reached over and closed her eyes, and pulled the sheet up over her face.

"She dead," he said to the room.

Mo woke up, or pretended to. He pushed his hat back from his eyes and looked at Sedge.

"Mizz Doreen dead, Mistah Tilly."

Mo stood and went to the bed. He leaned his ear against Miss Doreen's chest and listened, then he straightened and put his arm around Sedge's waist. "I reckon her time finally come," he said.

Sedge started crying. "She warn't always so bad."

"Naw. I know that. You been good to her, Sedge. Better than the law required of you."

I watched as Sedge leaned his head against Mo, his face resting on the top of Mo's hat. Mo patted Sedge on the back and caught my eye. "You done yo' duty," he said. "It ain't always easy to do what need doin'. I know that." Mo still looked at me.

"Yassuh," Sedge said. He raised his head

and dug the heels of his hands into his eyes. "I reckon I's free now."

"That right. You free now. You deserve to be free."

As I watched Mo comfort Sedge I made my decision about whether or not I would strike out on my own again or follow along to the Traveling S Ranch. It was not a hard decision. It was easy to see that these men were good men, and that I would be in good hands. I would follow.

We buried Miss Doreen that morning. The land and the air felt scrubbed clean by the storm. I dug a grave while Sedge built a casket out of some of the siding we had ripped off the barn. We buried her next to her husband. Next to him were the two children, and off in the plains somewhere, perhaps living with the Indians, perhaps dead, were the other two.

Before we left, Mo told us to take whatever we wanted. "Long as it don't slow us down," he said. "Ain't stealin'. I reckon Mizz Doreen owe Sedge back pay anyway. We jest evenin' the score."

"Yassuh," Sedge answered, but he only took two things of value if you don't count the horses: Mister Hill's rifle, which he had been hunting game with all along, and the lamp from Miss Doreen's bedside table. Sedge wrapped the lamp and its globe in a torn coverlet and packed them into a wooden box, which he wedged between the lumber and the walls of the wagon bed.

Mo shook his head. "Lamp gonna break all to pieces befo' we get there."

"Yassuh," Sedge answered, but he made no move to take it out of the wagon.

Of the three of us, Mo took the most: saddles and tack, lariats and blankets, a kettle, a lantern, a jug of kerosene. After having sent me up onto the swaying barn in order to dismantle it, and after having carefully sorted and stacked the boards, Mo had me remove them all from the wagon bed and then he sorted through them again, tossing some to the side and handing me others, saying, "This'll do. Set it in the wagon, Persy."

I took the boards and angrily slid them into place. "Why'd you risk my life up on that damn barn if we aren't taking the wood?"

"We takin' the wood, Persy. What you think I handin' to you? 'Sides, climbin' up on that barn ain't nothin' 'pared to the risk you 'bout to take. We headin' to the frontier, case you don't 'member. Might get catched by the Indians. Ain't too late to change yo' mind, Persy."

I shook my head.

"You ain't no quitter. That what I like 'bout you. You gonna find that gal of yo's." He handed me the bucket of bent nails. "Load these up too." Mo stretched his back. "We take the extra wagon empty," he said. "Supply up in Drunken Bride. Feel good to be gettin' on. But first things first, I reckon you bein' a curious sort and all is wantin' to know why we takin' bent nails."

"No sir."

"That good. We get out there on the frontier, won't be doin' no good to be askin' why all the time. Get yo'sef a haircut that way."

I was too anxious to get under way to remind Mo I'd heard from someone that the Indians did not like nigger hair. I wanted to move on from the Double H Ranch, where I knew Chloe was not, to Drunken Bride, where I hoped to gain news of her. As for plundering and pillaging Miss Doreen's possessions, I cared not for anything until Sedge showed me a small trunk full of books.

"Mizz Doreen a schoolteacher befo' she come here," Sedge told me. "You take 'em, Persy. They a slate and chalk too. You teach me readin' and writin'."

I hefted the trunk into the back of the spare wagon, against Mo's protests of course. Too heavy, he said. Slow us down. "Waste of time, readin'," Mo said, punctuating his displeasure with a well-aimed spit landing just short of my boot.

We began the first leg of our journey with Mo and I each driving a wagon, and Sedge riding Spring Dance, bringing along the string of horses. We angled north, along the edge of the prairie. The grassland seemed alive in the August wind, stretching all the

304

way to the horizon, and the sky above it like an inverse lake, which witnessed everything, and dominated everything, and could take on different personalities minute by minute by minute. Sometimes the sky was raging red. Other times, soft and golden. It could contain clouds that looked like dark boulders ready to drop onto our heads. Or it could be like a solid thing, a quilt turned inside out and spread on top of the world. Or it could be endless blue, weak or dark or brilliant, with no clouds at all, only the beating sun.

By the time we camped each night, I only wanted food and sleep, but Sedge always insisted on his lesson, and I would open the trunk of books and pull out one of Miss Doreen's Blue-Backed Spellers, the slate and chalk, and hand them to him. By the light of the campfire we went over the alphabet. I sometimes reached across Sedge and guided his hand into making the proper shapes. We said each letter as he wrote it, and then we repeated the sounds of that letter. Mo spat and grumbled about how we were wasting our time, but this did not keep him from getting up and peering over Sedge's shoulder at the marks on the slate.

After I had guided Sedge through a proper capital G several times, Mo said, "Listen here, Sedge. You gettin' it all wrong. It like this." Mo picked up a stick and traced a perfect G in the dirt. "You always wuz thickheaded," he said, and he tossed the stick onto the fire and sat down again, spitting and feigning disinterest. But every night it was the same thing, Sedge having trouble with some letter, letters in fact that he'd previously had no trouble with at all, and Mo sighing and coming to peer over his shoulder as I traced the letter once again. Then Mo would berate Sedge for being thickheaded and draw the letter in the dirt, break his stick, and toss it in the fire.

After some time I caught Mo drawing letters in the dirt off to his side, and one day as I doused the fire I noticed the letters M and O side by side where his bedroll had been. By the time we reached Drunken Bride, after having traveled ten days, Mo willingly joined us in our lessons. He reckoned he ought to, he said, seeing as how Sedge needed all the help he could get, and, seeing as how I wasn't much of a teacher, seeing as how we were both so damn thickheaded it wouldn't hurt to help out none. "We gotta stick together," Mo said, and then he changed the subject. "Now when we get close to Drunken Bride, you stay on the edge of town," he told Sedge. "Make us a camp. Guard the horses. Me and Persy . . ."

"Persy and I," I corrected him.

"Shit." Mo spat my way. "Persy and I . . ." He held one pinkie up in the air. "Gonna have high tea." He spat again in my direction and looked at me. "Me and Persy gonna take the wagon into town and supply up. He get a chance to ask round 'bout that gal of his. He gonna find her. I feel it, I tell you. I jest feel it. She close by, Persy. That what ol' Mo think. She close by."

I would enter the town of Drunken Bride only three times in my life. The second time was with a raiding party of Comanche. The third time was for my trial. This was the first time, and it was as sorry a town as I had ever seen. One wide street bore through the town's center, with squat, crumbling buildings on either side. Mud-caked boardwalks ran along both sides of the road, and the few people who were out ceased whatever they were doing and glared at us as we rattled in. "These people don't seem too friendly," I commented.

"They prob'ly 'bout as friendly as any other Texans. But I might as well tell you, watch yo'sef here. Town founded by a messa folk fleein' the Yankees, what I hear. They prob'ly still got a hair up they ass over losin' the war."

"Most folks do," I observed, and then added, "You told me you didn't know anything about Drunken Bride."

"I tol' you I didn't know how they got that name. Still don't. Don't make no damn sense, if you ask me. Hold the mules, Persy."

We stopped at a storefront with a few lanterns and rakes haphazardly displayed along the walkway. A pile of hides, I could not tell from what animal, was stacked next to a post. Mo pulled the brake on the wagon and we both jumped down. I stood in the street stroking the mules' noses while Mo went inside to purchase supplies.

A black pig wandered down the center of the street, rooting its snout into the dirt. A man stumbled by, the sour smell of too much whiskey wafting along in his wake. Across the way a woman, as scrawny as an ill-fed cat, stepped into a building. The sheriff ambled along the walkway I stood next to, his spurs jangling loudly as he passed by. A hot breeze blew, lifting the mules' manes and then dropping them back down.

One of the mules huffed and nudged its nose into my armpit. "Steady, now," I said. Then I saw him, a short man, looking down at his feet as he churned his way along the boardwalk toward me. His broadcloth suit was wrinkled and dirty, and a large black hat rested on his head. As he drew closer I saw his mouth move, as though in conversation, although no one was near him.

A familiar chill came over me. The spirit I had so often felt in Master Wilson's presence pressed its cold silvery fingers into my back, nudging me forward. I left the mules and stepped onto the boardwalk into his path. "Master Wilson," I said.

He stopped, looked at me. "I don't know you, nigger." He moved to get by me, and I sidestepped to block him.

"You know me, sir."

"I don't. Now get the hell out of my way."

"I'm Persy, sir." He stared at me blankly. "Persimmon Wilson. I used to work on Sweetmore."

He squinted his eyes. A cloud of recognition crossed his face, yet he stood perfectly still, staring. At last he spoke. "Persy." He slapped me on the shoulder and I winced. "Persy. I thought you were dead. Fell in the river is what I remember."

Behind me I heard jingling spurs and the hollow thump of the sheriff's boot heels against the boardwalk. "Joseph," the sheriff said as he passed by. He tipped his hat, and then he settled on a bench outside the store and watched us.

I took a deep breath. I would not be intimidated. I only wanted news of Chloe. Nothing more. "You remember correctly, sir, but I did not die."

"Well now, listen to you. You must have got yourself an education. I hear the niggers all wanting to read and write now. You learned fast, I reckon. The thing is, I don't really recall you being a fast learner. Well, what brings you to Texas, Persy?"

I was strangely calm as Master Wilson delivered this charade. It was as though that spirit that had always run between us held my anger in reins with cold, unruffled hands. It was as though that spirit whispered to me, "He is the master of nothing here. He is nothing but a dingy little man living in a dingy little town with the sheriff looking on."

I remained polite. I only wanted to know one thing, and then I need never see Master Wilson again.

"I am looking for Chloe, sir. Do you know where she is?"

"Chloe?" he asked.

"Yes sir."

"Well now." He scratched the back of his neck. "I had so many niggers I can't remember all their names." He tapped his fingers against his lips. "Chloe, Chloe, Chloe."

Still I was calm. I was closer to finding her than I had ever been before. Only this pathetic little display of power stood in my way.

"Oh, yes. Chloe," Master Wilson said at last, as though he now recalled a vague memory of someone who mattered little to him. He removed his tapping fingers from his lips. "I recall now," Wilson said. "House nigger. Took good care of my wife in her final days. Pretty little wench, for a nigger. Loyal."

"Yes sir," I said. Inside, I laughed at him. I thought that there was nothing he could do to hurt me anymore. "I am looking for her," I said again.

"Loyal," Wilson repeated. "Very loyal to me. A credit to her race. A shame though, Chloe died along the trail."

Master Wilson reached out and laid his hand on my shoulder.

"You had a little spark for her, didn't you? I recall she didn't care for you though. But I reckon it doesn't matter now. Well" — he laughed — "except that you came all the way to Drunken Bride to find her." He removed his hand from my shoulder. The sheriff crossed his legs and his spurs jingled.

Wilson's words swam in my head. Died. Along the trail. Loyal. Spark. The words took turns nipping at me, just like the fish in the river had done.

"Oh dear," I heard Wilson say. His voice was vaporous now and far away, even though I saw that he still stood just before me. "I hope you've not come all this way looking to me for employment. You do have work, don't you?"

I did not answer. The spirit left and it became hot. I saw Master Wilson smile. And then I heard my voice unpinning itself from my throat. "Yes sir, I have work." Through the window of the store I saw Mo moving about, pointing at this and that as the store-keep fetched things.

Master Wilson followed my gaze. "You're working for that man?"

I nodded. "Ranch work."

"Good. I can see that you're still strong." He reached out to feel my biceps. My mind snapped to attention at his touch, and I jerked his hand off me.

"Joseph," the sheriff said. "You needing help?"

"No," Wilson answered. He turned to look at the sheriff. His back was to me briefly, his pink neck exposed beneath the brim of his hat. "Just one of my niggers come to see me."

The sheriff leaned back against the wall of

312

the store. Wilson turned back to me.

"How?" I asked. "How did Chloe die?"

"Well now, let me see." He pretended to ponder again. "Died on the trail. Several of them did, you know. I'm not sure exactly why. Travel might have been too hard. We were hurting for food sometimes. You know, times were hard, Persy. Leaving Sweetmore was very hard on me. I don't know if you realize that."

"Where?"

"Where did she die? I don't know. It was Texas, I know that."

"Did you bury her?"

"Of course we buried her. What kind of man do you take me for?"

I did not tell him what kind of man I took him for. "Did you mark the grave?"

"With a rock. Didn't exactly have time to carve a pretty little cross. We were running for our lives from the Yankees, you know." He let out a hoarse laugh. "Leaving my home, leaving Sweetmore, leaving all that I'd worked so hard to build was very hard on me. You niggers don't seem to understand that."

"You didn't cover the grave with rocks?"

"Didn't have a lot of rocks, and y'all were feeling pretty mutinous by then. You'd traveled a long ways."

It crossed my mind to correct him, to remind him that I had not been along on this journey, that I had in fact been shot and left in the river to drown, but in the face of Chloe's death the words felt too complicated, the thoughts would not emit into language. I continued to stand there and the sheriff continued to watch and Master Wilson continued to talk.

"I am sorry to be the one to tell you about Chloe, Persy. I know you had a spark for her. I still don't recall her caring for you though. I need to get on now." He brushed aside and walked away, and I stood staring at the space where he had been. One of the mules snorted and blew its breath out, and I stepped back to them and stroked its nose. The sheriff stood and hitched his pants up and walked back the way he'd come. Through the store window I saw Mo continue to move around and point, the merchant continue to fetch. I felt my breath become uneven. It emerged from my throat in small huffs and then it occurred to me that I was crying.

I heard the clop of a horse coming nearby and looked up to see Master Wilson riding my way. He stopped at the wagon. "Persy," he said gently. "I was just thinking what a big mistake I made back at Sweetmore. You were a good worker. Strong and industrious." I nodded. "I should have been more thoughtful. With your strength and Chloe's loyalty, I should have bred you two." He grinned and laughed and reeled his horse away from me, thundering off before I could respond.

Mo came out of the store. "Help me load up, Persy."

I stepped up onto the boardwalk and began hefting sacks of flour and beans into the wagon bed, and then I picked up a sack of coffee, and I smelt its rich aroma, and I recalled the scent of coffee in Chloe's soft hair as she leaned against me in the barn of Lidgewood.

I think myself a fool now for believing Master Wilson, but everything he said was plausible. All those years, five years since I had last seen Chloe, I did not know where she was, and in my darkest moments, I had imagined her dead.

After Master Wilson thundered off on his horse, I could think of nothing but the fact that Chloe had died along the trail without me, nothing but her grave not properly covered with rocks, nothing but her body dug up and gnawed on by some animal.

I told Mo and Sedge in our camp outside of Drunken Bride, and then I spread my bedroll away from the fire and lay alone on the prairie, apart from my companions. There was a meteor shower that night. Stars shot across the sky, leaving trails of light in their wake. I rolled over away from the stars, and I touched the button at my throat and I sobbed. I am sure that Mo and Sedge heard me, but they did not come to me, for which I was grateful.

The next day, and many days thereafter, Mo spoke to me about Chloe. He tried to lift my spirits, tried to make me see that I might meet someone yet and fall in love again. He meant well. I know that now. Around the fire each night, he spat and poked another stick into the flames and said, "At least you know, Persy. At least you can quit her. Find yo'sef a new gal. You young yet."

I listened and nodded.

"I cain't get over it though," Mo said, shaking his head. "I sho you gonna find her. I felt it." He thumped his hand against his chest. "I felt it right here." Then he started up on trying to comfort me again. "You ain't as bad-lookin' as I tol' you befo', Persy. I believe some gal might take a likin' to you yet."

I gave him a weak smile and tore a bit of meat off whatever we'd cooked that night and jammed it into my mouth.

"You fall in love again. I seed it happen. Men with they hearts broke all over the place. Broke so bad you think they ain't never gonna get outta bed. Then some little gal come along and they be fallin' in love again. I seed it. I seed it plenty of times.

Heart broke one minute, trippin' over they tongue the next. It could happen to you."

"Did it happen to you, after your wife died?"

Mo spat and rolled away from me and became silent. I could always count on the subject of Mo's wife clamming him up, and I used this strategy, cruelly and often.

"What you go and do that fo', Persy? You jest gettin' mean," Sedge said. He reached over and gave Mo's back a little rub.

I did not care what Sedge thought of me, nor did I care for Mo's paternal overtures. I hobbled the horses at night and helped break camp in the morning. The lessons I had been giving Sedge and Mo ceased. I cared not for the trunk of books. I cared not for my companions. I cared not for the sun coming up each morning or setting each night. Five years apart, two years searching for her, and she had been dead all along. I slept. I woke. I fingered the button at my throat, and when it became too much for me I walked off into the prairie alone.

We rattled on day after day. The grassland swallowed up our wagon tracks as if we had never been there. I barely spoke to either of them any longer. I merely rode along, driving one of the wagons, or in the saddle on the back of Cups or one of the other horses.

I rode like this until one day, perhaps a week after we'd left Drunken Bride, Mo spat out his wad of tobacco and called out, "Whoa, whoa, whoa," to the mules and pulled the brake on the wagon. "Whoa, whoa, whoa," Sedge yelled, squealing his wagon to a halt. Mo jumped down and stomped over to me. He reached up and grabbed my belt, yanked me out of my saddle, threw me to the ground, and kicked me.

"Get up, Persy." Mo jerked me up by the back of my shirt and stood me before him, and then slammed his fist into my face. I fell back, and tasted the blood in my mouth. I wiped it with my sleeve and looked at the bright red stain blooming there. "Come on," Mo said, dancing in front of me with his fists raised.

I did not need any more invitation than that. I hauled myself up and was on him. He rolled into a ball and I pummeled my fists into his back. I kicked him. I yelled at him. I called him a son of a bitch, a bastard, a goddamn troll, and I grabbed him and rolled him back over. I pulled his head back by his long flowing hair that the Indians wanted for their shields, and I pulled my fist back, ready to slam it into his face. He raised his arms to protect himself. I hesitated and Mo rolled away from me again.

The grass kicked up around us as I pounded my fists into his back. I heard him grunt with each blow. I heard myself grunt as I delivered a second punch and a third and a fourth.

I do not know how long it went on, but at last I stopped. I was exhausted, and I lay down next to him, panting and bleeding. I looked over. Mo had rolled onto his back and lay in the prairie grass with his eyes closed. Blood oozed out of his mouth.

"Mo?"

He nodded. I thought I saw a tear glisten down his cheek, but he quickly wiped at his face, then pulled his bandana from his pocket and daubed the blood away from his mouth. I heard the wagon creak and the thump of Sedge's feet as he jumped down, and then the long liquid sound of his urine splattering against the prairie as he took a piss. The mules snorted. The horses ripped up the grass and chewed. Mo finally said, "Listen here, Persy. I know you done lost someone. I know how it feel. My wife, I done lost her. It near 'bout kilt me."

I lay my arm across my forehead to shield my eyes from the sun. "How did you lose her?" I asked.

I heard him take a deep breath. "Lost her in the war," he said. "I was fightin' fo' the goddamned Rebs." He looked over at me. "Biggest mistake I ever made, leavin' her there all alone."

"Where?"

"Back in the Piney Woods. A deserter raped her and kilt her."

"I'm sorry."

"Like she warn't nothin'." His voice choked. "I shoulda been there. I shouldn't of been off fightin' that damn war so some rich bastard like yo' Massuh Wilson could keep him some slaves and . . . and have Chloe. I sorry, Persy. I sorry fo' yo' loss and I sorry fo' mine." Mo rolled over and spit some blood out of his mouth, and said, "Damn if I couldn't use me a chaw. Sedge, bring me my haversack, will you?"

"Yassuh, Mistah Tilly."

Sedge ambled over, Mo's haversack swinging in one hand and a canteen in the other. He plopped down in the grass beside us. "Y'all done had a tussle," he observed, uncapping the canteen and pouring a little water onto a bandana. He offered it to me. "I believe you took the worse of it, Persy. You know Mistah Tilly be undestructible."

I took the offered cloth and touched it to my lip, which was cut, and above my left eye, also cut. Mo was rooting around in his bag, shaving off a piece of tobacco and settling it in his jaw. Then he pulled out a small, hinged case, opened it, and handed it to me.

"My wife," he said, pointing to one of the two tintypes inside. A young lady with an oval face, dark hair swept into a bun, piercing eyes, and black-lace-gloved hands resting in her lap stared back at me. The other tintype was of a younger-looking Mo, dressed in a Confederate uniform and holding a rifle. "My lovely Geraldine," Mo said. He reached over and took the case from my hands, stared briefly at her likeness, and then snapped it shut and slid it back into his haversack. "My name is Maurice. Maurice Tilly. That was Mrs. Tilly. You keep callin' me Mo if you don't mind." He spat. "You want a chaw, Persy?"

"No sir. Thank you."

"I take one," Sedge said.

"I ain't offer you one."

"All right." Sedge settled in the grass beside me and took a drink out of the canteen before offering it to me. I took a swig and offered it to Mo, who shook his head and pointed to his mouth.

"Tombaccer," he said.

The three of us sat quietly until Mo finally said, "I reckon we ought to be goin' on now."

"Yassuh," Sedge answered.

Mo stood up and offered me a hand. I grasped his arm and he hauled me up and as he did so, he pulled me into an embrace. His face pressed against my chest. "I need you, Persy," he said. "I need you payin' attention. It ain't jest yo' life. It mine and Sedge too. You fuck up, we might all die."

"Yes sir," I said. "I understand."

He let go of me. "I hope you done beat yo' grief out."

"No sir, I don't think so."

"I reckon not."

"I'm sorry. It did help to hit you."

"Yeah." Mo spat. "It help to hit you too."

We rode on. I was, of course, not able to leave my grief behind, but I owed the living, and that night we started our lessons again.

It was not long before we entered the edge of the frontier. Sedge and Mo had been armed all along, and now Mo provided me with weaponry as well, a Henry rifle and a six-shooter, along with a belt of bullets to wear around my waist, delivered, of course, with his ever-present advice to save one for myself, along with his ever-present observation that my hair would be of no interest to the Indians.

The truth is we saw no Indians, and the rattle of the wagons, the squeak of tack, the snorts of horses and mules, the rhythm of day in and day out travel and encampment lulled me into a stuporous disbelief of anything Mo had to say about them. *Eat the raw meat; don't show fear, save a bullet fo' yo'sef.* On the subject of Indians, Mo's voice had become a sort of buzz, like bees in a bush.

The tall lush grass of the prairie gave way to shorter grass, and then to land patched together with brush and stubble and cat claw and mesquite. The wind whipped up in bursts, sending grit into my eyes and nose and mouth, and creating little dust devils that twirled along the road ahead of us, as if in escort. Occasionally, tumbleweeds rolled across our path and out into the plains as if they were animals fleeing a hunt.

Oddly, the place did not frighten me. That I should find myself in such a landscape after losing Chloe seemed fitting and right. The very strangeness of it matched the strangeness of my heart. I fingered my button and rode on.

We passed, on occasion, graves along the roadside, some piled with rocks and marked with blank staring crosses, others marked only with one stone if they were marked at all, and of these some had been dug at by animals, the bones scattered. I saw a femur rolled beneath a mesquite bush, and the bones of a rib cage lay chewed and cracked in our path one day. We did not stop to re-assemble these dead or to give them a proper burial. Mo simply drove on, around them if necessary, politely taking his hat off at every grave and every human bone.

I was driving one of the wagons when up ahead I saw Mo take off his hat and nod his regards. It was a skeleton this time, nearly whole, lying alongside the road. The skeleton was clothed in a faded, dry-rotting dress. The bones, what parts of them were not missing or covered with drifts of sand, were bleached to a blinding white, and at the ends of this skeleton's legs a pair of women's shoes stuck out, simple and black, with a row of brass grommets.

"Whoa," I said, pulling on the reins, putting the brake on, and jumping down from the wagon.

"Whoa, whoa." Mo pulled back on his reins. The mules stopped and Mo twisted in his seat to look back at me. I stood now at the side of the road, staring down at the skeleton.

"Persy, what you doin'?" Mo yelled.

Sedge came riding up beside me. "What is it, Persy?"

"Do you see a button like this one?"

Sedge leaned over. I felt his hand rest on my shoulder. "They a thousand buttons like that one, Persy. Mizz Doreen had a dress with buttons like that. It don't mean nothin'."

I fell into the dirt and began pawing at it, sifting it through my fingers.

"You ain't gonna find no button, Persy," Mo hollered. "What the hell you thinkin' 'bout, anyway? Let's quit this place."

"No," I said, and I stood and walked to the back of the wagon and pulled the shovel out from beneath the tarp.

"What the hell you doin'?" Mo asked.

"I'm burying her."

"Why?"

"What if it's Chloe?" I said, and I shoved the blade into the earth.

"What?" Mo pulled the brake on his wagon and jumped down. "It ain't Chloe."

"How do you know?"

" 'Cause she passed on befo' Wilson reach Drunken Bride. She buried back behind us, Persy, not in front of us. This ain't Chloe. You think 'bout it. It don't make no sense. She ain't come this far."

I stopped my digging. Mo reached out and took the shovel from me. He lay his hand on my shoulder and led me back to the wagon, muttering the whole way. "Goddamn it all to hell. Sixty-seven gonna be one hell of a year. There you go, Persy, back in the wagon." And he helped me up as if I were an old lady. "I ain't as smart as you," he said, "least ways that's what I thought befo' now."

As we rattled along again Mo yelled back to me, "You got to quit pinin' fo' her, Persy. Ain't no good in this."

"I don't even know why I'm here," I hollered back.

"You here to help out you ol' friend Mo. You fo'get that somehow."

"He gettin' moony again?" Sedge asked as he rode along beside us.

" 'Pear to be," Mo answered.

"I'll give you the winter," I yelled, "then I'm heading to San Antonio or Austin. I got to make a new life for myself."

"Glad to hear it. I 'bout had it with you anyway."

"Are you going to be able to pay me when I leave? Mr. Sanders wasn't going to pay until he sold his beeves."

"I pay you somehow, Persy." Mo spat. "If you determined to leave, I give you some horses, that rifle there, some grub to get you started. If you can find water and hunt game and take care of yo' horses and don't get lost and don't get kilt by the damn

Indians, you be all right."

"Who gonna teach me readin' and writin'?" Sedge asked, turning his horse around and coming back to ride beside me.

"We'll just have to work hard through the winter," I said.

Ever the optimist, Mo yelled back, "They be plenty of time. Weather gonna be awful. You two girls be goin' dog-heat crazy by the time spring come on. Prob'ly be a wonder we all don't kill each other."

The casket maker came an hour ago and measured my height. For the last few hours, I have listened to the saws and hammers of the men as they build my gallows. Right now I hear the carpenters laughing as they test the trapdoor, which will drop away from my feet and leave me swinging. They test it again and again, and it makes a loud thunking noise each time. The men laugh, and one hollers out, taunting me, "That ought to do it."

Jack brought my lunch not long ago. I pushed it aside. I have twenty-four hours left. The men outside test the trapdoor one more time, and then they walk together in a clump, heading up the street to the saloon. One glances at my window as they pass. I do not know if he can see me, but all the same, for some reason, I lift my hand and wave.

It was the first of September, three days

after leaving the shoed skeleton unburied along the trail, that we arrived at the Traveling S Ranch, the remuda raising a cloud of dust behind us. Since its abandonment at the start of the war the ranch had been reduced to remnants of broken-down corrals, an adobe house with one wall cracked and crumbling back into the earth, a dingy bunkhouse, various outbuildings, and a barn that loomed incongruously against the sky. We swept out the bunkhouse and moved our gear inside, and then set to work.

Over the fall Sedge and I built up the corrals, cleaned the barn and outbuildings, scrubbed the bunkhouse and the ranch house, and made all the necessary repairs. We set up woodstoves that had fallen over or collapsed into the floor. We cleaned flues and chimneys and gathered wagonloads of twisted mesquite branches for firewood. We built a fence of lashed saplings around a garden plot that did not yet exist and pens for livestock that had not yet arrived.

Mo assigned himself the duty of priming the well pump, and when the prime did not hold, the pump's innards stiff and ornery from having not known water for so long, Mo took the thing apart and began rebuilding it while barking orders to Sedge and me. Right through the first days of winter's snap in the air, Mo had us working.

I flailed against the needs of the ranch just as I had once flailed against fields of cane. I needed no repose, wanted no rest or time off in which to think or feel. In fact I feared such rest, for the news of Chloe's death had reached so far into my heart that her memory had become an artery of sorts. With every beat she was there, just as my blood was there, just as my lungs involuntarily took in air, just as my skin prickled when a cold wind brushed across it.

After Mo finished with the pump he started in on another project, keeping his promise to Sedge that he would not have to bunk with the white hands by building us separate living quarters. For this Mo used the bit of lumber from Miss Doreen's barn. Our abode, once finished, was a small house, no larger than ten by ten. Inside were three bunks cantilevered out from the walls, a potbelly stove, purchased in Drunken Bride, set in the center, a door facing east, windows with shutters over each bed, and a little shelf running beneath the windows.

On the shelf above his bed, Mo placed the framed tintypes of himself and Geraldine, along with his block of "tombaccer" with a knife plunged into it. He banged a nail into the wall above and hung his haversack, and coat, and hat there. On the floor beneath the bed he tucked an old can in which to spit. On the opposite wall, along my own little shelf, I lined up the spellers and the few books from Miss Doreen's trunk, and I tucked the torn-off piece of map that I'd carried from Sou Sou between them. On his shelf Sedge propped up his slate and set his nub of chalk beside it, and then carefully unwrapped Miss Doreen's lamp, miraculously unbroken, and placed it on the corner shelf Mo had built especially for this purpose.

It was November now and the jaws of winter clamped their teeth upon us. On good days we worked, gathering more wood and continuing with repairs. On days that were too bitterly cold or stormy we spent our time doing what few chores were necessary, and then we played poker, placing bets with the bent nails Mo had brought by the bucketful from Miss Doreen's place. At night we had our lessons by the light of Sedge's lamp while the wind whistled around the corners and shook the little building, causing our piles of betting nails to tremble on the shelf.

Winter tediously moaned its way through the days and weeks, and soon enough it imprisoned us in blocks of time in which the weather was too cold and cruel to face more than daily chores. After we had tended the horses and brought in the firewood we could only play so many hands of cards, only bet so many nails, only have so many lessons, and only read so many pages of books, so there were times when we did nothing, when we each reclined in our beds and did not talk, times when even Mo was quiet. It was not uncomfortable between us, but just as I had feared, left without distraction, my mind always drifted to Chloe.

I envied Mo his tintype of Geraldine. I wished for an image of Chloe, although not for the reason one might think, for she was not fading from my mind, but becoming more and more vivid, more and more real. My remembrances became tangible. At times I even felt her breath across my neck as I lay in bed. A photograph, I reasoned, might lesson the intensity of my dreams and my dreams had begun to frighten me.

I need not tell you that I dreamt of her. I woke up certain that she was calling my name. There was distress in her voice, and more than once I got up and stepped around the glowing woodstove, and out into the night calling back to her, "Chloe. I'm coming. I'm coming."

The nights were bitter cold. The wind cut

through my long johns. Bits of snow and ice bit against my skin with sharp little stings. My socks stuck to the earth.

I did not know where to look for her. The rolling hills stretched out empty before me. The moon either shined or did not shine, was either full or a sliver, I could either see or not see. "Chloe?" I would call again. The cold air froze inside my lungs and made me cough. And then I would feel Mo's hand on my shoulder. "Come on in now, Persy," he'd say. "She ain't out here."

"I heard her."

"You been dreamin'."

"Where is she?" I asked. "Where do you think she is, Mo?"

"I don't know, son."

"Where do you think Geraldine is?"

"I don't know, son."

"How can you bear not knowing?"

"I cain't bear it."

"But you do bear it."

"Exactly. Now come on in. Come on in, I'm cold."

I allowed Mo to lead me back inside and put me in bed. He pulled the blanket up to my chin, and then he tucked it close into my body, just as my mother had once done when I was a little boy on the Surley place in Virginia.

I watched from my bunk as Mo opened the stove door and shoved another piece of wood in, the flames lapping their tongues out before he closed it. Between us Sedge snored. Mo would climb back into his bed and pull the blanket up. "Go on back to sleep, Persy," he'd say. "You be hurtin' jest as bad tomorry. Won't miss nothin' by sleepin'."

But it would happen again the next night, and the next. It was as though Chloe called to me, as though she had some message for me. I think now it was as though she wanted me to know that she was alive.

Master Wilson had told her. I know this now. He had told her that he had seen me in Drunken Bride, and that I was asking about her. He had told her the entire story, right down to her own death along the trail. Perhaps, if one believes in such things, I could feel Chloe reaching for me. For the first time in five years she knew that I had not drowned in the river, and that I was looking for her. Perhaps every time Master Wilson forced himself on her now, Chloe called my name.

Each time I heard her voice, I woke, and I answered her, and I stepped outside, and every time, no matter the weather, no matter the cold, or sleet, or snow, Mo came and

335

got me, and every time he'd lead me back inside to my bed, and he'd pull the blanket up to my chin, and then I'd lay there and watch the fire lap out of the stove door as he lay another stick of wood on.

I had been through two Texas winters before this one. I knew them to be harsh, but I swear that in 1867 the cold was colder, the ice icier. Winter howled. Some storms were worse than others. There were days that we were not sure if it was day. Had we fed the horses? Was it time for breakfast or dinner? The light so often looked the same.

Our loss of time was not just limited to days, but also weeks and months. We did not know if it was Christmas or New Year's or Monday or Wednesday. Our beards grew and we did not shave. Our skin became slick with oil and gritty with dirt that ground against our bedding at night.

There were blizzards. They could come out of nowhere. A sunny day could suddenly go dark, like the end of the world. The snow was blown so far across the prairie that very little accumulated on the ground. Mostly it banked itself against anything in its path, the buildings, the woodshed, our own little bunkhouse. Still, you would not want to be out in one of these storms, for although very little snow accumulated, it fell at times so thick and wild that you could not see your own hand in front of your face. Once or twice one of us would get trapped in the barn when a blizzard suddenly came up and we would simply stay there, huddled close to the horses for warmth. It was into these storms that I sometimes stepped out looking for Chloe, and it was into these storms that Mo stepped out behind me and pulled me roughly back inside.

Except for the weather, every day seemed the same. There were chores, a breakfast of cush-cush, a game of cards, a lunch of beans and sometimes bacon, more cards, taking turns reading a bit out loud from one of the books, Mo and Sedge laboring through this, then dinner same as lunch, and perhaps another round of poker.

The cabin took on the intermingled smells of our existence: beans, body odors, the scent of the woodstove and kerosene and tobacco. Winter pressed and breathed down on us like a dragon with ice in its lungs instead of fire. The hunting scene from Sedge's lamp cast its shadows on the walls, until, at last, we turned in each night, or was it day? Everything felt like its own equivalent until the morning Mo got sick.

He had been coughing. I would recall this later, but at the time I was not concerned.

This was Mo, and Mo was strong. He chewed his tobacco, and spit into his can, and stoked the fire, and beat me in poker, and hauled me in whenever I wandered into the night. I never thought it would be any other way, except that perhaps the details might change, but Mo would not. And then one morning I woke to the stove door creaking open, the roar and crackle of the fire against the sound of a blizzard hurling itself around the corners of our little house, and a wet, racking cough, filled with the sound of fluid. Sedge's lamp glowed in the dark cabin.

"Mistah Tilly sick," Sedge said.

I looked over. Sedge was sitting on the edge of Mo's bunk and Mo was shivering.

"Give me yo' blanket. Get mine too. Put 'em on him."

I got up and pulled the blankets off the beds and spread them across Mo, pinching them close to his body just as he had done for me only hours before. I opened the stove door and lay more sticks on. "Build it up good," Sedge said. "Build it up hot." I added more wood until the stove glowed red, the fire as big and hot as I dared to make it.

Just then Mo looked up at Sedge, his eyes as large as pecans. "Geraldine?" he said.

"Nawsuh, Mistah Tilly. It me, Sedge. And Persy right here too. Don't you worry none. We gonna get it hot in here. We gonna sweat this thing right outta you." Sedge stood and took Mo's leather coat off its nail and draped it across his feet. I handed him my pants and shirt and jacket, all hanging on my own nail, and Sedge draped them across Mo.

Still Mo shivered. Another fit of coughing. Sedge helped him sit up a little and I watched as Mo's body jerked through it. Sedge eased him back down, and Mo said once again, "Geraldine?"

"Get him a dipper of water," Sedge said.

I did so, and while Sedge raised Mo's head I dribbled a trickle into his mouth.

Sedge reached under the covers to feel Mo's skin. "He startin' to sweat some. I gettin' in with him. Give him mo' heat. You keep the fire up, Persy. We take turns." Sedge lifted the blankets and clothing and slid in beside Mo. He wrapped his arms around him and said, "It be all right, Mistah Tilly. It be all right."

Mo jerked and shuddered and called again for his dead wife. I reached up to the little shelf and took his tintypes down and placed them on top of the blanket.

Sedge nodded. "That good," he said.

"That good. There she be, Mistah Tilly. There she be." He held the picture up to Mo's eyes, but Mo's eyes did not focus on it. Sedge wrapped Mo's fingers around the tintype and said again, "There she be, Mistah Tilly."

Mo coughed, another fit of coughing that lasted five minutes, ten it seemed like as the storm screamed around us and rattled the shutters. I fed the stove and sat across from them and waited to feed the stove again, staring at Sedge's thin back as he lay wrapped around Mo. After some time we traded places and Sedge climbed out from under the blanket dripping with sweat, and I climbed into the bunk and wrapped my arms around Mo Tilly.

He shivered violently against me. His skin was moist and hot. The wind wailed. The cabin shook. I have said that it was morning, and I suppose that this is true, yet I do not really know, for no light leaked through the spaces between our shutters. I heard the stove door open behind me, heard firewood scrape across the floor as Sedge hauled it out from under one of the bunks, heard the crackle and pop of flames.

We spent hours trading off lying with Mo and keeping the stove stoked. We dribbled water into his mouth. We held him up as he coughed, and caught the greenish phlegm he produced in a bandana held to his face. Sedge heated broth from last night's beans and tried to feed him, but Mo would not take it. He turned away from the spoon.

"My mules," he said at one point, his voice thick and swampy. "Take care of my mules."

"We takin' care of 'em," Sedge said.

A little later Mo reached up and touched Sedge's hair. His eyes were glassy. "Keep yo' scalp, Sedge," he said.

Sedge laughed nervously. "I be keepin' it, Mistah Tilly. You be here to make sure of that."

Mo shook his head.

The storm died down at last, as did Mo's coughing. Sedge and I stopped rotating in and out of Mo's bunk long enough to make and eat a pot of cush-cush.

"We got to feed the horses," Sedge said.

I nodded.

"And bring in the firewood."

"We're going to need our clothes," I said, eyeing Sedge's and my britches and shirts and coats that we'd piled on top of Mo.

"He be all right. We stoke up the stove nice and high, work fast. I believe he some better. Don't you, Persy?"

"Yes," I lied. "I think he's some better."

I stood and opened the stove door, jamming in stick after stick. When the fire seemed good and hot, Sedge and I pulled on our clothes and opened the cabin door and stepped outside. The air was frigid, with pings of ice that stung against our skin. The sun shone weakly through a sky muffled with clouds. Sedge headed toward the barn and I toward the woodshed. I filled the handcart with a load of wood and hauled it to the cabin, dumping it outside and going for another load, figuring that I could stack it more quickly inside if I had it all nearby.

Mo must have built our little bunkhouse to invisible specifications that only he could have known how to calculate, or perhaps it was just sheer dumb luck that just enough wood for a few days would fit under the three bunks. We supplied up whenever there was a break in the weather, never letting our stock get too low. But we had used a lot of wood keeping the fire hotter than usual, and I made another trip with the handcart and then a third, and a fourth.

I opened the door to the cabin. Mo said nothing as I went in and out bringing in armloads of wood. Once he looked at me as though he did not know who I was. "It's Persy," I told him, though he had not asked.

Sedge came back soon. "Yo' mules is fine," he told Mo. Mo nodded, and we took this as a good sign.

For three days we nursed him. We took turns lying beside him, and we propped him up and made him drink dipperfuls of water and tried to get him to take some broth, or beans, or maybe a small bit of bacon. His cough came and went. Sometimes it sounded light and tickly, and other times strings of greenish phlegm stained his beard. He asked for "tombaccer" once, and Sedge told him, "Nawsuh. You ain't well enough fo' a chaw. You have one when you better." Sedge turned to me and smiled.

On the third day we woke to another blizzard. The wind whistled and howled, and against this backdrop, Mo's coughing seemed worse. Sedge got out of bed and stood over Mo and watched him wrack out cough after cough, the green phlegm dribbling down his chin. Sedge wet a cloth with warm water from the kettle and daubed it at Mo's beard and face, but Mo pushed him away and continued to cough.

When he was still at last Sedge lifted the covers and felt of Mo's skin again. "He got the fever back," Sedge said. "I gettin' in with him some mo'. Get us the extra blankets again."

He climbed into bed and wrapped his arms around Mo. I spread my blanket and

Sedge's blanket across them, and then stoked the stove and sat on my bunk and watched the rise and fall of Sedge's back. I thought of Miss Doreen, and how Mo had held the pillow over her face, and how he had done it for Sedge. I did not know their history, for I had been too preoccupied with my own grief and yearning to ask, but there was deep love there. It was easy to see, and I vowed that I would ask the story of their friendship when Mo was well again.

The storm died that afternoon, and Sedge and I built up the fire and pulled on our clothes and boots and went out to do our chores, him off to the barn again and me hauling firewood in the handcart.

As I brought in the last of the wood the sky went black and I shut the door against the second blizzard of the day. The tempest screamed around the corners of the cabin and shook the shutters. Sedge had not made it back in time, but he would be warm enough nestled between two of the horses.

I sat on my bunk and watched Mo, who was now slowly rolling his head from side to side and calling out Geraldine's name again. I got up and placed the tintypes on his chest. He ignored them and I brought his hand up and rolled his fingers around the little hinged case. "There she is," I said.

He weakly held the picture of Geraldine and said her name once again. Even in Mo's weak and faded voice I could hear the longing and the hope and the puzzlement as to why Geraldine did not come to him, and where she could possibly be if not by his side.

I stoked the stove again and sat on the edge of my bunk and stared at him. The tintypes dropped to the floor with a little clank. "Where you been, darlin'?" Mo said. His voice this time was different, so young and confident. His eyes were clear and focused. He smiled. "I been lookin' all over fo' you." I watched as his hand closed, his fingers curling gently around something that I could not see. "Sweetheart," Mo said, and then he was gone.

The living do not always believe what they see. I stood and held my ear to his chest and heard nothing. I reached over and pulled the knife from Mo's block of tobacco and held the blade to his parted lips and it did not fog. There was no breath.

As if on some staged cue, the storm intensified its howling and screeching. The cabin groaned as if it would blow apart. I turned up the flame on Sedge's lamp. I felt the wind suck through the walls, though I had never felt drafts in the cabin before.

The stove burned brightly, but its heat, even in this small space, was inadequate. I shivered a bit, and then it occurred to me to close Mo's eyes and to take one of his blankets and wrap up in it, and these things I did.

I wished that Sedge were here to talk to, to add body warmth, to take turns with, one of us sleeping, and the other tending the fire. I wished for his presence also to prevent my thoughts from gaining too much strength, but he was not there, and as I stared at Mo's body I remembered all the nights since we'd arrived at the ranch that he had stepped outside in the hacking cold to fetch me back in, and to answer my questions — "Where is Chloe? Where is Geraldine?" — with his simple reply that he did not know. He knew now, I thought.

After some time I became grateful that Sedge was not there, for I did not like the idea of him seeing me blubber like a baby, and that is what I did. I sobbed, and I bawled, and I cried for the loss of Mo, and the bitter thought that a man like Mo Tilly must die, while a man like Master Wilson went on to live and breathe air that he did not deserve.

The storm lasted the night. I slept fitfully on occasion. The next morning the world was quiet and sunny and Mo's body was cold, and when I opened the door I found Sedge frozen and dead not ten feet away.

I could not bury them. I tried. I picked a spot and I dragged Mo out of the house and Sedge up beside him. I pulled the dead grass away from the ground, creating two spaces large enough for graves, and I threw the blade of the pickax against the earth only to have the impact reverberate up the handle and into my arms. A small sliver of dirt, not even the size of Chloe's button, pinged loose and fell against my boot. I hit the earth again, and again only a small chip came loose, and again this did not stop me.

Whatever your opinion of me, I do not want you to believe that I gave up easily on this task, that I lazily hit the earth once or twice and then decided to wait for spring. I do not want you to presume, whatever else you presume about me, that I did not care about properly laying my friends in the ground.

I cared a great deal. I loved these men,

and I put my pickax and my back and every muscle I had to the task of giving them an immediate burial. I flailed at the ground. I swung down hard on it. After two hours, I had dug one hole, the size of the dough bowl on which I had floated to safety on the river.

I was sweating, and the air was chill, and I came to understand that I would not be able to bury Mo and Sedge until the ground had thawed. I loaded my friends into the hand-cart and wheeled them to the unused bunkhouse, where I lay them on the floor just inside the door. I retrieved feed sacks from the barn and used them to cover the bodies. And there I left them for the winter.

It was dusk when I closed the door to the bunkhouse. The sky was a beautiful eddy of red and pink and purple. I went into our own little house and lit Sedge's lamp, and built up the fire. I warmed a pot of beans and sat on my bunk eating. I was afraid to go to sleep that night, afraid that Chloe would call to me and that I would wander out into the dark cold, this time without Mo to step outside and pull me back in. I sat up until daybreak, the lamp flickering; the hunting scene on its globe cast in shadows against one wall.

In my mind I can see the interior of that

cabin: the empty bunks, the disarray of blankets, Sedge's lamp and his slate and his nub of chalk, Mo's block of "tombaccer," his haversack, our separate piles of rusty nails, and the dog-eared deck of cards sitting next to the tintypes of Mo and Geraldine.

When morning broke I went to the barn to tend the horses. I brought in more firewood, emptied our slop pot, and refueled Sedge's lamp. Then I ran a rope from the door of our cabin, my cabin now, to the barn. I do not understand why we had not thought to do this before. It was so simple, a guideline to hold on to if I was caught out in a sudden, blinding blizzard, a rope that might have saved Sedge's life.

Mo, who guided us from the Double H Ranch all the way up here along the Colorado River, who lay in enough provisions for us and the horses and mules, who built this cabin to withstand any wind and any blizzard, who came out to get me and bring me back inside night after night, this man, Mo, who had done all this had not thought of a guideline from home to barn.

Mo had done his best by me. He had pulled me off my horse and beat me with the hopes that he could loosen my torment. He had shaken me, as best he could, out of my stupor, but he could not stop the dreams from coming at night. He could not stop Chloe from calling to me. He could not stop me from rising out of sleep and opening the door and stepping out into the cold darkling hours. Yet somehow I must stop it, for I was alone now. The only solution I could think of was to lock myself in.

To this end I fashioned two brackets from lumber left in one of the barns, and I secured them to either side of the cabin door, and each night before I turned down the lamp and went to sleep, I lay a thick heavy board in them to bar my way out.

Chloe must not have called for me that first night, for I woke in my bed the next morning, and the next few after that, but then it happened one morning that I woke slumped against the door, exhausted, I supposed, from trying to open it.

I cannot tell you exactly how many months I spent alone at the Traveling S Ranch. Perhaps if I tried, I could count for you the number of storms I endured, or the times I woke up on the floor, or the sticks of wood I burned, or the hours I spent staring at Mo and Geraldine's tintypes, at my friends' empty bunks, at their possessions. I cleared away none of it. I even left Mo's spit bucket until its contents fermented one night and bubbled over the rim, sliding like algae to the edge of his boots left at the foot of his bed.

I visited their corpses throughout the winter. On good days, days without blizzards or too much ice in the air, days in which I had done all my chores and had some time to spare, I pulled up a chair and sat next to their feed-sack-shrouded bodies and spoke to them. I told them of my life, my dinners, my breakfasts, the book I was reading through again. I thanked Sedge for his lamp. I told Mo that I'd shaved off a piece of his "tombaccer" and chewed it, inadvertently swallowing it, and I would not be trying that again, thank you very much. "I miss you," I said.

The dreams of Chloe continued. Her memory would not release me. She would not release me. "That winter," she once told me, "that winter after he told you I be dead, I pray fo' you. I pray you come back. I pray you knowed I warn't no dead thing out on the prairie. I pray you knowed he was lyin'. I was prayin' you find me, Persy."

Perhaps I should have prayed that winter. It would have at least been something to do. But I did not pray that winter, or any other. I do not pray still. While I was with the Comanche, I left the praying to the medicine men, and sometimes the medicine worked and sometimes it didn't.

Chloe's medicine worked, for I cannot ignore the fact that she prayed for me. I cannot help but think that her prayers might have been the source of my dreams, the reason I could not sleep through the night. I woke many times slumped against my barred door, the fire out in the stove and my urine frozen in the slop pot.

Spring came, as it always does, just when I believed it never would come. After a spell of warm weather the ground thawed and I buried Mo and Sedge. I dug the holes deep. I rolled them in, and by the grace of something, they both landed faceup. Into Mo's grave I dropped the tintypes of him and Geraldine, and into Sedge's grave I dropped his slate and the nub of chalk and a braided lariat. I covered them up and mounded their graves with rocks. I pulled two boards from one of the stalls and carved their names into them, and these I planted.

I still did not know what month it was. The only thing I knew was that the coming of spring assured me that the year had definitely passed from 1867 to 1868. I wanted to leave this place. I had no desire to stay and wait for the other ranch hands to show up. I had no desire to be here without Mo and Sedge.

In order to leave, I would need to take some of the horses and set the others loose, thus committing the first act for which I am to hang, horse thievery, although I did not think of it as such at the time.

I shaved, and I rolled up my bedroll, and I crammed a few things to take with me into Mo's haversack: a book, the deck of cards, my piece of map. I culled the horses I wanted from the herd, Cups and Spring Dance, three others so that I could trade off riding them, letting some rest as we went along. I took Mo's team of mules. I took a good saddle and what little was left of our provisions: cornmeal and coffee and beans. I took my rifle and all the ammunition. I left the wagons. I left Mo's block of "tombaccer." I left Sedge's lamp.

I had not thought of Indians for a long time. I did not think of them still. The long winter and the loss of my friends had lulled my sense of danger and survival into an apathetic torpor. Hadn't I managed to hold on, companionless, through blizzards, endless days of sameness, and Chloe's voice calling to me in the night? Wasn't the worst of it over, the weather warming now, the danger gone? I needed only to make my way back to civilization. I needed only to find some sort of work and a way to support myself. I needed only to find a way to forget about Chloe.

I set free the horses I was not taking with me. I watched them thunder off into the plains, tossing their heads, their manes and tails lifting in the wind, some of them turning back once to look at me before disappearing over a rise.

I visited my friends' graves one last time. I promised Mo that I would take care of his mules. I swore to Sedge that I would take care of his horses, and that the rest were free. I told them they were as good friends as I'd ever had, as good as Henry and Sup. "You would have liked them," I said. "Maybe I'll find them." And then I put on my hat, and mounted Spring Dance, and quit this place, heading southeast, angling toward the town of Drunken Bride. From there I thought I would go to Austin, and then back to New Orleans. Perhaps I really could find Henry or Sup. Perhaps I could even find my own pa or ma or sister, Betty.

Along the way I made camps beside streams and trickles of water. I killed prairie chickens and jackrabbits and developed a taste for rattlesnake. I saw a herd of buffalo, like a slow-moving black stain against the faraway hills. Antelope sprang across my path. Vultures spun in air currents above me. I watched, one day, as two rattlesnakes mated on a sun-warmed rock beside the trail, and even though I was hungry, I did not kill them. It seemed a sacred act, this twining and twisting around each other.

I dreamt of Chloe only once. It was not the same as the dreams that had plagued me throughout the winter. She did not call for me. I did not get up and wander into the plains looking for her. Instead she was walking toward me in the moonlight. The white gown she wore shimmered, like the Mississippi River had shimmered in the starlight when I'd awakened pressed against that snag of limbs and debris, clutching my dough bowl to my chest. In my dream Chloe held her hand out to me, and said a word, which I did not recognize. I took her hand, and woke from the dream feeling peaceful, the same as I had felt whenever in her arms.

I traveled on. Another creek. The water was clear and cold, the air warm. I thought I might be nearing Drunken Bride, and I wanted to clean up before I did so. I shaved and washed my clothes. I had neglected to empty my pockets before washing my britches and as I dipped them in and out of the water the little noose from One-Eyed

Jim's hanging floated out and began to travel in the current across the rocks. I grabbed it and put it in Mo's haversack, and then spread my clothes across a bush to dry and sat on a sun-baked boulder to eat a bit of leftover rabbit. My saddle sat on the ground close by. Mo's haversack and a belt of bullets lay on the ground behind me. I had not been so stupid as to leave my rifle out of grabbing distance. With the exception of Chloe's button on its leather strip still tied around my neck, and my hat, I was naked.

The horses and mules were not hobbled. They were gathered in the stream, drinking contentedly, when all of them at once raised their heads and smelt the wind. And then I saw a figure splashing in the stream among them, raising his hands, waving his arms, and the horses took off, running across the plains away from me, and just as quickly the first arrow whistled by my right ear. I did not know what it was. I stood watching my horses retreat in the distance, still not comprehending what was going on when the second arrow sang by my left ear.

The Indians came over the hill in front of me, a dozen or more. Their shrieks and yelps sounded as though pulled from the throat of the devil himself. I jumped behind the rock for cover. I grabbed my rifle, aimed and fired and aimed and fired again, but they swarmed around me like an angry nest of hornets. They turned their horses this way and that, spinning here and there, always moving. I could not take aim, they moved so fast, like a twister, swirling as if one funnel cloud, changing their positions constantly, trading posts as though in an orchestrated dance.

The arrows fell thick around me now. Some pinged off the rock. Others stuck in the ground. Still more flew into the brush, landing with a whump into my clothes left drying in the sun. Several of the warriors rode up to me and touched me with their bows or the butts of their rifles, but before I could fire at them, they were gone with a shrill whoop, vanished back into that hot swirl.

One warrior threw a lance, and it stuck in the ground next to me. I do not know why, but I reached over and pulled it out, and hurled it back to him, and somehow he caught it by its shank. The Indians found this amusing and for a brief time they stopped fighting while they laughed and rode around and around as the warrior held his lance in the air. And then it all started back up again.

I was allowed to reload and continue shooting. Not one of the warriors took cover or showed any concern that I might kill him. They were toying with me, the same way that a cat will toy with a mouse. I know this now. Still, that I am alive today, that I am here, breathing and ready to hang, is a wonder to me. I swore to myself that as long as I had ammunition I would not surrender, but I did not know what I would do when it came down to that last bullet, the one that Mo advised I save for myself.

I kept shooting. They kept firing arrows at me. Some of them had guns, but few were fired. I know now that they had a cache of ammunition, but they did not care to waste bullets on one easily taken naked man.

It seemed forever that I was behind that rock, defending my life, and then it seemed no time at all that it was over. In the heat and surge of battle I had not paid close enough attention to my supply of bullets, and suddenly I reached to reload and there was nothing to reload with. A warrior galloped his horse right up to me.

It was as if this had all been planned, as if everyone involved knew the cues and the dance but me. He jumped down and held out his hand, nodding his head toward my rifle. I looked into his eyes and shook my head no. He smiled, reached over and grabbed the rifle, then hit me in the head with its butt.

I came to, slung belly down, like a deer carcass, tied to the rump of a galloping horse. My head bounced and jostled and hurt. I had the impulse to touch the tender spot where the rifle butt had made its impact but found that my arms were trussed to my feet, the rope passing beneath the horse's belly.

The ground below was orangey and rocky and hard and dry, when the horse slowed down enough that I might get a glimpse of it, and then, when the Indian above me urged the horse to pick up its pace, the ground was hidden by billows of dust. I felt something soft whipping into my face, and I turned my head to find that it was hair from one of three scalps tied to the belt of the Indian. The scalps were fresh, the skin around them raw and dark with blood.

My stomach lurched and my last meal, the rabbit I had been eating just before the attack, came up, leaving a burning residue of bile in my mouth. I spit and then spit again, and apparently a bit of it landed on the moccasin of the brave riding the horse behind me, for he rode up and thumped me hard on the back with his bow. A shower of pain sparked across my skin and I realized that I was sunburnt, for I was still naked, my butt and back taking the full beating sun.

I raised my head and looked to my right at the foot and leg of the brave mounted on the horse with me, avoiding as much as possible the sight of the scalps. The foot was moccasined, the leg without hair, the calf bunched with muscle, the skin bronze.

Others rode beside us, the horses' hooves kicking up dust, causing me to blink against the grit in my eyes. A herd of horses without riders also traveled with us, and it took me a moment to realize that some of these were mine. I saw Spring Dance and Cups among them. I saw Mo's mules.

My stomach lurched again, but nothing came up. With each involuntary heave, the rope strained against my feet and arms, cutting into my skin. At last I lay still, my stomach settled, as settled as it could be under these circumstances.

We entered a brushy area; mesquite bushes

362

scratched and stung at my legs and arms and neck. I felt blood dribble and then cake along my calves and forearms. I closed my eyes now. Watching the ground go by only made me dizzy, and I feared a mesquite might brush against my face and lodge a thorn in my eye. I tried to will my body to rest. I tried to loosen my spine just as Sedge had taught me to do when riding bucking broncos. And I tried, as I was bounced along, to remember all that Mo had told me about dealing with the Indians, all the inane and puerile bits of advice he had given, other than kill yourself before you get captured, for it was too late for that.

The truth is I had never fully trusted Mo's information, but I had nothing else to go on. He had of course been wrong about one thing. The Indians were not so put off by my hair that they would leave me alone.

Be brave, I remembered Mo saying. Don't show fear. The Indians admire courage. If they offer you something to eat, take the raw meat.

At this thought my stomach lurched again and my mind turned to torture. Cut off your nose and your fingers and your dick, Mo had said. Cut holes in your arms and run leather thongs through and hang you from a tree.

I seed it, I heard Mo's voice say. *I seed it.*

"Mo." I heard my own voice. It sounded so faint that I could not believe it had come from me. "Mo."

Don't call fo' yo' mama or yo' God. Be brave. Don't show fear. If they offer you food, take the raw meat.

Be brave. Don't show fear. Take the raw meat.

Be brave. Don't show fear. Take the raw meat.

Somehow I fell asleep with Mo's voice chanting through my mind. When I awoke again we had stopped traveling. It was night. I felt the rope being loosened from my body and then I was dumped on the ground. I rolled onto my back. Above me were a pale gibbous moon, and the braves standing around me in a ring. They were but dark shadows in this faint light. I pulled myself to my knees, and tried to stand, but my legs would not support me. They were as flaccid as strips of flannel cloth, and as I slumped to the ground I heard the Indians laugh.

I tried again, and again my legs caved out from under me, and again the Indians found this entertaining. One of them stepped forward and lifted me by my arms and stood me before him. As soon as he let go I crumpled to the ground. They guffawed at this, and stood around me laughing at my misery, and then once again one of them lifted me up and stood me before them and again I fell.

They laughed as if they were children and I a trick toy. They slapped their thighs. They lifted me again and again and they never tired of the game until at last my legs held, and I stood there in front of them swaying like a reed. One of them, he was wearing my hat, reached over and touched my shoulder, and I grabbed his hand and removed it from my person, and this they thought hilarious.

And then another of them suddenly stepped forward and before I knew it I was on the ground again, and my feet were tied together with strips of rawhide, and then my hands behind my back. He pulled me upright, and I stood there wobbling, willing the muscles in my legs to gain strength before the next abuse.

It seemed they had camped here before, for my bed for the night was already prepared, two forked sticks driven into the ground. A long pole was pushed through the rawhide tying my hands and feet, and two of them picked me up by this pole, and set it in the forked sticks so that I was suspended like a sow, but with my face to the ground, my back arched. Apparently they did not consider this to be painful enough, for one of them placed a heavy rock on my back, and as he did so, I willed my voice to be silent. I willed my body not to respond with any sound.

I could see, after the rock was placed on my back, their feet standing around me. They were looking at me. I stayed silent. I forced my breath into shallowness, for deep breaths were excruciating with this weight on my back. They made noises to each other and turned away. One of them said something in a language I did not understand and then I heard them moving about.

Soon I saw the light of a fire flickering across the ground. I could tell by this light and by the fact that its heat did not reach me that it was a small fire. I could see the shadows of the Indians settling down around it. They conversed in their strange language, paying no attention to me that I could tell. I am certain that they had no food this first night out, for I smelt no meat cooking, and heard no grease dripping into the fire, and I think I would have heard chewing or grunts of satisfaction had they been eating raw meat. Eventually the flickering shadows of the fire died down, and I heard the Indians, one by one, settle in to sleep.

I spent the night thus. If you think hanging can hurt me compared to this, you are wrong. The rock that had been placed on my back was nearly the circumference of a large fry pan. I wished it were a fry pan for a fry pan would not have been so heavy. The rock pressed into the small of my back until it felt like a thousand people were sitting on me, causing the rawhide to pull at my legs and arms and cut into my skin. I sagged toward the ground but I did not touch it. My head hung down. The only thing that I could move was my neck, and I occasionally stretched it, although this movement sent sharp knives of pain into my shoulders and down my spine.

I had not yet let out so much as a whimper, and I vowed that I would not. I would not show fear. I would not show pain. These were the only two things I had within my power, and I would use them. I was sure that in order to do so I must stay awake. When I felt myself passing out I forced my neck to move just a little, the excruciating arrows of pain a welcome fix on consciousness. I expected the pain, and I sucked in my breath as it hit me. But I did not cry out. I never once cried out. All night long, whenever I felt myself nodding, I again moved my neck and caused the sharp pain that would keep me awake.

This travel between the worlds of consciousness and unconsciousness required, ironically, that I be exceedingly conscious, that I not allow myself one speck of comfort, and that I concentrate on everything my body was feeling; the rock, the unnatural arc of my back, the stiffness of my limbs, the soreness of my skin, the rawhide cutting into my wrists and ankles. And so I spent the night wandering to the rim of senselessness, the rim that bordered the canyon of relief, and forcing my way back from it every time.

Daybreak came. The light gradually changed. The ground in front of me became a little more visible. I heard the Indians stir. One came to me. I could see his feet standing at my right shoulder. One foot lifted and the rock was kicked off my back, a large swath of sunburnt skin taken with it. But I made no noise, not of pain at the abrasion, nor of pleasure at having this weight removed from my back. I made no noise at all. The Indian reached into my hair and pulled my head up, and then seeing that I was alive, he pulled a knife from a sheath held by a belt around his waist. He held the knife to my throat and slid its blade across, just barely pressing into my flesh, so that a thin line of blood bubbled along my neck. I showed him no fear. I gave him no satisfaction.

It is true that I had made up my mind that this is the way I would be, but it is also true that at that moment I would have welcomed death. Lying in the desert with my throat slit, my blood pouring onto the dry, orangey earth, my body food for the vultures would have been a welcome change. The Indian grunted at my lack of response and moved his knife to my back and quickly cut the rawhide strips.

I fell to the ground with a thud, the impact nearly knocking the breath out of me. I rolled onto my back. I tried to move my arms to the front of my body but they were empty of blood and I could not make them move. It was as if they were dead, yet somehow still attached to me. The Indian reached down and lifted one and then the other and laid them on my chest, and then he walked away, his moccasins making soft padding sounds against the earth.

I lifted my head to look at my hands. My wrists were bleeding from the rawhide strips. I could feel that my ankles also bled. I lay my head back and closed my eyes. I could hear the Indians moving about, the horses nickering, the Indians speaking to each other words I could not understand. I did not know if they were preparing to leave, or preparing some new abuse, but for the moment, no one bothered with me. I opened my eyes and stared at the pale blue sky. A bird circled high above. I dared not close my eyes again, for I still feared unconsciousness.

I decided that if they did not kill me, if we were to travel again, then I would sleep on the back of the horse. Slowly the tingling of returning blood filled my arms and legs like a thousand pinpricks. I tried again to move my limbs but was unable. I kept waiting and trying until finally I found that I could lift my right arm, and then my left, and my feet, and legs. I sat up, teetering.

It looked as if we were to travel, for they were breaking camp, and gathering the horses, and placing blankets and saddles onto their backs. Soon enough one came to me and lifted me and placed me on the back of a horse behind another warrior. I was grateful to be placed upright this time. My feet were lashed together, the rope running under the horse's belly. My hands were placed around the brave's middle, and he clamped his arms down against mine in a muscled vise. I tried to move them but found that I could not, and he laughed as I discovered this. It seemed as though they had nothing better to do than laugh at me.

I'd had nothing to eat or drink since before my capture. My muscles cramped with dehydration, and my stomach rumbled with hunger. The torture of the night before transformed itself into another sort of torture as my body tried to readjust to this new position, my back no longer forced into an arch, but straight. This Indian I had been placed behind must have been the same Indian I had ridden behind the day before, for I recognized the scalps tied to his belt, the hair now tickling my knee. I looked down at them.

One was a long braid of dark hair, another a drift of golden hair, the third long brown hair, and from it a comb dangled askew. The scalps, I noticed, were starting to stink. I felt my stomach lurch again. There was nothing to come up, for which I was thankful, for who knew what might have happened had I vomited onto the back of this man.

I pushed the rising stench of the scalps away. I knew not what they had in mind for me tonight, but this was my time to rest. I was about to lean my head against the man's back when I saw that his hair was crawling with lice. It seemed likely though that getting lice was the least of my problems and so I went ahead and leaned my head against him. He made a small humming noise, deep in his throat, but he made no effort to dislodge me from this position. I closed my eyes and I slept with the stench of the scalps drifting into my nose.

It was afternoon when I awoke. The sun, at its zenith, baked onto my neck. I was still naked, and scorched, and the air was a dry heat that traveled like an avalanche of gravel down my throat, causing me to cough, which turned my windpipe into a tunnel of fire. I began working my mouth, trying to produce spittle, some slight bit of moisture, but there was none.

For the rest of the day I went in and out of consciousness. I remember telling myself that I should orient to the sun, I should determine the direction we were traveling in case I had the chance to escape, but the surrounding land was so strange and haunted that I could never tell if I was dreaming or hallucinating, or if everything I saw was real.

I remember flat scrubby earth stretching all around me. Stunted trees twisted and hanging on to ledges as if they were sentries watching our passage. A place with piles of human bones bleached to a blinding white. An antelope with the mask of a white man springing across our path. Large rocks rising out of the ground like an army of tremendous statues whose legs were buried in the sand, and whose heads had long ago rolled off and been lost. In the distance two round caves in a cliff like the hollow eyes of a ghost.

It was all so extraordinary; I cannot tell you, even now, what was real and what was not. I saw that antelope wearing that mask. If I close my eyes, I see it still. I will not say it was a hallucination, for it seemed no more peculiar than the land itself.

I do not know how many miles we traveled that day, or any day. The Indians kept up a relentless pace. We tore through the country, a cloud of dust kicking up as we went. I fell asleep once again, and was awakened this time by a slowing in pace. I opened my eyes and saw only the flat land, and the big sky, and then suddenly a gash opened in the ground, and we were traveling down into a small canyon. I could feel the air become cooler and I smelt the water before I saw it, a wide stream shimmering in the sun. I leaned toward it, and the Indian in front of me said something and pushed my body back with his.

When we reached the stream the horses waded in and bent their heads down to it and drank. The Indians, including the one I sat behind, slid out of their saddles, their feet splashing as they landed. They bent and cupped the water to their mouths. They left me tied onto the horse, and sitting there, wanting the water I could not reach, was as torturous as anything they had done yet.

My body yearned for this water. My eyes could see it. My nose could smell it. Drops of it hit my legs as one of the Indians playfully splashed some toward his companion. The horse I was on wandered a little ways upstream, placing the Indians behind me. I looked up at the canyon walls. The sun peeked over the edge now. I leaned over and tried to reach the rope tied around my feet beneath the horse's belly, but could not. I heard the Indians speak to each other and finally I heard one of them splashing his way toward me. He grabbed the horse's mane and led it back downstream. There he untied me and I fell into the water and drank of it like a dog. After I'd had my fill I rolled onto my back, and let the stream cool my sunburnt skin.

It occurred to me then that I could perhaps let the stream carry me away. The Indians were once again paying no attention to me. But I still could not swim, and I was weak with hunger, and the canyon walls were steep around me. I had no clothes, no rifle, no knowledge of where I was, so I just lay there in the shallows, the horses wading around me, and bending their necks and dipping their snouts into the water and raising them with droplets falling and glistening in the sun.

After a time one Indian waded into the stream and began taking the saddles off the horses. I had not noticed the three antelopes, two babies and their mother it looked like, slumped on the backs of some of Mo's mules. The Indian untied the carcasses and I sat up to watch. Soon I heard the crackle of a fire and I smelt meat cooking and I saw the antelopes roasting on spits across the flames. I stood and waded toward the meat. I did not think. I reached for some, even though it was not fully cooked. One of the Indians slashed my hand with his knife. I reached with my other hand, and again he slashed me. Then I sat and watched the food cook.

It was not long before one of them stood and said something, and they all stood and looked toward the eastern rim of the canyon. Three of them pulled spyglasses from their bags and peered into the distance with them. I had not noticed before that they had spyglasses. They passed them around to each other and pointed them east. After a time they settled down again and started speaking to each other, and it was not long before I heard a collective yelp coming from upstream. The Indians stood again, and let out an answering call and soon another party of braves appeared herding another group of horses. There must have been fifteen more Indians, and the horses they herded numbered in the thirties.

All the Indians gathered around the fire now. The antelopes were taken off the spit and they tore into them, ripping off pieces of meat and pulling the bones apart. They ate their fill and I watched. Occasionally they looked at me. I sat there, naked and hungry. I did not make a noise. I did not whine or beg. I would not do this.

After some time they had filled themselves and one of them lay a stick on the fire and they sat back and started talking. They looked at me and gestured toward me as they spoke. I sat impassively. I'd had good practice for this in my life as a slave.

They continued to talk. After a time one of them gestured to me, nodding his head toward what was left of the antelopes, and I fell upon one, ripping the paltry strips of meat left on the bones off with my teeth, chewing and swallowing almost simultaneously, gulping it down as if it were air. They let me have what was left, although I was still hungry, for they had eaten most of it. Then I was tied up again, this time in a sitting position, feet to hands. They made their beds all around me, and fell asleep.

Once again I tried to stay awake through the night, and I managed for some time, listening to the rise and fall of the Indians' breath, watching their dark forms, the fire gently flickering its shadows, but my body, for the first time in two days, felt some sense of comfort, for although I was still naked and aching and burnt, I had at least had food and water. My eyelids drooped, and eventually I let my head nod and I fell asleep.

The next morning the two parties joined each other, almost thirty Indians now, and more than twice as many horses. For the first time I noticed that there were a few young boys among them, and that one of them was white. He spoke their language fluently. I wondered if I could get him alone somehow and talk to him, if he might help me escape, but it was a foolish thought. He was as thoroughly Indianized as if he had been born to them.

I do not know how many more days we traveled, for we went once again for a long period of time without food or water, and I became, once again, delirious and weak and unable to make sense of things. I do remember that each day, as we traveled, I was tied to the back of a horse behind the same brave, and that each night I was tied in a sitting position, feet to hands, and that this position tormented me. Every morning I could barely stand, and as the Indians prepared to break camp, I stretched and hobbled about in order to retrain my legs and back to unbend and carry me. On the last night out we camped near a spring and I was given water, but no food.

I did not know what day it was, or how many days had passed since my capture. I cannot tell you when we reached the Indian village, only that I'd had water the night before, and that as we drew closer to the village the party of Indians I was with let out yelps of joy, and urged their horses to go faster.

It was this that woke me from my slumber on the back of the horse.

We were at the edge of yet another canyon, this one larger than the previous one. Down below a mile or more of tipis lined one bank of a wide glistening stream, and on the other side a huge heard of horses grazed. I saw people moving about, and ropes of smoke from cook fires rising here and there outside the lodges. As we scrabbled down the face of this canyon, our horses turned sideways and picked their way carefully, occasionally dislodging a stone and sending it clattering into the basin. Our party was soon spotted and a great undulating cry went up from the women of the village. The Indians I was with whooped and hollered and as we approached people poured forth across our path, women and children and men, all chattering and smiling and welcoming their warriors home.

Mo's voice came to me again.

Don't call fo' yo' mama or yo' god. Be brave. Don't show fear.

There must be, I thought, thousands of them.

It was the women who went at me first. They surrounded me, cut my rope ties and pulled me from the horse and threw me on the ground, slapping me, beating me, kicking me. One fat old woman sat on my chest so that all the air pushed out of my lungs as she smacked her large hands against my head. All the while they kept up their shrill cries. I made no effort to stop them.

Off and on, when my ears weren't being boxed, the noises of the camp came to me, the muted sounds of men in conversation, erupting laughter, children chattering excitedly, the thunder of the horses' hooves as they were driven to the larger herd across the stream, and of course the women's shrieking as they continued to abuse me. And then the large she-devil sitting on my chest smiled at me and leaned back and reached between my legs with the intent of twisting my balls, and to this I quickly rolled over, dumping her onto the ground. The other women laughed and paused in their treatment of me, while the large woman pulled her skirt down and stood up and delivered one final kick to my thigh before stalking off.

And then, as though orchestrated, the women fell back, and a group of young bucks began charging at me, feinting with their lances as if to stab me, and at the last minute plunging their spears into the ground beside me. I lay still. They shot arrows all around me, but none hit, and soon enough this game ended and another began.

Two Indians whom I had not seen before hauled me up and dragged me to the center of camp. I felt blows and slaps as I stumbled along. I was taken to a pole set in the ground and my feet were tied to it, my hands clasped around it and lashed behind me. A boy ran by wearing my hat. Another stood in front of a tipi, closing my little noose around his finger. A third, he could only have been five or six years old, ran up and shot a toy arrow at me. I felt it bounce hard off my chest. An old man came up to him and smiled and patted him on the back. He then encouraged the child to try switching the bow to his other arm, and the child did so. I watched as he pulled another toy arrow from the quiver on his back, placed it in the bow, and fired it at me. Again it bounced hard off my chest, and the man praised the boy, ruffling his hair and smiling.

The party of men who had brought me in was standing off to the side. They seemed to fall into a discussion as to my fate, looking at me and talking, gesturing with their hands to each other. The Indian whom I had ridden behind said something to another, who then ran off and returned with a white boy, dressed in a buckskin shirt and leggings. He was not the same white boy who had been with the party that had brought me in. This boy was a little older and had red hair.

The man whose horse I had shared, the one who'd hit me over the head with the butt of my rifle, my Indian, for this is how I had come to think of him, handed the boy a pistol and motioned toward me. The boy walked up to me. He looked into my eyes. His red hair was long and crawling with lice, his skin leathery from the sun, his eyes hard and filled with loathing. He lifted the gun, and held it to my face. I stared at the barrel, trying to show no expression, although I was certain that this was it. I was about to die. The boy pulled the trigger, and a black powder exploded across my skin, for unbeknownst to me, and possibly to him, the lead had been taken out of the shell. I dipped my head down to my shoulder in order to wipe the powder away from my eyes. "Yay," my Indian said, and they all looked at each other and nodded.

The women scurried off and returned carrying loads of sticks and kindling, which they piled at my feet. Dying, I realized, would be a welcome relief, and then I thought of Chloe. I wondered if I still had her button around my neck. I could not remember feeling it when I came to, slumped across the rump of the horse following my capture, or if it had been there the night they suspended me between the forked sticks with the rock on my back, or if I'd felt it anywhere along the journey to this village.

Why would I have felt it? My body was feeling so many other things. But now, as the women continued to pile sticks at my feet, I thought that perhaps the strip of leather that held it had broken, and Chloe's button now lay somewhere, the same as her bones lay, alone in the frontier. If I must die this way, and it seemed as though I must, I wanted more than anything to have Chloe's button around my neck.

I felt my fingers straining with a memory of their own, trying to reach up and touch it. But with my hands tied, I could do nothing. Instead I concentrated on that one small part of my body, trying to isolate it from all the other parts still screaming at me from stings and slaps and kicks and aches and the scrape of kindling being piled against my sunburnt calves. At last I felt it, the small weight of it against my throat. I straightened and looked out over the village.

The men who had captured me were still gathered in a clump, surrounded by other men now. I watched as one gestured. I could not understand the language, but I was certain he was telling the story of my capture, pointing to me and crouching to mimic me taking cover behind the rock, pointing to me again and raising his arms as if firing a rifle. He nodded, made the gesture again, and then pantomimed the night I was suspended between the poles with the rock on my back. The man pushed his foot forward and said something, and the others turned as a group to look at me. I recognized the storyteller as the man who had kicked the rock off my back and slid the knife across my throat, and he made this motion now, his finger sliding across his own throat, saying something. They turned again to look at me and they nodded to each other.

I focused my attention away from them. The scalps they had brought home now hung from the tops of long poles set in a tripod, and, except for the braid, the hair waved in the breeze. On the other side of the river, the great herd of horses grazed, peacefully bending their necks toward the grass in a lush meadow. The tipis were plain but beautiful. The sun hitting some made them seem as though they glowed. The two children who had been given my hat and my little noose were now chasing each other, fighting over their toys. A pack of dogs roamed between the lodges, and one wandered over to me, sniffed at the kindling piled at my feet, then lifted his leg and urinated.

I caught the eye of one of the women laying on sticks of firewood. She was young and pregnant. She smiled at me, and laid her sticks at my feet, and went to get more.

There was a great pile of tinder surrounding me now. One woman made gestures to me, telling me with her fingers flickering upward like fire, what they had planned. As if I had not already guessed. It would be painful. It would be very painful, but it would soon be over. My life would end here. We would see if I could keep my stoicism once the flames were leaping up my legs. For now I showed no expression. Another woman brought a burning stick. She jabbed it toward the kindling at my feet but she did not let it touch. I thought that once dead, there would be nothing anyone could do to hurt me again. I thought of Mo's last breath, of the way his voice had changed. "Sweetheart," he had said. If ever there was a time to believe in God in heaven, in being reunited with Chloe, then this was it. If heaven was true, and if I was going there, then I would welcome seeing her again.

The woman with the burning stick laughed and danced and jabbed its flame at me, but still I gave no response. I looked at her impassively, and she jabbed again, passing the flame quickly across my legs. I felt its heat and showed nothing. A great cry went up among the women, and one of them ran over to the men, jabbering and pointing to me. They came and gathered around me, and looked me over. The woman with the burning stick jabbed it again toward the tinder.

It is odd to think of it now. I had, at this point, given up on everything. I did not even feel the need to talk to myself about dying, about being brave and showing no fear. I felt as if I had perhaps already left my body. The movements of the villagers in front of me did not seem to be happening in a time in which I now lived. They were as if wading through water. The sounds — the women's excited cries, their jabbering, the call of a hawk above us, the conversations of the men in the language I did not understand — it all curled around me as if it were wind coming around the corner of my mind. I thought of Mo and Sedge, of Henry and Sup, of my mother and father and sister. I thought again of Chloe, of the first time I had seen her on the trader's display-room floor, of Master Wilson telling her to unbutton the bodice of her dress that he might examine his future property. I thought of her leaning against me in the barn at Lidgewood. I thought of the first time she came to me in my cabin, our falling together onto my pallet, the fire guttering in the hearth, the way the shadows flickered against her skin. I thought again of Mo calling for Geraldine before he died, of his hand curling around something. Behind me I felt my fingers close around Chloe's hand, for I imagined it there, her hand in my own, her breath on my neck.

It was just then that another raiding party

entered the village with more horses and scalps and another captive. The villagers left me there, tied to the post, and surrounded these men. The women made their excited noises. The men yelped and whooped. The braves who had just come in dismounted, and the women pulled the captive from his horse and beat him just as I had been beaten. I watched him roll on the ground, holding his hands and arms to his face. I heard him scream as the braves feinted at him with their spears. I saw two more scalps tied to poles. The hair rippled in the breeze, and I thought of Chloe's hair.

The captured horses were led away, and the captive was pulled to his feet and brought over to the pole where I was tied. He was dirty, thin and bearded, naked like me, a white man. The Indians kicked some of the kindling aside and tied him behind me and then pushed the tinder around his feet. I am going to die tied to a white man, I thought. And then I heard something. My name. "Persy?" the man was saying. "Persy? Is that you?"

I twisted my head. I could not see him of course.

"Persy?" I thought he said again. "From Sweetmore? It's me, Holmes."

I laughed. My mind was playing tricks on

me. The image of the women swam in front of me as they piled more wood around our feet. I thought of the river. How peaceful it had been to give in to it. I thought of the dough bowl, I thought of it as Chloe's dough bowl, floating along in that big wide river and bumping into me.

Biscuits. Pies. All kinds. Blueberry, peach, apple. With crusts all buttery and flaky.

Chloe. Chloe.

My fingers could no longer curl into her hand, for I was wedged up against this man now. And then the voice spoke my name again. "Persy?" it said. "Isn't that you, Persy? From Sweetmore? It's me, Holmes. We worked together."

I twisted my head again. By my peripheral vision I could see the man's wrists and forearms and muscles fighting and coiling against the restraints. Holmes? My mind was surely gone to have conjured up Holmes with whom to die. I laughed again when the woman with the burning stick returned.

"Persy," the man said again. "Get me out of here."

And then I heard my laughter cease and my voice say, "Show them no fear."

"What?"

"Show no fear. They admire bravery," I told the white man.

389

"Ha. Is that why you're here, about to be burned alive? For being brave?"

"Die your own way," I answered.

The woman pushed the flaming stick toward the kindling, and neither of us made a sound. She poked the stick closer, and then she prodded it into the tinder, once on each side, so that a thin blue plume of smoke began to rise at my feet, and another at the feet of the man behind me.

I heard the slight crackle of fire. I felt the heat against my toes. The Indians fell back away from us and watched, and then the Indian who had captured me started to argue and laugh with another. I could now see the fire, bright and orange, licking its way toward me. It climbed up my calf, and I fought against the pain, and then suddenly my Indian walked over and kicked the fire away, and we were cut off the pole and led away in different directions.

I was taken to a tipi where I was given a breechcloth and a blue wool shirt, as well as food and water. A bed was made for me of a pad of grass and thick buffalo robes and I fell into it, too exhausted to let the uncertainty of my situation keep me awake. I did not even know, until the next morning, that there were others, who had come later in the night, sleeping in the tipi with me: my

Indian, two women, and three children.

I was given food again, and more water, and I was led to the stream, where I bathed and soothed the burn on my leg. The Indian I was with, the man who seemingly owned the lodge I had stayed in, came to me and said something and looked at my leg. He grunted and splashed more cold water on the burn and said more that I could not grasp.

Back in the tipi I was clothed again, this time in buckskin britches. Every hair on my face was pulled out with a pair of bone tweezers, and this was as much torture as I had yet endured. Then my hair was cut with a knife, and two white streaks were painted across my cheeks, and I was led to an open area, and I saw that from the opposite side the man I had been tied to was being led here also, and that his facial hair was also gone, and that he was dressed as I was, and that it was indeed Holmes.

A crowd gathered around us, and my Indian pushed me into the arena while across the way Holmes was also pushed. We stood there, just staring at each other, and then Holmes said, "I think we're supposed to fight."

"All right, then," I answered.

"Persy," he said, "we can escape. We can

fake the fight."

The Indians yelled at us, and one of them came over and slapped Holmes. Then he grabbed Holmes by the arm, and motioned toward me and frowned, nodding his head at me again. I did not wait for Holmes to make the first move, for fight each other we must, and truth be told, I had no qualms about it. I fell on him. I fought him with all my might, for here before me was Holmes, and while it was not Master Wilson, he would have to do, wouldn't he, as the white man I would kill before I died?

Perhaps, though, I had already killed a white man, for I could never be certain during the war if I hit what I aimed for. But here, in this battle, there would be no question.

Yes, I killed him, and you may add that to your list of charges against me, although I do not believe it necessary at this point. He fought hard. It took some time. He muttered to me at one point that he did not mind killing a nigger, and I told him that I did not mind killing a white man, and there we were, scrabbling against each other, first one and then the other on top.

Around us the Indians yelled and jeered. Those who had bet on Holmes shouted and pumped their arms whenever he got me down, and those who had bet on me did the same whenever I got him down. I do not know how long the battle went on, but I remember my toes digging into the earth as I held him down, and I remember him getting his hands around my throat and squeezing the breath out of me until I got my thumbs into his eyeballs and pressed in so that he let me loose. And I remember that he rammed his fist into my face and knocked me down and began kicking me and that I then grabbed his leg and pulled him down with me. Blood ran out of my nose. We rolled in the dirt. He bit me on my shoulder and held on with his teeth until I tore loose from him, and then he spat a chunk of my flesh out of his mouth before continuing on.

It was meant to be a fight to the death, and it was. I felt life leave his body as I pounded his head against the earth, yet I kept on pounding. And then a last puff of dust rose up from beneath him as I let him drop.

The Indians quieted. I got off him and slumped onto the ground with my head between my knees. A brave came into the arena and pushed at Holmes with his foot. Then he shook his head and the Indians who had bet on me gave up a great cheer, and I watched as another man stepped into the arena, and picked up Holmes's head by his hair, and ran a knife around his skull. I heard the pop his scalp made as it let loose. The brave handed me the bloody scalp and I took it.

I took it, not because I was proud of what I had done, although I was not ashamed. I took it, not because I considered it a trophy, although that would come later. I took it simply because it was handed to me, and because I was tired, and because I was among people who held my life in their hands.

The Indians let out a great roar when I accepted the scalp, and then a teenage boy stepped into the arena and dragged Holmes away by his feet, his head leaving a bloody furrow in the dirt.

In spite of what is said about me, I am not an insensitive man. I know that my search for Chloe after the war was just one among many searches for loved ones. I know that families were never reunited, that husbands and fathers and brothers never came home. I know that men and women disappeared into the frontier, their fates unknown. I helped, sometimes, to make this happen.

But I have not forgotten what it is to scour

the land looking for someone, and even if that person is dead, to want to know the truth about that death and where or if she is buried. So I will tell you, in the event some relative is looking to learn the fate of an uncle or a father or a brother or a son, and thinking that perhaps the man I killed is he, I will tell you now that I never knew his full name, nor that he had any family, and I do not know from where he was captured. I only knew this man as Holmes, one of Master Joseph Wilson's overseers on Sweetmore Plantation, Saint James Parish, Louisiana.

The white boy who had fired the pistol at me led me back to the tipi. He pried my fingers loose from their grasp in Holmes's hair and said things in the Comanche language I could not understand. I nodded, thinking he was telling me that the scalp was not mine to keep, hoping he was saying this, for I did not want it. The boy also nodded, as if we understood each other. He set the scalp aside, and then he cleaned my wounds with a wet cloth and spread salve across the tear in my shoulder and the burn along my leg. I tried to speak with him. "Where are you from? What is your name? How long have you been with the Indians? What do they have planned for me now?" He looked at me strangely and shook his head. If he had ever known my language, he did not know it now.

Before he left the tipi, he set beside me a bladder of water and a bit of food, strips of dried meat and hardtack. I lay back on the bed of buffalo robes. Outside I could hear the movement of the camp: the hooves of horses, the occasional growling fights of dogs, the strange language. The top of the tipi walls glowed red with the fiery slip of the sun and then faded to pink and amber. The flap opened and a young woman stepped in. She nodded to me and built up the fire in the middle of the floor. She saw that I had not eaten the food, and pushed it toward me with the toe of her moccasin, nodding and saying, *"Tuhkuh. Tuhkuh."*

Her meaning was clear. "Eat."

I thought that perhaps the food was poisoned, for even though I had eaten the food offered the night before, and even though the boy who had tended my wounds had been tender with me, and this young woman seemed genuinely concerned, I had seen enough already to believe, now that my fight with Holmes was over, that I was of no value to these people.

She pushed at the food again, and then she sat down on the buffalo robe beside me and picked up the strip of meat. She took a bite out of it, chewed and swallowed, then handed it to me and I took it. She did the same with the hardtack, and I took that too. She nodded and stood, and then reached into a fold in her dress and held out her open palm to me. In it was the little noose. I took it from her, and she nodded again and opened the flap to the tipi and stepped out into the night. I never did get my hat back.

Outside I heard gunfire close by and the squeal of mules. I lay listening, wondering if soldiers had come, and if I would be rescued. Then, just as quickly, the thought crossed my mind that I might be arrested for the death of Holmes. But there were no more gunshots, and I know now that the tribe was slaughtering a few mules in their herd in order to have something to eat.

This was the year of 1868, and there was a shortage of food among the tribes. I did not know this as I ate the food that had been left for me. I then lay back on the buffalo robes and slept. It was still night when I woke.

Someone had tended the fire in the tipi, and it crackled cozily and made shadows on the walls and the smoke drifted up in a twisting column to the vent in the top. Light from a larger fire outside flickered against the upper walls, and against this light huge shadows occasionally loomed and glided as a person outside crossed by.

I felt something in my hand and opened

my palm to see the little noose the woman had returned to me. I had no place to put it. The buckskins I had been given to wear had no pockets. Mo's haversack was gone. I untied the rawhide strip from my neck and strung the little noose next to Chloe's button. My shoulder, where Holmes had taken his bite of me, throbbed as I did so.

It took some time for me to decide that I should step outside the tipi and meet whatever fate the Indians had in store for me. There seemed to be no escaping it. There was nothing I could do for myself. I had no horse, and no gun. Chloe was dead and I thought that I might as well also be dead. I no longer even cared about showing bravery. I would scream and cry if I wanted, and then, once my breath had left my body, I would scream and cry no longer.

I rose and opened the tipi flap and stepped out into the night. There was a large fire off to my right, and many Indians were gathered around it. I smelt the roasted meat, and in spite of my bravado and determination to die, my stomach growled so loudly that it caused a brave walking by to laugh. He took my arm and led me to the fire and a place was made for me between two men. I was handed a bone full of meat. I took it. I fell into it, gnawing and chewing and swallowing all in one motion. It did not occur to me until later that this was one of Mo's mules.

The Indian beside me smiled and patted me on the back. They continued their talk. The strange words rose and fell around me. Their language sounded like stars would sound, but also like chunks of lard, and the wind in trees, and arrows zinging through the air. I could make no sense of it.

The white boy who had tended my wounds was across from me, with a group of boys around his age. They chattered and laughed and roughhoused. Among them were two more white boys, and across from me was a white man, and to my right a white woman nursed an infant. Captives. Captives turned savage.

I finished eating and continued to sit there. I wondered if I was still being held. It did not seem like it. I stood and grabbed my crotch, indicating to the man next to me that I needed to go relieve myself. He nodded. The fellow to my other side raised his arm and shooed me away, as if I had no need to explain myself. I walked a little ways off from the firelight and the camp and did my business.

When I turned back they were paying me no attention. They were eating, talking, and laughing. I took a few steps back from them and they ignored me. And a few steps again. I squatted there in the shadows, watching the firelight flicker on their faces, listening to their laughter and conversation.

The moon was full and high. I had no doubt that they could see me if they wanted to. I sat there ten minutes, twenty minutes and still they paid me no mind. The two men I had been sitting between shifted closer to each other, closing the gap where I had once been, and I understood in that moment that I was free to go if I wished. I stood and walked away toward the herd of horses and then I turned to look at them again.

A young woman stood and put more wood on the fire. As she sat back down, the man next to her patted her ass and she giggled.

I turned again to walk away. I faced the moonlight, the walls of the canyon, the vast open plains beyond. I faced the freedom to take my leave and return to my own life, but what was that life? Chloe was dead having never known freedom. Mo and Sedge also dead. I had traveled around Texas, and I had seen what white men were still doing to black men. Even if I made it out of Texas alive, what lay beyond it? I turned again and looked at the people gathered around the fire, the families, the children, the women, the men, the elders, the village. I did not know what sort of life I could make in the white world, and I would never know, for that night I wheeled away from it and walked back toward the fire. As I came up two men moved aside, not the two I had sat between before, but two others making a space for me, and I sat down and in this way I joined the Comanche Indians.

You will want to know, I am sure, what I thought lay ahead. It is not as though I reasoned it through while sitting in the canyon in the moonlight, watching my captors around the fire dine on Mo's slaughtered mule. Nor did I know what would be expected of me should I become part of the tribe. But this seemed to be what was being offered and I took it.

I have thought about it quite a bit since, and I believe that what I felt at that moment might have been akin to power, or at least to the potential of power, and this was not something I had ever felt at any other time in my life.

Perhaps I had enjoyed killing Holmes more than I have admitted to you. He was, after all, Master Wilson's loyal underling, and for that, did he not deserve to die? It felt good to hold his scalp in my hand, to wrap my fingers into his hair, to let his blood drip onto my leggings.

I cannot say for certain what the tribe saw in me, but they needed warriors. They needed brave men, and I had shown this quality. But a brave man must also be a man willing to help protect the tribe, a man willing to hunt and bring home the buffalo, a man willing to fight the soldiers, a man willing to raid the settlements, to steal horses and cattle and mules, to kill white men, to kidnap women and children. A man who would not mind running a knife around the skull of another human being and popping his scalp off. I became such a man as this.

The next morning my Indian woke me by nudging his foot into my ribs. When I opened my eyes I found him standing above me, a leather bag strapped across his chest and a pistol stuck in his belt. He motioned for me to follow him. Outside his horse was already saddled, and his shield propped nearby. He picked up the shield, grabbed the horse's reins, and began walking.

It was early. There was scant light, but already cookfires were smoking and tipi flaps propped open. Men sat on a blanket outside one lodge, throwing what looked like dice. Two dogs growled and fought over a bone from last night's mule. Three boys chased one another, each with a quiver of toy arrows on his back and a bow slung across his shoulder.

A woman who was scraping a hide looked up and smiled at me, nodding an acknowledgment before bending back to her work.

An old man came up to me. His chest was shriveled and hairless. He touched my wounded shoulder and said something, and then stepped aside. We passed a group of young women carrying bladders of water from the creek, and they looked at me and leaned into each other and giggled.

The man I followed paid these people no mind. We waded across the river, and through the herd of horses. I had never seen so many horses, and as we plowed through them I looked for Spring Dance or Cups, but among such a large herd I could not pick them out.

I looked up at the canyon walls as we walked. It was a deep canyon. I would learn later that the Mexicans we traded with called it Palo Duro. In 1868, the year of my capture, your soldiers had not yet seen it, and for the Comanche it was a place of absolute safety. I felt a sense of peace and contentment there. I cannot say why. After all, I still did not know my fate with these people, and a man with a pistol in his belt was leading me to a place I was uncertain of. Even so, I took a deep breath of the cool morning air and let the spirit of the Palo Duro settle over me. The sun now peeked over the rim and shredded into rays that fell in stripes across the canyon floor.

The Indian stopped. We were in a large scruffy field, away from the village and the herd. He let loose of his horse's reins and it wandered off to graze. He then pulled the pistol from his belt and handed it to me, holding it by the barrel. He pulled the bag off his shoulder and opened it, showing me a stock of bullets and dropping the bag on the ground at my feet.

He turned and walked several paces away before turning to face me again. He held up his shield and made motions with his index finger and thumb, shaping them like a gun. His thumb went down. "Pow," he said. He lifted his shield and nodded. "Pow," he said again. And then he held the shield in front of him.

Was I to shoot at him? I looked at the gun, and back at the Indian, and shook my head no.

He nodded slowly and made the gesture with his finger and thumb again.

I raised the pistol, and pointed it at him, and then let it drop.

He shook his head, made a string of sounds I could not understand, and then made the gesture again with his fingers. "Pow," he said.

I raised the gun and pointed it at him. He nodded, and spread his legs a bit apart, and held the shield up to his chest. I squeezed the trigger, but at the last minute lifted the gun so that the bullet went above him. He frowned, came to me quickly, and smacked me across the cheek. Then he returned to his position.

I raised the gun, took aim, and fired. The Indian, I would later learn his name was Thin Knife, quickly moved the shield. The bullet pinged off it and bounced into the grass. He nodded at me again, and held his shield up. I squeezed the trigger, and again he deflected the bullet. I shot at him until the chamber was empty.

While I reloaded, he caught his horse and mounted and indicated that I should shoot at him as he rode. I did so. He moved masterfully. The bullets thumped into his shield and bounced off into the grass, some of them reflecting the sunlight and falling like little stars.

I fired the last bullet and he rode back to me. He dismounted and held out his hand for the gun. I passed it to him. He looked me in the eye and smiled and handed me the shield.

This was the way of the Comanche. They did not teach gently. There was no theory or discussion, no diagrams drawn in the dirt. To learn to use a shield effectively I must be shot at. I would succeed or I would die. It was as simple as that.

I succeeded. At first I thought I needed to see the bullet in order to deflect it, and of course I was worried, for can a bullet fired from a gun be seen? I was to learn though, that so much depends not on the eyes, but on the instincts, and perhaps on magic.

I have spoken of power, but I have not spoken of magic. I do not believe in prayer and incantations as much as I am told I should, but magic is what I felt as I rode Thin Knife's horse across the field that morning. The horse was fast, and responsive, moving this way and that with only the slightest prod. The shield felt as though it was telling me what to do, rather than the other way around. The shield felt alive in my hand, like a snake, as I lifted it to meet each bullet.

As we returned to the village Thin Knife reached over and patted me on the back and said something. Something friendly, I thought, delivered with a grin and an approving nod of his head.

I was given the bed where I stayed that first night.

I was given clothes and food.

I was given Mo's haversack as my own once again, empty of its contents now.

And I was given my name. Kweepoonaduh Tuhmoo. Twist Rope. Named after the little noose I wore now next to Chloe's button.

A week after my arrival in the canyon I saw vultures circling in the air. Perhaps they were circling the body of Holmes. Already my fight with him seemed a long ways back. I lay in my bed at night and looked at the stars through the smoke vent in the lodge. I watched the moon closely, for it, and the hair on my face, was my only connection to the passing of time. And then it was just the moon, for as soon as my beard began to grow back, I was thrown to the ground and sat on, while once again every hair on my face was tweezed out.

Thin Knife seemed to have adopted me, and I shared his lodge with his family: his wives Feather Horse and Crawls Along and their children, a son named Salt, a daughter named Elk Water, and another daughter named Fall Up.

It took me some time to discern who was mother to whom, but at last I worked it out that Crawls Along had given birth to Salt, and Feather Horse, who was Thin Knife's first wife, had given birth to Elk Water and Fall Up. I would estimate that at the time of my capture, Salt was about three years old, while Elk Water was nearly seven, and Fall

Up about five.

Thin Knife was a short man, although not as short as Mo had been, and muscular, with an angled face and dark matted hair. He had hit me over the head with the butt of my rifle, had participated in slinging me between two poles and placing a rock on my back, had watched as the women piled tinder at my feet. He had bet on me in the fight against Holmes. And he bet on me still. Every day that he was not otherwise occupied, he gave me a lesson in survival and skill.

I do not wish to make my assimilation into the tribe seem easy. It was not easy. It was not quick. It took time for many in the tribe to trust me. It took time to become the warrior I am today. It took time to learn the ways of my new family, the customs, the food, the culture, the language. But I was immersed. There was no leaving. There was no turning back. I had made my choice when I turned away from escape into the plains, and instead had sat in the space made for me around the communal fire. I knew that I had made this choice, and I lived with it.

Assimilate or die. Merge or separate. Learn or perish.

Thin Knife and his friends, upon finding

out that I could not swim, tied a rope around my middle and threw me into the deep part of a river. At the point of nearly drowning, they hauled me out, smacked the water out of my lungs, and threw me in again. After five times, I had figured out how to swim.

I learned to use a bow and arrow. I learned to use them well, with deadly accuracy, and with either hand, just as I learned to fire a rifle with either hand. I learned to hang on to a horse galloping at full speed, by one leg slung across its back, my body hanging down, pressed against the horse's side so that its body provided cover in battle. I learned to ride up close to the enemy this way and to shoot an arrow or a gun from beneath the horse's neck. I learned to do this without breaking speed. Eventually I learned to go days, weeks if necessary, without food, and I learned to find water in places where it seemed there was none.

It was the Comanche way of life to move, to leave one place for another. We often moved camp. There were many reasons to do this. Our horses were in need of fresh grass. We followed the buffalo during hunting season. We had favorite places to stay during certain seasons. We knew where we could get wild plums or grapes. We went to trading parties with Mexicans and with other tribes. We broke camp and disappeared after a raid. Sometimes a chief simply said it was time to go, and so we went. It took me some time to understand all this.

I had been with the tribe almost four moons when I went on my first raid. Thin Knife led the raid. I had learned enough of the language to know that he said it was time for me to prove myself, and that if I did not do so, there might be trouble for me. We were no longer camped in Palo Duro and were now out on the plains. We rode a long ways. It took many days to reach the group of cabins along the Llano River in Hill Country. It was daylight when we rode in. Down below were a cabin and a barn and three children in a wheat field chasing birds from the crop.

We stopped, and Thin Knife told me to stay behind. I was sure that the group I stayed with was watching me closely. I was sure I was being tested, that Thin Knife wanted to know if I would remain loyal to the tribe or break for the white settlement. I would have been killed had I tried to leave, but that is not why I stayed. I stayed because the Indians offered me something that had never been offered to me before. Here I could become a warrior, and a man of means, while down there, in that valley of white people I could never even be a man.

I sat on my horse and watched as Thin Knife's group wove their way down the hill. The vegetation sometimes hid them from view, and then they would appear again, and then disappear behind some scruff of growth. The children in the wheat field stopped and watched the riders approach. And then they ran and the Indians bore down on them. Two riders leaned over and scooped two of the children up. The third child dove into a thicket. The group looked for him, but before they could find him a man came out of the cabin and fired his rifle and Thin Knife raised his own rifle and shot the man. He rode quickly to him and scalped him and mounted his horse.

From there we rode to another cabin. I was left, along with another man, in charge of guarding the children. The boy was placed on the back of my companion's horse, and the girl on the back of mine. Her hands were placed around my middle and I clamped my arms down on them so that she could not move, the same way Thin Knife had once clamped down on my arms.

Off in the distance I watched as Thin Knife and the others entered the cabin. It seemed to be empty. They pulled a mattress out and ripped it open, and the feathers filling the air reminded me of Sweetmore, and of shooting my gun into Master Wilson's bed.

The cabin was set on fire. Five horses were stolen. We rode on. Two more raids on little farms and ranches, the cabins burned, one more scalp taken, a total of twenty horses stolen, all done within just a few hours.

We rode hard away from there. We put many miles between us and the white men who would surely come after us. We went through the hardest part of the country, where water was scarce. We confused our trail by doubling back on it, and we rode through the night. When we finally stopped, we did not build a fire. One of the men in our party had killed an antelope, and we ate it raw.

The girl we had captured, who shared my saddle, stayed quiet during our ride. She did not shiver or cry. She did not squirm to get loose. She would make, I thought, a good Indian.

How could I, you will want to know, I, a former slave who understood the experience of being separated from my parents, feel nothing for this child or any of the other children I lifted onto my saddle and carried away from their homes?

To this question I answer with a question of my own. Did the white man not understand what he was doing before selling children away from their parents? Did he not rip babies out of mothers' arms and pull crying, clinging toddlers away from their skirts? How convenient the memory of a white man is, and how inconvenient you wish mine to be. If we did not trade them, the children we took would become Comanche, while the children you took would always be slaves.

I, too, became Comanche. I did as the Comanche did. I ate what they ate, and I starved when they starved. I moved when the camp moved. I learned the language. I learned the signs we used with other tribes whose language we did not share. I learned to track the movement of animals and enemies. I learned to locate a buffalo herd, the tahseewo by the steam cloud of its collective breath on the plains.

We rode from Texas into Colorado. Utah. New Mexico.

Mexico. Kansas. Arkansas. Arizona. Nebraska. And we rode into what you call Indian Territory, that too-small squeeze of government land you had set aside for so many tribes to be held, and contained, and given rations at your agencies. We were not held or contained. We did not receive your rations. Our land was large and open, and we rode hard and far and often, and these are but some of the states and territories that I know we visited. The truth is we rode so much and pulled up camp so often and made so many raids that most of the time I did not know exactly where we were.

I remember rivers and mountains and prairies and plains. Salt licks and bee caves. Quicksand and dry lakes. Canyons and caprock and limestone ridges. I remember the black smoke of burning cabins, the squeal of pigs as we killed them, a brave dog filled with arrows, feathers filling the air as we dragged out and cut open bedding, for this was the way of a raid. Burn, destroy, kill. To this day I cannot see a feather floating in the wind without being reminded of it.

We met trading parties of Mexicans, and we swapped horses and sometimes captives for metal and cooking pots and blankets. And then we went to another place and made camp there, and we filed the metal into points and made arrows and lances, and then we raided again. If the soldiers chased us, we vanished. Sometimes we retreated across the Red River onto the government land where the agencies were, for at that time there was a policy forbidding the soldiers to follow us there, and we knew this, and we made good use of it.

By winter I had three scalps decorating my shield, the one belonging to Holmes and two others from men I had killed during two different raids. Thin Knife trained me well. He had seen, I suppose, that I could be counted on, that I would kill and take scalps, and that I would ride back into fire to pick up the wounded.

Thin Knife was generous with me. He gave me the buffalo hide with which to make my shield. He showed me how to crumple paper from stolen books and cram it between the two layers of hide to make the shield even more impervious to bullets. He let me take and keep a fine bow and quiver of arrows belonging to a Blackfoot he had killed, a warrior from a band that had raided into our territory. He shared his food with me, and I played with his children.

In a game of gambling with a man named Beetle, the man who had drawn his knife across my throat, I won back my horse, Spring Dance, and with Spring Dance I rode into more raids, and stole more horses, and in this way I became a man of some means.

I was never a wealthy man. I did not own hundreds of horses as some men did. I was never a chief or a leader or a medicine man. I was merely who I was. A good warrior, and that seemed enough to me.

I saw everything that Mo Tilly had warned me about. I saw death, and plenty of it. I saw bloody scalps lifted up onto poles as we danced around them. I saw children caught and turned into Indians. I saw the torture of our enemies. I saw the mutilation of bodies, the arms and legs of the dead hacked off and hung in trees. I saw the "utter degradation" of captured women, and I participated in all of it, except this last.

For this, I had not the stomach. Think of me what you will. It is true that I killed and scalped, and that sometimes the victim was still alive as I ran my knife around his or her head. It is true that I took children away from their parents. It is true that I participated in the grisly aftermath rituals of battle. But while I never stopped it, I also never participated in the rape of a woman. I merely walked away and tried to close my ears to her screams and pleading.

I had been with the band almost a year the first time the soldiers came into a village. It was in the fall. We were camped along the Washita River, and it was very cold, and a blanket of snow covered the ground. There were many Indians there, for it was not just Comanche, but also some Kiowa, and the entire winter encampment of the southern Cheyenne and Arapaho.

The Cheyenne chief Black Kettle's village was upstream from the Comanche, and it took the brunt of the attack, which came at dawn while the village slept. By the time we heard of it, the village was done for, many of its inhabitants killed, lodges looted and burned, and the soldiers, still not knowing of our presence, were shooting the horses, which ran off bleeding and dying into the snow.

I was among the warriors who mounted up and rode off for battle. These soldiers were stupid. They had not scouted well. They did not know, because they had not bothered to find out, that around the bend, downriver from Black Kettle's village, there were fifteen miles of tipis, each tipi usually housing at least six Indians. After seeing so many of us painted up and mounted, ready to fight, the soldiers retreated, and beyond a few skirmishes we could not engage them, but the damage for Black Kettle was done. He lay with his wife, both dead in a stream, splashed with mud from the soldiers' horses.

We rode through Black Kettle's village on our return to our own. I saw scattered across the ground the bodies of women and children. I saw outside a tipi, which was miraculously still standing, a woman with her baby on her back, both shot through. I saw the dark shapes of a thousand dead horses, their trails of blood mapping bright red rivers across the snow. Fires smoldered, tipi hides and buffalo robes tossed onto them, black smoke roiling into the sky, adding fumes to the stench of death and blood that filled the cold air. By the time we reached our village the women had broken it down. The horses and travois were packed, and we disappeared away from there.

I do not recall where we traveled after we left the Washita, but I can tell you this: it was after seeing the destruction of Black Kettle's village that I began to feel my life as a slave slipping off me, like a snake leaving its shed skin caught on the branch of a tree. I could feel that I was leaving it all behind me somewhere, empty and draped and forgotten.

The year that followed the death of Black Kettle was much the same as the first year, except that I was Comanche now. I was thoroughly Comanche, and nothing could change this.

So many nights I stepped out of the tipi and gazed at the stars thick in the sky above the plains. I listened to the ripple of the river we were camped along, to the sound of our thousands of horses milling about on the other side. It felt like I had lived with the people forever. It felt like I had been born to them. The breastplate I wore rested in just the right way across my bones. Memories of my mother and father, my sister, my early life in Virginia and my later life at Sweetmore, the war and even my search for Chloe, my life with Mo and Sedge, all this blended in my brain now into a stew of indecipherable ingredients. And yet here was this button, and here was this little noose, both of which I still wore around my neck on the leather thong I had made from a dead man's belt.

I had been with the people two winters, when one morning Thin Knife sat beside me outside the tipi and, reaching over, lifted Chloe's button from where it lay against my throat. He rolled it between his fingers. "What does this mean to you?" he asked.

I told him. My woman. Chloe was her name. A house slave. I hated the man who once owned us. He abused her. I was never able to get her from him. She is dead now, I said.

Thin Knife let go of the button and I felt it drop against my throat. "Perhaps you wear it too long," he said, and then he rose and left.

Moments later Crawls Along and the children left the tipi, and Feather Horse poked her head out and said, "Come sit with me, Kweepoonaduh Tuhmoo."

I went inside and sat across from her. She said, "You must get your own lodge."

"If you say I must, then I will," I answered, although I was hurt to be expelled like this. I had been happy these past few years living with Thin Knife, and I wondered why he wished me gone.

Feather Horse shook her head as if I had spoken this thought out loud. "No," she said. "It is not because we do not want you here. You will soon find a woman, and you must have your own tipi."

"What woman?" I asked.

"I see it," she answered. "I see a woman and you together, riding your horse. She loves you and cares for you and you must provide a home for her. It is all she's ever wanted, a home, with a man who makes her feel safe."

"There was a woman. I did not manage to keep her safe."

"I heard what Thin Knife said. He is wrong about the necklace you wear. The woman I see is happy that you have kept it and worn it so long. You must prepare for her. She is coming soon. I see it. You bring horses to Thin Knife, and Crawls Along and I will make you a lodge."

"How many horses?" I asked.

Feather Horse thought for a minute, then answered. "It will take fifteen skins to build you a good lodge. Fifteen horses."

"That is all I have."

"Get more."

"What if I bring you the skins instead and

you scrape them and sew them? Then how many horses?"

"Even more," she answered.

There was no arguing with Feather Horse. Vision or not, she usually got her way. So I went on more raids and I captured more horses and I gave them to Thin Knife in exchange for his wives' work on my tipi.

When Thin Knife heard of Feather Horse's vision, he suggested that his recently widowed sister-in-law Cocklebur might make a good wife. I was not interested, although Thin Knife said I might give it some time. He told me that she was too early in her grief to consider another husband. I replied that I was too early in mine as well. "You grieve this woman too long," he said. "It is not healthy for a man to mourn a woman so long."

Feather Horse was quiet, but when we were alone together again she said, "Cocklebur is not the woman I see. She is a fine woman. She would make a good wife. But she is not the woman I see."

"Tell me the woman you see," I said.

"You and Thin Knife should go gather poles for your lodge. This vision is very strong."

So Thin Knife and I went in search of a stand of cedar. We cut poles and I peeled them and let them season and trimmed sticks into sharp lacing pins. My work on the tipi was done, but when the work on the cover and the liner was completed, Feather Horse and Crawls Along kept it a secret from me. They wished to surprise me, and they did.

We were camped in another canyon. I remember it being west of a hill that was made of white rock, like a huge pile of salt, and that the river had stairsteps of wide flat rocks that the water ran over into pools below. I remember the musical sound of these little waterfalls filling the air. Two tribes had come together and there were many horses, and many tipis, all with their flaps open toward the east. I had gone out with a group to hunt buffalo. We were gone for five days, and we were successful. Crawls Along and her sister Cocklebur and some of the other women had traveled with us to process the meat and make it transportable back to our village. I myself had killed two buffalo, and I was proud of this. The meat had already been cut up and rolled into the hides by Crawls Along and Cocklebur. I would give some to Thin Knife's household and some to Cocklebur's in thanks for her help. Already, at our village, the scaffolds were built on which to hang thin strips of meat to dry for our winter provisions.

I remember riding into camp and hearing the women set up their trilling calls at our arrival. *Li-li-li-li-li-li.* They swarmed around us, patting the hides covering the meat on our travois, smiling and laughing. I dismounted, and a boy took my horse and led it away.

And then I saw it. A new tipi standing next to Thin Knife's. My shield sat outside the door. I stood staring at it. Feather Horse laughed and took my hand and led me inside. Thin Knife and Crawls Along followed, and outside many of the tribe gathered around as I entered my home for the first time.

Words fail in telling you the beauty of a tipi, and particularly my tipi. Its red cedar poles met at the top, the blue sky visible though the smoke flap. A bed had been made for me with a mat of fresh prairie grass and a buffalo robe. To one side of the door was a stack of buffalo chips, and to the other, a kettle and stabbing sticks and a buffalo horn ladle. I learned later that several people in the tribe had contributed these things to furnishing my household.

"Is he to cook?" Thin Knife asked. The group laughed at the absurdity of this.

"These are for his woman," Feather Horse

answered.

Thin Knife shrugged and shook his head. "You will eat with us until she comes. My wife says you will find your woman soon."

Feather Horse turned to me and held out her hands. "Give me your things," she said. I handed her my bow and quiver and Mo's haversack, and she hung them from the poles of my lodge.

And then I noticed, hanging from another lodge pole, a cradleboard, beautifully lined with raccoon fur. "Your faith in this vision is very strong to have made this," I said to Feather Horse.

She nodded.

"Perhaps you will have a son," Thin Knife said, clapping me on the back.

That night I lay alone in my new lodge and stared up at the smoke spiraling out toward the stars. I rolled over and stared at the empty spaces across the fire. Above the emptiness the cradleboard hung expectantly from a cedar pole. Outside the river ran over its rocks, gurgling and splashing.

I wanted to believe in Feather Horse's vision. I wanted to believe in it as strongly as she did, but I did not think I was ready to love anyone besides Chloe, and it seemed that I must sleep alone until I got ready. It was too quiet in the tipi. I fingered the button at my throat.

I remembered Chloe's fingers trawling the fabric of her dress as we sat on the deck of the steamer that was to take us across the Mississippi River. I remembered her begging Master Wilson as he held his gun on me. All I had ever wanted was to get her away from him, and I had failed, and now I was told that a woman was about to appear in my life, a woman who would make me happy, but I could not believe it. I stared again at the empty spaces across the tipi. I got up and placed another buffalo chip on the fire and watched the sparks rise into the sky. I missed my family. I missed listening to Thin Knife rolling around with one wife or the other. I missed the soft breath of the sleeping children. For the first time since I had been with the people, I cried, stifling the sounds of it against the fur of my robe made from the tahseewo.

The tribe took on a collective excitement over Feather Horse's vision. They were as happy for me as if my woman had already arrived, as if she were already heavy with my child. I could not speak my true feelings to any of them. I would not insult them in this way. I would not insult Feather Horse's vision.

As I walked through the village old men patted me on the back and nodded their approval. Old women smiled and tittered to each other. The young girls looked at me expectantly, and my friends pointed out various women as they walked by carrying firewood or bladders of water. When we broke camp and were on the move Thin Knife or Beetle would often come riding up to me and mention a name. "She is the one riding up there on the red horse. She would make a good wife."

I tried to go along. I tried to notice if a

woman was pretty, or seemed strong, or cared for her sister's children particularly well. More than once Thin Knife nudged me in the ribs when Cocklebur walked by. "She would make a good wife," he said again.

I shook my head.

"Perhaps her cousin," he said one day. "She is young. You would have to give some horses to her father."

I shook my head again.

"Kweepoonaduh Tuhmoo, you must get more horses. A woman is not easily acquired without horses. We should raid that settlement. What do the whites call it? The one near the edge of the plains."

"Drunken Bride?" I answered.

Thin Knife laughed, and then repeated the name phonetically, so that it sounded like the German I'd heard spoken in the Hill Country. "Drun-ken-bride. Haa. We should go there. You will need more horses."

Our village was then four days' ride from your little town. Many of the men chose to go on this raid, twenty or thirty of us. As we prepared to leave, the women surrounded us and smiled and laughed. The children called to their fathers to bring them something. Thin Knife leaned down from his horse and kissed his wives, and Crawls

Along held up the children for him to pat and say goodbye to. Feather Horse came over to me and laid a hand on my leg. "It will not be long," she said. She smiled and stepped back as I wheeled my horse around and we left the village.

It was a leisurely ride. There were no women with us, and I appreciated the reprieve from the constant commenting and nudging I had experienced in the village. Halfway there we stopped along a stream that seemed familiar to me, and Thin Knife told me that this was where I had been captured. I recognized it then, the boulder I had taken cover behind, and where Thin Knife had hit me in the head with the butt of my rifle.

Outside Drunken Bride we painted up and then rode right through your town, in broad daylight, right down the middle of the street. Two of our men stampeded the horses out of a stable, and let loose every one that was tied to the hitching posts. Another smashed the window of the store, and then dragged the merchant out into the street and stabbed him and took his scalp.

I chased a white woman on my horse, simply for the fun of chasing her. I did not want her. She did not know this, and I laughed to watch her run as I wheeled my horse in and out, in front of her now, beside her now, behind her now, on the other side of her now. She screamed and stumbled over her stupid skirts. She fell in the mud. I bore down on her as if I would scoop her up and carry her away with me, and then at the last minute I rode off, whooping and yelling. I wheeled again, turning around, as though I would come for her once more, and she scrambled away, and crammed herself under a house, her skirt disappearing like the tail of a rattlesnake.

The townsmen were shooting at us now, but they were panicked and shot wildly, and our medicine was good. A few captives were taken. Two young boys who were twins, and a young girl. A man was killed and scalped in the graveyard beside the church. Another in front of the jail. A third outside the saloon. I can look now through the bars of my window and see these places.

We rode on. The horses we'd stampeded were gathered into a herd. We stopped in a small ravine nearby and decided to split up, one party going with the horses and captives out into the plains for safety, the rest of us in the other direction, toward some of the farms outside of Drunken Bride. I went with the latter party.

We rode to a farm where again we stampeded the horses, then entered the house. There was no one there. We stole food and some red flannel and a Bible. We pushed over furniture. We broke dishes. We pulled the mattress out into the yard and cut it open, letting the feathers fly into the wind. We killed the pigs and left them there, for we did not eat pork. And then we set the house on fire and rode on.

At the next farm we found a man and a woman cowering in the loft of the cabin. We shot them and ransacked the house the same as we had done to the one before. We took the horses. I found and took two books, for I still liked to read, and once I had satisfied myself with them, I could trade them. I slipped the books into Mo's haversack.

It was late afternoon as we moved on to the next farm. We watched it from a distance. Smoke puffed from the chimney. There were three horses in a corral, and one of the boys riding with us sneaked down and creaked open the gate and let them loose. And then a man came wandering across the yard. A short man, singing "Old Dan Tucker." He was drunk, but I recognized his gait. I recognized his swagger. Thin Knife raised his bow, but I reached over and pushed the arrow down. "No," I said. "He is mine."

"Why should you have his scalp and not me?"

"He is the man who used to own me," I said.

Thin Knife nodded. "This one," he said to the other warriors, "belongs to Kweepoonaduh Tuhmoo." The men gave their agreement. I would be the one to kill the drunken white man singing his way across the yard.

Seeing Master Wilson there, right in the open, was almost more than I could bear. My past, which I thought I had shrugged off, flooded back into me. My memories became distinguishable and vivid again. The cane fields waving in the breeze. The hard handle of the knife in my hand. The stench of the swamp as I waded in to cut wood. Breech and his broken neck. The lash whistling through the air. The sound of the gun when Wilson shot me. The splash of river as I fell in. Chloe pleading with me to get her away from him.

I could have shot him right where he stood, but I wanted Joseph Wilson to die knowing exactly who had killed him. I climbed onto my horse and the rest of the warriors followed. We whooped and yelled and called out our war cries. The others surrounded the house while I rode down hard on Master Wilson. He fell to his knees. He had no weapon, nothing with which to defend himself. I held the point of my lance against his chest. I stared into his eyes. I enjoyed the terror I saw there. He begged for his life. "I am but a poor man," he said. "Please do not kill me."

And then the spirit that always passed between Master Wilson and myself trailed its cold fingers down my arm and into my own fingers clasped around the lance. Master Wilson began shivering.

By now my companions had entered his house. I heard furniture being overturned and dishes breaking. I heard the squeal of the hogs as they were killed. I heard gunfire, as my friends fired their rifles into the air. Chickens squawked and scurried all around us, while in the distance, a dog barked.

I kept my eye on Wilson. I kept the point of my lance pressed into his chest. I did not kill him yet. I watched and listened to him plead for his life, while inside the house was Chloe.

I did not know this of course, but she was alive and she was there. She had hidden herself tightly between a corner cabinet and the wall, a masterful hiding place that Wilson had built should raiding Indians ever

435

attack their farm. This must have been the only thing he ever did well on his own, the only thing for which I am grateful to him, but then he always did care about his property.

The corner cabinet was secured to the wall and could not be turned over, and the board covering the crack between the wall and the cabinet, the board behind which Chloe hid herself, could be secured from the inside. It was easy in the frenzied heat of a raid to overlook this little illusion.

"I have a woman," Wilson said to me. "You can have her."

I pushed the lance a little harder against his skin.

I laugh now to think of this irony, that he saved Chloe this way, saved her for me, and that he now offered her to me, if only I would spare his churlish life. And is it not also ironic that a man could build something such as this cabinet yet could not seal all the cracks in his cabin? As I held my lance on Master Wilson, Chloe was now able to watch through a crack at the corner of the house as he begged me for his life.

Did I look familiar to her, even with my war paint and my leggings and my breastplate? She knew now that I was alive, that I had not drowned in the river, for Master

Wilson had tortured her with this information ever since I spoke with him on the streets of Drunken Bride. And she had heard of the nigger Indian, for I had been seen raiding with the tribe. I had been seen killing a man. I had been seen lifting a child onto the back of my horse. I had gained a reputation among the Texans.

And now Chloe, from her hiding place, having heard all the talk of the nigger Indian, having been told by Master Wilson that I was alive and looking for her, suddenly realized who was on the horse, holding a lance against the chest of the man who had owned her and raped her and called her his wife.

And just as she realized it Master Wilson also realized it, for he suddenly looked at me and said, "Didn't I own you once?"

"My name," I said in English, "is Kweepoonaduh Tuhmoo, but you know me as Persimmon Wilson."

"I owned you," he said again, and it was right then that I ran the lance through his chest, and right then that I leapt off my horse and scalped him, and right then that Chloe pushed her way out from behind the corner cabinet and walked, somehow walked unharmed, through this din of warriors to me.

There was no time to think that what I was seeing might be an apparition. Indeed I did not even care, for real or not, this woman coming toward me was some semblance of Chloe, and I climbed onto my horse, and I stuck out my foot for her to step onto, and I switched Joseph Wilson's scalp to my other hand that I might hold this hand out, covered in the blood of a man she hated, to help her up.

She did not hesitate. Chloe did not hesitate. She took my hand. She stepped onto my foot. She slung herself up behind me, and she was real. Her body pressed against mine. Her warmth, Chloe's warmth covered my back. She reached her arms around my waist and held on. "Persy," she said. I could not speak. Around us the warriors circled and whooped and torched the cabin. The flames rose quickly into the air, the wood was so dry. Thin Knife came riding up beside me. He nodded and smiled and rode away, and I followed with Chloe holding on.

We rode hard away from Drunken Bride. We covered the distance, normally four days' ride, in two. We rode through the night, stopping only briefly for water and to change horses at the place of my capture. There was no time to talk with Chloe, no way to prepare her for the life I was riding her into. I did not even think of these things. I only felt her body behind mine, felt her arms circling my waist, felt her head lean against my back, and rode hard, away from Drunken Bride, away from the body of Master Wilson still pinned to the ground with my lance.

When we reached the village the women fell upon Chloe. They grabbed at her and I wheeled my horse around, kicking at them, calling out.

Kay. Kay. No. No. *Kwahee. Kwahee.* Back. Back. *Kay. Kay. Kwahee. Kwahee.*

The women moved away and stood watching and frowning. *Kwahee,* I said again, and I dismounted. Feather Horse pushed her way to the front of the crowd and watched as I helped Chloe down and set her on the ground. "It is his woman," she said to the people.

"Ahh," the women said, and they smiled and nodded and looked at Chloe, nudging each other and chattering.

"Kweepoonaduh Tuhmoo's woman is white," someone observed.

"This was not in my vision," Feather Horse replied.

"She is not white," I told them, and the crowd laughed.

Chloe clung to me. She did not raise her head to look at them. A boy came up and took my horse. The crowd parted as I walked her to my tipi, lifted the flap, and led her inside.

"Sit," I said. She looked at me. I did not realize I had spoken in Comanche. I motioned to my bed. She sat and ran her hand along the buffalo robe that covered it.

I built a fire. I brought her food and water. I squatted down across from her, watching as she pulled the meat off an antelope bone and gulped the water from a tin cup I had found during a raid. When she was finished I motioned that she should lie down. She shook her head. I knew what she was think-ing, that I would want to be with her. "You sleep," I said. "Just sleep. I will not bother you."

She frowned and shook her head again, and I realized again that I had been speak-ing Comanche. "Sleep," I said in English. "Just sleep. You must be tired."

She lay down and pulled the buffalo robe up around her, closed her eyes, and slept for most of three days. I suppose it was too much for her, that moment of realizing where she was. I suppose that she could not fathom how she had gotten here. I suppose she could not fathom whom I had become. I sat across from her for that entire three days, rising only to bring her water or help her outside to relieve herself. The rest of the time I watched the firelight flicker across her face, just as I had done that first night together in my cabin in the quarters of Sweetmore.

I could not resist sometimes stroking the backs of my fingers across her cheek as she slept. I lifted her hair and smelt of it. I climbed under the buffalo robes with her, and without waking, she settled against my chest. If she whimpered, I rocked her. If she cried out, I hushed her, speaking Comanche again without thinking. *Puh sooah-*

tsoomyee. He is dead. *Puh sooah-tsoomyee.*

But even as I lay with her, and held her, and comforted her I felt a great stabbing in my heart. That Master Wilson had lied to me was clear, and I was a fool for having believed him, but other questions plagued me. Why was Chloe at Wilson's house? There seemed to be no other former slaves on the property, so why had she not taken her freedom with the rest? Why had she stayed with the man who had repeatedly raped her and who had left me to drown in the river?

Still, I nursed her. I held her every night. I kept the fire going. If the buffalo robe slipped from her shoulder, I moved it back. I did nothing but watch Chloe and wait for her to wake up that we might talk. And on the fourth day she finally did. She looked around my lodge with an awareness of her surroundings that I had not seen in her eyes the previous three days. She seemed to know exactly where she was, and she gazed at the walls of my tipi, my bow and quiver of arrows hanging from one of the poles, the fire at the center of the lodge, me hunkered down across from her. "I reckon you wantin' to know what I doin' there," she said.

I nodded.

"I thought you dead. I seen you drown in the river. Then he tell me you in Drunken Bride lookin' fo' me."

I didn't understand, and I shook my head.

"I passin' fo' white," she whispered, bowing her head. "I passin' fo' his wife. You got any water?"

I shook my head. "I don't understand," I said.

She looked up and glared at me. "I need some water."

I complied, dipping some into the tin cup and handing it to her, and then sitting on the other side of the fire from her. She drank, and then put the cup down and wiped her sleeve across her mouth.

"I passin' fo' white," Chloe said again, this time looking straight at me. "All them folks in Drunken Bride, they think I be white. I passin' fo' his wife. I thought you dead," she said again.

And then she told me the story in its entirety. She told of watching me drown in the river. She told of Wilson raping her in the barn after the steamer landed. She told me of what he said. "You can have it this way, or we can make some other arrangements." And she told of the day she climbed into the wagon beside him, the day she became "Mrs. Joseph Wilson." She was the mother of his children, a boy and a girl. Both had died from scarlet fever, within weeks of each other.

When I found all this out, and when she cried telling me of the deaths of their children, I felt my heart rear up and gallop away from her. I could not help this. It was too much to take in. Chloe and Master Wilson living as husband and wife. Children. A family. "Can you fo'give me?" Chloe asked. "Fo'give me fo' marryin' him?"

I buried my face in my hands. Outside I heard Feather Horse and Crawls Along working and talking, the scrape of their tools across hides. Chloe whispered, "I done lost you, Persy. I don't know what to do after that. I care 'bout you, and he done shot you. He hold my head up and make me watch you drown. You was gone, and I headin' to Texas, and he . . . he havin' me all along the way. Somethin' snap in him when we leave Sweetmore. Somethin' go wrong with him, Persy. He meaner than he ever been befo'. He hittin' me now. He say he won't hit me no mo' if I let him make me white. I didn't know you was alive, Persy. I didn't know it."

I kept my face buried in my hands. Across the tipi I heard Chloe softly crying. I think today, although I did not then, of how excruciating those moments must have been for her, sitting in a tipi in a strange place, among people she only knew as savages. She must have wondered what would become of her if I rejected her. What would become of her if I chose my pride over the love she offered to me, the love she had always offered? Once again her life hung in limbo as she waited for the decision of a man.

I left her in this state of limbo longer than I care to admit, but at last I lowered my hands from my face. I looked up at the red cedar poles meeting each other, and at the smoke spiraling up to the pale blue sky. I looked at the cradleboard Feather Horse and Crawls Along had made. I looked around my lodge, at my bow and quiver hanging with Mo's haversack. I thought then of Mo's hand gently curling in death, as if holding something. I thought of him saying, "Sweetheart," and then dying. I thought of him telling me that if his wife Geraldine had been taken by Indians, he would still want her. I had told him the same thing about Chloe.

I wiped my tears away. "You didn't marry him," I said. "There is nothing to forgive." I crawled across the tipi to her and wrapped my arms around her, and she fell into my lap and wept.

I suppose that if you have read this far, if you believe all that I have told you, then you will want to know why Chloe did not quit Master Wilson at the end of the war, and you will want to know if I truly did not blame her for staying, for continuing to pose as his wife, for continuing to pose as white. I did not blame her then, and I do not blame her still, for what, I ask you, could she have done differently?

One by one, all of Master Wilson's slaves quit him until Chloe was left there with no one but Wilson knowing her true identity. To all the neighbors, to all you people in Drunken Bride, Chloe was white. Chloe was Joseph Wilson's wife. So I ask you, had she chosen to leave, where could she have gone? What could she have done to earn a living? Who would have taken her in? And how can I blame her for staying in a life as tightly constricting as this jail in which I now sit?

"I loved my chirren," Chloe said now. "I love 'em still. I hate they father, but I love Jason and Anna. That the one thing he let me do, name the chirren. And I name 'em after my mama and papa."

I nodded.

"I hate him."

"He is dead now, Chloe."

"I hate him."

I nodded again. In that moment it did not feel like enough that I had killed Joseph Wilson. It did not feel like enough to have merely run my lance through his body. It did not feel like enough to merely have his scalp drying on my shield. If I were not scheduled to hang so soon, I would take the time to write for you exactly what I would have done to him, but torture is a leisurely pursuit, and I have not the time to do it justice here.

"I thought you was dead," Chloe said again. "I'd of never done it if I'd knowed you was alive."

"You had to survive. We all had to survive."

I pulled her to me and I held her tight and I resolved that I would never let her go, that I would look after her, that she would finally be safe, for she was with me, and while I was not a wealthy man, I was no longer a poor man either. I had a lodge, and I had horses, and I had weapons, which I knew how to use. I would protect her. I would provide for her. Is that not what any man who is worth his salt wishes to do for his woman?

I cannot tell you how long she sobbed, except that it seemed forever. She took in great gulps of air, and I felt her tears dampen my shirt. Her shoulders shook violently as she let it all out, and I muttered in Comanche again and again, *"Puh sooah-tsoomyee. Puh sooah-tsoomyee."* At last she slowed her crying and she looked up at me and asked, "What that mean?"

"He is dead," I answered, which renewed her weeping. "I thought you wanted him dead," I said.

"I did. But . . . I . . . I thought you was dead," she said between sobs.

"I am not dead," I told her. "You are here with me and I am not dead. This is my lodge. I have a herd of twenty-five horses. I can take care of you."

She pulled back and looked at me. "How you come to be here?" she asked.

"I was looking for you," I said, and then I told her everything, and we pieced our stories together like a quilt stitched with needles and thorns. She started laughing. I could not see what was funny, but she continued to laugh, and whenever she managed to stop, it was only briefly before she started again. I think now that she was hysterical, that she could not take it all in, my capture, the fact that these people, the people I lived among, had once planned to burn me alive. I think now that the death of Wilson was catching up to her, the sight of his body pinned to the ground with my lance, the sight of his bloody head, his scalp in my hand.

"Massuh Wilson dead," she finally said between fits of hysteria. "He dead. I thought you dead. You don't be dead. You thought I dead. I don't be dead neither. Joseph dead. Holmes dead. We not dead."

I flinched at the use of Wilson's first name, but Chloe did not notice. She laughed some more and then dissolved once again into tears.

I stood and reached into Mo's haversack and pulled out a handkerchief, which I offered to her. You will perhaps be surprised that I had a handkerchief, but I had many of your white person's things, stolen in one raid or another. I cannot remember which raid the handkerchief came from; it was a wagon train I think. The handkerchief had initials embroidered into one corner with pale blue thread. Chloe wiped her eyes and then fingered the stitching. She looked up at me. "These yo' letters?"

"No."

"This belong to someone else?"

I shook my head. "It belongs to me. I took it."

She looked around my lodge. "What else you take?"

449

"I took this shirt," I answered, lifting the hem of the blue wool. "I took some of the horses I own. I took that gun. I took these books." I lifted one of the books I'd stolen from the farm outside Drunken Bride and handed it to Chloe.

She held it in her hands like a broken bird, and then she opened it to the front page and ran her fingers across an inscription written there. "What it say, Persy?"

I took the book from her and read, " 'To my darling wife, Jane, from your loving husband, Richard. On the occasion of our marriage. May 19, 1860.' "

"That be the Coopers. Jane and Richard Cooper. I knowed 'em. They dead now?"

"Most likely."

She nodded. "I hated 'em."

"Did they treat you badly?"

She shook her head. "Naw. They was nice enough, but I couldn't never be myself there. Didn't no one know 'bout me. And they all say, I heard 'em, they say I Mistah Wilson's uneducated wife. I heard 'em say they reckon he want me 'cause I purty, it sure ain't 'cause I smart. They say, 'Listen to the way she talk.' I ain't never knowed no other way to talk, Persy."

"They are probably dead," I said. I closed the book and wrapped my arms around

Chloe again.

She looked up at the smoke vent, where the red cedar poles met and were lashed together. "You say this yo' place?" she asked.

"Yes."

"You own it?"

"Yes."

"You got a woman?"

I smiled. "No."

She nodded at the cradleboard hanging from one of the lodge poles. "What that doin' here?"

"My friend's wife made it for me. She had a vision that I would find a woman, and that I needed my own lodge to bring her to. She believes this woman will provide me with a child."

"Is that right?"

I nodded.

"Am I that woman?"

"Do you want to be?"

She did not answer.

"If you do not I will take you back to Drunken Bride. You can tell them you escaped. You could sell his farm, use the money for passage back to New Orleans."

"What 'bout you?"

I hesitated. "I need to stay here," I finally answered.

"Why?"

"You can go back and be white, Chloe. In fact you won't be able to be anything but white. You're his widow now, but I will always be a nigger. We could never be together out there."

She was silent. Outside the sun began to set, and its light made the tipi walls glow pink.

"I have missed you," I finally said.

She did not answer. The light changed to golden and then the sun dipped away.

"I should build the fire up." I crawled away from her, and added tinder, and blew on the coals and lay on another buffalo chip. When I turned back she had taken off her dress, the same dress she had been wearing all this time, smeared with Joseph Wilson's blood. She let it drop to the ground. "Throw it out," she said, and I picked it up and pushed open the door flap and tossed it outside. I turned back to her. She lay down into the buffalo robes. "Ain't you gonna love up on me?"

It had been eight years since I had been with Chloe, eight years since Master Wilson had shot me and I had gone bobbing down into the Mississippi River. Chloe was older now. I was older. I was no longer a field slave and she no longer a fancy. I pulled off my shirt and kicked off my moccasins and my leggings. I crawled under the buffalo robe with her. She tugged on the little noose hanging from the necklace at my throat. "You wear this all the time?"

"Yes."

She lifted the button and rolled it between her fingers.

"It's yours," I said. "I found it when I was in the army, in Wilson's room at Sweetmore."

She shook her head. "You have my button?"

"Yes."

"You have it all this time?"

"Yes."

She let the button drop to my throat with a cool little thump. She wrapped her arms around me and traced her fingers across the scars on my back, and when I felt that touch, Chloe's touch against my skin, I wept.

You tell me that I captured Mrs. Joseph Wilson in October of 1870. I suppose that I must agree with you on the date, if not the identity of the woman who climbed onto my horse with me. At that time I had no use for calendars, or clocks, or to mark years with numbers. I knew the year by what happened inside it. I knew the month by the weather and the moon. Just as I know now that it is Saturday morning, April 3, 1875, and that tonight, I will be buried somewhere beneath the prairie grasses.

Jack stirs in the next room. I see him moving papers about at his desk, pinning a wanted poster to the wall, idly eating a biscuit. By the jailhouse clock I see that I have five hours before my hanging. I reach up and touch Chloe's button. Her life with me was not one of terrible servitude as you claim it to be. I want you to know this. Chloe wanted a home, and I gave it to her. I would have taken her anywhere else had she asked me to. She did not ask. She stayed. I see the clock hand move. I must keep writing. I must keep telling you what I know. If you do not hear it from me, you will never hear it.

Feather Horse and Crawls Along noticed the bloody dress tossed outside our lodge that night. They picked it up and threw it on the midden and arrived the next morning at our tipi with a buckskin dress that had once fit Crawls Along. They shooed me outside and clothed Chloe. They gave her moccasins. They combed out the tangles in her hair. They chattered to her in a language she could not understand, and then they pulled back and admired her, made her turn in a circle, and brought her outside to show me her transformation.

Chloe had always been beautiful, no matter what her clothes; the simple dress of a slave in a showroom, the slightly better dress of a house slave, the plain farmwife's dress I had captured her in, and now, this buckskin dress fringed at the bottom and tasseled across the breast. It was good leather, elk hide, cured and worked to suppleness by

Crawls Along, and the dress draped across Chloe's shoulders like something liquid. She smiled shyly at me, and then Feather Horse and Crawls Along shooed me away once more as they began to teach her how to break camp, for after that raid into Drunken Bride, we had best be on the move once more.

She was given a name. Nakuhakeetuh. It means Come in Sight. She was named for the way that she suddenly appeared to the other warriors on the back of my horse after the raid. They had not seen her walk to me. She had come in sight to them, just as she had to me, wondrously, mysteriously, and miraculously.

Every day back then was a miracle. My heart opened. It opened wider than I ever knew possible. No matter where we went, Chloe was with me. Nakuhakeetuh shared my bed, rode one of my horses when we moved, dipped water down by a stream and brought it to our lodge, learned the ways of cooking and camp. I cannot tell you the pride I felt in her, for she adapted. She did not cleave to her former life, or any fantasy of another life, in another place. If she looked to the east, it was not to civilization, but to the sunrise.

It was not easy for her. I know this. I, too,

had had to learn the ways of the people, learn the language, and learn the culture. How she must have loved me to do this. To stay. To patiently, day after day untangle Feather Horse's and Crawls Along's words to her. I translated some, but I could not be there as the women did their work each day. I could not tell her the proper angle to hold a hide-scraping tool, how many hot rocks it took to drop into a leather pouch in order to warm a stew, or how to put up and take down the tipi single-handedly. I was grateful for Feather Horse's and Crawls Along's gentleness, for they did not box Chloe's ears or otherwise hurt her in order to make their points. The band did not treat her, ever, as a captive. She was treated as my woman, the woman of Feather Horse's vision. "White," the people said of her.

"No," I told them. "She is not white."

"You have gone blind," Beetle once said to me. "Nakuhakeetuh is white."

In our lodge we spoke our common language, until one night Nakuhakeetuh said to me, *"Tuhkuh."* Eat. She handed me a stick with which to spear the chunks of meat in the stew. *"Tuhkuh,"* she said again.

I did not move.

She prodded the sharpened stick toward me and said in English, "What wrong with you?" And in Comanche, *"Tuhkuh."*

"You are speaking the language," I said in English.

She stopped motioning with the stick. She stood by the kettle and looked at me, and then at our lodge. She looked back at me and smiled. *"Tuhkuh,"* she said again.

Every day more and more of the language slipped into her, until one night we were making love and she whispered my name in a heat of passion. Kweepoonaduh Tuhmoo. Kweepoonaduh Tuhmoo.

It makes me cry now to remember it.

Her life was not easy. I know this. Chloe worked hard. She scraped hides. She cooked. She sewed. She kept the fire. She cut the tahseewo meat into thin strips and draped them to dry over the scaffolding that she had built. Every time we moved the village she took the tipi down and put it back up again so that it opened to the east. She arranged the interior just as it was supposed to be.

I will not lie to you, for I have no reason. If Chloe were still alive, I would not be writing this. Instead I would tell you everything you long to hear. I would confess to you that, yes, she was my captive, and yes, she was my slave, and yes, I abused her terribly. I would do my best to make her white again,

458

in the hope that being white would lead her to an easier life. But I haven't any reason to humor you. For the first time in Chloe's life she was no one's slave.

Chloe told Feather Horse and Crawls Along that she was not white. She told them that she had belonged to Master Wilson, and that at the time of her capture, she was posing as his wife. I do not know if Feather Horse and Crawls Along are still alive, but if they are, they are living on agency land. Perhaps you can find them and ask. They will tell you that what I say is true. Nakuhakeetuh told them the same story I am telling you now.

"Why would you do this thing?" Feather Horse had asked.

Chloe told me that she could not explain. She had answered it was a trick.

"A trick on who?" Crawls Along said.

Chloe could not answer this either.

"You were only doing what you thought might make your life more bearable," I told her.

In Comanche, Nakuhakeetuh said, "Joseph was not fooled. He knew I hated him. Every day he knew this. He owned me worse then than he had ever owned me before. I think he liked it that way."

"Puh sooah-tsoomyee," I said. He is dead.

His scalp dried nicely, by the way. His hair flowed pretty on my shield. I thought you might like to know that a part of him became useful after his death.

The first time I told Chloe that I must go out on a raid, she did not cling to me. She did not cry or beg me to stay. She had observed the other women sending their men off on raids, smiling, holding up their children for one last kiss before the warriors spun their horses and rode off toward the settlements in the east.

"You must go," Chloe said to me. "Make me proud."

It was early spring. We rode a long ways, all the way into the Hill Country, where the white settlements were, and we took many horses, and no captives, and killed, I remember, three men and one woman, and burned houses. I took no scalps on this raid. One of our party, Beetle's brother named Poehoevee, Sweet Sage, was killed, blasted in the face by a woman with a shotgun. Beetle stabbed her and scalped her, and we loaded Poehoevee's body onto the rump of one of the horses and began our ride home.

The village was gone when we returned. Signs had been left to tell us where they had moved and we found them easily enough, but the moving of the village during my absence had frightened Chloe. Feather Horse and Crawls Along explained to her that we would know how to find them. Still, she worried, and when we rode in Chloe forgot to make the welcoming yips the women made to announce returning warriors. She ran to me, and I slid off my horse and we were in each other's arms.

But the welcoming yips of the women turned to wailing as Poehoevee's body was discovered. His first wife ran to him slumped across the rump of the horse and she threw herself onto him, and then his second and third wives joined her, and then his sister, his aunts, his mother.

That night these women traveled to a lonely rise and wailed and gashed their arms and breasts. There is no other sound like a Comanche woman in grief. It is a sound that insists on being heard, like the call of a wolf. In our lodge with the fire guttering at its center, Chloe pulled away from me. "What that?" she asked in English.

I told her.

"They cuttin' theyselves?"

"Yes."

"Cain't you make 'em stop?"

"No." I reached for her again. I kissed her neck and moved my lips down to her breasts. The wailing of Poehoevee's women filled the air.

"How many nights they gonna do this?" Chloe asked.

I stopped kissing her. "I don't know," I answered. "I don't know what makes them stop. Forget this. We're together. I am home, safe."

She pushed her hands against my chest. "Naw," she said, and she rolled over, facing away from me, and pulled the buffalo robe around her.

I pressed my body into her back. I pressed my erection into the fleshy cheeks of her buttocks.

"Don't make me," she whispered in Comanche. "Please, Kweepoonaduh Tuhmoo. Don't make me."

I loosened my hold on her. I moved my body, my erection away from her skin. "I would never do that," I said. "I would never make you."

She rolled over and wrapped her arms around me. "I wish they would stop."

"Here." I pulled the robe over her head and pressed my hands against her ears. "Don't listen."

We moved the village a few days later. I was among a party of scouts that saw soldiers riding through the plains. We stayed out of sight and passed a spyglass around to look at them. The man who was leading the way had stubs for fingers on one of his hands, and he impatiently snapped them in the air as the soldiers rode forward, looking for Indians.

I had heard of this man. Bad Hand, we called him. You will know him as Colonel Randal MacKenzie.

The troops he led were Negroes. Thin Knife asked me if I wished to join them, and I said no.

"You say Nakuhakeetuh is not white. You could take your wife and go and be with your people," he said.

"I am with my people now," I answered.

"It would perhaps be an easier life for you."

"Why do you say this? It would not be easier. Nakuhakeetuh is white in the minds of the whites. She would be taken away from me."

Thin Knife raised the spyglass and looked again at the soldiers. "Do you know any of them?" He passed the glass to me.

I looked. I did not recognize anyone. I returned the spyglass to him. "I hope not," I answered.

"Will you fight them if you have to?"

"Of course."

He looked at me and raised the spyglass

again, and then we began backing our way out of our hiding place. The soldiers did not find us. We did what we were best at. We melted into the plains. We vanished. I have never found out if Henry or Sup or any of my other friends at Sweetmore, or even my own father, were among the soldiers in search of us. I did not want to know then, and I do not want to know now.

I wish this story were different. I wish I could write about many years in which Chloe and I were together without the pursuit of soldiers, many years together in which our story was only our story, and not a part of the larger fabric of history. But our time together without the outside world pressing into us was brief, and there are things I must write about that defined our life together, things I participated in, and things I had nothing to do with.

I had been with the tribe for three years, and Chloe not quite a year when we heard of a raid made against a wagon train at a place you call Salt Creek. White men were killed, so you labeled it a massacre. Three men were arrested at the agency. I knew them all. Satanta, Satank, and Big Tree. They were good men.

You held a trial that summer. The month before, Satank had been killed trying to escape, but Big Tree and Satanta were sentenced to hang, and this made us angry. We vowed to get our revenge on the whites, for not only were you killing two of our leaders, but also you were planning to slice our country in half with your railroads. Besides that, there were just too damn many of you, and you kept on coming.

We were sick of you that summer, sick of your arrogance, sick of your farms and sheep and cattle. Even the agency Indians were mad enough to leave that place and come back to the plains, back to the old ways. It made my heart glad to see our numbers swell, our herds multiply, and our villages stretch for more miles along a river.

But it was hard on Chloe. She had not been with the tribe long enough to feel secure with us, and just when she had begun to know the people in our band, other bands arrived to join us. Besides this, the men left often that summer. We went on many raids. We killed many white people. I frequently left Chloe to ride to the settlements with Thin Knife. When I was gone she stayed with Feather Horse and Crawls Along and the children. She did not feel safe alone in our tipi. She was still considered white, and there was much hatred of whites that summer. She feared, as did I, that someone from another band might hurt her.

But it was not long before this chapter was over and another begun. We heard that the governor, fearing that we would kill many more whites if the execution was carried through, had reduced Satanta's and Big Tree's sentences. Instead of hanging, they were sent to a prison. This subdued the agency Indians, and most of them drifted back there. Our numbers shrank again, and we were back to smaller raiding parties, and fewer scalps.

Chloe had seen, though, what she had stepped into. She had seen the scalps on my shield. She had seen the dances and heard the drumming. She was living and traveling with warriors. If she knew that she had stepped into the losing side, she did not express this to me. She welcomed me home every time. She accepted what little gifts I brought to her from the white world. A woman's hairbrush, a hand mirror, a reel of ribbon not unlike the strip of ribbon I had given her at Sweetmore. This last she sewed into a shirt for me, so that the ribbons billowed when I rode my horse across the plains.

We were all over that land. Our hearts knew it in a way your hearts never will. The older warriors could sit down with the younger ones and tell them how to reach a place they had never been. They could draw a map in the dirt and show the young braves rivers and rocks and valleys and canyons. Show them where to find the hidden water holes. Tell them how long the ride between waters. The land to us was more than land, more than something we skimmed across on our way to other land. The land, the sky, the rivers, the buffalo, these were our companions.

I close my eyes sometimes. I sit still and do not write. I think of how it was to step outside my tipi and see the moonlight sparkle in a rippling river. I think of the walls of Palo Duro Canyon rising up above our village. I think of the collective breath cloud of a herd of buffalo along the prairie's horizon. And then she comes to me. She comes in sight, my Chloe, my Naku-hakeetuh, sitting across from me in our lodge while the fire makes its talk and its light. She is sewing and, with her teeth, she pulls a thin piece of sinew from a strand to use as thread. She looks up at me. I have been reading a book taken on a raid. She looks down to thread her needle, and smiles. "I am to have a child," she says.

A month ago, here in Drunken Bride, a soldier came to visit me in my cell. He showed me a picture of a white girl about eight years old. "She was with a band that turned themselves in," the soldier said. "She doesn't recall where she was captured. She doesn't recall her name, or even her language. We are trying to find her people."

I reached through the bars and took the photograph from him. I recognized the child.

"We caught her with her brother," I said. "The boy was traded to the Apaches. I do not know what became of him. Their mother is dead."

"Where was this?"

I tried to remember.

"There were sheep, I think," I told the soldier. "The Hill Country maybe? Perhaps along the Llano? A man traveling with an ox along a road was killed. Maybe you can look up a record of this."

The soldier sighed. "We can't look up a record if we don't know where to look. I'm sure her father is anxious to get her back. Parents are writing to the agency all the time, trying to find their children. It's a damn mess piecing this shit together. Can you remember anything else?"

I shook my head. "There were many raids. This is all I remember about that one." I passed the photograph back to him through

468

the bars of my cell.

He took it and looked at it sadly before tucking it into his pocket. "Do you know her name?"

"We called her Koe-ko. It means chicken."

"Her white name?"

I shook my head. "I do not know it."

The soldier turned to leave.

"So she is captured now?" I asked.

He turned to look at me.

"By the whites, Koe-ko is captured?"

He took a deep breath. "She is recovered," he said.

Recovered. This is what is said about Chloe. She was recovered. Mrs. Joseph Wilson was found and recovered. Rescued from a life of savagery and degradation. This is the story you tell, but it is not the story I tell. I loved her and she loved me. Together we would love any child we were blessed with.

Until I moved into the tipi with Thin Knife and his family I had never, as an adult, lived with little children. I loved Elk Water and Fall Up and Salt almost as if they had been my own. I wrestled with them at night. I fell down, pretending to be dead when Salt hit me in the chest with a toy arrow. I made a little doll out of corn husks for Elk Water and Fall Up to share. Now I was to have a child of my own, and Chloe and I were stupid with happiness, stupid with love.

Outside our tipi Chloe staked a hide and scraped it and worked it until it was smooth and supple. And then she cut it into a pattern for a toy quiver. At night she sat in our lodge by the fire and began stitching it together while I sat across from her, stringing the toy bow I had made and fitting the toy arrows with soft tips. We looked up often from our work and smiled at each other, and even laughed at our foolishness in making such things so early for a child yet to be born.

"Feather Horse says that we will have a son," Chloe said, as if to convince herself that we were not wasting our time.

"I will love the child no matter what," I told her.

"What if it is a girl?"

"I told you, I will love her."

"What of all this work?"

"What of it?" I answered. "Do you think this will be our only child?"

She smiled at me and shook her head. "I believe in Feather Horse's vision," she said.

"I, too, believe," I told her.

How could I not? Feather Horse's vision of my woman sat across from me, pregnant with my child, foolish and happy and stitching a toy quiver. Our child would be a boy. A black circle would be painted above the door of our tipi to indicate that a warrior had been born. I could see it. I could see it all, as if it were my own vision. This was the happiest and most content that I have ever felt, these few months I spent with Chloe in our own lodge in preparation for our child.

Thin Knife and his wives laughed at us. "Is this child to be born four years old?" Thin Knife joked, he and his family sitting in our lodge after having shared a meal with us. It was late, and the children had eaten their fill and now lay in our buffalo robes, sleeping. Elk Water lay with her head resting against Chloe's thigh, and Chloe idly stroked her hair.

"Ah. Leave them alone," Crawls Along said. "It is their first. Kweepoonaduh Tuhmoo and Nakuhakeetuh are too excited to help themselves."

"It is not wise to make these things too early," Feather Horse told us. "It is a lot of work, and much can happen between now and then."

Chloe's hand left Elk Water's hair and went to her stomach, resting on its mound. "What you know gonna happen?" she asked, slipping from Comanche to her original language.

They looked at her, not understanding. I translated. Feather Horse smiled and crawled across the floor and rested her hand on top of Chloe's. "To this one? Nothing.

You will have an easy birth and a fine baby."

Chloe smiled, and her hand returned to stroking Elk Water's hair. Feather Horse returned to her place. She glanced at the little bow hanging from the lodge pole next to my bow. The toy arrows were lying in a bunch on the floor, tied with a rawhide thong. Feather Horse picked up the unfinished quiver and examined Chloe's handiwork. "It is good," she said. "You are doing good work. I hope it does not get lost in the plains, is all."

"It won't," Chloe said.

But it did.

Chloe completed the work on the quiver the night before the soldiers came. She filled it with the toy arrows I had made and hung it next to the little bow. She smiled and walked across the floor to me. I opened the buffalo robe that she might climb in. She was well along now, five or six moons, her belly round and taut. The fire flickered shadows across the tipi. I wrapped my arms around Nakuhakeetuh and I hugged her tight, and I stayed awake as long as I could, just to listen to her breath.

The next day was warm, the sky a deep blue with patches of clouds. The women were busy cutting strips of meat and hanging them to dry on the scaffolding. A thicket of wild grapes had been discovered and in the afternoon, a woman and her son went off to gather some. Several of our men were on a buffalo hunt. Already our hunts had been successful. We would have plenty of meat for the coming winter.

There were many bands camped here along this northern branch of the Red River. We were in safe and plentiful territory. The grass here was thick and the horses grazed peacefully, a breeze occasionally rippling their manes and tails.

In the afternoon I left our tipi. "I am going to find a game," I said to Chloe. She was outside on her knees, cutting meat into strips. She looked up at me. The breeze lifted her hair and she lifted one hand to wipe it from her face, a knife held in the other. She smiled. I licked my thumb and used it to wipe a smear of dirt from her cheek. "Win many horses," she said before bending back to her work.

I sauntered through the village. Outside the tipis the women were bent to the same work as Chloe was. At Beetle's lodge I joined a group of men sitting on a blanket, gambling with colored wooden dice. I lost two horses in this game and had won one back when Beetle said, "Look," and pointed out into the prairie. We stood. There was a cloud of dust forming in the distance. We watched for a while. "Our men are hunting," another man said, and we settled ourselves again on the blanket, and tossed the dice.

It was a bad mistake. That cloud of dust was the only warning we would have. One minute all was peaceful and good, the next we lifted our heads at the sound of hundreds of hooves pounding the ground, and we saw a cloud descending on our camp, and from that cloud burst your cavalry.

We had no time to reach our horses, to put on our war paint, to group together and form a counter charge. At the first sight of the soldiers, I stood up from the blanket and fled. We all did. We were running this way and that, each man trying to reach his own lodge, his weapons, his horses. We dodged women and children also running. I grabbed my bow and my quiver and my rifle from our tipi. Chloe was not there.

By now the soldiers were thick among us, riding right through our camp. They plowed their horses into our lodges, and the lodges toppled, the skins caving in and the poles falling. Women and children screamed and ran and fell and were sometimes trampled. We were in absolute frenzy trying to get away. Our men could not cover the retreat of our women and children. There was no time. The air thickened with smoke and flashes and booms of gunfire; the air thickened with screams of terror.

We all fled in different directions. We scattered like ants. I saw, as I ran, a parfleche dropped on the ground. I saw smoke curling from the tops of tipis that had not yet been squashed. I saw hides left pegged to the ground, half scraped, tools dropped beside them. I saw the soldiers ride into the scaffolding where our winter supply of meat lay drying. I fired into their ranks. I stumbled over a dead horse, and picked myself up, and fired again. I do not think I hit anyone.

I ended up with many of the men, along the river. We hid ourselves in the long grass that overhung the banks. By then most of our horses had been captured, but we had a few that had been in camp when we were attacked. We grouped up with these few horses and charged the line of soldiers shooting at us from a ravine, but we were driven back, and we lost men. We threw our dead into the deep water to prevent them from being scalped by the Tonkawa scouts who always helped the soldiers. The blood of our dead swirled with the river water, and then the river was no longer the color of water, but was instead the color of blood.

We could do nothing down in that river. We did not know where anyone was, except for those in our group. I did not know where Chloe was. Thin Knife did not know where Feather Horse or Crawls Along or the children were. The other men did not know where their families were. All was confusion in camp. All was lost. We could not prevent the soldiers from taking our village. I escaped, along with Thin Knife and three others, by hugging the bank and creeping upstream. All we could do, any of us, was save ourselves.

It was quick and it was horrible. The entire destruction of our village took perhaps thirty minutes. We watched from our hiding place in the prairie, lying low in the grasses, as our possessions were thrown onto fires: our buffalo robes, our winter supplies, our clothes, our tools, the weapons we had dropped or left behind. The soldiers set our lodges on fire. They herded our horses together and led them away. I recognized Bad Hand MacKenzie riding among his men, snapping his bad fingers in the air. And then we saw, as the soldiers rode away, a large group of our women and children being herded along among them.

One of the men I was with pulled a spyglass from the dripping wet bag slung across his shoulder. He wiped the river water away from its lens, and we took turns looking through it to see who was among the captives. Beside me, I felt Thin Knife let out his breath as he looked through the glass and recognized Feather Horse and Elk Water. Another man recognized his sister and aunt. A third man, his young daughter and son and first wife. I did not see Chloe. I did not know how to feel about this. I was relieved that she was not captured, but not being among the captives might mean that she was among the dead.

When it was safe we made our way back to the village, as did the others who had been in hiding. One by one or in groups we crept into our camp and wandered around in a daze. Bodies were thick on the ground. Some had been scalped and mutilated.

Our village was destroyed. My tipi, burned. The little bow and quiver of arrows we had made for our child, gone. Our buffalo robes, gone. Our kettles and tools, gone. Our food, gone. Nakuhakeetuh, gone.

I turned over bodies, looking for her. The wails of the women started up as each discovered a relative who had been killed. I kept on turning over the unclaimed dead. Soon all the bodies were claimed, and the wailing of the women left in camp intensified. Now I was certain that Nakuhakeetuh must have been among the captured women with the soldiers. Perhaps I had not seen her because she had been mistaken for white. Perhaps she was no longer Nakuhakeetuh but was once again Mrs. Joseph Wilson, the captured white woman from Drunken Bride, pregnant now with the child of a savage.

There was no time to let my heart break over this. I had to help the men gather the horses that had not been captured. We had to lead a raid. We had to get our women and children back. I had to do this, even if Chloe was not to be among them, even if she was being kept apart, interviewed perhaps by Bad Hand himself.

At dusk we rode out after the soldiers and found them camped in the sand hills. From a distance we could see our women and children closely guarded in the center of the camp. Darkness fell and we began circling them, making our war whoops and firing, the soldiers firing back at us. Our efforts were of no use. Only a few of the captives were able to escape during the ruckus. At midnight we stampeded a herd of our stolen horses that had been corralled into a sinkhole, a group of sleeping Tonks left in guard of them. We got most of them back, as well as a few of the Tonks' mounts.

We ran the horses back to the stream beside our destroyed village. As we approached, even over the sound of the horses' hooves thudding against the earth, I could hear the moans and wails of grieving women. I could smell our meat for the winter, our hides, and our tipi covers burning. I could see the fires set by the soldiers still glowing and smoldering in the distance.

We turned the horses into the grasslands and found some boys to guard them. I dismounted and walked back through the village.

Even though we had not been successful, I was grateful to have gone on the mission to rescue our women. I was grateful to help with the recovery of our horses. I was grateful to have had something useful to do, for without that I do not know how I would have survived those first few hours without Chloe. Now there was nothing to prevent my fear and sorrow from engulfing me. I called to her, but she did not answer. There were others wandering the village, calling out names. The moon and the smoldering fires of our lodges and possessions lit our way. I saw Crawls Along pulling a tipi hide behind her, piling on anything not destroyed that she could find. "Have you . . ." I began.

She shook her head. "You had better get what you can find," she said.

"Nakuhakeetuh?" I said.

"She is as good as gone," Crawls Along scolded. "Now take this." She unrolled another partially burnt skin from the pile of things on her tarp. "Go find things."

I did as I was told. I found a knife. A spyglass. Some arrows. A pot. Down by the river where we had been fighting, I found a five-foot bow. In the ravine where the soldiers had been, I found a canteen. And then as I was climbing out of the ravine, I saw her. Nakuhakeetuh. She came in sight, walking across the grass toward me, like a mud goddess, for her skin and hair and face were caked and smeared with the stuff. Her hands rested on her pregnant belly as she walked.

"Nakuhakeetuh," I called, and I ran to her, and I caught her in my arms.

"I be all right," she said, unaware that she was using the language of a previous life. "I be all right, Persy. I go to the river. I don't know why I go there. But I dig into the bank. I dig in along some tree roots and I stay there till it over. That why I be so dirty." She looked down at herself and swiped her hands against her dress, then rested them on her belly again, and stood there swaying.

"Are you sure you are all right? Is the baby all right?"

"I be all right," she said again.

"Let's get this mud off of you."

"That be good."

She stumbled as she began walking and I reached out and caught her by the elbow.

"Is the baby hurt?" I asked again.

"I's real careful with the baby, Persy. I has to claw out a pretty big hole. I think the baby be all right. I needs to ask Feather Horse 'bout it. I needs to ask her if he be all right."

"Feather Horse is captured," I said.

"Uh."

"Elk Water is captured too. A lot of women and children are captured. We tried to get them back, but we couldn't."

"Oh no. Po' Thin Knife," she said. "Po' Crawls Along. Oh no. Po' Salt and Fall Up."

I took her to the river, to a shallow rippling spot away from where the fighting had taken place, away from where the water was colored red and the bodies were sunk. I lifted her dress over her head and she stood naked in the moonlight as I cupped water in my hands and poured it over her. Rivulets of mud and dirt trickled down her skin. "Can you sit down?" I asked. "Can you dip your head back? Let me wash your hair?"

I held her arms as she eased herself down. She lay back and I sat down and ran my hands through her hair, working out the cakes of mud. When I was done she lay there looking up at the moon while I rinsed her dress.

"You can't wear this," I said. "It's wet. Come with me."

We went back to the ravine. I moved everything I'd found off the burnt hide, and I wrapped it around us and held her close. And there we slept for a few hours, in the cavity in the earth where the soldiers had been.

The next day we counted our dead, and we saw who was missing from our village. There were few among us whose families were not affected. Many women and children had been captured, more than a hundred gone with the soldiers. We did not know where they would be taken, or how they would be treated. We were inconsolable. We wrapped our dead in whatever we could find. We carried them off, away from what was left of our camp, and we dug shallow graves and buried them and tried to cover the graves with rocks, but there were not enough rocks to be had. We did not burn their possessions, for this had already been done by your soldiers, for both the dead and the living. Each night the grieving women withdrew from us and moaned and slashed themselves. It was a horrible time. Every night Chloe and I covered ourselves with the burnt lodge cover and slept in the ravine where the soldiers had been.

I stayed close to her, for in the days and weeks following the raid on our village hatred for whites swelled like a dead body left in the sun. It swelled until it would burst, and for many of the women who had lost husbands and sons, the hatred burst onto our white captives. Some women swore that they would kill a white person, even if that white person was one of the boys who guarded our horses, who had gone on raids with us, who had risked his own life and killed when killing needed to be done.

The women were crazed with loss. Husbands were gone forever. Sons, dead. These men would not be coming back. Nor would daughters and mothers and sisters and aunts be returning. The women, when they looked at our white Indians, saw only their skin. It did not matter that our white Indians had remained loyal to the tribe, had not tried to sneak away in escape, had learned our ways and lived among us. It did not matter that they knew less about how to be white than how to be Indian. I could not trust that when a grief-stricken woman looked at Chloe she would not consider her white. If I had to go into council with Thin Knife or any of the other men, I made certain to leave Chloe in the care of Crawls Along.

I went into council often and I did not like what was being said. But I could not fight it. I could not argue against it. None of us liked it, and none of us could think of an alternative. We had few lodges left to us and no winter supplies. In order to survive the winter, we must move onto government land. We must move in closer to the agency. We must take the handouts, the rations offered in order not to starve.

I look out the window now and see that you are arriving for my hanging, wagons and buggies and four-in-hands parked at the edges of the street. I watch your women unload baskets of food and cloths to spread on the ground. I see your men heading off to the saloon for a drink. I see your children climbing out of the backs of the wagons, all scrubbed and cleaned and excited.

You have arrived early to jostle each other for a good seat. I lean my face as close to my barred window as I can, and I look up the street to see my gallows and the crowd of people in front of it, the colorful patchwork spread of cloths and quilts on the ground, the women's skirts fanned out like flowers on a vine. There are many of you wanting a clear view of my execution. Good. You will be the first to smell the shit my body is bound to release as I drop through the hatch.

I watch a man setting up a table across the street, a board spanning two barrels. He props a crudely painted sign in front. "Sooveneers," I see painted there. A larger sign proclaims, "Membrences of Mrs. Joseph Wilson. The Most Tragik Figer of the Fronteer." He begins to lay out his wares. I look away. I cannot watch.

Beneath my window, a group of children gather. They gaze up at the bars, hoping for a glimpse of the wild nigger Indian. I am looking right at them but they do not see me, for the angle of light is not behind me, and I am dark skinned, and besides this, it is the way of the Comanche to see but not be seen.

One of the boys nudges his friend with his elbow. Then he starts up a little chant, and soon they have all taken it up, and they stand there, with their earnest little faces tilted up as if they are singing me a Christmas carol.

Persimmon Wilson, Twisty Rope
Your last meal is in the poke
Watermelon, corn bread, sweet potato pie
Today's the day you're going to die

I open my mouth and take a deep breath. I breathe all the air I can into my lungs, and

I let out a war whoop. They scream and scatter. The whole street becomes quiet. Jack comes into the hallway outside my cell and tells me to stop that shit. I am frightening innocent children, he says.

I look at the jailhouse clock behind him. It is ten. I hang at twelve.

I look out the window again. A woman is comforting the boy who started the chant. He leans into her dress and cries and she looks up and glares at my cell. Across the street the store is doing a brisk business. The saloon is packed, I am sure. Already the man selling souvenirs has people standing in line.

I must speed along now. I must not pause to reflect on what it means to die, for it does not matter what it means, nor has it ever mattered. What matters is Chloe. What matters is this story that I must leave behind.

We moved our camp to Cache Creek on agency land. There was no other choice. Chloe and Crawls Along managed to cobble together a tipi from salvaged lodge poles and bits of covering they pieced together. We moved in with Thin Knife's family, as did Crawls Along's sister, Cocklebur.

Each week a party of our men rode in on ration day and brought back to us the stringy beef, which we divided among the tribe. We dug a few roots, but there was little to eat that winter, and we watched as our children and women lost weight, their complexions becoming dim, their eyes dull.

I worried about Chloe and the baby she carried, not just because of our lack of food and warm buffalo robes and decent lodging, but also because the soldiers might come to our camp and see Chloe as a captured white woman. And if this were to happen, they would take her away from me. To prevent it I darkened her skin with pecan hulls.

The agent, we called him Bald Head, soon made it clear that he would not release our women and children until we had returned all our white captives, as well as any horses stolen from the military. We did not even know where our captured women and children were being held, but at this news the tribe became divided.

There were those among us who looked on our white Indians as the answer to the return of their loved ones. But others thought that the white Indians who had lived with us deserved more loyalty than this. And besides, the young boys who had been captured and had lived with us for a long time, Backecacho, Cachoco, Toppish, and others, were not willing to go. I spoke with Backecacho, and I know that the idea of leaving us, of returning to white society terrified him, just as it terrified Naku-hakeetuh.

She would not leave my side, nor would I leave hers, for I saw in some of the people's eyes that Chloe was a catch now, a bargaining chip, and a route to getting a mother or a sister or a child back. There was much talk among the tribe, much debate among the men, and in the end it was decided. We would take one or two of our white Indians and some horses to the agency, and our relatives would be released. We could see no other way.

Backecacho and Cachoco were the two boys taken in. We told them to allow this for the tribe. We told them to escape once the captives were returned to us. Before he left, Backecacho told me he would return to his life with us. Take care of my horses, he said. He would see me again. He never returned. I never saw him again. None of our people were released. Two more young warriors, white Indians, were taken in. And still our women and children were not released.

During all this Chloe shook with terror. She spoke of it every night to Crawls Along and Thin Knife and Cocklebur and me. "I have nothing to return to," she said. "Return to where? Drunken Bride? Those people? I never had a husband there. Here I have a husband. I never had friends there. Here I have friends. I never had a home there. Here I have a home."

Thin Knife told me that on that first trip into the agency when Backecacho and Cachoco were taken in, Bald Head asked about Mrs. Joseph Wilson. Thin Knife and the others shook their heads. They did not know the name, they said.

"The woman taken on the raid in Drunken Bride," Bald Head replied. "Her husband was killed."

"Ah," Horseback answered him. "That woman died."

"And where is her body?"

"I do not know. But she died. It was somewhere along the trail. She was not strong."

"How did she die?"

They looked at each other and shrugged. "I do not know what killed her," Horseback answered. "She was not strong."

I wonder now what it must have felt like to Backecacho and Cachoco to listen to this talk, to know that they were being sacrificed while Nakuhakeetuh was being protected. It is to their credit that they said nothing. And it is to Thin Knife's credit that he never considered turning my wife in to the agency, in the hopes of the return of Feather Horse and Elk Water. I felt no fear inside his lodge. Chloe and Crawls Along and Cocklebur worked together to cook what food the agency provisions allowed, and to take care of Salt and Fall Up. Often I saw Crawls Along and Cocklebur flanking Chloe, holding their hands to her belly to feel our child kick.

I do not know why Bald Head did not press harder for information regarding Mrs. Joseph Wilson. Perhaps he believed what Horseback told him, or perhaps he did not really care, for surely the parents of the young boys who stood before him now had written more letters asking for help in finding their children than anyone in Drunken Bride had ever written about Chloe. It would not be until later that you would make a martyr of her, and give her this mantle of "the most tragic figure of the frontier."

We wintered over at Cache Creek, on the government land. It was a nasty and putrid place, the water contaminated by Fort Sill, which was upstream from us. All the same, we would not move any closer to the agency. Nor could we go out onto the plains, for we would starve. Our women and children were not returned to us. They were being held, we learned, at Fort Concho, not at Fort Sill where the agency was.

It was here that a comet appeared, bright in the night sky. It was here that a Quahadi medicine man named Isa-tai predicted that the comet would disappear in five days' time, which it did. But while that comet still hung in the sky, Chloe gave birth to our son. I named him Mohats Tahtseenoop, Bright Star, and the black circle was painted over the door of the tipi we shared with Thin Knife's family, to show that a warrior had been born.

There are no words to say what it is like to hold one's own child. He was a brown little baby. He slept between Chloe and me, and I woke sometimes in the middle of the night to hear Bright Star suckling and Chloe cooing to him. In spite of the conditions of our lives, our diet of stringy beef instead of the tahseewo we had hunted and prepared for the winter, the stinking creek we camped beside, the shame I felt at having turned in our young white warriors for nothing, in spite of all this, I had never been more in love, more amazed at the miracle of Chloe lying beside me with our child. The skin around her nipple returned to its pale color where Bright Star's suckling licked away the pecan-hull dye, and to me that color of Chloe's true skin represented our eventual freedom.

We would leave this place. We all knew it. We needed only to endure this winter along Cache Creek on the government land and get our captured women and children back, and this we did. The women and children were returned to us the next summer. Such a joyous reunion you cannot imagine. The women making their *li-li-li-li-li* sounds. Thin Knife and Feather Horse and Elk Water reunited at last. It was not a quiet night in our camp. We built a fire and celebrated. There was still little to eat, but we ate it communally, and we shared our stories. We had all been captives that winter, those caught by the soldiers and held at Fort Concho, and those forced onto the government land below Fort Sill. But we would no longer be captives. We packed up the next day and rode out to the plains, where we belonged, and we started anew.

There was a locust infestation that summer. It was my last year out on the plains, and it is this that allows me to count back and come up with your measurement of years. 1873. All summer long the locusts chewed at the plants, while all summer long we raided and stole more horses and mules.

We ate the mules, and in the fall we rode beyond the locusts, looking for the collective breath cloud of a herd of tahseewo. It was not easy. Your buffalo hunters arrived that year. There were not many yet, only a few brave and greedy souls, but we saw what even one white hunter could do. We saw a field of bloated carcasses, only the skin taken, all the meat spoiled, millions of flies buzzing around.

We found another herd and killed some. Our women skinned and tanned the hides, and sewed them into tipi covers. We searched out lodge poles and peeled them and let them season. The women built scaffolding and cut the meat into thin strips and hung it to dry for the winter. Slowly we built back up, but we could not keep far out of our minds the sight of the slaughtered buffalo, the bodies rotting in the sun.

These were the things of our lives now. As I write this story I can feel the gathering cloud of our demise. It feels so obvious now, it is remarkable that I did not feel it then. Again, I wish that I could write only of Nakuhakeetuh's and my joy over the birth of our son. I wish that I could write only of bliss, of building another lodge, of making another toy bow and toy arrows for Bright Star, of watching Nakuhakeetuh sew another quiver, of seeing these things hanging in the lodge beside my own bow and quiver of arrows. But there was no time for this. All our work must be toward survival, and Chloe and I were never to have our own tipi again.

But we had robes to wrap up in, and the tribe had more lodges, and we had meat for the winter, or so we thought. We did not, it turned out, have enough for that particular winter. The winter of '73, '74 was a winter that no one on the plains is likely to ever forget. It was worse than the winter with Mo and Sedge in the little bunkhouse on the Traveling S Ranch.

One after another, blizzards bore down and howled through our village. Our horses suffered and some froze to death. Some of the old and sick in our band died of the cold. A few children died.

It seemed that each day found us huddled inside the tipi. Chloe and me, Thin Knife and Crawls Along and Feather Horse and the children, and Cocklebur, who stayed and became Thin Knife's third wife. We listened to the wind howl, sometimes for hours. The sound of it whining and scouring through the camp, thumping itself against the tipi walls, letting up and starting again was enough to drive a man to madness. The blizzards went on and on, one after another. And after a blizzard had ceased, a fearful quiet fell across us as we listened for the sounds of someone having died, the wail of a daughter or a wife, or the thudding footsteps of a runner as he went through the village to alert the relatives. Sometimes Bright Star cried as if he, a little baby, could feel the loss before we even knew of it. Or perhaps he was just hungry and cold.

And what can I tell you of Chloe during this time? That she was cold. That she shivered with Bright Star in her arms, under a buffalo robe. That she was hungry. That she lost weight. That her breasts ceased to produce milk for our child.

He slept between us, Chloe's arm wrapped tightly around him, and Bright Star holding on to my finger. I remember so well his little fist, his little fingers and nails, the look in his big brown eyes when I held him. I remember so well waking in the night to the feel of my son desperately sucking on my finger, as if it were a nipple.

I have since read in your newspaper that the blizzards lasted until April 1874, so you can imagine that there was plenty of time that winter and plenty of hungry anger with which to make talk against the white man.

We had heard that we were not the only Indians who were starving. It was even worse for the agency Indians, for they did not hunt as we did, and you did not provide the promised food. Many raiding parties left the government land to get what they could for their families, and they stopped sometimes in our village and told us how it was for them at the agency, how they were always told to wait. Wait while their women and children starved.

And we told them our own news: two new towns that had sprung up close to Drunken Bride, new ranches with the cattle eating up all the good grazing, and buffalo hunters that had arrived the previous fall.

We all knew, agency Indians and free Indians alike, that your hunters had killed so many buffalo above the Canadian River that the herds would no longer migrate there. We all knew that you would be coming down into our lands to take the buffalo. It was all happening so fast, settlers and railroads and towns and buffalo hunters. We talked angrily in our tipis that winter while the blizzards swarmed around us. We agreed that the buffalo hunters must be stopped. If, come summer, for surely summer would come, we could get all the tribes of the southern plains together we might stand a chance, and to this end, when the blizzards finally ended we held a sun dance.

We were not sun dancers. That was Kiowa medicine, but Isa-tai, the medicine man, said we needed something to bring us together, and he invited all the bands of the Comanche to join us. Isa-tai and a charismatic young warrior named Quanah spoke at the sun dance of war against the whites. We smoked the pipe. If a man took the pipe, he was with us; if he refused, it meant that he did not want to fight. I took the pipe. I would take the pipe again if it were offered to me.

We talked it over and decided that our first target would be the place you call Adobe Walls, the supply station for buffalo hunters that had materialized that spring. And once we had murdered all the buffalo hunters and merchants there, we would ride out and attack everywhere at once, all the hated Texans, all the white people who wanted only to see us die.

We called for other tribes to join us: the Kiowa, the Cheyenne, the Arapaho, the Apache, the Kataka. As we rode through the plains toward Adobe Walls, smaller parties of Indians merged and joined with us, and our numbers swelled to hundreds. Isa-tai told us that our medicine was strong, but he lied.

We did not surprise a sleeping camp, as Isa-tai told us we would. We did not kill the many white men he had promised. We took only two scalps. Upon our attack the people in the supply camp holed up in several sod houses, and they punched holes through the walls, and they shot at us with guns that we had not seen before, guns that were powerful and frightening and could fire long distances, and we were hit, and many of us died. Isa-tai's medicine was no good. Isa-tai's yellow paint that bullets could not penetrate was no good. His horse, also painted yellow, was shot out from under him from a long ways off. Quanah was hit, the bullet creasing his skin between neck and shoulder, bleeding little but leaving his arm paralyzed for several hours.

I cannot describe to you the helplessness I felt as we finally gave up that fight and rode away, for in riding away we were leaving behind many of our dead. We could not reach them without being killed ourselves. This had been proven, as some of the dead were men who had tried to retrieve the bodies of their brothers. Our anger over our defeat surged through our ranks, and the party divided and we spread out and struck blindly against any whites we ran across.

Wagon trains and settlements and farms and buffalo hunters. We killed more brutally than we ever had before, and then we returned to our village and reported our failure at Adobe Walls.

That night I covered my head with a buffalo robe to block out the sound of the widows' wailing. Chloe wrapped her arms around me and rocked me as if I were a child. The next morning I could not hide from seeing these women with their arms and faces and breasts slashed, their blood-stained dresses, and from knowing that I was among those warriors who had failed to protect my brothers, who had failed, even, to bring the bodies home.

Chloe told me again and again that it was not my fault. She spoke in Comanche, reminding me of all that we had been through. She told me that I had been the only strength she had at Sweetmore. She told me that I had given her comfort there. She reminded me that I could have escaped with Henry and Sup, but had instead boarded the boat to Texas to be with her.

"These are not the deeds of a coward," Chloe said.

We were, Chloe and Bright Star and I, sitting along the bank of a river near our camp. The weather was dry, but not so dry yet that the river did not sparkle against the sun. The sky was clear, a solid pale blue. Bright Star pulled himself up along my leg and stood teetering against me. He smiled at me and reached out to tug on my nose. I took his hand from my face and kissed it and looked out over the river.

"We should have escaped Sweetmore," I said. "I should not have waited so long. We should have escaped long before the boat to Texas. It is my fault that we are here."

"That's right," Chloe answered. "It is your fault that I no longer live with Master Wilson, that I am no longer being raped by him."

"We could be in New Orleans." I wrapped my arms around Bright Star and lifted him to my lap where I began his favorite game of smacking him lightly on the bottom. He giggled and squirmed. "You could be making biscuits and pies," I said. "Do you even remember how to make biscuits?"

She smiled at me. "I will never forget," she said.

"You could be living in a house. You could have dresses. Our child would never be hungry. I might have found work, teaching school. I might have provided for you. You deserve to be . . ." I could not find the Comanche word for what I wished to say, and so I finished in English. "You deserve to be a lady."

"I be a lady," Chloe answered in her own English. She entwined her fingers in mine as they rested on Bright Star's back. "You provide for me," she said in Comanche.

She stood and lifted Bright Star from my lap. She jiggled him in her arms, and I knew that she wanted him to go to sleep. It did not take long. "Take your shirt off," she said. And so I did, and I spread it on the grass and Chloe laid our son onto it. She took me in her arms then. She held me. She traced once again, the scars on my back, first with the light touch of her fingers, then with her tongue.

I remember this day. The whisper of the breeze through the prairie grasses. The way they caressed themselves all around us. A tiny bird landing on a stalk of grass nearby, the grass bending gently under its weight. I remember the way that Chloe's skin glowed in the sun, and the way that sun warmed my back and my buttocks. I remember the gurgle of the stream, and the feel of my wife opening up beneath me.

The summer of Adobe Walls, the summer we made our war on you, marked my sixth year with the tribe, and Chloe's fourth. Salt was nearing nine years old now, Elk Water and Fall Up were becoming young women, and Cocklebur's belly was big with Thin Knife's fourth child.

It hurts me to write of the final days of this summer, for this was the last summer that I would be on the plains, the last summer that I would be free, the last summer that Chloe and Bright Star and I would be all together, the last summer that I would be surrounded by the people who knew Nakuhakeetuh as my wife. It is hard to believe that this summer I speak of was not even a year ago.

When I left on raids or to hunt, Chloe held Bright Star up to me as I sat on my horse, and I kissed his black hair while he kicked his little legs and sank his little fists into the scalps on my shield. I remember so well Chloe untangling our son's fingers from the hair of a man I had killed. I remember so well the way she pulled Bright Star down into her arms, and kissed his face, how she stepped away, and smiled up at me, and said, "Make me proud."

Bright Star, in spite of the hardships of his early months, was growing strong. He tottered around the tipi and the camp, clinging to the hem of Chloe's dress. When he saw me he lurched into my arms. He had a fat little brown belly. He knew the word for horse. He knew the word for dog. He knew the sign for tahseewo.

One night we were all home. Thin Knife and I were both stringing new sinew onto our bows. Across the tipi the women, four of them now, all bent their heads to their sewing. Cocklebur rested her work on the mound of her belly. Elk Water and Salt and Fall Up lay under the buffalo robes, their arms wrapped around each other, quietly watching the fire. Bright Star lay sleeping in the crook of his mother's legs. Nakuhakeetuh looked up from her work and said, "Kweepoonaduh Tuhmoo, there is something I must tell you."

"Yes?"

She smiled. "We are to have another child."

At this news my breath came out of me in a little huff.

Thin Knife laughed and nodded and said, "This is good. We will have two babies in our lodge. Perhaps little warriors for both of us."

I laid down my bow and went to Naku-hakeetuh and kissed her cheek. "My heart is glad," I said.

I would like to close my eyes. I would like to close my ears to the noise of the people gathering outside my cell. I would, if I could, suspend time and live every minute I have left in this one moment in Thin Knife's lodge, where my family surrounded me, where my wife and child sat across the fire from me, and inside her belly our second child grew. That summer was not so long ago, and yet it is forever ago. It was not an easy summer.

We had declared war on you. I went on many raids. We attacked your hunters, your wagon trains, your little farms and camps. We struck and killed, and struck and killed again. We tortured any man we caught alive. We scalped the dead, and the soon to be dead. All summer long, we did this.

You may think us cowards for attacking

your civilians, but do not tell me that they were causing no harm. Were they not fouling our watering holes and rivers with their cities and towns? Were they not staking out the best grazing ground as their own forevermore? Were they not building the railroads and killing our buffalo? There would have been no war at all without them.

All we wanted was to follow the buffalo, which were becoming fewer and fewer. Even that first summer of the hunters swarming across Texas we noticed this. We had to travel farther and farther to find the herds. The white hunters had spread out and set up many camps. Too many times for our comfort we passed by slaughtered herds, the bodies rotting in the sun, and too many times for your comfort you found your hunters killed and scalped.

There was little rain that summer, and much work in providing for our families, and in killing the white people, but we went on about the business of it. Your army made some sort of rule that summer that all Indians were required to come into the agency and register, and if we did not do so, we would be considered hostiles. Do you hear how absurd you sounded to us? We must come in like little children, you said, and you would register every one of us and then we would be safe. You would count us as if we were sheep and herd us onto the land where you said we must stay forever. But we were not little children. We were not sheep to be herded and restrained. Besides, we heard of your rule far too late to meet the deadline, for we were not hovering about your forts awaiting word from you as to what we could and could not do. We were out on the plains, living and hunting as we had always done.

Fall came and the drought broke and the heavy rains turned the plains into a carpet of mud. Because we had not registered, and were not contained, you sent your army out to find us. You sent into this miserable mire, not just one troop but many. We saw them looking for us, the Tonkawa scouts riding ahead, reading our trails, each troop criss-crossing the plains searching, searching, searching. We could not fight against such a large force, and so we did what we had always done. We slipped away and melted into the land. We were masters at this.

There was a place, a special place, a favorite place to us all, the canyon known as Palo Duro, where I was first taken when I was captured, and where we would often winter. I have told you about it. The grass was good. The river was clean and beautiful, its banks lined with cottonwood, juniper, hackberry, wild cherry, and mesquite. The canyon walls were steep, so steep and so high that if you stood on the edge and looked down into our village, the tipis seemed no larger than Chloe's button, which I still wore around my neck.

It was a fortress and we went there. Many Indians went there, many tribes and many bands. We thought the soldiers would give up. The army had never campaigned into the winter before. But they crossed the land, and each other's tracks, over and over, as if the pressure of their horses' hooves across the ground could squeeze us out of hiding.

There was no talk among our men of giving ourselves up. We had no reason to. We had winter provisions. We had warm robes and lodges again. We had many horses. We had scouts who would see the soldiers long before they saw us. And we had this canyon in which to hide. They could not find us here. We were sure of it, and while the soldiers lived out in the plains and rode about in the miserable gumbo of mud, we tucked in. We cooked our meat, and ate our meals, and we talked, and laughed, and repaired our clothes, and carved new arrows and waited for spring.

Chloe's belly became a little marble. I lay

my hand often on her stomach. The women sewed, Chloe making a new shirt for Bright Star. Thin Knife and I spent our time finding games in which to gamble. Cocklebur gave birth to a son, and Thin Knife named him Tuhkohnee, Little Frog Croak. Again the black circle was painted above our lodge door to show that a warrior had been born.

And then one day our scouts told us that Bad Hand MacKenzie and his soldiers had set up a camp, too close to our canyon for comfort. We formed a war party. Hundreds of us. As I have said, there were many Indians, many tribes, many bands come together in the Palo Duro Canyon. Besides Comanche, there were Kiowa, Cheyenne, Apache. We planned to attack that night, stampede the horses and kill whatever men we could, and then the next day we would lead them on a chase away from our canyon, away from our women and children. We would lead the soldiers across the plains and get them lost. We would split up, and split again, and again, and confuse our trail until it could no longer be followed. It would be a simple thing to lead the soldiers to places without water. It would be a simple thing to take their horses. An attack always began with the horses.

But when we attacked that night we

discovered that the horses had been so thoroughly hobbled they could not move. They stood in terror as we rode among them whooping and hollering and firing our guns trying to make them stampede. When that failed we began circling, and the soldiers fired on us. But it was no use for either side, and early in the morning we gave it up.

At daybreak the soldiers pulled out of camp and we watched from a high ridge. We did not try to hide. We showed ourselves, hundreds of us, painted up, the feathers of our war chiefs' bonnets flicking in the breeze, our rifles and lances held in clear sight. We drove down toward them and shot at them, and they attacked, and we retreated, laying a trail southwest, away from our village.

We were well satisfied when our rear-end scouts told us that Bad Hand and his men were following. We kept on, southwest, baiting them, showing ourselves and not showing ourselves, shooting at them, and taunting them, and keeping them on our tail all day long, leading them farther and farther away from our village.

At sundown the soldiers went into camp. We stayed hidden and watched to see that it was not a feint, and as they started their cook fires and hobbled their horses we were convinced that our strategy had worked, and we doubled back and rode hard north to return to the Palo Duro.

A Kiowa medicine man predicted that we would be safe there, but even if he had not done so, the talk among the men, the warriors, me, was that we could not be found. And besides, they would not follow us at night. Not across the muddy plains to a place they had never been before. No. They were making camp. We all saw it. We had led the soldiers twenty-five or thirty miles away. We had left them camping in another canyon. They did not know where we were. The plains were too muddy for them to make this trip. We believed all this, and it was our undoing.

When I reached my home, Chloe dished out some stew for me, and as Thin Knife and I sat eating she asked, "Are we safe now?"

"We are safe," I answered.

Thin Knife nodded to his wives. "Do not worry," he said. "We have led them far away. It is night. The plains too muddy to travel. They don't even know where we are." He shrugged. "Do not worry," he said again. He stood and Cocklebur handed him Tuh-kohnee. "My Little Frog Croak," he said.

"You are my Little Frog Croak."

"You must see the shirt I made for Bright Star," Chloe said, and she held up the finished garment. It was made of soft cream-colored buckskin, and she put it on our son and tugged it around his little chest. I fingered the leather and complimented her on her work. Bright Star climbed into my lap. We ate and crawled into our beds and fell asleep, and we woke up only when it was too late.

The attack came in the morning. The soldiers had scrambled down the cliffs of our canyon while we slept. It was a long ways down, and if only we had awakened, we could have easily picked them off as they clung to the sides of the canyon walls. But we did not wake. We were tired from fighting and our hard ride home. There had been one rifle shot, and then nothing, and upon hearing it, I had assumed an Indian was hunting deer. I had rolled back over and lifted Bright Star's little hand to make sure that I did not crush it, and wrapped my arm around Chloe. And then I had fallen back asleep.

Was it the thundering of hooves that woke me, or was it the alarm being sounded, or perhaps the screaming and yelling and shooting? I cannot say, for all the sounds erupted at once. I was up. Thin Knife was up. We grabbed our guns and ran outside. "Run," I yelled to Chloe as I lifted the tipi flap to follow Thin Knife out. "Run to the cliffs and climb out of here."

Thin Knife and I ran to the horses, as did all the other men. The women and children were everywhere, fleeing, screaming, and dropping things that they had tried to save. The ground was littered with dropped pots and empty cradleboards and sacks of flour and buffalo robes and blankets. The soldiers came on, riding into our village, shooting and trampling the lodges.

I was mounted now, and I rode with the other men toward the cliffs, and there we climbed up, and covered the retreat of our families, shooting down into the crowd of soldiers. Behind us our women and children clambered up to the top of the canyon. I reloaded, and as I did so I saw down below a woman kneeling in the dirt touching something that lay before her, something that was brown and red and dressed in a cream-colored shirt. The soldiers' horses surged around Chloe and what I knew to be the body of Bright Star.

Bullets hit the dirt all around her, pinging up bits of grass. I slid back down the cliff. I dodged the charging horses. I reached her and grabbed her arm and pulled her up. "I tripped," she said. "I was running and I fell and the horses . . ." She did not finish, and I glanced down only briefly to see Bright Star's trampled body. I did not have to see this for long to have the image seared into my mind. He was unrecognizable, bloody and flattened beneath the hooves of a horse, or perhaps many horses. It had been not an hour before that I had lifted his little hand so that I would not crush it as I rolled over to wrap my arm around my wife.

I pulled Chloe away from there. She wailed and fought against me, but I tugged on her arm and pulled her out of the middle of the action. I told her that she must move, she must come with me. There was no scooping Bright Star's body up from the ground. I would not lose Chloe too. This is what I thought as I tugged on her arm and pulled her along.

It was too late to run to the canyon walls. The men who had been covering the retreat of our village had done so, and they had now climbed the cliffs and disappeared. We were alone among the soldiers. Somehow we wove through them without harm, and when we came to a bush I shoved Chloe into it to hide, and I followed. She cried and clung to me. I hushed her. "Be quiet," I whispered.

The sounds of the battle died down. Fewer and fewer shots were fired. We heard now only the sounds of the soldiers as they ransacked our village. Tipi poles clattering as our lodges fell or were knocked down. The neighing of horses being herded together. Shouts and exclamations from soldiers as they found things worth keeping. Soon we heard footsteps nearby. I spread the branches of the bush and looked out to see a soldier poking a lance he had found into the shrubs, searching for hiding Indians. It would not be long before we were discovered. It would not be long before we would be either killed or taken, and I did the only thing that I knew to do in order to protect my wife and our unborn child.

"Chloe," I said. "Nakuhakeetuh, I love you." I pulled her to me, and held her, and then I pushed her away to look into her eyes. I rubbed my fingers across her cheeks to wipe the tears away. "You must go to the soldiers," I said. "Tell them that you are Mrs. Joseph Wilson."

The sudden jerks of her sobs ceased. Her eyes became large with fear and surprise, for this must have been the last thing she ever thought to hear from me. She shook her head. "Naw," she said in her old language. "Persy, naw. I ain't married to him."

We could hear the soldier's boots grinding into the dirt as he moved closer. We could hear the lance, stabbing into the brush nearby.

"It is the only thing to do," I said. "They are going to find us. He is just out there. You can hear him. They are going to think you are white anyway. You have to tell them that you are. Be white," I said, "so you can live, so our baby can live." I touched her hand. "I love you," I said.

"Kweepoonaduh Tuhmoo," she said. "Kweepoonaduh Tuhmoo." It was the last thing she ever said to me, and she said it twice. My name.

I grabbed her arm and I dragged her out of the bush and I pushed her toward the soldier. "Take her," I said. "I do not want her anymore."

She looked at me with panic. Six soldiers suddenly surrounded us, and just as suddenly they divided and three surrounded Chloe and three surrounded me. They held their guns on us. I thought that I could not bear to see the pleading in her eyes, but I made myself look and I held her eyes with mine and I said, "I caught her near that town you call Drunken Bride. She should go back to them I guess." I raised my hands

517

in surrender. "It is all over for me."

Chloe wailed.

"Poor thang," one of the soldiers said. "She damn near hysterical."

"It gonna be all right, ma'am," another soldier said to her.

And then a third: "I think this is that lady we heard of, Mrs. Joseph Wilson."

At the sound of her white name, Chloe let out another wail.

"What the hell did you do to her?" a soldier asked me.

I shrugged. "I killed her husband and I took her. She was treated no differently than any other white woman." I spat. And then the soldier raised the butt of his rifle and hit me in the head. The last I heard was Chloe speaking Comanche. "Kweepoonaduh Tuhmoo is my husband," she said. "Kweepoonaduh Tuhmoo is my husband."

When I came to, Chloe was nowhere in sight and Bad Hand himself was leaning over me. "You're that nigger Indian," he said. "And that woman is Mrs. Joseph Wilson? Am I right?"

I moaned and tried to make my eyes focus. I was still in the canyon; I could see that. The sun was high overhead now. The scent of scorched buffalo meat filled the air. I rolled over and threw up into the dirt.

"We're saving you for the noose," Mac-Kenzie said.

I suppose that Nakuhakeetuh was taken out of the canyon, that she was guarded and watched over, and that some sort of escort was formed to return her to Drunken Bride to be among "her people." I, too, was escorted under heavy guard out of the canyon, as were our captured horses. At the top of the cliffs the best horses were culled for payment to the Tonkawa scouts, and some for Bad Hand's own use, and the rest were shot. A thousand of them or more. I watched as they were led in groups to a firing line. As the grim task went on they became more and more difficult to handle. They screamed and stamped and reared up, and it did not matter. At the end of the day there was a pile of dead horses at the top of the Palo Duro Canyon, the place where we had felt so safe. Down below, our villages still burned. Down below was the crushed body of my son. Inside, I wept. Outside, I stayed the defiant warrior, the nigger Indian who had kidnapped and raped Mrs. Joseph Wilson.

I saw Chloe one last time. It was the day that I was driven into Drunken Bride for my trial. It was the end of February, after I had spent the winter in the jail at Fort

Concho. A large crowd had gathered in the street to witness me being led in. I sat chained in the back of a wagon, just as Chloe and I had once been chained in the back of Master Wilson's wagon. As we approached the town one of the guards turned to me and said, "You're quite a celebrity, Persy. Gonna be a lot of people here for your trial, I bet."

"A lot more for your hanging," another guard said.

They laughed. I had heard this teasing before. All winter long my guards at Fort Concho had told me that I was famous, the famous nigger Indian.

"You're gonna hang in Drunken Bride," I was told. "After what you people did to that town, they'll be out in droves to watch you dangle from a rope."

All winter long I had listened to this, as well as the updates my guards gave me on the Indians I had ridden with. White Horse surrendered. Tabananica, White Wolf, Big Red Meat, Little Crow, all captured. This band has come in and surrendered, I was told, whenever they themselves got the news. That band captured. Another band surrendered. The Cheyenne. The Arapaho. The Kiowa. The Kataka. Most of the Comanche. As I listened to this news, to the fates of my comrades and the fate planned for me, I fingered Chloe's button and thought always of her.

Now, as we traveled into Drunken Bride, I heard a boy call out, "Here they come."

"Quite a crowd," the driver said.

I sat up to look. There were so many of you lining the street. As the procession approached you became quiet. The soldiers in front rode in, followed by the wagon, and then the guard following behind. A man walked up and spit in my face. I lifted my hands to wipe the spittle from my eyes. My chains rattled. I let my hands back down, and then I saw her. She was standing at the edge of the crowd, her hands resting on her stomach, big with my child now. We smiled at each other, just as we had smiled over the casket of Gerald Wilson when the vulture had strutted across it.

She wore a dark blue dress. Her hair was up, under a bonnet. She looked, for all the world, like a white woman. I saw the sadness in her eyes, as I imagine she saw the sadness in mine. But she was alive, and our child was alive inside of her, and she was smiling at me because this distant smile was the only way she had to tell me she loved me.

It was only a brief moment. The wagon

rattled by, and as it did a white woman came up to Chloe and put her arms around her and leaned down to whisper something before leading her away. I pled guilty to all the charges against me so that she would not be required to testify.

She was known in Drunken Bride as Mrs. Joseph Wilson. She is known that way still. There was not one person in this town, Chloe once told me, with whom she was close, not one person whom she could trust. There was no one, with the exception of Master Wilson, who had ever called her by her first name or knew that she had once been a house slave.

It is written in your newspaper that Mrs. Joseph Wilson's story is even sadder than that of the white captive Cynthia Ann Parker, whom Mo Tilly told me about all those years ago, and who, it is said among the white citizens, at least had family to return to.

You called Chloe degraded and ruined. You whispered behind her back. No white man would ever want her now, you said, as if being wanted by a white man was the ultimate compliment. And when our baby was born dead, Nakuhakeetuh, still in the birthing bed, was told that it was a blessing to lose that heathen child. A blessing, you told her. This was written in the newspaper. "He would have never fit in. Every day of Mrs. Joseph Wilson's life this child would have been a reminder to her of the utter degradation which she suffered. The Lord in His blessed glory did not mean for this child to live."

The church bell rang when he was stillborn. I watched from the window of my cell as the people gathered in the street and hoorayed. I did not yet know what this celebration was about, and I asked Jack, "What's going on out there?"

"Your bastard son died," he said. "Praise God that Mrs. Wilson won't have that burden to carry." He ran the barrel of his pistol across the bars of my cell. "Praise God," he said again.

I watched the people pour into the street. They gathered below the jail and shook their fists at my window. The church bell pealed and pealed. Men shot off their guns and hooted and hollered while somewhere in Drunken Bride, I did not know where, Chloe lay in a bed listening, white women in attendance, holding her hand.

You gave our son a Christian burial, in a solitary grave out on the prairie. I watched from my cell as the wagon rolled down the street away from town, the little casket clattering in its bed, the preacher with his Bible and black hat, riding shotgun. The wildflowers were blooming, the prairie covered in color.

Two weeks later Chloe made a batch of biscuits in the kitchen of the house where she was staying, and after taking them from the oven she stole a pistol from a cabinet and walked out into the prairie and shot herself. She was buried in the cemetery behind the church, next to Master Wilson and their two children. Their names, I remember Chloe once telling me, were Anna and Jason, after her mother and the man she called father.

I watched her burial from my cell. I watched the women dressed in black, like crows, bringing handkerchiefs up to dab at their eyes. I watched the men lower her casket into the ground and the preacher holding his Bible open and praying. And I watched, after all these white people had left, a colored man shovel dirt into the grave and tamp it down, and then pound the cross into the ground.

Down below, the man at the souvenir table is doing a brisk business. I force myself to look now. Locks of dark hair, each tied with a blue ribbon, are lined in a row along his table. This is the enterprising man who cut

Chloe's hair before she was buried. He cut it and he washed the blood out of it, and he packaged it up into little bundles to be sold today, the day of my hanging. Jack bought one. It sits on his desk. I can see it from here. A lock of Nakuhakeetuh's hair tied with a blue ribbon, sitting on my jailer's desk.

The street is filled now. Those who arrived early did well to do so, for there seems to be no more room for anyone else, yet every minute I hear the creak of tack and the rattle of buggies and wagons as more arrive. I hear friends and neighbors greeting each other. I hear snatches of conversation. I imagine men, down the street in the saloon, hoisting their glasses to my pending death. Some thoughtful woman has brought a plate of food to Jack. I smell the fried chicken. My body wants to be fed. My hand no longer desires to write. My mind no longer desires to focus.

I let my fingers slip to my throat and fondle Chloe's button, and the little noose that lies next to it. That little noose, One-Eyed Jim's name long faded away from it, the string frayed and worn. I rub it between my fingers and it falls apart in my hand, leaving only Chloe's button cool against my throat.

It is hot in this cell. There is no air. I have loosened my collar, unbuttoned my sleeves and rolled them to my elbows. Sweat drips from my forearm onto the paper, smearing the ink. I can only hope that this is legible, but to whom, I do not know.

"Fifteen minutes, Persy," Jack calls to me, with his mouth full.

I must stop my writing and prepare for my death. I must change my clothes, for these clothes I wear now are not the clothes I intend to die in. Those clothes, my buckskins, my moccasins, and the faded checkered shirt I took in a raid, the clothes that I was captured in, are spread out at the end of my bed.

I see Jack finish up his food and take his feet down from his desk. He stands and wipes his fingers on his britches. He picks up the lock of Chloe's hair and slips it into his pocket. His boots clump across the floor and he lifts a rope off its peg. The rope with which to tie my hands.

Outside the noise rises. I think that it could not become any louder, and yet it does. It has been so difficult to concentrate these last few hours. I do not know what will become of these pages. I do not know what will become of this truth. All I know is that my children are dead. My woman is dead. My people have mostly surrendered to you. The buffalo, the tahseewo, will soon be gone. My casket is ready.

A NOTE FROM THE AUTHOR

It is difficult to write of things gone by, times in which I did not live, and cultures of which I have no firsthand knowledge, but I believe that writing fiction is always about pushing up against what I do know in order to learn what I don't know. I learned a great deal while writing this book: about the institution of slavery in America, the growing and processing of cane, the fall of New Orleans in 1862, the Civil War and the era known as Reconstruction, and the culture of the Comanche and their clash with the settlers and the army in Texas during the 1870s. That said, there are many things I simply can't know. My goal in writing about the slave culture of Louisiana's cane country and the Comanche culture of the 1800s was to honor and respect the people of those times and places.

In writing this story, I have used dialect to show the difference in Persy's speech and the speech of those around him. The use of dialect was not limited to black characters. I understand that dialect is a sensitive matter. Normally I am not a fan of it, but I believe it has its uses, and I felt it was needed for this story. Also, the use of derogatory words was intended to reflect the era's language and history, not to condone or exploit what I believe are abhorrent terms. I believe these words were needed to convey the reality of Persy's life on Sweetmore and in Texas.

I apologize to anyone who finds these usages offensive.

As the Comanche had no written language during the time Persy was writing his story, I chose to use phonetic spellings of Comanche words as I understood them. I referred to *Our Comanche Dictionary* published by the Comanche Language and Cultural Preservation Committee. Comanche names were also tricky business, and while I studied and tried to see patterns to all the names I could find, many names were interpretations made by white culture, and therefore some guesswork was involved. Any mistakes made are my own, and again I apologize for any offense I may have inadvertently caused.

In addition, I used a novelist's power by

choosing not to name the particular band Persy belonged to. Not only did I not name this band, I chose to ignore the issue completely. I did this in order that Persy might experience firsthand certain historical events and battles. I believe this made for a better story, and I hope that it brought the reader's attention to the overall plight of the Comanche tribe, rather than narrowing it down to the troubles of one particular band. It is easier to see connective events in hindsight than it is in real time, and I wanted to give the reader that experience.

In the end I am a novelist and not a historian, and a novelist must make many choices. In the case of these particular choices my hope was to create a good story with real tension while remaining respectful to my characters and the times in which they lived.

This is always my goal with every story.

ACKNOWLEDGMENTS

Writing is often a solitary activity. For the fortunate writer it is also an activity of community. I am a fortunate writer and am grateful to the following people, who saw me through the work on this book, chapter by chapter and draft by draft: Nora Esthimer, Joyce Allen, Ruth Moose, Paula Blackwell, Kim Church, Pat Walker, and Laura Herbst.

I had other early readers to whom I am also grateful: Betsy Joseph, Land Arnold of Letters Bookshop, Anna Jean Mayhew, John Yow, and Ben Campbell.

Special thanks to my Wednesday Night Group — aka the Iron Clay Writers — for giving me support during some difficult times and celebrating the good times: Rebecca Hodge, Claire Hermann, Barrie Trinkle, Agnieszka Stachura.

I'd also like to thank Ronlyn Domingue for being one of the most incredible writing friends I've ever had.

Extraordinary kisses go to my husband, Ben Campbell, for the multiple, always careful readings of this novel, and his participation in the endless conversations that took place in our household about Persy, the Comanche, sugarcane, the slave trade, the fall of New Orleans, and a million other little details and historical facts that I uncovered as I worked. And for picking me up off the floor many times.

I would also like to thank the Hope James Foundation for providing me with the funds I so badly needed for a writing retreat in my studio, the tree house. Gratitude also goes to Ann Davis for being my generous landlady at the tree house, Mary Ruth for easing me into social media, Sharon Wheeler of Purple Crow Books for welcoming me to Hillsborough and into this community of writers, and the folks at Flyleaf Books for hosting my monthly Prompt Writing class: Jamie Fiocca, Sally Stollmack, Erica Eisdorfer, and Jeremy Hawkins, as well as unnamed but generous staff for always being warm, funny, and supportive of readers and writers.

Finally, thank you to Henry Wiencek for always supporting me in my career and for helping me find a great agent, to Howard

Morhaim for being that agent and for always being straight and honest with me, and to my editor, Sarah Branham, for pushing me to write a better book.

My sincerest gratitude to you all.

ABOUT THE AUTHOR

Nancy Peacock is the author of the novels *Life Without Water* and *Home Across the Road*, as well as the memoir, *A Broom of One's Own: Words on Writing, Housecleaning, and Life*. She currently teaches writing classes and workshops in and around Chapel Hill, North Carolina, where she lives with her husband Ben.